The fiery brilliance of the Zebra Hologram Heart which you see on the cover is created by "laser holography." This is the revolutionary process in which a powerful laser beam records light waves in diamond-like facets so tiny that 9,000,000 fit in a square inch. No print or photograph ·can match the vibrant colors and radiant glow of a hologram.

So look for the Zebra Hologram Heart whenever you buy a historical romance. It is a shimmering reflection of our guarantee that you'll find consistent quality between the covers!

PASSION'S KISS

Judith's whole body quivered when Strong Hawk stopped abruptly in front of her and drew her suddenly into his arms. He raised his fingers to the nape of her neck and gently urged her lips to his.

Never having been this close to a man before, Judith began to shove at his chest, alarmed. Then her alarm gave way to wonder as her body became fused with his and she felt the brute strength of Strong Hawk's thighs pressed sensuously against her. His lips were warm and sweet, yet demanded response. The feelings created inside of her stole her breath away, and she was soon lost in hopeless surrender.

Overwhelmed by this drugged passion he was weaving into her heart, Judith returned his kiss. She closed her eyes and let this new sensation wash over her, until she could have sworn that she was melting forever into his embrace. . . .

THE BEST IN HISTORICAL ROMANCE
by Sylvie F. Sommerfield

BETRAY NOT MY PASSION   (1466, $3.95)

The handsome sea captain's hands felt like fire against the raven-haired Elana's flesh. Before giving her heart she wanted his pledge of everlasting love. But as the prisoner of his fierce desire she only prayed . . . BETRAY NOT MY PASSION.

TAME MY WILD HEART   (1351, $3.95)

Fires of love surged through Clay's blood the moment his blue eyes locked with the violet of Sabrina's. He held her bound against him with iron-hard arms, claiming her honeysweet mouth with his own. He had bought her, he would use her, but he'd never love her until she whispered . . . TAME MY WILD HEART!

CHERISH ME, EMBRACE ME   (1711, $3.95)

Lovely, raven-haired Abby vowed she'd never let a Yankee run her plantation or her life. But once she felt the exquisite ecstasy of Alexander's demanding lips, she desired only him!

TAMARA'S ECSTASY   (1708, $3.95)

Tamara knew it was foolish to give her heart to a sailor. But she was a victim of her own desire. Lost in a sea of passion, she ached for his magic touch—and would do anything for it!

DEANNA'S DESIRE   (1707, $3.95)

Amidst the storm of the American Revolution, Matt and Deanna meet—and fall in love. And bound by passion, they risk everything to keep that love alive!

Available wherever paperbacks are sold, or order direct from the Publisher. Send cover price plus 50¢ per copy for mailing and handling to Zebra Books, Dept. 1739, 475 Park Avenue South, New York, N.Y. 10016. DO NOT SEND CASH.

SAVAGE TORMENT

CASSIE EDWARDS

ZEBRA BOOKS
KENSINGTON PUBLISHING CORP.

ZEBRA BOOKS

are published by

Kensington Publishing Corp.
475 Park Avenue South
New York, NY 10016

Copyright © 1986 by Cassie Edwards

All rights reserved. No part of this book may be reproduced in any form or by any means without the prior written consent of the Publisher, excepting brief quotes used in reviews.

First printing: January 1986

Printed in the United States of America

Dedication

*With much love and affection I
dedicate* Savage Torment *to
my niece Debbie Jackson, her husband
Jerry, and children Lorie and Mark.
Also, I dedicate this to my niece
Darla, her husband Steve, and children
Kevin, Greg, and Andy Sabens.*

—*Cassie*

All paths lead to you
  Where e'er I stray,
You are the evening star
  At the end of the day.

All paths lead to you
  Hill-top or low,
You are the white birch
  In the sun's glow.

All paths lead to you
  Where e'er I roam.
You are the lark-song
  Calling me home!

—Blanche Shoemaker Wagstaff

Chapter One

Duluth, Minnesota . . . 1899

Red and brown sandstone bluffs loomed wild and bold from Lake Superior, while pleasant hills and stately elms, pines, and cedars suggested a cool serenity. It was springtime in the lake country, and everything was rich with promise. Green shoots of flowers reached sunward, and buds were appearing on the skinny branches of all the trees.

From somewhere close by a repeated gunfire rang out, silencing the songs of the nuthatch, sparrows, wrens, and chickadees. And then there was a soft laugh, a laugh comparable to the softest note that could be played on a harp.

"Father, what's got into you? You couldn't hit the side of a barn this morning, should one even be there right before your eyes," Judith McMahon laughed, blowing smoke away from her own personal lady's pistol. "Perhaps we've waited too long for this target practice. But there were the winter months getting in our way. Thank God the snows have finally melted so we can get out and do things like this." She wiped her pistol clean against the coarse material of her jeans.

Travis McMahon, Judith's father, smiled toward her, his lower lip quivering in his nervousness. As of late he had felt the weakness increasing and had experienced many spells of a crushing sort of pain around his heart. Tall and extremely thin, he had wondered for a while if Judith had noticed the thinning of his sand-colored hair and how faded his blue eyes had become.

Square-jawed and clean shaven, attired in his Texas jeans and shirt and his leather cowboy boots, which shone this morning, he had meant to recapture something of what he once had been when he was a rancher in Texas.

But even he knew that was impossible. What was past was past. He had Judith's future to consider now, after he was gone. If only his mind wouldn't continue to wander back to Texas so often of late. Was that a bad sign? Was his end really so near?

Yes. With Judith now eighteen, she had to be first on his list of priorities. . . .

But, ah, Texas, he thought to himself, his face shadowing. Damn how I do miss it!

His heart had forced him to leave the grueling work of running a ranch behind him and invest his monies in a lumber and land development company in the thriving town of Duluth, where he ruled his men from behind a desk.

"Father?" Judith said, a brow lifted quizzically as she stepped to her father's side, enjoying the breeze that escaped down the opened throat of her plaid cotton blouse where two buttons were left unbuttoned. "What is it, Father? You've suddenly become so . . . so gaunt. Don't you feel well?"

She understood quite well the extent of his illness, but knew better than to ever try to baby him. He was a man of pride and would never want to be reminded of his failing heart, though at times it tore at Judith's insides not to be able to speak of it openly. He, in truth, was all that she had. Her mother had died many years ago in Texas, and her older brother, Rory, had cut ties with the family and now practiced law in St. Paul.

Yes, it was just Judith and her father, and her loyalty to him ran deep.

Travis replaced his pistol in his holster and eased Judith's pistol from her hand. He aimed it toward the large bundle of straw positioned at the edge of the bluff that overlooked Lake Superior. On the straw had been placed a drawn red circle on a sheath of leather and the sun danced like a glaze against it as Travis steadied his aim and fired.

"I'll be damned," he chuckled. "It must've been my pistol causin' me to miss all those times this mornin', Pug." He lowered Judith's pistol and squinted his eyes, shielding them with his hand. "Just look at that. A bull's-eye, Pug."

Pug. Judith smiled to herself, having learned to accept her nickname long ago, when her father had first called her that because of her cute, upturned "pug" nose. As she had developed into full womanhood, her nose hadn't changed as the rest of her had. Her father often had said that she was dangerously, shatteringly pretty, with her golden blond hair worn long to her waist and her sky-blue eyes.

He had explained to her that he had used the word dangerous because he worried that her statuesquely tall and voluptuous figure would cause her to have to be too cautious in this northwoods territory, where rough-talking lumberjacks and seafaring sailors were more in abundance than there were women to keep them satisfied. That had been his reason for teaching her the art of shooting a gun. She needed the protection from the animals who walked around on two legs more than from those that ventured out of the forests on four.

Graceful in all her movements and with her eyes twinkling, Judith went to the target and placed a forefinger to the fresh bullet hole in the exact center of the red circle. "My word," she said. "Father, it couldn't be a more perfect hit."

Then she swung around as he came to her and she smiled up at him. "You missed all those other times on purpose," she giggled. "You couldn't possibly have missed so terribly those ten . . . twenty shots in a row and then hit a bull's-eye. Are you playing games this morning, Father, or what?"

The sun reflected onto the barrel of Judith's pistol and then up into her eyes as Travis placed it in the palm of his hand. The pistol was dwarfed, by the largeness of the hand in which it lay. "Pretty good firearm, wouldn't you say?" he chuckled, glancing from the pistol to Judith. "Should do the trick if you need it for protection. Shoots damn straight, this gun."

Judith sighed. "Yes. It shoots damn straight," she

said. "Seems neither of us missed the target with that gun this morning, but you're evading my question. Why is it that you missed so often with yours? You weren't trying to make my ego swell on purpose, were you?"

"Naw," Travis said, his pale blue eyes dancing as a smile lifted his lips. "I wouldn't want to do nothin' as dumb as that. Let a lady outshoot me on purpose? Never."

Judith took her pistol from his hand and placed it in her holster at her hip, then idly kicked a loose rock at her feet with her cowboy boot. "Maybe not just any lady," she teased, her eyes lowered. "But a daughter?"

Her eyes rose to meet the kindness in the depths of his. "Yes," she murmured. "You would for a daughter . . . even a daughter dressed like less than a lady, in jeans and cotton shirt."

Travis bent his back and placed his lean arm about her waist and guided her to the bluff's edge. With his free hand, he gestured toward Lake Superior. "Beautiful this mornin', ain't it, Pug?" he said thickly. "Kinda nice bein' alive, wouldn't you say?"

"Yes. Quite," Judith said softly, almost choking on his hidden meaning. She absorbed the setting, feeling the peacefulness of it clean into her bones, it seemed, for a brief moment able to put worries of her father from her mind. The pine-fresh air of the northwoods was at her back where the forest stretched out far beyond where even her imagination dared to reach. In front of her the air was fresh and cool, smelling of lake water where the red sandstone cliffs jutted into Lake Superior.

Judith looked out across the lake to where the blue

sky that met the blue of the water was only distinguishable from the water by an occasional ship on the horizon. It was a dizzying, swimming landscape, a blue, luminous carpet.

Then Judith looked in another direction, downward, toward the city of Duluth, a seaport now known even as far away as China. Duluth extended for twenty-six miles along the west end of Lake Superior, lying on Saint Louis Bay. It had been built on a bluff that rose gradually from Lake Superior to a height of six to eight hundred feet and had grown rapidly after 1880, when lumbering and iron ore industries had developed.

Many varied kinds of ships now lined the piers, and black smoke coughed and circled from the four- and six-story brick warehouses and assorted businesses that made up the city of Duluth. Church spires broke the monotony of buildings, shimmering white up into the sky. Judith let her gaze wander to the houses that had been built into the side of the steep hills of Duluth. Her father had chosen not to build among the other houses of the city. He had wanted to be different. He had wanted to retain a touch of Texas, though he had left it behind him several years ago. A Texas-style ranch house spread out across the land only a few yards from where they now stood, close to the open land and forest that her father owned. From there they could look down at the city, instead of up from the city to the forest.

"There's so much for you to learn," Travis said thickly, suddenly breaking through the silence that had fallen between them. He dropped his arm from

14

around Judith's waist and began moving toward the ranch house, his shoulders slumped and his head hung.

Judith stood, momentarily stunned, as he walked away from her. He was more moody this day than usual, and this frightened her. What if he was feeling worse and hadn't wanted to worry her? Without him her life would be empty. Up to this point, no man had captured her interest. Most of the men she came in contact with were burly, loud, dirty, or had lust-filled eyes when they looked her way. So often she had wished not to be a part of the Duluth scene, and she knew she was only there because the city had been of her father's choosing. Should he die, she couldn't see herself remaining there. Surely she could find a more alluring future for herself somewhere else, where gentlemen were gentlemen.

Taking quick steps with her long legs, Judith went to fall in step beside her father. "What you just said," she tested, giving him a guarded glance. "What did you mean by saying there's so much for me to learn?"

His face pale and lined with worry wrinkles, Travis flailed a hand into the air, refusing to look her way. "My business, Pug," he growled. "My business. You've got to show more interest. You've got to learn all aspects of it, should I . . ."

Judith swallowed back a lump in her throat. "Should you what?" she said shallowly, fearing to hear the answer.

"Should my ticker stop working," Travis said, his eyes now snapping as he looked down at Judith. "Damn it, girl, don't pretend you don't know what

15

I'm talkin' 'bout. You've known for a long time how my health is worsenin'.''

Shaking her head, Judith gave him a determined look. "No. I don't want to hear it," she said.

Travis stopped and turned to clasp his hands onto her shoulders. "Whether you want to hear it or not, you'd best listen," he said. "Since your brother Rory has chosen to leave us to practice law in St. Paul, you're the one who will inherit McMahon Enterprises. *Only* you. And this means you've got to let me teach you everything I know before . . . before it's too late."

"But, Father . . ." she said in a bare whisper, wanting to elude the subject of her taking over his business. How could she tell him that she hated the thought of it? That *alone* could kill him. . . .

"There's even more to my business now than before that's gettin' in my way of relaxin' nights, and you've got to know about it, Pug," Travis said, dropping his hands to his side. "Tomorrow we'll be ridin' into Indian territory. You've got to learn all aspects of my business. Even the uglier side."

Judith paled. She took a step backwards. "Indians? Uglier side?" she gasped. "What do you mean?"

"Even though my company is the largest in Duluth, we still have the need to move farther north to find more trees," Travis said hoarsely. "Duluth is becomin' sparse of trees. They've been overworked because there are so many lumber businesses in the area."

"You don't mean to move into Indian territory, do you?" Judith said, her eyes wide, partially from fear and partially from excitement. Life had become dull. But would an involvement with Indians be leaning a bit too much in the other direction . . . ?

"I don't see why we can't reason peaceably with Chief Gray Wolf about the rich forests near his village beside the St. Croix River," Travis said, shrugging. "My plans are to go to Gray Wolf and warn him that our men will be arriving there soon with equipment to begin cutting the trees."

"But, Father, surely the land is theirs," Judith murmured. "How can you just go in and begin cutting?"

"The land belongs to no one by contract," Travis argued, once more moving toward the house, Judith close by his side. "Even the government hasn't yet made claim to that area of the forest. I must before they do."

"Are those the Chippewa Indians of whom you are speaking?"

"The same."

"They are known for their peaceful ways," she said, shaking the hair back from her shoulders. "But I am sure that will change if they are pushed too far by the white man."

"That's another reason why it's important that you go with me to the Indian village," Travis said, giving her a half glance.

"My? Why?"

"It's common knowledge, Pug, that two of the Chippewa chiefs have married white women. Surely having you at my side will make for more bargaining power. Their respect for white women is widely recognized. You'll be a great asset.''

Judith eyed him with a deep, silent questioning, never before having felt in a position of being "used" by her father. This made her fear for his health even more, for only a desperate man made desperate moves.

Chapter Two

Strong Hawk sat handsomely tall on the bare back of his black stallion, his copper skin shining beneath the soft rays of the sun. He was attired in a fringe-trimmed buckskin shirt, leggings, and moccasins, and his black, coarse-textured hair was drawn back from his face into two neat pigtails, with a loop of his hair left free, from which hung his yellow feather.

Strong Hawk rode away from the maple grove. It was *zee-gwun*, spring, the time of *oo-shi-gah-e-gay*, when the maple trees were tapped and the sap poured into the kettles and bubbling troughs of the Chippewa. For several days and nights now Strong Hawk had worked diligently alongside his father Chief Gray Wolf's people, collecting birchbark buckets from the dripping wounds of the trees. Even now the most hardy of the Chippewa maidens stood beside the troughs made from hollowed logs stirring the boiling sap around and around with paddles.

At the age of twenty, with his features set, seeming to accentuate his high cheekbones and causing the color of his eyes to appear even darker than their usual black color, Strong Hawk's mind was troubled. He looked ahead, across the shimmering meadow full of blossoms of yellows and purples and toward his father's village, which sat beside the St. Croix River. Smoke spiraled upward from the smoke holes of the dome-shaped wigwams clustered about, a peaceful enough scene; yet Strong Hawk feared for his father's people. There was an unending struggle to satisfy the elementary wants of the Chippewa . . . particularly the need for food, which constantly drove the Indians from hunting ground to maple grove, from berry patch to wild rice bed.

Wenebojo, the spirit who made the world, had protected the St. Croix band of the Chippewa and had seen to it that none of them had starved through the long, hard winters. If a lucky family had more food than it could consume, the surplus was shared with the needy.

But Wenebojo had seemed to turn his head this past winter, pretending not to see the Chippewas' plight, for there had been barely enough food to spread out among his father's people. The wild rice beds had thinned from overuse, the deer had moved farther north, and the white man was stealing the fish from the river upstream, far from the Chippewa village, yet close enough for it to matter. This was the reason for Strong Hawk's frown and heavy heart this day. He knew the need to move the St. Croix village north. But his father . . . the great Chief Gray Wolf, was of the old family of Chippewa, and he continued to believe that Wenebojo would once more bless his people with food . . . with skins . . . with peace from the white man.

Drawing his reins taut, Strong Hawk urged his stallion to stop. Patting the sleek mane, he peered toward two log cabins that had been built in the Indian village. One now sat vacant, where his grandfather Chief Yellow Feather had lived with his beautiful white-skinned wife, Lorinda, whose Indian name had been Red Blossom, and who had been Strong Hawk's beloved grandmother. Both were now a part of the happy hunting grounds, together forever, in their special love.

Strong Hawk reached a hand up and smoothed his fingers over the yellow feather that hung from his coil of hair. On Yellow Feather's deathbed he had handed the feather of his childhood vision to Strong Hawk, saying that it was only right that Strong Hawk should wear the sacred feather, since Strong Hawk was the firstborn of Gray Wolf, Yellow Feather's son, and would one day also be a great chief of the St. Croix band of the Chippewa.

A knot of sadness formed in Strong Hawk's throat, oh, so missing his grandfather. He hadn't only been a fierce leader but a kind, warmhearted man as well, one loved by all. It had been easy to see how a white woman as beautiful as Lorinda Odell had fallen in love with such a man, leaving her way of life behind to live with him in his Indian village.

Closing his eyes, Strong Hawk could see in his mind's eye the flame of his grandmother's hair, the twinkle in her green eyes, and he could always recapture the gentleness of her voice in his thoughts.

Shaking his head sadly, blinking his eyes open, his heart was burdened with loneliness for his grandmother now, as though having just said that final good-bye to her all over again. . . .

He nudged his knees into his stallion's side and flicked his reins, now moving in the direction of the other, quite large log-built house. In it he had developed into manhood, under the loving influence of his father, Chief Gray Wolf, and his mother, Sweet Butterfly, another white woman whose love for her Indian husband had drawn her from the white man's way of life. It had been his white mother who had taught Strong Hawk his love of books and poetery that most said made him the gentler and wiser of the twin sons born to Gray Wolf and Sweet Butterfly. Rarely did Strong Hawk let his thoughts wander to his brother who was merely seconds younger than he, as time is counted on a watch. Silver Fox had become caught up in greed, loving the feel of the green American dollar between his thumb and forefinger. Now in full control of his mother's Duluth-located lumber company, Silver Fox had even taken a white man's name, as well as his way of dress and manner of living.

Strong Hawk felt too much shame for his brother to even let himself wonder about his welfare from day to day. Silver Fox had chosen his way of life . . . Strong Hawk had chosen his own.

"He will follow the white man. I will *lead* the Chippewa," Strong Hawk proudly boasted to himself. *"Ay-uh*. I will be a great *chee-o-gee-mah*, a powerful chief, a leader. My father will have chosen wisely between sons of the same womb. My grandfather was right to say that seconds between births of sons made Strong Hawk the future leader of the Chippewa!"

Strong Hawk rode on into the village and wove his stallion around the many wigwams and the Chippewa people busy at work, some making canoes, others grinding maize, and others turning a spit over a large outdoor communal fire upon which hung the carcass of a deer, dripping grease from it and into the fire.

At the far edge of the village where the forest lay dark and deep behind a wigwam that stood isolated away from the rest, Strong Hawk dismounted from his stallion and secured its reins to the low-hanging limb of an elm tree.

Glancing at his wigwam and then at the large log house, he thought it best to go to his parents' house before entering his own private dwelling. He had the need to see if his father was feeling better. Of late, the strange heaviness in his father's chest and the pain that accompanied it gave Strong Hawk just cause to be concerned about his father's welfare. Though he was the epitome of a strong man, and still looking handsomely young, Chief Gray Wolf's health was quickly failing him. It was for this reason and because of Strong Hawk's respect for his father as father and chief that he failed to pursue the issue of moving the village farther north. His loyalty to his father ran deep. He dared anyone to bring trouble for his father into the village of the Chippewa.

Strong Hawk frowned, knowing that he was recently guilty of having troubled his father. Gray Wolf had only just begun to understand Strong Hawk's need to live alone in his own wigwam. One day soon he hoped to find a woman to take into his dwelling, to fill the lonely, empty corners of his heart with love. So far, none had pleased him in the way he expected to be pleased. He longed for the special one who would forever fill his wigwam with sunshine.

He had been pleased that his carnal needs had been dealt with by willing Indian maidens, but knew that most of the women who had shared his blankets had done so because he was not only an Indian of great physical attributes, but also because he was the next chief-in-line . . . not because of soft whispers in their hearts guiding their kisses and bodies.

Taking large strides, his tall, straight figure casting an even taller shadow on the ground beside him, Strong Hawk hurried on toward the house. As he approached it he caught a glimpse of his mother in her upstairs studio window with a paintbrush in her hand. Strong Hawk smiled. His mother was capturing this lovely spring day on canvas. It made him proud to know that many of her paintings had once hung on display in a white man's bank building in Duluth. As a child, he had been in awe of those earlier paintings, which at *that* time had been hanging on the walls of this house in the Chippewa village and the house of his mother's ancestors high on a hill in Duluth, overlooking Lake Superior.

Her talent was only surpassed by her incessant need to continuously be painting something. The loss of another daughter, and then another, seemed to have given her an even stronger need to fill the void in her life that had been made by only being able to bear two healthy children in her lifetime.

With a spring in his step, Strong Hawk moved on into the house, then stopped when he saw a spiral of tobacco smoke winding its way up from behind a high-backed wing chair that was facing a roaring fire in the fireplace. His father. He was taking a relaxing smoke before the fire. It seemed that he was doing more of this sort of thing lately, which in itself was peculiar to Strong Hawk. Gray Wolf had always before been such a strong, energetic, vital man. Was his will fading along with his health? It made a gnawing ache of sadness at the pit of Strong Hawk's stomach to see all of these things that meant even harder times ahead not only for his father, but for his people as well.

"Gee-bah-bah?" Strong Hawk said, walking across the room to step around in front of the chair. *"Gee-dah-kooz-ee-nah?"*

Strong Hawk's mouth grew dry, seeing that his question about his father's being sick was answered with one look at him. There was a weakness in his father's green eyes and an ashen color to his high cheekbones. Other than that, he looked well enough, in his fringe-trimmed shirt and leggings with fancy beadwork on both articles of clothing, and his black hair had a sheen to it from an application of deer tallow and hung neatly to his shoulders.

Gray Wolf took his colorfully painted pipe from between his lips and looked up at Strong Hawk, smiling to himself over how soundlessly Strong Hawk moved, even in a house. This had been taught Strong Hawk at an early age when Gray Wolf could pull his son away from his books, teaching him the need to be silent, in the forest, on the trail of a deer. . . .

"I am fine, my son," Gray Wolf said, lifting an

eyebrow in amusement. "Do you continue to worry yourself about me? Between you and your mother, I've one foot in the grave."

Strong Hawk clasped his hands tightly behind him as he frowned down at his father. "Can you tell me that you have had no strange heaviness in your heart this day?" he asked. "I can see it in your eyes, father."

"Your *gee-bah-bah* is fine," Gray Wolf assured him. He handed his pipe toward Strong Hawk. "Knock the tobacco from my pipe and place the pipe upon the mantel. The tobacco isn't as sweet and pleasing to my taste today."

Strong Hawk did as his father asked, and having the need to change the subject to something more pleasant, looked toward the staircase. "I saw *gee-mah-mah* at the window upstairs," he chuckled. "Is she doing a new painting?"

"*Ay-uh*," Gray Wolf said, nodding his head. "And Aunt Rettie is asleep in her room. Seems she sleeps much too much these past weeks."

Strong Hawk looked toward the closed bedroom door. "For a lady who is now one hundred years old, I don't see how she does anything but sleep," he marveled.

"The time is nearing when we will have to take her to Duluth, to live with North Star and Silver Fox in your mother's ancestors' house," Gray Wolf grumbled. "She needs to be closer to her white doctor. She makes too big a fuss when I suggest the shaman work his magic over her. Aunt Rettie is set in her ways. But you know that. Everyone knows that."

Gray Wolf coughed into a cupped hand, then leaned forward in his chair and pushed himself up from it. As he straightened himself beside Strong Hawk, he placed an arm proudly around his son's shoulders. "And the sugar camp? How is it going, son?" he said thickly, missing the days when he was known to have emptied more buckets of sap into the troughs than anyone else. *Ay-uh*, the heaviness in his chest had slowed him too much. Yet, it was important that Strong Hawk take charge and learn the full duties of a chief. Time seemed to be running out for the reigning chief of the St. Croix band of the Chippewa.

"The trees are giving the Chippewa much sap this year, *gee-bah-bah*. There is no threat to our forests, and as long as there is an abundance of maple trees, sugar will continue to be plentiful," Strong Hawk said, then gave his father a guarded, sideways glance. "And I see no problem there, since new trees spring up every year. But it is the wild rice . . . the deer . . . that we are lacking, father. . . ."

Strong Hawk ceased speaking when he felt his father's arm tense upon his shoulder, and Strong Hawk knew that once more he was displeasing his father. He had vowed never to worry his father about these things again, and here he had done so without even the blink of an eye! He was a thoughtless son, but was always forgiven by a father of deep love and warmth.

Gray Wolf stepped back away from Strong Hawk, his eyes moody. "Wenebojo has never truly failed us, Strong Hawk," he growled. "And Wenebojo won't fail us now." He doubled his fist and pounded it on his chest. "My heart tells me this. Your heart should also, since you are my son and next-chief-in-line."

Strong Hawk hung his head. "I'm sorry, Father," he murmured. He tried to console himself by remembering that they *did* have an abundance of maple trees. At least that remained in their favor. . . .

Chapter Three

The sound of the horses' hooves and the rattle of the buggy's wheels sent an almost ominous echo into the forest, which now spread out on both sides of the narrow dirt road they traveled. One horse led the buggy and one followed behind, fastened with a lean leather rope.

"We'll have to abandon the buggy soon and travel the rest of the way on horseback," Travis said, giving Judith a quick glance, wondering about her silence. Was she afraid to move into Indian territory? Was he wrong to have brought her? He still had to believe that the Chippewa were not unreasonable Indians and would receive their unannounced visitors into their village with a handshake of friendship.

Surely the Chippewa had no need for all of the trees that shadowed their village. There were miles upon miles of uncut timber. It made Travis's heart pound even harder realizing the money that could be made by this new venture. Judith would never want for anything again in her lifetime.

"How much farther?" Judith asked, fidgeting with the heavy folds of her dark riding skirt. Her crisp white long-sleeved shirtwaist blouse was buttoned to the neck, and she had tied a colorfully printed neckscarf around the collar. The scarf's silk ends fell across the swell of her right breast without hiding her voluptuousness. Her golden hair lifted and fell with the breeze, her blue eyes were alight with excitement. Though she had been bored all the other times when her father had insisted that she sit and listen to his instructions about his business, she was glad that he had chosen to include her this time on this newest venture of instruction. It would be interesting . . . meeting the Chippewa Indians one on one.

"One night by a campfire is all that will be required," Travis said, flicking the horse's reins. With his left hand he loosened the neck of his shirt by unbuttoning the top button. A cold sweat had suddenly engulfed him, but he couldn't let Judith know that even now he was experiencing wave after wave of chest pains.

"I'm glad that the evenings are no longer nippy," Judith said, looking into the forest, but even as she said it she caught the smell of the snow in the air that drifted out of the deep woods where it still lay under ledges of rock never touched by sun.

If she listened hard enough she could hear the drumming of the pheasant and the rattling of a squirrel in its hoard of acorns. Blue jays squawked overhead, and a mockingbird made its multiple sounds—first that of a catbird, then a cardinal, and then a red-winged blackbird.

In the shadow of the forest the wind moved among

the branches, carrying along with it an even more pleasant freshness. Wild berries trailed over alder branches, and the partridge vine, claytonia, and bloodroot were in evidence everywhere. And, also marking the new season of spring, delicate, exquisite flowers grew in the shade and under the damp thickets of the young balsams.

Travis drew the horse and buggy to a halt. He peered all around him, trying to find something by which to mark the spot so they could hide the buggy and return to it after the meeting with the Chippewa. He caught sight of a rippling stream through the thickness of some blue spruce trees and then saw the mouth of a cave.

A smile touched his lips. "This should do it," he said, stepping down from the buggy. "We'll hide the buggy in that cave. It won't be hard for us to find it later, but no one else will happen along and discover it."

He walked stiff-legged around to Judith's side and reached a hand to help her from the buggy. "We'll secure the buggy, fit the saddles and camping gear on our horses, and head out again," he said. "So far so good, Pug."

"Kind of like back in Texas when we left the troubles of the ranch behind and took off on our own out on the range when I was a little girl, isn't it, Father?" Judith laughed, jumping from the buggy. "I loved those times alone with you. You've always been such a busy man."

"I know my past mistakes," Travis grumbled, now guiding the horse and buggy around trees and through the thicket. "Your mother would probably still be alive if I had been more attentive to her. As it was, she sometimes didn't see me for weeks when I left for a roundup."

Judith walked alongside her father, stumbling when a briar pierced her skirt, then her leg. With her boots she kicked the remaining briars away. "You shouldn't blame yourself for Mother's death," she said softly. "It was the fever that killed her. Not you or your absence."

"She was so lonely, Pug."

"She had me and Rory."

"Children ain't the same as a husband. One day you'll understand. There'll be a man who sets your heart to racin'. Then you'll see the importance of a man at night when the sheets grow cold in bed."

Color rose to Judith's cheeks as she blushed, clearly understanding his meaning, though yet to have felt the embrace of any man who could set her to *wanting* him to share a bed with her. But maybe one day . . .

"Help unleash the horses, Pug," Travis said, winded. They had reached the mouth of the cave and backed the buggy into it. "I'm going to take a rest beside the stream. Seems the tiniest bit of exertion wears me out. Some man I've turned out to be in my midlife."

"Nothing could make you any less a man," Judith fussed, going to him to embrace him. She placed a cheek to his chest, hearing his erratic heartbeat. First it would beat and then it would not. . . .

"Just shows how much you know about the makeup of a man," Travis chuckled, patting her back fondly. "Now get along with you. Ready the horses. Then we'll follow this stream farther into the forest. It surely reaches to the St. Croix River. Once we find that river, the Indian village won't be hard to find. The Chippewa we are in search of named their band of Indians after that particular river."

"The St. Croix band of the Chippewa?" Judith asked, drawing away from her father. With the butter softness of her leather gloves she scooted some stray locks of her golden hair back from her face.

"Exactly," Travis said, nodding. "The *friendly* Indians, we hope. Right?"

Judith emitted a soft, nervous laugh. "I would certainly hope so," she said.

With a turn of a heel she went inside the cave to unattach the horses. A shiver ran up and down her spine as a chill passed over her from the intense dampness of the cave. From somewhere in the distance she could hear the rippling of water, and she gathered that it came from the far end of the cave where it was black as night. Above her she could see sparkling bubbles of moisture clinging to the cave's roof. Crystallized formations made the floor of the cave rough, and it was slippery where moss had grown in spots.

Working diligently, hungry for the sunshine's warmth, Judith released both horses from the buggy, blanketed and saddled them both, then loaded them with their camping gear. She took both their reins and guided them out into open space, worried anew when she saw her father kneading his brow as he hung his head.

"Ready, Father?" she hurriedly said, smiling nervously toward him as he jumped with a start and looked her way.

His eyes lit up when he saw the camping gear and saddles in place. "I guess I taught you well," he chuckled. "Done as well as a man, Pug."

Judith sighed. "Yes, I guess so," she said, handing him his horse's reins as he came to her. "I can shoot like a man, ride like a man, lasso like a man. Do you wish that I were a man, Father? You've always compared me to a man."

"No son could ever give me what you've given me, Pug. I know how sons behave from having Rory," he said thickly. He placed a foot in the stirrup and swung himself up and into the saddle. "When I've needed gentler handling after a hard day's work, I could depend on gettin' that from you. You're a blessin', darlin'. A blessin'."

Judith eased up into her own saddle, straightening the coarse material of her travel skirt around her legs. With her boots securely in the stirrups and the reins coiled around her right hand, she felt more at home than she ever did in a buggy.

"Gentle, am I?" she teased, giving her father a mischievous glance. "We'll see about that."

She flicked her horse's reins. "Hahh! Hightail it outta here, boy!" she shouted. She giggled, knowing that these wilder spurts of her personality never ceased to amuse her father.

"Wait up!" Travis shouted after her, spurring his own horse quickly onward. "You gol' darn fool daughter. Don't you know to be more careful in the forest? A low tree's limb could whip you right out of the saddle!" He was breathless when he pulled his horse up next to hers.

Seeing the flush of his cheeks and the heaving of his thin chest, Judith was immediately reminded of her father's condition and knew that she had to put more restraint into her actions. Why didn't she remember? But he hadn't been ailing that long. Before, *he* could brag that he was the one to outdo everyone in any challenge.

"You're right, Father," she said hoarsely. "I should be more careful in the forest. And it seems, in my haste to show off, I led my horse away from the stream."

Travis shrugged. "Won't take no doings to get us back there," he said. He looked toward the forest ceiling. The tips of the trees were aflame with color as the sun began its descent in the sky. "We'll ride awhile longer. Then we'll make camp."

"Then tomorrow . . . we'll meet with the Chippewa," Judith said, thinking hard on the prospects, wondering just how they would be greeted in the village. Thank God it was the Chippewa and not the Sioux. The Sioux were known to still be eager for a white man's scalp.

"Tomorrow . . ." Travis said blandly, suddenly fearful of this venture. This far from Duluth, he felt insecure. Why hadn't he thought to bring a crew of his men for protection?

Wiping a nervous bead of perspiration from his brow, he urged his horse onward beneath the dark shadows of the elms, maples, and oaks.

Chapter Four

Birds rose with a clamor as Strong Hawk rode his stallion along the winding creek. Evening was his time to commune with nature. Through the break in the trees overhead he could see the birds now winging their way across the fiery sunset-splashed sky, on the way to their nests among the rushes.

A deep contentment mellowed his insides, having cast all his doubts and worries aside for this moment, his time to be alone.

The wind rushed against his face as he sent his stallion into a gallop, and he swelled his bare copper chest out to inhale the freshness of the air. In the dimming light forest spider webs glittered, and the huge virgin pines caught the last rays of the sun in fiery reds in their tops. The air was heavy with the smell of pine and damp earth—but there was suddenly another scent, which caused Strong Hawk's heart to leap and his eyes to narrow.

Tightening his reins, he drew his stallion to a shuddering halt. His nose twitched, his eyes searched.

"Ish-sko-day," he said in a low growl. "Fire. And where there is fire, there is also man."

Dismounting from his stallion, he secured its reins beneath the weight of a rock on the ground, then stood tall, straight, and quiet as he once more sniffed the air.

Slowly he let his eyes begin the search through the trees, seeing nothing. But his nose would not mislead him. There was a fire ahead, and he had to discover why, and built by whom. This was the land of the Chippewa! All trespassers had to be dealt with and sent back in the direction from whence they had come!

Taking his rifle from its leather sheath at the side of his stallion, he grumbled beneath his breath as he began inching his way alongside the stream. "Strong Hawk will find out who so foolishly enters Chippewa land," he said. *"Boo-chee-goo-nee-gah-ee-shee-chee-gay!"*

His moccasined feet made scarcely a sound on the deeply piled pine needles as he made his way through skin-tangle, ground pine, juniper, and *kinnikin-nick,* which softened the slope that led down into the water.

Looking upward, through the break in the stately Norway pines ahead, he caught his first glimpse of smoke. His shoulder muscles tensed, his jaw tightened, and hate entered his eyes. Though he was seeing only a soft spiral of smoke, he knew that even that could be a danger to his people—as well as to the persons responsible for having lighted it!

He had to expect to find that the intruder was white. The Nadoues-Sioux, the Chippewas' snakelike enemy, knew best to not show themselves by way of fires so close to the Chippewa villages. That would be excuse enough for any Chippewa to attack and slay his arch enemy.

Yes. It must be a white man. *Ay-uh*, it had been a while since a white man had challenged a Chippewa. Strong Hawk hungered for such a challenge, yet knew that it would not be best for his father *or* his father's people.

Peace! Strong Hawk had to continue the tradition of peaceful ways with the white man. How could he forget for one moment that his mother was white, as was his beloved grandmother, who was only with him now in spirit?

A sudden sound of laughter caused Strong Hawk to stop in midstep. His heart did a strange sort of flip-flop, having never heard such a soft laugh before. It had most definitely come from the throat of a lovely lady, because in the laugh he could read gentleness . . . warmth . . . kindness.

Eager, more anxious now than angry, Strong Hawk proceeded on his way in the fallen dusk, following the scent of white man's coffee. As the aroma grew stronger, his footsteps slowed, not wanting to reveal himself, only wanting to see, before confronting for questioning.

A splashing of water made him tighten his grip on his rifle, and after taking two more steps he found himself with a clear view of a campfire and beside the fire a man stretched out, asleep, on a bedroll.

"It is the *chee-mo-ko-man*," Strong Hawk growled beneath his breath. "A white man intruder, just as I suspected!"

Another splash of water and the same sort of soft laugh that he had heard earlier was cause for Strong Hawk's head to jerk around, toward the sparkling waters of the stream. The sun had long fled from the sky, and it was the soft glow from the moon that revealed to Strong Hawk's eyes the opulent whiteness of the woman's flesh, the rich gold coloring of her long and flowing hair, and the curves and dips of her enchanting body as she continued to splash water up over her. She stood knee deep in the water, with a blanket hung from a tree limb to separate herself from the white man asleep by the fire.

"Mi-tah-qwah-shay," Strong Hawk whispered huskily, letting his glazed eyes drink in her nakedness. As a blaze of desire fired his insides, he let his gaze move even more slowly over her. Had he ever seen such satiny, large breasts? Had he ever seen such a tiny waist? They flared out to rounded hips, which then led to a patchwork of gold, downy hair between her thighs. She was like a flower growing from the water, so delicately beautiful, beautiful, ready to be plucked . . . ready to be savored.

Then he looked more intensely at the soft lines of her face as she leaned her head backwards to comb her wet, tapered fingers through her lustrously long hair. She was so beautiful it made his loins ache and his heart pound. Though the moon was all that was lighting her, Strong Hawk could see her long, feathery lashes as they closed over her eyes, her very unusual but pretty nose, which turned slightly up at the end, and her seductively full lips, wet now after she had just licked them.

Never had Strong Hawk been so taken by a

woman! Never had his heart felt as though a hundred drums were beating in unison inside him! He wanted to reach out and touch her. He wanted to caress her and tell her how lovely she was. His mouth wanted to taste the jasmine of her lips . . . her breasts . . . the soft core of her desire that was hidden beneath the gold patch of hair between her thighs. His tongue wanted to probe every secret part of her and have her beg for more!

Almost obsessed by this sudden need for this white woman, it was becoming a torment to him to continue looking at her. His loins ached . . . his heart raced. . . .

Forcing his eyes away from her, swallowing hard, Strong Hawk circled his free hand into a tight fist at his side. He had just experienced a weakness in his character that he had never known to be possible. And it had been caused by the loveliness of a white woman instead of a Chippewa! Was it destiny that he continue the sort tradition begun by his grandfather Yellow Feather and his father, Gray Wolf? Was his heart also to be handed to a white woman!?

Letting his eyes move slowly back to this lovely creature bathed in moonlight, passion reigned supreme inside him. Then his heart jumped. Was she . . . looking . . . his way? Had . . . she . . . seen . . . ?

He shook his head to clear his thoughts and forced himself to turn and move quickly, stealthily away. Surely she hadn't seen him. It was his mind playing tricks on him. He now knew, though, that he could not go on into this white man's camp. He was afraid that his words would fail him. He was afraid that his eyes would mirror his soul, revealing how this lady with the hair the color of soft summer wheat had stirred his insides to an inferno. Though he knew that this white man and woman should not be allowed to travel farther into Chippewa land, it could not be *he* who stopped them. Somehow he felt the danger was more to his heart than to his father's people. He would return to his village and warn his father and let him decide what must be done.

He shook his head slowly back and forth. "*Gah-ween-endah-gush-gay-too-sin,*" he whispered to himself. "I just can't do it. If I tell father of this white woman and man's presence in the forest, then he will send many braves and force them to leave. In truth, I could not bear not to see her again."

His jaw suddenly grew tight and his eyes narrowed. "The white man asleep," he wondered. "Is he the woman's husband?"

Feeling a slow twisting of his gut, knowing that surely the man and woman were man and wife, he thrust his doubled fist into the air. "*Gee-wah-nah-dis!*" he growled beneath his breath. "How could I have been so foolish as to let a white woman affect me in such a way when she belongs to another?"

His stallion was reached. He mounted it without a look backwards. "*Gee-wah-nah-dis,*" he grumbled, knowing that he now would go and warn his father after all. He had been wrong, anyway, to think not to. The white woman's loveliness had almost blinded him to his loyalty to his father.

Riding away, back toward his village, he couldn't shake the vision of the golden hair and the sensuous curves of her silken body from his mind.

41

Chapter Five

When a deer started from the thicket, Judith gasped and yanked hard on her horse's reins. The horse neighed as it stopped and turned halfway around.

Travis rode up next to Judith. His forehead wrinkled with a worried frown as he reached and took her reins from her. "What is it?" he softly questioned. "Pug, everything seems to be spookin' you today. Are you that afraid of where we're going?"

Judith swept her hair back from her shoulders. She was aware of the flush of her face and the rapid pounding of her heart, but she would not reveal the reason to her father. Why alarm him needlessly? Just because she had caught a glimpse of an Indian the previous night just before she left the stream didn't mean that they were in danger. The Indian hadn't returned with others after having discovered them, though Judith had huddled, hidden behind a tree for most of the night, waiting with her loaded rifle. She hadn't awakened her father then for the same reasons she wouldn't tell him now.

Flashes in her mind of the Indian reminded her of his handsomeness as he had stood there in the shadows of the trees, watching her. Her moment of seeing him had been brief, because it was at her moment of discovery that he had turned and fled.

She couldn't help but wonder how long he had been standing there, with her so vulnerable . . . with her so nude. The air had been white with moonlight. Surely every inch of her had been revealed to his eyes.

"Judith? Damn it, girl, what's botherin' you?" Travis said sternly. He leaned toward her and took one of her hands in his. "Do you want to turn back? Is that what you want?"

Hearing her father call her by her given name instead of her nickname was cause for Judith to look quickly toward him. She now knew just how much he was reading into her different behavior, and she knew that wasn't wise. She had his health to protect. She must think of him. It was foolish to let her insides thrill when she remembered the handsomeness of the Indian whose eyes were as black as the blackest nights. Wasn't she being wanton for not being more disturbed by having been a victim of the Indian's voyeurism?

"No, Father," she quickly blurted, covering his hand with her free one. "I don't want to turn back. I'm sorry if I've worried you. I guess I am a mite uneasy about riding into an Indian village, but not so much that I don't want to do it. If you didn't feel strongly about this you wouldn't have come. I'm with you, Father. All the way."

She didn't tell him that nothing could dissuade her

43

now from going on into the village where hopefully her eyes could search and find the handsome Indian. But could she bear to look him square into his face, knowing that he was the only man, ever, to have seen her nude? Hadn't his eyes even branded her as his, by being the first?

"Well, then, let's get on with it," Travis said, handing Judith's reins back to her. "It shouldn't be too far now. I believe I see the shine of the St. Croix River through the trees just ahead apiece."

Together they moved out of the forest and onto a meadow bright with sunshine and assorted wild spring flowers blowing gently in the breeze. Only a short distance, and they reached the banks of the St. Croix River.

Travis looked across the river and to his left, smiling broadly. "Seems we've hit the jackpot, Pug," he chuckled, pointing to a grouping of dome-shaped wigwams across the river. "That's the Chippewa village, all right. Take a look at the uncut timber spreading out behind and beside it. And the river can be used to carry the lumber away, for sellin'."

Judith's eyes wavered as she quietly studied the village. From this vantage point she could see some activity around the wigwams and smoke rising lazily from all the smoke-holes. An occasional dog ran into view, yapping, and a child at play ran to the river's edge, stopped, and stared down into its blue-green depths.

"Seems peaceful enough," Travis said. He flicked his reins and clucked to his horse. "Come on, Pug. Let's get this chore behind us."

Judith was experiencing a strange weakness at the

pit of her stomach and in her knees as she nodded a yes to her father. She was eager yet apprehensive at the thought of seeing the handsome Indian again. Would he know her from the night before? Would she know him? Or was he perhaps from another Indian village . . . ?

She clung tightly to her reins and pressed her knees into her horse's side as the horse slipped and slid down the embankment that led them into the river.

Feeling the water soaking up into the bottom of her travel skirt and seeping down into her boots, Judith urged the horse quickly onward. And once the other side was reached and climbed and the horse was once again on flat land, Judith followed alongside her father, wordless.

But her thoughts were many. What would the next moments bring? How would it all affect the rest of her life? Was the Indian truly as handsome as her brief glance had shown him to be?

A bend in the land and Judith looked at the cave she was now passing. The entrance was large and void of any ground tangle, and the grass was packed solidly before it, as though the cave was entered quite often. And then her gaze moved to several mounds of earth on the far side of the cave, on the side that faced the village. There were four small graves and three larger ones. But without gravestones marking each, Judith was left to wonder whose . . . ?

But her thoughts were quickly diverted as the wigwams drew closer. As each Indian saw the approach of Judith and Travis, he or she stopped and stared momentarily, with stark defiance on his or her face, and then just as quickly disappeared into a wigwam.

Judith and Travis exchanged glances as they moved on into the outer edges of the village. Now, it seemed, the village was deserted. Even the dogs had been taken and hidden from sight. Only the carcass of an animal hung over the hot coals of an outdoor communal fire, giving off a rancid odor of burned flesh and dripping grease.

"I'm not so sure about this," Travis said, patting his rifle nervously where it lay in its leather sheath at his horse's side.

"Father, surely you didn't expect a celebration when we entered," Judith said, laughing softly. "These people must not have many visitors from Duluth. I doubt if any, ever."

"Well, we're here, and I intend to speak with Chief Gray Wolf or die trying," Travis said flatly. "Damn if I'll let an empty village scare me out of words. Now if there were Indians with guns pointin' our way, that'd be another matter. As it is . . ."

Suddenly several Indian braves attired only in brief loincloths stepped from behind a wigwam with rifles poised, aimed at Judith and Travis.

Judith's heart plunged and her mouth went dry. "Father, what . . . were . . . you just saying?" she whispered harshly. Her gaze traveled from Indian to Indian, now afraid, for in their dark eyes she saw no semblance of welcome or friendship. Nor did she see any who looked like the Indian of the past night.

One of the several Indians stepped forward. He lowered his rifle as he looked cautiously from Travis to Judith and then back again to Travis. *"Andi-aszhion?"* he said in a low, gravelly tone.

Travis straightened his back and looked with a sober face down at the Indian. "I do not understand your Chippewa way of speaking," he confessed. "But I know that your chief speaks fluently in the English tongue. I ask that you take me and my daughter to him. We would like to have council with him."

"Mah-bee-szhon. Come," the Indian commanded as he nodded with his head and pointed with his rifle toward a large lodge that sat on a hill, back away from the rest of the village, where it had a commanding view of the St. Croix River. This lodge, the Chippewas' council house, was a long, narrow structure, handsomely fashioned of bark and appearing to be sixty feet or more in length and about twenty feet wide. The ends were beautifully rounded and the roof gracefully arched. The snow-white birchbark sides were decorated with striking totemic designs in brilliant but harmonious colors. Slow spirals of smoke rose from four smoke-holes and an Indian stood guard on each side of its front door.

"It's as though the Indians were expectin' us," Travis said, giving Judith a quick glance. His eyebrows forked, wondering why that statement should cause a blush to rise to his daughter's cheeks and her eyes to lower, as though guilty of some unpardonable sin of the flesh.

Damn! She continued to puzzle him today. And this wasn't the time for her shenanigans. Apparently this Indian Chief Gray Wolf was no easier to deal with than his predecessor Chief Yellow Feather, and it was going to take all of Travis's charm along with his daughter's to succeed at what he had come here to do!

"Pug . . ." he said beneath his breath, reaching to shake her by shoulder, "what did I say to set your face to flame?"

Not wanting her father ever to know that the handsome Indian had silently watched her bathing in the nude, knowing that would cause his temper to flare so that he might do something foolish, she raised her eyes and met his bold stare.

"It is their loincloths," she lied, nodding toward the Indian braves who now walked alongside them toward the council house. "Father, it is embarrassing for me, to say the least. I've never . . ."

Travis chuckled. He patted her hand, then focused solemnly on the council house that was now only a few feet away. Out of the corner of his eye he had caught the shadows of two log houses . . . one small and one large, sitting back on the outer edges of the forest. This gave him hope, reminding him of the two white women who had been taken as wives by the Indians and how they had willingly come to live among them, even to bear Indian children.

Then a strange fear grabbed at Travis's heart. He looked quickly toward Judith. God! Why hadn't he thought to worry about her before this moment? Wasn't she a white woman, unwed, and so beautiful? An Indian brave could become completely captivated by her and want her as his woman. He hadn't thought to worry about that sort of danger.

Yet, he knew his daughter well and did not expect that an Indian could turn her head or steal her heart. Surely she would want more out of life than to have a future as an Indian squaw in an Indian village. She had been brought up with the finest things money could buy, though she still preferred her jeans to her dresses. But why shouldn't she? She had been born and bred a Texan . . . and the Texas blood in her made her different from most women that he had run across in these parts.

Judith jumped as one of the braves suddenly turned and grabbed the reins from her hands, stopping her horse right before the door of the council house. His dark pits of eyes bore holes through her flesh as he looked up at her.

"Nee-si-ee-ee," he growled, gesturing with a hand toward the ground.

"I believe he's sayin' to dismount," Travis said, doing so himself as an Indian brave also took his reins from him.

"I wonder if all Indians lack in manners as this one does," Judith said hotly, slipping on down from the saddle.

"Just smile, Pug," Travis encouraged her as he began walking alongside her to the council house. "We must impress them that we are here as friends. Not enemies."

"I would think they would already know that," Judith softly argued. "How could a man and daughter be anything but friendly? We most surely can't appear to pose a threat to this whole community of Indians. What would they do if many men rode into their village? What will they do when your men swarm to these forests to cut down the trees? Father, I think you just may have to be the one to back down this time."

"Never," he growled. "My mind is made up, Pug. I have always succeeded at gettin' what I want. This

49

time ain't going to be no different."

She had always known him to be a shrewd businessman, yet kindness seeped from his pores when he left his corporate mind behind at his office. With the Indians, would it be any different? Which approach would he take? Would he charm his way into their hearts, or would he come across as cold and calculating, since riches were involved here?

Either way, she had no choice but to help him succeed.

With her chin held high and her back tall, straight and slender, she entered the council house with her father and their Indian brave escorts. Though there were four open fires burning in the firespaces in various locations in the council house, the light was dim, compared with the brightness of the outdoors.

Judith blinked her eyes nervously, waiting for her eyes to adjust, then stopped when she was slowly able to make out the figures of two other Indian braves sitting side-by-side before the largest firespace of the four, in which a gentle fire burned. They were on raised platforms spread with a fine display of bearskins. Strewn balsam boughs and cushions ran entirely around the wigwam next to the outer wall, and Judith tensed when the spaces of the dwelling began to fill with even more Indian braves.

Wiping her eyes with the back of her hand, Judith looked once more toward the two more commanding figures of the many who still sat in silence while the others slowly began to seat themselves in a circle. With her vision finally completely cleared now, Judith's heart did an erratic dance. Her eyes were now locked with those of the handsome Indian who had been her silent visitor of the night before. He was one of the two most distinguished figures of the group of Indians on the raised platform, dressed fully in buckskin, as was the older man sitting by his side.

Remembering his having seen her nude, Judith's face warmed with color, now knowing that he, indeed, recognized her. It showed by the twinkle in his dark, fathomless eyes and the soft smile forming on his lips.

Judith tore her eyes away from him, almost swallowed whole by her heavy heartbeats. But before she did she had seen and memorized every detail of his handsome copper-colored face with cheekbones high and pronounced, a commanding nose, and sensually full lips. She had even seen the wide, muscled strength of his shoulders and chest, and the way in which he wore his coarse dark hair drawn back in pigtails, with a yellow feather showing from a coiled lock of the hair at the back. On his fringed buckskin shirt had been sewn beautiful colored beadwork designs of flower petals and leaves, unlike the man who sat next to him, who wore a white buckskin outfit and a five-foot-long Chippewa tribal headdress with brightly colored feathers stitched onto leather.

Now forcing herself to ignore the handsome Indian's steady stare, hoping that he wasn't envisioning her nude, Judith looked toward the Indian who most surely was Chief Gray Wolf. He was an exact older replica of the handsome young Indian who sat at his left side—which made Judith suddenly become aware of just who the Indian at the chief's side must be. He most surely was the chief's son!

Swallowing hard, now even in more awe of the Indian, who still studied her with the darkest of eyes, Judith still focused her eyes on Chief Gray Wolf. He was quite distinguished in his white attire. He puffed on a pipe, which was beautifully gay with feathers of the scarlet tanager. Though older, he was not only distinguished but was still handsome, with only minute wrinkles at the corners of his eyes.

Judith's mouth dropped open and she stared even more openly at Chief Gray Wolf. His eyes were green, not dark like most Indians'. How . . . ?

Then Judith remembered that he had been born of a white mother. Surely he had inherited the color of her eyes, instead of his father's.

Noticing even more, Judith was aware of the faded shade of the green color of his eyes and of the tiredness in them. It was almost the same as in her father's, and she had to wonder if this man was also ailing. . . .

Chief Gray Wolf took his pipe from between his lips and looked studiously first at Travis and then at Judith. He did not rise, instead bowed graciously, bending from the waist, raising his hand in greeting.

"*Nah-mah-tah-bin,*" he said, nodding his head. "Sit down and have council. Tell Chief Gray Wolf why you have entered the land of the Chippewa."

Travis placed a hand to Judith's elbow and guided her down onto a bulrush mat before the fire, then sat down beside her.

Across the fire from Judith and Travis, up on the platform so that he could look down at the intruders, Chief Gray Wolf patiently waited for the white man to talk. He let his gaze slowly drift over to the white woman. She made him recall his youth, when he had first seen his wife, Danette, his Sweet Butterfly. There was a strong resemblance to his wife in the stubbornness in this woman's eyes. They were even the same color. They were the color of the sky and rivers . . . a penetrating blue, which now challenged him back, as though defying his right as chief.

A slow smile lifted his lips. He had always liked fire in a woman. Then his smile faded when he saw her gaze move to Strong Hawk. There appeared to be a keen softness now in her eyes as she studied his son. It had to mean that she possibly saw his handsomeness and his mark of greatness in the way in which he sat so tall and proud beside his chief father.

Full of wonder, Chief Gray Wolf gave Strong Hawk a sideways glance. His jaw tightened when he saw a look of recognition in his son's eyes. Yet—why not? He had seen the woman before this day. Strong Hawk had ridden back into the village early this morning with the news of the white man and woman's intrusion into the land of the Chippewa.

But there was more in his son's eyes. Strong Hawk was seeing more than an ordinary woman. He showed an intense attraction to her . . . which made her special to Strong Hawk. And they had not yet even exchanged words!

Having mixed feelings about this discovery, Chief Gray Wolf once more looked toward the white man. "You do not say yet why you have come," he said dryly. He placed his pipe aside, leaving his hands free to gesture with as he spoke. "You do not say why you bring a white woman into the land of the Chippewa with you. White man, now is the time for you to speak. *Gee-gee-doon. Ah-szhee-gwah.*"

Travis cleared his throat nervously. He was aware of the muted silence in the council house. What he had to say would be heard by many, not only the chief. The fear of this sent a spasm of pain through his heart. He placed a hand to his chest, then lowered it again as he saw Chief Gray Wolf's face light up with what appeared to be recognition. Yet how would this chief understand his illness? Hardly did he even understand it himself.

"*Gee-gee-doon,*" Chief Gray Wolf once more said, softening his tone of voice, realizing the man who sat opposite him was, like himself, not a well man.

"My daughter, Judith, and I have traveled from Duluth to speak openly with the great Chief Gray Wolf, to have council with you about something of vital importance," Travis blurted. He looked over his shoulder at the Indian braves crowded around, sitting in a circle.

Then he once more looked directly toward Chief Gray Wolf. "But we had wanted private council," he said quietly. "Can that be arranged?"

Chief Gray Wolf weighed the white man's words in his mind, then raised a hand and spoke to his braves. "*Mah-szhon,* my braves," he ordered.

There was a sudden stirring in the council house and a rush of feet as the braves began to leave. This gave Strong Hawk a moment to think of other things besides pleasing his father and why the white people were wanting council. Strong Hawk had heard the white man make the declaration that the woman at his side was not his wife, but instead, his daughter. Strong Hawk's heart was beating like a drum against his chest, so happy was he to know that this beautiful lady was free, as was he. It was now easy to envision her at his side, perhaps even forever!

He once more smiled toward her as she gave him a slow stare. It amused him to see her beautiful thick lashes flutter so nervously, and how his attention to her made a blush rise to her cheeks.

Letting his gaze lower, he could see the greatness of her breasts, though they were covered by a white blouse. All he had to do to know what lay beneath her blouse and skirt was to remember how she had stood, so perfectly nude in the water, bathed in moonlight. . . .

"My braves, all except for my son, have left us alone as you requested," Chief Gray Wolf said, leaning to place another log on the fire. "Now, white man, you are free to speak. What brings you here?"

Travis ran a forefinger nervously around his shirt collar, easing it away from his throat. He stretched his neck, turned his head slightly back and forth, then placed his hands on his knees and leaned forward. "I have come here to speak of the land and trees which are of abundance on all sides of you," he finally blurted. "I have come to tell you of my plans and hope that you, being the wise chief that you are, will listen and understand."

Judith straightened the folds of her skirt more comfortably around her, then paled when she saw the reaction of Chief Gray Wolf . . . and his son.

Their eyes had grown cold . . . their lips and jaws had tightened as well as the muscles of their shoulders, which were noticeably suddenly corded, tightening their shirts across their shoulders and massive chests. Both locked their arms across their chests, staring icily toward Judith's father.

A deep frown furrowed Chief Gray Wolf's brow. *"Ah-neen-ay-kee-do-hen?"* he said in a low growl.

Travis once more cleared his throat nervously, his pale blue eyes wavering. "Eh . . . ? Pardon . . . ? What was that you said?" he said thickly. "I do not understand the Chippewa language."

"Gah-ween-nee-nee-sis-eh-tos-say-non," Chief Gray Wolf said with a jerk of his head, his eyes blazing with hate.

"Sir . . . chief . . ." Travis said in a strained voice. "Please speak in English. There's no way we can have council if you continue to speak in . . . in . . . in Chippewa."

"Neither Chief Gray Wolf nor his son Strong Hawk, the next chief-in-line of this St. Croix Band of the Chippewa, have ever discussed the land of our people with a white man," Chief Gray Wolf said flatly, holding his chin proudly high. "Nor shall we now. You have wasted your time coming here. Take your daughter and leave. The council is over between us."

Color rose into Travis's face, his eyes burned with humiliation, and his heart raced and fluttered ominously. He wiped the fingers of his right hand over the sudden dryness of his lips.

Judith saw her father's reaction to Chief Gray Wolf's denial to listen to him in her father's expression and worried anew about him. She reached a hand to his arm. "Father . . . ?" she whispered, jumping with a start when he brusquely brushed her hand aside. She swallowed hard when she saw his stubborn, set stare as he silently challenged Chief

56

Gray Wolf.

Judith then glanced over at Chief Gray Wolf's son. Strong Hawk, he had called him. The next chief-in-line . . . ah, so much a younger replica of this powerful chief of the Chippewa. She caught him looking her way, and though he was displaying the same bold hate and mistrust as his father, Strong Hawk momentarily let his eyes soften and his lips loosen into a quick, yet even more quickly vanishing smile.

This confused Judith. But she had to remember the intimacy they had shared beside the stream. Surely as he looked at her now, he was remembering. Had it affected him as sensuously as it had her . . . ?

Shaking her head, trying to clear her thoughts of such foolishness, Judith stole her gaze away from Strong Hawk, to once more look at Chief Gray Wolf as he rose to his feet, to glower down at Judith and her father, even dwarfing them with his added height.

Travis just as quickly stood, his shoulders squared, his arms locked stubbornly across his chest. Judith eased up beside him. Strong Hawk rose to stand proudly beside his father.

"I insist that you listen," Travis said, breaking the silence. "Surely what I plan to do can be done in peace."

Chief Gray Wolf locked his own arms stubbornly across his chest. "The Chippewa have had few battles with the white man through the many moons of our forced coexistence," he growled. "That is because we Chippewa have lived in isolated areas."

He unlocked his arms and made a sweeping

gesture with his right hand. "This land of the Chippewa is far from the cities of Duluth and St. Paul. Those cities will not be allowed to be brought closer by white man's ways. What you would want to say about my land will fall upon deaf ears, white man."

He pointed toward the door. *"Mah-szhon.* Go. Do not linger. You are not wanted here."

Travis took a step forward, to the very edges of the firespace, daring Chief Gray Wolf with an even harder stare. "My name is Travis McMahon," he said icily. "I own McMahon Enterprises, a lumber and land developing company in Duluth. I need to spread out to find more trees. The trees in the forests that surround Duluth are thinning too much. Houses are quickly filling the spaces where the trees have been felled. I plan to bring my crew north, to fell some trees close by your village. I plan to use the St. Croix River to transport them to Lake Superior. You can cooperate or you cannot. I thought I was being fair to come to give you fair warning."

Chief Gray Wolf turned to Strong Hawk. "Please take the white woman from the council house for your father," he said, clasping a hand fondly to Strong Hawk's shoulder. "I don't wish to have the white woman a part of the discussion ahead."

"Ay-uh. I understand," Strong Hawk said, nodding. He stepped from the platform and went to Judith. "Please step outside with me. Our fathers have much to discuss that is not for a woman's ears to hear."

Judith looked up into Strong Hawk's dark eyes, seeing much in their depths and feeling a strange sort

58

of passion quite unfamiliar to her.

"Go with him, Judith," Travis growled. "I won't be long."

As though in a trance, Judith let Strong Hawk ease a hand to her elbow and walked alongside him from the council house and into the bright sunshine of late morning. The touch of his hand, his manly presence, caused her insides to begin to slowly melt.

But then she remembered her father and knew that Strong Hawk and his father were her enemies!

She broke free from Strong Hawk and walked hotly away from the council house and toward the forest's edge, aquiver with many various emotions invading her senses.

Chapter Six

Feeling torn between wanting to stay close to the council house should his father need him and wanting to go after the lovely lady who showed spirit in the flash of her eyes the color of the sky and rivers, Strong Hawk clenched and unclenched his fists. He looked toward the council house and then at the gold hair bouncing as Judith moved even closer to the edge of the forest.

"*Gee-mah-gi-on-ah-shig*," he suddenly whispered.

Having made his mind up that he had to find out more about this white woman before she left the village with her father, Strong Hawk swung around on his heel and followed after her. Chief Gray Wolf had never failed in his counseling before, and he wouldn't now. No son . . . not even a next-chief-in-line . . . should interfere!

In her brisk steps, the wind caught in the hem of Judith's skirt and whipped it up, baring her knees and thighs. "Oh!" she said irritably, brushing it back down again with a hand. Nothing was working out as it should! And she was full of concern over her father. When his temper got heated up, there was no stopping his rage, and rage was the last thing that he needed at this time.

Then her thoughts wandered to eyes as dark as midnight and how their intense study of her had set her insides aglow. Would she ever be able to blot those eyes . . . the Indian's handsomeness . . . from her mind . . . from her *heart?*

Yet this attraction was futile. She was white. He was Indian. And their fathers already had enough to disagree over, let alone a son and daughter becoming infatuated with one another.

"Andi-dush-ay-ah-szhi-on-nee-gee?" Strong Hawk said as he fell in step next to Judith.

Judith stopped with a start, swallowed up by her heartbeats, glad, yet wary of his having come after her. Having the need to show him the deep loyalty to her father, she spun around on her heel and glared up at him, her arms locked defiantly across her chest.

"You only moments ago spoke to me in English," she hissed. "Why do you speak in Chippewa to me now? And why do you even follow me? We have nothing to say to each other. The differences between us were revealed in the council house."

Her insides tremored and there was a strange hollowness at the pit of her stomach as he once more branded her with his eyes. Why was it that he could disturb her so, when no other man had yet had that sort of power over her?

Nervously she shifted her feet . . . unlocked her arms . . . and clasped her hands together behind her as she fluttered her lashes up at him.

61

"I hear venom in your words, but I see something different in your eyes," Strong Hawk said, lifting his lips into a slow smile. "Why is that, white woman?"

Judith lifted her chin. "My name is Judith," she said hotly. "And I believe you had better look again, because I feel only anger at this moment. Your father proves to be a most unreasonable man. In your case, is it like father, like son? Do you share his views about the land and trees that lie adjacent to your village?"

Strong Hawk's smile faded. How could he confess to this lovely lady with the gentle name of Judith that he would lead the Chippewa away from this land and the trees, guide them farther north, should he be their chief? He couldn't tell her or anyone that he no longer agreed with his father about what was best for the survival of his people. But until he could, he had to help defend this land . . . these trees . . . the sugar bush. . . .

"It is not for us to discuss," he said dryly. "Your father . . . my father . . . are in council now. It is best that you and I talk of other things."

"And what would you suggest?" Judith challenged, placing her hands on her hips. She jerked her head haughtily, flipping her hair from across her shoulders. "What could we possibly have to say to each other?"

Strong Hawk took a bold step closer to her, his hands clenched to his side. "So you are one of the white people who thinks you are better than an Indian?" he growled, his dark eyes narrowed, his jaw set. "Your heart is *gee-seen-ah,* cold. I was wrong about you. And you are right. We have nothing to discuss."

With an angry jerk, Strong Hawk turned and walked briskly away from her. He was confused. Most generally he was a good judge of character. But this time he had been wrong. It ate away at his insides, this being wrong. For he knew that no matter how she felt about the Indians, *he* felt much for *her* that couldn't be denied. He wanted her. But this wanting was wrong. The blue of her eyes *and* the gold of her hair had blinded him to what was right for him, and perhaps even the future of his people!

Judith stood momentarily stunned. She watched Strong Hawk storm away from her, his muscled back stiff with anger, his hands still clenched at his side. Though his back was to her, she would never forget the hurt and humiliation in his eyes as he had accused her of thinking she was better than the Indians. What had she said to make him draw such a wrong conclusion? She didn't have any such ugly feelings inside her. How could she, when this one Indian made her realize what she had missed by not yet having discovered love for a man? This man caused a delicious feeling to swim around inside her. But she had felt that it was best to not reveal this to him!

Yet what was she to do now? She couldn't let him think her insensitive and cold. He couldn't walk away from her not liking her. There was so much unsaid between them—and to hell with what should or should not be where her father and his father were concerned! She would not let Strong Hawk forever think wrong things about her!

Raising her hand, Judith began to run after Strong Hawk. "Please," she said. "Please wait!"

Her voice . . . the knowledge that she wanted to stop him . . . stoked the fires within Strong Hawk that he wanted to refuse feeling. He closed his eyes and stopped, barely breathing, not understanding this weakness of his character that this white woman seemed to bring out in him. It was as though she had commanded him to stop and he had complied!

"Strong Hawk," Judith murmured, stopping, facing his back, with which he still shielded her from him, "I'm sorry. I didn't mean to lead you to believe that I . . . that I was talking down to you. It's just that I get so concerned over my father's welfare. His troubles are my troubles. His concerns are my concerns."

She was keenly aware of the wide expanse of his shoulders . . . the narrowness of his manly hips . . . and the strength of his muscular legs. Oh, only to be able to touch this man. She would probably be transported to heaven if ever she got such an opportunity. When he turned abruptly to face her, her body turned to liquid as his eyes touched her.

Her words had softened his mood and his heart. He now knew that she had spoken coldly before only because of loyalty to her father. He admired her for this! He, too, knew such loyalties, to his own father, and was glad that he and Judith could share some same emotions.

"We are the same in thoughts of our fathers," he said hoarsely. "That is good."

"Will you accept my apology for having offended you, Strong Hawk?"

"*Ay-uh.*"

"And what answer did you just give me in Chippewa?"

"Ay-uh is the Chippewa way of saying yes," he said, now softly smiling. "I am telling you that your apology is accepted. Now we can become better acquainted. Or do you want this?"

Judith cocked her head as a blush rose to her cheeks. *"Ay-uh,"* she giggled. "I want this."

Strong Hawk nodded toward the forest. "Shall we go into the forest where we can have more privacy to talk?"

Judith's eyes wavered as she turned and looked to where his gaze had traveled. No wigwams were close by, and where the sunshine didn't reach the forest it appeared to be so dark . . . so foreboding. And she was remembering seeing him looking at her, nude! But she wouldn't let him know that she had seen him!

She turned questioning eyes to him. "Now I am the one who has to ask . . . are you afraid to let your people see you talking to me, a white woman?" she queried. "Is that why you want me to go into the forest with you? To keep your people from seeing you with me?"

Strong Hawk chuckled. He lifted a hand to her hair and ran his fingers through its soft ends. "My mother is white . . . my grandmother was white," he said thickly. "How could I ever be ashamed to be seen with a white woman?"

His gaze moved to her hair. "Especially a white woman with such lovely hair that is the color of the golden winter wheat," her murmured.

His eyes lowered, to look into hers. "And, especially, a white woman with such a gentle name as Judith," he added softly.

A sensuous tremor coursed through Judith. She

tore her eyes away from him, fearing the feelings invading her senses. This was downright foolishness! What was the mystique about this Indian, giving him the power to make her forget everything about him? It wasn't only foolish . . . it was dangerous.

With a trembling hand, she eased his hand away from her hair, flinching when his flesh came in contact with hers. As she had thought it would be, touching him was pure heaven.

Feeling awkward and speechless, Judith toyed with the pleats of her skirt, smiling coyly up at Strong Hawk.

"Weh-go-nen-dush-wi-szhis-chee-gay-yen?" Strong Hawk asked huskily, once more looking toward the forest and then her. He knew that she had seen him watching her bathe, but he would never admit to having done it! But he realized that this was probably behind her sudden timid behavior. This amused him . . . this timidness.

Judith swallowed hard, then laughed softly. "Again you speak to me in Chippewa," she said. "If you want to become better acquainted, how can we, if you do not speak in English?"

Strong Hawk chuckled. "I asked you what you are going to do. Go into the forest to share the soft whispers of spring with me, or go and wait on your horse, for your father?"

"Soft whispers of spring," Judith sighed. "That's so beautifully put."

"I only speak of feelings," Strong Hawk said, his eyes showing an innocence that Judith hadn't noticed before. Though handsomely mature, he had a boyish nature about him when he was relaxed and not harboring anger inside him.

"Well, then, what are we waiting for?" Judith said, lifting the tail of her travel skirt up into her arms. "I choose to go into the forest with you. Shall we?"

Strong Hawk gently placed a hand to her elbow and guided her on and into the woods, to where the ferns were thickly green and twisted grapevines clung to the trees laden with huge grapes in tempting purple clusters. Strong Hawk stopped and picked a rich bunch of grapes, then once more guided her by an elbow beneath the trees and over thick moss and cushions of fallen leaves.

"Where are we going?" Judith finally asked, trying not to reveal a building alarm at being so far from her father. Though Strong Hawk seemed dependable enough, there was the smallest chance that he might not be.

"I know of a spot where we can truly relax," Strong Hawk said. "There is a creek where we can sit and drink up the drowsy, dreamy sunshine while we sit and talk."

He held the grapes out before him and chuckled. "And eat," he added.

"I can't stay long, Strong Hawk. My father . . ."

"Neither of us will be missed."

"But it may not take father long. . . ."

"Now that our fathers are alone, they will fully discuss their differences. This will absorb much time. So let us enjoy our time alone together."

Judith looked back over her shoulder, strangely

enough still able to see the council house, even better now than when they had first entered the woods. Somehow Strong Hawk had taken her in a half-circle, never truly moving too far away from where he could hear his father if he was called. Yet, in this section of the woods, the underbrush and trees were more dense, which did give them the privacy he desired.

Turning her head, once more looking straight ahead, Judith saw a break in the trees. There the sunshine appeared to be a shimmering cloak of gold as it spilled from the sky and into a bubbling creek only a few footsteps away. It was a lovely, esoteric setting.

"Mah-bee-szhon," Strong Hawk said. He hesitated for a moment, questioning her with his eyes, then suddenly grabbed her hand as he broke into a run. "Come. Do you see why I have brought you here?"

Judith laughed softly as she ran alongside him. "Strong Hawk, when I said I was afraid that I didn't have much time, I didn't mean that we were so short of time that there was a need to run," she said, becoming breathless.

Her whole body quivered when he stopped abruptly and drew her suddenly into his arms. He dropped the grapes to the ground and raised his fingers to the nape of her neck and gently urged her lips to his.

Judith began to shove at his chest, alarmed. Then her alarm gave way to wonder as her body became fused with his, and she, for the first time, ever, felt the brute strength of a man's thighs pressed sensuously against hers, and lips warm, sweet, and demanding upon hers. The feelings being created inside her stole her breath from her, and she was soon lost in helpless surrender. Limply, she let her arms creep about his neck and locked her fingers together. Overwhelmed by this drugged passion he was weaving into her heart, Judith returned his kiss. She trembled as his tongue entered her mouth and flicked at her tongue, igniting strange fires inside her.

The blood pounded in Strong Hawk's loins. His mind was a dizzy mass of rapture. *Ay-uh*, he was glad that his father had chosen to let the white man and his daughter ride on into the village instead of going to them to force them back to the city of Duluth! He was experiencing feelings he had never before felt with any other woman. He let his hand travel down the slender curve of her back, to her hip, and then up again, and around to where he chanced a touch of her breast through the cotton of her blouse. As he fully cupped her breast he heard Judith emit a soft moan, and he eased his lips from hers and looked down at her with hungry intent.

"Mee-kah-wah-diz-ee," he said huskily. "You are beautiful."

Judith could feel the heat in her cheeks and eyes. She slowly looked down at his fingers, which still circled her breast. She knew that she should feel ashamed for letting him take such liberties with her body, but there was something no longer within reach inside her brain, which usually guided her common sense. She wanted these delicious feelings—spiraling through her like a warm glow from a candle—never to stop. It was as though she was in a dream, and she didn't want to wake up.

Strong Hawk's fingers trembled as he moved them from her breast to the buttons that held her blouse securely in place in front. Watching her, seeing how her eyes now stared hazily into his and how her lips were slightly, seductively parted, he loosened first one button, then another. When all were set free, he spread the blouse open, pulled it off, then gazed with a dark passion at her breasts, which were no longer impeded by clothes, not even underthings, and stood firmly round from her chest.

Lowering his hand to one of her breasts, he fully cupped it, than ran his thumb over its dark, hardened nipple.

Judith closed her eyes as she took in a deep breath. She was melting, slowly melting. And when she felt his lips and then his tongue on her nipple, she placed a hand to his head and forced him even closer. She let out a soft gurgle of pleasure. But when he suddenly drew away from her and lifted her up and into his arms, she was jolted back to reality.

As he carried her to the creek and lowered her to the grass, spreading her out as though she were a rag doll, she realized the danger of letting this go any further. Her drunken stupor could make her do even more that she would later be sorry for, and it had to stop, and now!

She gasped and felt a sweet euphoric joy leap up inside her as Strong Hawk stretched out atop her and gathered her in his arms, urging her lips to his. Once more his lips were warm . . . sweet . . . gentle. One of his hands was kneading her breast, one of his knees was forcing her legs apart.

Panic rose inside Judith. She jerked her lips from

70

his, she shoved his hand from her breast, and she closed her legs. "Please stop. . . ." she softly cried, struggling to be set completely free. "My blouse. I must put my blouse back on. I don't know what I was thinking . . ."

Strong Hawk wove his fingers through her hair and gave her a hot, passionate stare. "You are sharing more than talk with Strong Hawk," he said huskily. "You have felt this strange power surging between us that I have also felt. It is right, this being together sensually, Judith. I believe destiny has brought us together. Do not fight it."

"Strong Hawk, please let me go," Judith softly argued, still tremorous from the erotic feelings that confused her insides. "I've never ever done anything like this before. I shouldn't . . . even . . . now."

Strong Hawk lowered a kiss to the hollow of her throat. "You've never done this before because we had not yet met," he murmured. "Don't you see? It was meant for you to only be with me in such a way. No one else."

"That's crazy," she laughed nervously. "I even think *I've* gone crazy."

She began shoving at him in earnest. "Let me up. I must get my composure and then return to your village. Coming here with you, alone, was wrong. My father . . . your father . . ."

"Our fathers have had their own moments of paradise with their chosen women," Strong Hawk argued, yet rising brusquely to his feet. "They would not expect less from us."

Shakily, Judith pushed herself up from the ground. Now aware of her exposed bosom, she covered her breasts as best she could as she inched toward her blouse, which lay on the ground. "Yes, they would," she said. "But only after wedding vows are exchanged between a man and woman is it right. I feel so . . . so ashamed for having done this."

Strong Hawk took a wide step and stopped her. He clasped his hands onto her shoulders, letting his gaze once more absorb the full ripeness of her breasts, then looked determinedly into her eyes. "Nothing you and I will ever share will be reason to feel ashamed," he growled. "Now that we have found each other, we are like the bees are to the honey. One would not exist without the other."

"But it is impossible," Judith said, swallowing hard. "We are . . . from . . . different worlds. . . ."

"So were my father and mother. So were my grandmother and grandfather," he said hoarsely, then drew her roughly into his arms, reveling in the touch of her breasts crushed against his chest. "I love you, Judith." He didn't kiss her. He just held her, sharing heartbeats and pure joy in being with her.

Loud shouts rang out from the council house, echoing through the forest. Judith wrenched herself from Strong Hawk's arms. "Father!" she gasped, having recognized his voice.

Strong Hawk's insides knotted. He turned with a start and stared toward the council house. "Father!" he gasped, having recognized *his* father's voice.

Strong Hawk and Judith then exchanged worried looks.

"They are quarreling," Strong Hawk growled. "Your father has upset my father."

Judith grabbed her blouse up from the ground and

72

pulled it on. "What do you mean my father has upset yours?" she argued, quickly buttoning the blouse. "It's apparent that your father has upset mine."

"How can you say that?" Strong Hawk argued back. "Your father is the one who came to my father's village with demands!"

"It is your father who is being unreasonable by denying my father what he needs," Judith spat, combing her fingers through her hair to straighten it.

"Gah-ween-nee-nee-sis-eh-tos-say-non," Strong Hawk said bitterly.

"There you go again," Judith sighed. "You're talking mumbo jumbo."

Strong Hawk's eyes narrowed and his nostrils flared. "Mumbo jumbo?" he gasped. "You will mock the way in which I speak?"

He turned and began running away from Judith, leaving her to stand staring after him.

"Oh, Strong Hawk," she whispered. "I didn't mean it. . . ."

When he disappeared from view, she gathered the hem of her skirt up into her arms to go to her father's assistance, still tasting Strong Hawk's kiss on her lips and the gentleness of his hand on her breast. How could she let herself . . . fall . . . in love . . . with him? They were worlds apart. Hadn't their last strained moments been proof of that?

Chapter Seven

Having been unsuccessful in convincing Chief Gray Wolf that the white man and Chippewa could share the abundance of the forests peacefully, Travis sat before the campfire, glowering, circling a cooled tin cup of coffee around between his hands. He stared into the soft embers of the fire, in another world, thinking about his younger, more spirited days. He hadn't backed down to anyone . . . especially an Indian! He wasn't used to losing, and it was hard being graceful about it.

Judith sat beside her father, silent in her own thoughts, sipping on her coffee. The night had an aura of softness about it. The fog swirled up and over the creek, creating an ethereal setting.

Judith's face warmed when she let herself once more recall how she had so wantonly let Strong Hawk touch . . . even kiss her breasts! Shame coursed through her veins, yet the memory of the delicious feelings that he had stirred inside her took precedence over all other feelings, and she knew that if she could live those moments over again, she would be guilty of behaving in the identical way. There was a magic between her and the Indian, a beautiful phenomenon that would forever be hard to understand, but harder yet to deny.

"Damn him," Travis suddenly growled, disturbing Judith's train of thought.

Looking quickly toward her father, for only a moment she thought that it was Strong Hawk of whom he was speaking, and that he had done so because he somehow knew of the relationship begun between Strong Hawk and his daughter.

"Father, what . . . did . . . you say?" she softly queried, now seeing the torment in his eyes as she focused her full attention on him instead of on herself. The day had been hard on him. It had probably done more harm to his health than she could even fathom. Knowing that Strong Hawk's father was responsible made her want to hate Strong Hawk, but she knew the utter impossibility of that! He had stolen her heart from her during their first brief eye contact.

"Chief Gray Wolf," Travis said, giving Judith a half glance. "He's one stubborn Indian. If you hadn't come and dragged me away from him when you did, we would have struck blows. He ain't a reasonable man, Pug. He ain't reasonable at all."

Judith eased the tin cup from his hands, placed hers on the ground, and refilled his cup with steaming hot coffee from the blackened coffee pot positioned in the outer hot coals of the fire. She offered the cup back to him.

"Here, Father. I think you need this," she said,

nodding toward the cup. "Then I think you need to climb inside your bedroll and get some shut-eye. Father, you just can't get this upset about things. You know it's not good for you."

Travis took the cup with a jerk, splashing coffee up over its rim. "I've told you over and over again that I don't need to be babied," he growled. "Wait until you have a house full of youngsters to practice your babying, Pug."

Judith unbuttoned the sleeves of her white shirt-waist blouse and then the buttons at her collar, sighing deeply. "If you don't take care of yourself, you won't be around to enjoy what children I may eventually have," she said soberly. "I know you don't want to hear that. But I had to say it. Now, Father, I'm going to call it a night. Then maybe you will."

She yanked one boot from her foot and then began struggling with the other.

"Some supreme being must be watchin' over those Indians," Travis said, ignoring her reference to retiring for the night. His pale blue eyes became gold with the flame's reflection as he once more stared into the fire. "Surely some sort of spirits guard the Chippewa and their land, because it don't seem natural that the government hasn't even bothered them. That's land ripe for developin'. Surely I'm not the only white man to come across it. Damn it, Pug. It's nearing the turn of the century. Most Indians have been forced to live on reservations by now. Why not the Chippewa?"

"That's not for us to figure out," she said, finally able to yank the boot from her right foot. "So why worry yourself so over it?"

"Why?" he said, furrowing his brow. "'Cause I fear the unknown. If it is spirits watchin' over the Chippewa, they might even be hoverin' over us now, watchin' us."

He looked over his shoulder at the lazy swirls of fog that persisted in hanging over the waters of the creek. "Just look at that," he said with a jerk of his head. "That fog's strange. There was no fog the other night when we slept here. Looks ghostly, it does."

Judith laughed nervously. "Father, I've never heard you talk like this before," she said. "I've never thought of you as being afraid of anything. Surely you are only jesting now, saying you're afraid of Indian spirits."

Color rose from Travis's neck to his face as his eyes met Judith's stare of wonder. "Sure I'm jestin'," he said hoarsely. "Sure I'm jestin', Pug."

"Thank goodness," Judith said, again laughing. She set her boots close to the hot coals of the fire to leave them there for the night. Her bare toes curled down into the cool grass as she rose to her feet.

"Hittin' the sack for real, Pug?" Travis asked, lifting an eyebrow toward her.

"Yes," she said, stretching her arms over her head, forcing a yawn. "It's been a hard day, even for me."

Travis splashed his remaining coffee onto the fire, causing a fretful hiss to rise into the air. He groaned as he pushed himself up from the ground. "Did the chief's son cause you some sort of problem this afternoon, Pug?" he asked, placing his hands to the small of his back as he straightened himself more fully. "You seemed flustered when you came from the direction of the woods. He even appeared a bit unruffled. Did you argue, or what?"

To hide the shock of blush suddenly enveloping her cheeks, Judith turned her face from him. "Yes," she said dryly. "We argued. But it's nothing to concern yourself with."

Travis chuckled as he ambled toward his bedroll. "I know that," he said. "If there's a daughter who knows how to take care of herself, you're it. I bet you showed that Indian, didn't you?"

Judith still avoided his eyes as she settled into her bedroll beside him. "Yes. I showed him," she murmured. "He won't ever be a bother to me, Father."

Her skin tingled, again remembering Strong Hawk's lips and hands. She hungered even now to be with him, sad to think that their differences would be the barrier that would keep them apart.

"Figured as much," Travis said, pulling a blanket up to his chin, stretching his weary bones out on the hardness of the ground.

Judith turned on her side to capture the colors of the fire against the backdrop of the white spray of fog. She was wondering what Strong Hawk was doing at this very moment. She let her gaze move to the sky. Through the fog's haze she could make out the perfect circle of the moon. Even it was haunting tonight. Was Strong Hawk experiencing these same thoughts . . . the same memories?

"I'm determined to get those trees and land," Travis suddenly growled. "If I don't, my company will go bankrupt for sure."

Judith turned quickly to face her father. Her heart lurched. "Bankrupt . . . ?" she gasped.

"Yes. And if I don't take the land and trees, someone else will," Travis said.

He yawned deeply, then said, "Night, Pug. I guess I'm even more tired than I thought. You get some good shut-eye, do you hear?"

A cold shiver ran up and down Judith's spine, as she stared blankly at her father's back while he turned on his side, facing away from her. Bankrupt, she thought to herself. She hadn't known there was that sort of threat hanging over her father's head. Now she understood his inability to control his stress. His whole future . . . *her* future, as he saw it . . . was in jeopardy. He had to feel free to move his crew to these untouched forests that were still called the land of the Chippewa. Somehow, Chief Gray Wolf had to be made to understand.

Hearing deep, restful snores already surfacing from her father, Judith smiled weakly. At least he was able to not let his troubles get in the way of his need for sleep. And when he was asleep, nothing could awaken him until he was ready to be awakened.

But Judith could not relax her muscles or remove her troubled thoughts from her brain so easily. First she saw Strong Hawk's passion-filled eyes looking down at her, firing her insides, and then she saw the pained look in her father's paling eyes.

Suddenly she felt torn between these two men and couldn't understand why. The time she had spent with Strong Hawk had been brief. The time she had spent with her father had been forever. . . .

Rolling over on her stomach, with her right cheek resting against the soft curve of her right arm, Judith tried to force her eyes shut. She wanted to sleep. She wanted to block out all remembrances of the handsome Indian.

Yet how could she? Wouldn't even her dreams now be disturbed by him? He would now be a part of her every moment . . . awake or asleep.

The lethargic floating feeling settled over her, the usual prelude to her falling asleep. She tensed when she heard the snapping of a twig close by in the woods, then exhaled peacefully when everything became quiet again except for the songs of the crickets hidden in the grass and the frogs croaking from the banks of the creek. She settled more comfortably onto her blanket, reaching to pull the top blanket up over her.

Then her eyes flew widely open and her stomach churned wildly as a hand clasped suddenly over her mouth so tightly that she couldn't emit a sound. Her arms flailed as she tried to hit her assailant, but she felt utterly helpless as another hand took her by her wrist and forced her up from the bedroll and away from the campfire. Stumbling, Judith tried to see who was abducting her, but her face was forced to stay in one position by the fingers still clasped tightly over her lips.

Anger and fear fused inside her when she was forced on farther away from where her father peacefully lay. The forest was dark. The forest was foreboding. Judith could feel the damp coolness settle on her face . . . she could smell a pungent odor drifting up from the rotted leaves. Her bare feet ached from occasional sharp-edged twigs piercing them, she stubbed a toe painfully on a rock that jutted up from the ground, and her wrist throbbed where her assailant still held her so unmercifully tight.

Then she was abruptly set free beside a beautiful black stallion reined to a tree limb. Breathless, she spun around, ready to pound on whoever was responsible for this wrongful deed. But when she found herself face-to-face with Strong Hawk, she was rendered speechless, her eyes wide and her mouth open in total surprise.

In the streamers of moonlight filtering down through the roof of the forest she could see Strong Hawk standing tall and erect, strength displayed in the corded muscles of his bare chest and shoulders. He wore only a loincloth, and his copper skin glistened beautifully, as though a thin application of grease had been spread over his skin.

Judith could hardly distinguish between his eyes and the night, both being of identical darkness. His lips were firmly set, as was his jaw, and his arms were locked angrily across his chest.

Seeing him so scantily attired was slowly unnerving Judith. The strength of his manhood was only a thin layer of deerskin away. . . .

"We must talk. *Ah-szhee-gwah*," Strong Hawk growled. "Much was left unspoken between us."

With her heart thundering inside her, Judith stood cautiously still, rubbing her raw wrist, forcing her eyes to look straight ahead, not down at his skimpy attire.

"What do you mean by abducting me in such a way?" she finally managed to say in a low hiss.

Strong Hawk released his arms and took a step toward Judith. "Did not you hear what I said?" he said thickly. "Much was left unspoken between us. I have come to right all wrongs."

"Ha!" Judith said with an angry toss of her head. "I do believe your approach is all wrong, Strong Hawk. And what makes you think that I want to talk to you about anything?"

"Your eyes told me more than your words when we were together," he argued. "I was aware of the response of your body to my caresses. Do you forget who I am? A next chief-in-line is wise in all ways of life. Even more so in matters of the heart."

He reached a hand toward her, but she flinched and took a quick step backward.

"How dare you to even try and imagine what I feel," she said angrily, yet wondering how long she could hold up under the command of his eyes, which set her pulse to racing. And what was this sweet pain between her thighs? She had felt it only one other time in her life, and that had also been when she was with him. . . .

"I know how you feel," Strong Hawk said, once more reaching for her and this time succeeding at grabbing her by the waist. With a gentleness he drew her next to him and looked intensely down into her eyes. "You feel as I. As though another night cannot be allowed to pass without our being fully together."

His lips bore down upon hers, his hands forced her body fully against his. He could feel the heat rising in his loins, grinding himself even closer into her. This need of her was eating away at his insides. Yet he wanted her to want him as badly. He would never take her by force. That was not the way of Strong Hawk. . . .

Judith was pinioned against him so hard she

scarcely could breathe, and his kiss seemed to be stealing even her sanity from her. She knew that she should struggle, but it wasn't in her to do so. She wanted to be with him. She would not deny herself this moment, for this one would surely be the last.

With a soft moan, she responded to his kiss and the sensual feel of his body moving seductively against her. She twined her arms about his neck and writhed with the intense pleasure of the moment.

Strong Hawk's lips moved gently away from hers. "My beautiful Judith," he said huskily. "You do understand that this was meant to be. You will let yourself enjoy the beauty of joined bodies?"

Though in a drugged state, the words "joined bodies" jolted Judith's sense of right and wrong. She jerked free of his embrace and began running blindly away from him, her bare feet hurting from foreign materials digging into them with each step that she took.

Then she was overwhelmed by his arms as Strong Hawk caught up with her and swept her up into his arms and held her tightly in place. "Do not fight me or your feelings," Strong Hawk murmured, raining soft kisses on her face.

One of his hands reached around and grazed the swell of her left breast, causing her breath to catch in her throat and rapture to take an even greater grip on her.

"My father," she said, shaking her hair back from her eyes. "Should he awaken . . ."

"He is asleep. He won't awaken until morning," Strong Hawk encouraged, now gently kneading her breast through her shirt. "Let us make love. Let us think only of each other for a change. You see, I suspect that you live your life through your father, as I am also guilty of doing. But for now, let's live for us."

"I can't, Strong Hawk," Judith softly cried. "It isn't right. I've been taught differently."

He lowered his lips to hers and softly kissed her, then drew away from her to look gently into her eyes. "Do you feel that kiss was wrong?" he asked, smiling.

"No . . ."

"Did the kiss make you feel peaceful and good inside?"

"Yes . . ."

"Then it is right."

He once more let his hand gently cup her breast. He saw passion glaze her eyes and was glad.

"Did my touching your breast make you feel peaceful and good inside?" he tested, barely breathing.

She closed her eyes dreamily. "Yes . . ." she barely whispered.

"Then it is right," he boldly stated.

Watching her reaction, he let his right hand slip up the coarse cotton material of her travel skirt, tremoring from the exquisite silk feel of her flesh where her legs reached up to tapered thighs.

His insides knotted when her underclothes seemed like a shield, protecting the very core of her womanhood. But that was no deterrent for him. His heart thundered wildly inside him as his fingers crept up and inside her silken underthing and then came in contact with her downy mane of hair, where her thighs met.

Judith hardly breathed now, her body one massive heartbeat as she let him have his way with her. It was as though she was under a strange spell, one that she could not shake herself from, making her want to experience . . . fully experience. . . .

Strong Hawk's fingers gently probed and stroked her between her thighs. "What I am doing now," Strong Hawk said huskily. "Does it make you feel peaceful and good inside?"

"Yes . . ."

"Then it is right," Strong Hawk said, bending to place her on the ground. Leaning down over her, his eyes absorbed her fully. "I've been only half alive until now . . . till you."

Caught up in this strange passion, Judith reached a forefinger to his lips and softly traced them. "I can't believe that I am willing to be here," she murmured, smiling shyly up at him. "But I am. And I want to be kissed, Strong Hawk. Please kiss me again. Please kiss . . . me . . . now. . . ."

His mouth was scalding as his lips crushed down upon hers. She writhed in response, feverish with desire now as his hand once more found her breast and he fiercely kneaded it through her shirt. His mouth was sensuous. His tongue surged between her teeth. And when his other hand began its ascent up her skirt, her limbs became weak . . . her heart wild.

Drawing away from her, Strong Hawk began stroking her flesh, then removed his hand and began unbuttoning her blouse, never moving his eyes from her lovely face. "It will be *mee-kah-wah-diz-ee, ay-uh*, so beautiful," he said throatily. "We will soon be transported to a world of momentary bliss. We will soon be as though one."

His words . . . his eyes . . . the touch of his fingers on her breasts sent shivers of rapture along her flesh. She raised up on one elbow and then the other as he set her completely free of her shirt. But she tensed as she heard the click of her snap as he unfastened it at the waistband of her skirt.

Trembling now from many emotions, Judith raised her hips and let him rid her of all her other garments. Then she lay nude on her skirt, which was now spread out beneath her, breathless as she watched Strong Hawk rise to his feet and slowly begin slipping his loincloth down away from him.

In the soft spill of the moonlight, Judith became keenly aware of his torso, perfectly sculpted to manly proportions. Her gaze swept slowly over him, to the muscled strength of his legs . . . to his narrow hips and waist . . . and to his broad chest and shoulders.

Then she felt heat rising to her cheeks when she found herself looking at the part of him that soon would be introduced fully into her body. Seeing this part of his anatomy brought her quickly to her senses. She began inching back on the ground, now aware of the shame that she should be feeling at being so wanton as to even be in the position of looking at a man in such a way.

Strong Hawk dropped his loincloth away from him and stepped out and away from it, then hurriedly knelt down over her, stopping her escape from him by imprisoning her with his body as he stretched out over her.

"Do not be afraid," he said huskily, framing her face gently between his hands. "Let me guide you.

Let me teach you the ways of making love. The world is full of many sorts of pleasure, but what we are about to share is the ultimate of pleasures."

"This isn't the time . . . ." Judith whispered, lowering her lashes, now embarrassed that she had let him undress her and that she lay nude on her rumpled travel skirt. A soft breeze touched the part of her flesh that wasn't covered by him, causing a chill to ripple through her.

Strong Hawk traced the line of her jaw with his finger. "This is the time," he said huskily. "But if you really feel awkward, you are free to go."

Judith tensed as he leaned away from her, completely freeing her. She pushed herself up on an elbow. "I really must return to my father," she said shakily. "Please understand, Strong Hawk."

"You do what you must," Strong Hawk said, gesturing with the sweep of a hand toward the open spaces. *"Mah-szhon.* I will not stop you." ·

Judith watched him closely as she rose fully to a sitting position. "I wouldn't ever have thought you capable of . . . of . . ." she said, but couldn't say the ugly word "rape."

"Rape . . . ?" Strong Hawk said with the lift of an eyebrow.

Her lashes fluttering nervously, Judith laughed softly. "Yes. Rape," she said.

"When we make love, it will be equally shared," Strong Hawk said huskily. His gaze burned along her bare skin as he once more absorbed her nudity.

Judith began gathering her clothes up from the ground. "There will never be a 'when,'" she murmured. "I will never allow myself to get caught

87

up . . . caught up . . . in . . ."

"In rapture?" Strong Hawk said, completing her words for her.

"I'm not sure if that's how I would describe this position I now find myself in," Judith said, hugging her clothes to her bosom. "Now, please, Strong Hawk. I just want to get dressed . . . and . . . leave."

"Just one more kiss, Judith?" he asked, running his fingers along the slender curve of her throat.

With passion-heavy lashes, Judith looked up at him. His nearness was smothering her. He was even anchoring her with the hold of his eyes. Her heart was racing out of control as his fingers lowered and sent butterfly touches across her breasts. She swallowed back a soft cry of ecstasy as his lips were suddenly there on the hardened nipple of her breast. His tongue flicking over the nipple was crazily intoxicating her into mindlessness. She hadn't wanted this. or . . . had . . . she . . . ?

"The kiss?" he said in a husky whisper. "One last kiss, Judith?" His eyes were hot coals, scorching her as he now gazed intensely down at her.

Tossing her clothes aside, Judith reached her hands about his neck and drew his lips to hers. "Yes . . ." she whispered. "Kiss me. Love me. I need you, Strong Hawk."

A soft sob rose from the depths of her throat when his mouth came down upon hers, scalding her, relighting the flame of desire inside her. She now knew that no matter how hard she fought this need, she couldn't help but give in to it. She gave herself up to the rapture as Strong Hawk stretched her out beneath him.

With a thick, husky groan, he continued to search her lips with his meltingly hot kiss as he nudged her legs apart with his knee. Trembling, he guided his manhood to her soft mane of golden hair, then probed . . . softly probed. He smiled to himself, realizing that he was the first man to be with her in such a way because of the effort it was taking to enter her.

He drew his lips from hers and gently framed her face between his hands. "The pain you will only briefly experience will be quickly replaced by a wild pleasure," he softly explained.

Judith was so enraptured by Strong Hawk and his hands now running sensuously up and down her heated flesh that she was only half aware of his words. Pain? She was already experiencing pain. But it was a sweet, melting sort of pain, and she welcomed more of the same. . . .

Strong Hawk once more lowered his lips to hers. As he thrust himself inside her, finally fully entering her, his mouth smothered her outcry. And then he felt her body relaxing against him and understood the passion that she was now feeling. He was feeling it also. . . .

Guided by some unknown instinct, Judith raised her hips to meet his eager thrusts. She closed her eyes, feeling the drunken spinning of her head. When Strong Hawk's lips lowered to her breast, she pulled his head closer until she even felt his teeth pressed into her flesh.

Then her hands began to run over his nakedness, down to his muscular male buttocks. Her fingernails dug into his flesh as his body moved in and out of hers. She moaned . . . she writhed. And then something seemed to explode inside her brain as a delicious feeling engulfed her and transported her momentarily away from herself. She softly cried out. She clung fiercely to him as he began quivering from head to toe, then grew quiet, breathing hard as he fell away from her.

Feeling amazed, yet wickedly content, Judith eased over next to Strong Hawk and fit herself into the curve of him. "It was beautiful," she murmured.

"And anything as beautiful cannot be wrong, Judith," Strong Hawk said thickly, wrapping an arm about her, snuggling.

"No. I no longer feel as though I've done anything wrong," she murmured, giggling. "Yet, I'm sure my father would argue that point with me."

The mention of Judith's father caused a coldness to sweep though Strong Hawk. He eased out of her arms and reached for his loincloth and pulled it on. "Your father," he grumbled. "It would seem that he is a man who enjoys an argument."

Judith's eyes widened. She moved to a sitting position. "What?" she softly gasped. "What did you say about my father?"

Strong Hawk went about gathering her clothes, then handed them to her. "*O-mah*," he said. "You should get dressed. The night air could cause you a chill."

Judith accepted her clothes. She gave him a quizzical stare as he walked away from her to stand beside his stallion with his head half hung.

After hurrying into her clothes, Judith went to Strong Hawk. She felt pain when she stepped on a sharp rock, which caused her to grab her foot and teeter sideways, falling against him.

He swung around, his lashes heavy over his dark eyes. Steadying her, he then inspected the sole of her injured foot. "Does it hurt?" he asked softly.

"Only barely," she sighed, easing her foot away from him. She tested it as she placed it back on the damp ground. When the pain appeared to be completely gone, she stood straight-shouldered before Strong Hawk, questioning him with her eyes.

"What you said about my father," she said. "I believe you are assuming wrong things about him. He is a kind, lovable man."

"He did not behave in such a manner toward my father," Strong Hawk grumbled. He once more placed his back to her and began stroking his stallion's sleek black mane.

"From what I heard, your father was no saint today," Judith argued. "His voice was just as loud, if not louder, than my father's."

Strong Hawk spun around on his heel, his eyes flashing with anger. "Your father had no right to make demands of my father," he growled. "Your father has no rights to this land."

Strong Hawk firmly clasped Judith's shoulders. "You must convince your father that he was wrong to come here. I have come here tonight to ask you to talk to your father. Make him understand the wrong that is plaguing his mind."

Judith paled. She jerked free of him. "You came here tonight only . . . to . . . plead your father's case?" she gasped. "You didn't come here to see me, to be with me as you earlier said you did? Making love to me was only a . . . a . . . ploy . . . to . . . to get what

91

you wanted from me, which in truth was not love . . . but for me to agree to talk my father out of his plans.''

She looked away from him, choking back a sob. A sick feeling circled around inside her. She felt degraded . . . humiliated . . . totally ashamed.

Strong Hawk placed a forefinger to her chin and urged her face around, forcing her eyes to meet his. ''That is not so,'' he said thickly. ''I love you, Judith. From the first time I saw you, when you were bathed in moonlight, cleansing yourself in the creek, my heart suddenly no longer solely belonged to me. What we just shared. Did you not realize that was special . . . that I could never feel the same about another woman?''

Color rose to Judith's cheeks. ''So you finally admit to being guilty of voyeurism that night?'' she hissed. ''You stole my private moment away from me that night?''

''The night has a thousand eyes,'' he said hoarsely. ''Mine were just a part of the night.''

Judith jerked away from him and began storming away from him. ''You won't get a chance to share any more nights with me,'' she spat. ''Strong Hawk, I don't care ever to see you again.''

Strong Hawk's pride would not let him go after her. Instead, he mounted his stallion and rode away from her, hurt . . . angry.

Hearing the muffled sound of the stallion's hooves moving away from her, Judith stopped and turned, to try and get a last glimpse of him. Her insides knotted. Had she spoken in haste? Had she wrongly accused him?

Raking her fingers through her hair, she went back to the campfire, feeling low in spirit. She settled down on the ground close to the fire, watching the dying flames. Picking up a twig, she scattered the orange glow of the ashes about, wondering about the exchange of heated words between herself and Strong Hawk, and how she had felt, thinking he had used her for his own benefit.

"I don't want to feel used," she whispered. "I can't believe he made love to me for all the wrong reasons."

Hurtful anger made her throw the twig into the fire and go back to her bedroll, to stretch out between blankets. Her eyelids mercifully grew heavier and heavier, until she finally entered the pleasant void of sleep.

Chapter Eight

Safely back home, with her golden hair tied back from her face, attired in her pale blue velveteen night robe and soft fuzzy slippers, Judith left her bedroom, worried. The house was too quiet, and that wasn't like her father. He was usually up at daybreak, loudly discussing the day's activities with the servants, handing out orders right and left.

But this day, nothing. Judith had to believe the journey to the Indian village had been too traumatic for her father. It had been for her . . . but in a much different way. She was still tender between her thighs, where she had so shamefully, willingly, been introduced into the ways of making love.

Circling her fingers into tight fists at her side, she softly cried. "How could I have been so . . . foolish? Strong Hawk doesn't even care about me. He tricked me into making love, only to use me."

Her eyes grew intensely bluer in color. "Never again!" she hissed. "I would die first."

Yet she wondered if any other man could ever take

Strong Hawk's place in her mind and heart. He seemed to be constantly with her. His face would suddenly appear before her eyes . . . his hands would be molding her breast . . . his lips would be on hers urging her once more into total surrender.

A fit of coughing from another room drew Judith's mind back to the present. "Father!" she gasped.

As she hurried down the wide hallway her house slippers echoed almost ominously on the waxed oak floor. The morning was gray with a threat of rain, and gaslights in bronze wall sconces in the shape of western lanterns lighted her way to the closed door of her father's combined private bedroom and study.

Judith stepped up to the door, barely breathing. She placed her ear to the door, wondering if her father was still asleep. If so, she wouldn't want to disturb him. Rest could be the best medicine for him now.

Another bout of coughing from inside the room was cause for Judith to hurriedly open the door, knowing that in no way was her father peacefully resting. His health was worse. And she felt totally helpless.

The drapes were still closed at the windows and only a faint light burned from a smoking kerosene lamp on her father's desk, far across the spacious room from where he lay. The lamp's soft glow showed a desk of cluttered papers and opened ledgers and a mass of cigar stubs in an ashtray. From all appearances her father hadn't gone to bed as early as he'd promised he would, but had, instead, poured over his ledgers and filed through his papers probably into the wee hours of the morning.

An oval braided rug muffled Judith's footsteps as she inched her way to the massive oak, four-poster bed. In the semidarkness she could only see a faint shadow of her father's form beneath rumpled blankets. On the splay-leg nightstand beside the bed sat a half-emptied bottle of whiskey and a glass knocked over on its side.

Judith's nose twitched as she reached the bed and stood silently staring down at her father. She smelled the mixture of stale cigar smoke and alcohol, and thought that both of her father's bad habits were only helping to make him worse.

Her eyes now adjusted to the darkness of the room, Judith studied her father even more closely. Only his face was visible above the blankets. His thinning sandy-colored hair was partially covering his closed eyes and his cheeks were of an ashen color and sunken, his mouth gaping open in a soft snore above his open-necked nightshirt.

Judith placed a hand over her mouth and tears shone at the corners of her eyes. Never had her father looked so old as at this moment. Somehow she felt like an intruder, observing him in his sleep, when even the most handsome man or beautiful woman could look their worst.

Yet she was compelled to stay, to make sure that he was in a natural sleep, not a sleep caused by a weakened state. She jumped when the whole bed shook as her father began coughing once more. Biting her lower lip nervously, Judith leaned over and lightly placed a hand to his brow, checking for a temperature.

As she touched him, Travis's eyes flew wide open.

"Pug, what're you doing?" he asked, brushing her hand aside.

He leaned up on an elbow, kneading his brow as he looked up at her and then toward his cluttered desk. So she had seen. She knew that his worries of bankruptcy were a reality and had kept him up most of the night. The ledgers never lied.

Judith took a step backwards. "Father, your coughing drew me to your bedroom," she said softly. "And the fact that you've yet to rise for the day is cause for my alarm."

"Babying me again," Travis growled.

"Oh, Father, I don't mean to," Judith sighed. "It's just that I worry so. The cough. It sounds so bad."

"Ain't nothin'," Travis growled. "As you discovered by the palm of your hand on my forehead, I have no temperature. It's just the shortness of breath that causes me to cough."

"Even . . . in . . . your sleep?" Judith quietly tested.

Travis's face shadowed. "Even in my sleep," he grumbled. He reached for his maroon satin robe at the foot of the bed and slipped his arms into it, rising from the bed on the opposite side from where Judith stood, tying the robe securely in place at his waist.

Stepping into leather house shoes, he lumbered over to the desk and rifled through some papers. "We need the push north, Pug," he said hoarsely. "If not . . ."

He clutched at his heart and paled, gasping for breath. Shakily he leaned against the desk, wheezing.

"Good Lord—" Judith cried, rushing to his side. "Father, you're having another spell. I must go and get Doc Somerset."

Travis angrily flailed an arm into the air. "Damn it, Pug, will you cut it out?" he said between more wheezings. "Just help me back to my bed and you go on your way today and let me be. I want to be left alone by everyone. Do you hear?"

"But, Father . . ." Judith softly protested.

"*Everyone*, Judith," Travis said darkly.

His not calling her by her nickname made Judith know that he meant business, and she was afraid that further argument with him might rile him more. Instead she placed an arm about his waist and began helping him to his bed.

"I'll have orange juice and coffee sent up," she said, hoping that he would at least agree to that. She glanced toward the bottle of whiskey and empty glass. "And I'll remove the alcohol from your nightstand."

"Leave the whiskey," he grumbled.

"But, Father . . ."

"It makes me rest, Pug. And rest is what I need after that meetin' with that damn stubborn Indian, Gray Wolf. And it won't be any different when his son Strong Hawk becomes chief. He's a younger replica of his father in appearance and manner."

A wave of remembered pleasure crashed through Judith at the mere mention of Strong Hawk's name. She swallowed hard, not wanting Strong Hawk to mean anything to her. She meant nothing to him.

"Let's not talk about the Chippewa today," she softly urged. "For today, just try and place all of your worries aside."

"But what about tomorrow?" he said hoarsely, easing down onto his bed. "And the day after tomorrow? You can't run away from problems that easily, Pug."

"We can take it one day at a time," she said, helping him off with his robe. "Just rest today. Tomorrow will take care of itself."

Groaning, Travis slipped beneath the blankets and stretched out, staring weary-eyed up at Judith. "And you?" he said thickly. "How about your tomorrows should my ticker just up and stop? I'd be leavin' you in one hell of a mess."

"Father, don't talk like that," she murmured, lowering a kiss to his cheek. "After resting today, you'll be as good as new. You'll see."

But she didn't believe this. As each day passed, she had felt a slow panic rising and had begun wondering, herself, what the future held for her. She didn't want to inherit his business, bankrupt or not. It didn't appeal to her in any respect. And any time she had begun making any sort of plan of her own for the future—she had even wanted to attend college— her father had stood in the way, making her then feel guilty for talking of leaving him alone. Rory, his son, had not been so easily dissuaded and had succeeded in making a life for himself. But a daughter's place was in the home with a father, her father had always said, especially when there wasn't a mother.

Judith's eyes brightened. Rory! He had to be the answer. Surely he wouldn't refuse to return home for a little while to help in this family crisis, especially after hearing how ill his father was. Surely Rory still had feelings for his father, though something in Rory's youth had happened to keep father and son at arm's length.

Travis reached up and patted Judith on the cheek. "Now you get outta here and let your pop have his beauty rest," he chuckled, his mood lightening.

"You'll be all right?" Judith softly questioned.

"Just fine," he said. "And what are your plans? What are you going to do to keep yourself out of mischief today?"

She now knew that she had to travel to St. Paul, to talk to Rory. And she felt compelled to do it immediately for fear of what the future might hold.

"I think I'll take a trip to St. Paul," she said, watching his face for the haunted expression that appeared when any mention of Rory had been or was going to be made.

Travis dropped his hand to the bed, his eyes hollow as he gave Judith a somber look. "To St. Paul?" he said. "To buy a new hat . . . or to see Rory?"

Judith forced a giggle. "Both, I guess," she said. "Is that all right, Father? Will you truly be all right while I'm gone?"

He looked away from her. "He won't have time for you," Travis growled. "He's too busy at the state capitol, usin' his knowledge of law."

Judith straightened her back. "He'll have time for me," she said softly. "We usually go horseback riding. It's kind of nice, being with Rory like that."

"Harumph," Travis grumbled. "I wouldn't know. Seems he's forgot where we live. I'm surprised he even still knows how to ride horseback. I'd think he'd be more proper in a lady's buggy. Why, he ain't even taken a wife yet, and he's twenty-five. Ain't much of a man, that one."

"Father!" Judith gasped, blanching. "What a thing to say!"

Travis chuckled and reached to pat her hand. "I don't always mean everything I say. You know that," he said. "Especially where Rory's concerned. Now you go on. Buy the fanciest hat in St. Paul. Then bring it home and model it for me. Is it a deal?"

"It's a deal," Judith laughed. She sat down on the edge of the bed and placed her cheek to her father's, then softly kissed him. "I'll be back tomorrow."

Then she hurried from the room, anxious to see Rory, even if for all the wrong reasons as far as he would be concerned.

After a fine spray of soot blew into the train window, causing Judith to sneeze and to fret about whether or not the black specks might ruin her hat or dress, she quickly slammed the window shut. With a lace-trimmed white linen handkerchief, she dabbed at her nose and chin, then placed the handkerchief inside her purse, knowing that St. Paul was only a few more miles down the track.

Watching the forest slipping by outside the window, she remembered tales told by people in Duluth and St. Paul of the great fire that at one time had raged through the forest, killing anything and everything in its path. That had been twenty years ago, before Judith was even born, and her mother and father had been living in Texas. It was said that a train on these very tracks had tried to outrun the fire by traveling in reverse away from the flames, but the flames had moved more quickly. The passengers who hadn't yet fled for safety in a nearby lake had burned to death and even some of those who had succeeded in getting away from the train had burned from falling debris and trees.

A shudder shook Judith's body. She found it hard to imagine such a tragedy, when now the forest was alive with spring blossoms, so peaceful in its beauty.

"St. Paul!" the conductor's voice boomed out as he made his way down the aisle of the passenger car. "Next stop, St. Paul!"

Judith's heart began to race. It was too long between visits to St. Paul. Though she was angry at Rory for seeming to have forgotten he had a father, Judith missed and loved him.

Her fingers went to her hat, hoping that it was sitting straight enough on her head. She had swept her hair up into a swirl atop her head, and she wore an afternoon hat stylishly displaying an egret plume, with a pale blue satin-faced brim to match her powder-blue tailored suit. The double-breasted suit accented the voluptuous swell of her breasts and the tininess of her waist where the skirt flared out. Beneath it were silk petticoats that rustled enticingly whenever she even slightly moved her legs.

She hated corsets, which not only confined her but choked her as well, though all proper ladies wore such things when they dressed stylishly. It was only when she was in jeans and a shirt that she could relax. But to visit her successful brother in St. Paul she had to dress the part of his affluent sister from Duluth.

Seeing houses now coming into view alongside the tracks outside the window, Judith picked up her white gloves and began working them on, a finger at a time. When this was done, she took a small mirror from her purse and peered into it, smiling back at her image, liking what she saw. Her cheeks were rosy pink, her teeth sparkling white, and her lips a soft crimson. Her lashes were thick and heavy over her eyes, which shone back at her in exquisite blue, more vivid today because of her eagerness to spend some time with Rory and hopefully to talk him into returning home to confer with their father.

Yes, Rory was her only answer! He was truly their father's only answer!

The train's brakes squealed as it came to a shuddering halt. Everyone seemed to rise from their seats at the same time, filling the narrow aisle before Judith had had a chance to slip from her seat. Drumming her fingers nervously on her lap and watching impatiently as everyone moved onward, she finally felt free to rise and leave herself.

Reaching overhead, she took her small valise down from the luggage shelf, then eagerly walked toward the door, catching glimpses of the mulling crowd outside the passing windows, but not yet seeing Rory. She had sent him a wire informing him of her arrival. Hopefully he had received it in time to meet her. There was a chance that he might not even have time for her.

"I will see to it that he does," she determinedly whispered to herself. "For one day, at least, he can have time for his sister!"

Holding on to her hat, she took the three steps that led out of the train. As she placed her feet on cobblestones, she heard her name being yelled through the crowd. Her eyes shot around her; then she saw his towering height and coal-black hair above the rest of the crowd as he worked his way toward her. He was waving . . . he was smiling. He was just as glad to see her! Judith was relieved.

Still holding on to her hat with one hand and her valise with the other, she inched her way through the crowd, momentarily losing sight of Rory. And then he was suddenly there, hugging her tightly to him.

"Sis," he said, "it's good to see you."

Then he stepped back away from her and looked her up and down. "I don't know how it's possible, but you're even prettier than the last time I saw you." He kneaded his chin and lifted a brow quizzically. "Hmm," he murmured. "Which is the most prominent? The glow of your cheeks or the sparkle in your eyes?"

Then he chuckled. "A man has to be the cause of that special glow. Want to tell me about him?" he teased.

Judith's lashes lowered over her eyes and she felt the flame rise to her cheeks. "There is no man, Rory," she fussed.

Rory broke into a fit of laughter. "You say there's no man, yet you're blushing," he said. "Sis, you wouldn't blush at only my suggestion. There is a man. Want to tell your big brother who the lucky man is?"

With annoyance flashing in her eyes, she quickly looked up at Rory. "Am I pestering you into telling me about your private life, Rory, whether or not you have a special friend?" she challenged.

"Touché, little sister," Rory chuckled, winking at her. "Now, before the crowd swallows us whole, let's get to my buggy."

He took her valise and guided her by an elbow until they reached the buggy. Judith let him assist her up and onto the seat, then studied him out of the corner of her eye as he also climbed aboard and began steering his stately brown mare away from the train depot.

There was no resemblance to their father, except for Rory's tall and lanky height. On his face he wore features that belonged to only him. His nose was long, his nostrils wide, his eyes green, his jaw squared. He was tan, but naturally so, having been born with the darker tone to his skin.

This day he wore his expensive, tailored blue pin-striped suit well, with a detachable collar on his white silk shirt and a diamond stickpin shimmering from the folds of the blue satin cravat at his throat.

He was a man of distinction, and when he spoke it was in a succinct manner, having left his Texas drawl behind him.

Hatless, his black hair blew gently in the breeze, and his lips were lifted in a soft smile as he suddenly looked her way.

"I've moved since you were last here, sis," he said.

"Oh? You did?" she said. "In which part of the city are you now living, Rory?" She clung to the seat as the horse and buggy swerved around carriages and men on horseback.

Rory snapped the horse's reins. "You'll find it quite to your liking," he said, flashing his straight white teeth as he grinned at her. "We'll be there shortly."

"You seem pleased with the move," Judith said,

returning his smile. "I'm sure it must be impressive for you to be so mysterious about it."

"It will do in a pinch," he chuckled. Then he sobered. "In your wire, you didn't give me a specific reason for your visit, sis."

He gave her a quick glance, then steadied his gaze straight ahead again, on the road. "There is a reason, isn't there? You've never come to St. Paul before on such short notice."

Judith wasn't sure how to approach him, remembering his reaction to her requests on many other occasions. She didn't answer right away. "The city of St. Paul is so much nicer than Duluth," she sighed. "I always feel as though I'm traveling beneath a giant umbrella, the way the elm trees' limbs hang over the streets. And, Rory, the leaves are on the trees here. In Duluth, there are only buds. You wouldn't think that the few miles between the two cities would make that much difference in the seasons. . . ."

"Sis!" Rory interrupted. "You've procrastinated long enough," he said. "No one knows better than me the difference between the two cities. That's why I chose the one over the other. So don't try to evade my question by rambling on over the trees . . . the weather. . . ."

"The houses are so neat. The paint on them is so white and fresh," Judith said, still purposely avoiding what she knew was a sour subject for her brother, yet not understanding why. "And the lawns. They are so green."

"Judith!" Rory stormed. "Cut out the small talk. Tell me why you're here. It's Father, isn't it? He's prodded you into coming, to talk me into going to

Duluth, isn't that so?"

Something tugged at Judith's heart. She turned her face to her brother. "Why is going to Duluth to be with Father such a hard thing to do?" she blurted. "Good Lord, Rory, what is this thing between you and Father that keeps you apart? Will I ever know?"

"I don't know how you'll ever know, when I don't even know myself," Rory growled. "All that I know is that the tension between us began as far back as when I was seven. It was at that time that he quit doing much with me. After a spell I got used to it, and it became a way of life with me."

Rory guided the horse onto Wabasha Street where the state capitol building was now in sight, its tall dome reaching into the sky. This was Minnesota's second capitol building, the first having burned in 1881. A third building was now under construction to take the place of the second, because a larger building was needed to house all the activities of those who ran the proud state of Minnesota. It was to be a magnificent building, the cornerstone having been laid by Alexander Ramsey in 1896.

"Rory, if you were seven when you first noticed this, that was close to the time when I was born," Judith said shallowly. "You don't think Father treated you this way because he . . . because of me, do you?"

Rory cleared his throat nervously. "I can't deny that I've had my moments of being jealous of your relationship with Father," he said thickly. "But no need to worry. I no longer ever think of it one way or the other. Like I said. His treating me that way became a part of my way of life. And now I have a life of my own. I sure as hell don't need him."

"Rory, Father is quite ill," Judith said in a rush of words.

"Rory's head jerked around, his green eyes wavering. "Ill? In what way? Is his life . . . uh . . . threatened by the ailment?" he tested.

"You do care," Judith sighed, relaxing her shoulder muscles. "I hear it in your voice and I see it in your eyes."

"Sis, tell me if his life is in danger," Rory insisted.

"Perhaps . . ."

"What do you mean . . . perhaps?"

"It's his heart. He has spells."

"God."

"And he's having financial problems. There seems to be too much competition crowding the lumber industry. He's worrying about going bankrupt. I'm afraid the worry is going to kill him," Judith said. "Rory, I believe if you went home, that could help lift some pressures he is feeling. Perhaps you can advise him."

"He doesn't need or want my advice," Rory grumbled. "He never has. Why is now different?"

"Because he is worrying about the future," Judith said softly.

Rory laughed bitterly. "Sis, I'm not a part of that future he's worrying about," he said dryly. "You and I both know the terms of his will. You will inherit the business. Not I."

"Only because you made it clear that that was the way you wanted it," Judith softly argued. "One word from you is all that is required for it to be yours, Rory."

"And what would I do with my law practice?" he said, once more laughing bitterly. "I'm in demand now. Most of my clients are senators and congressmen. I like that, Judith. I like that damn much."

"There's more, Rory," Judith said, oblivious of the fact that he had drawn his horse and buggy to a halt in front of a two-story house across the street from the state capitol building.

"More?" Rory said, letting the reins go lax in his hands. "What have you left unsaid, sis?"

"Father has the notion that if he could buy up some land and trees farther north, his business could be saved."

"Sounds like a good idea. But I see that something about the idea bothers you, sis. What is it?"

"By north, I mean Chippewa country," she said cautiously.

Rory's eyes widened. "Are you trying to tell me that Father is wanting to try to make a deal with the Chippewa?"

"He's already tried. Chief Gray Wolf and Father came to harsh words over it. But Father is still determined. . . ."

"Well, now I know why you're here," Rory said, nodding. "And you have every reason to worry about this fool idea of Father's."

"Why do you say that?"

"Because as far as I know, Father's the first to try."

"Why is that, Rory? I don't understand why the government hasn't claimed the land."

He shrugged. "Beats me, sis," he said thickly. "But something has stood in the way of the white man's settling there. I think it's best to leave well enough alone."

"Then will you go to Father and talk some sense into his head?"

"Let's talk about it later," Rory said, patting her hand reassuringly. "Let me show you my house, and then we'll take that horseback ride. It will have to be a short ride today, because I have some commitments. But we can take a long ride into the forest tomorrow."

"Sounds good to me," Judith agreed.

"Well?" Rory said, nodding toward the house. "What do you think?"

Judith's head turned slowly around and she gazed intensely toward the two-story white frame house. A wide porch stretched across the front, and white wicker furniture and a porch swing made it appear cozy and alluring. But it was so big for only one man!

"It's quite nice," she said, and then she laughed softly as she looked toward Rory. "But is it big enough for you, Rory?"

"It was once a boardinghouse," he said. "It was at one time run by a colorful figure of a woman by the name of Rettie Toliver. But I've made many changes. I've knocked out many walls to make the rooms larger. And that's not only where I make my residence, I also run my business from there. It's quite handy, wouldn't you say, with the capitol only across the street?"

"Yes, quite," Judith said, smiling. "And now how about the grand tour, big brother? Show me how you've converted Rettie Toliver's boardinghouse into your own private domain!"

Chapter Nine

The night had been a restless one for Strong Hawk. No matter what he tried to focus his thoughts on, Judith was there, taunting him, accusing him of having made love with her for all the wrong reasons.

Ay-uh, there could be many reasons for making love, but when the right woman was found, only one reason reigned supreme. Love from the heart . . . and the need of fulfillment of such a love.

Nude, Strong Hawk flipped over on his bare back on his bed of blankets beside a crackling fire in his firespace and watched the spirals of smoke rising and leaving the wigwam through the smoke hole. Ah, if only he were at this moment a puff of smoke, escape from his torments could be so easy. He could rise into the sky, blend in with the clouds, and float peacefully away, into eternity!

But, *gah-ween*, he was quite alive, and the dull ache around his heart would not leave him. He knew that to have Judith . . . to fully possess her . . . was his only answer. But how? Without her, he was not *gah-kee-nah,* he was not whole.

A rush of footsteps sounded outside, drawing closer to his wigwam and causing Strong Hawk to rise quickly to his feet and draw on his loincloth. He brushed his fingers through his long, coarse black hair and took a step toward his entrance flap just as his mother's soft voice spoke through the young morning's silence.

"Strong Hawk? Son? Are you awake?" Danette asked, her voice tremoring with quiet alarm.

Strong Hawk's insides tightened, his mouth went dry. He knew that his mother would only be there that early in the day for one reason. It had to be his father. Surely his father's health had worsened. Strong Hawk could hear fear in his mother's voice.

Throwing back the deerskin flap, Strong Hawk stepped hurriedly outside, barefooted. In the dim twilight he could only see his mother's outline in her ankle-length deerskin dress, but he could smell her perfume. It always reminded Strong Hawk of a field of lily of the valley flowers, so sweet, just like his mother's personality.

"Gee-mah-mah?" he asked, towering over her. "Why are you here? *Ah-neen-ay-szhee-way-bee-zee-en?"*

Danette stepped closer, into the soft light emanating from the glow of the fire. She reached and took Strong Hawk's hands, looking up into his face. Something tugged at her heart, and she knew that it was the memory of another young, handsome Indian, with the same beautiful copper skin and perfect Indian features. Looking at her son was the same as looking at Gray Wolf as a young man, when their young love was new.

In her son she would always have a part of Gray Wolf when Gray Wolf was gone. But Strong Hawk could never really be a replacement. . . .

"Strong Hawk, it is your father," she blurted. "He's had a spell. You must go to him and talk some sense into his head. Will you? Will you go and tell him what he must agree to let us do? To not do so could mean his death."

Strong Hawk's heart began to pound against his ribs. His eyes narrowed into two dark slits as he peered through the soft haze of morning toward his parents' two-story log house.

"He again refuses to let you send for a white man's doctor?" Strong Hawk grumbled. "Is that what you are saying, *gee-mah-mah?*"

"*Ay-uh . . .*" Danette said, lowering her eyes, feeling a tear splash to her cheek.

Then she once more lifted her eyes to Strong Hawk. "Son, I know that you are not from the old school of the Chippewa in thoughts and beliefs, as is your father. You see the need of a white man's doctor as I do. But what can we do to convince your father of what must be done?"

"Has he gone to the sweat lodge or has he called for a shaman to come to his bedside?"

"He has gone to the sweat lodge, as he has all the other times," Danette mournfully sighed. "Being there alone could kill him in his weakened condition. It's too much of a strain on him."

She squeezed Strong Hawk's hands tightly. "Please do something, Strong Hawk," she begged.

"Father is stubborn," Strong Hawk said, nodding.

113

"As was Great-Grandfather Chief Wind Whisper and Grandfather Chief Yellow Feather."

"As even you are, my son," Danette softly argued. "But you do not let your stubbornness stand in the way of what is best for you."

"That is because I had a special mother," Strong Hawk said, smiling gently down at Danette. "You have guided me in ways that most Indian children weren't. You have given me wisdom no father ever could, be the father a chief or not. This is why you see in me this difference . . . this need to not let my every deed and thought be ruled by my ancestors and their beliefs."

"You will go to your father? You will ask him to return to his bed? You will demand that he agree to let you ride to St. Paul to get a doctor?"

Strong Hawk chuckled. "Now, *gee-mah-mah*, you know that is much easier said than done," he said. He drew her into his arms. "But I shall do my best."

Danette clung to him, placing her cheek to his solid chest. "What would I do without you?" she murmured. "My son. My beautiful son."

Strong Hawk urged her away from him and stood at arm's length from her. "*Gee-mah-mah*, you go and prepare *gee-bah-bah's* bed. I will do everything within my power to see that he returns to it, but I ask that you be patient. It may be difficult to interrupt the rites in the sweat lodge. Shaman Thunder-In-The-Sky will be quite displeased with me if I do this thing."

"For your father, you must," Danette softly encouraged him.

"*Ay-uh*. For my father," Strong Hawk said. He

nodded toward his parents' large log house. *"Mah-szhon.* Go and dry your tears and try to quit being so full of worry. It isn't good for you. You must also think of yourself as well as your husband."

Danette reached a hand to Strong Hawk's cheek. "I know," she murmured. "You are right. I must keep myself healthy so that I can care for Gray Wolf."

"Then you will go? You will do as I say?"

"Yes, my wise and beautiful son," Danette said, standing on tiptoe to kiss him lightly on the lips. "I will obey the next chief-in-line."

Strong Hawk chuckled hoarsely as he watched his mother turn and quickly disappear into the dark cloak of night.

But then he quickly sobered as he squinted his eyes and tried to see the sweat lodge in the distance. It, too, was disguised by the black of night, and Strong Hawk had to imagine what was happening inside the small dwelling. Oh, how often he had wanted to speak openly to his father, to tell him that the heat of the sweat lodge only succeeded in weakening him more instead of giving him strength, as the shaman and his followers had always taught. Strong Hawk's mother had good reason to be alarmed, for she also knew this and, too, had not yet become bold enough to tell her husband that what he was doing was not wise. No one told the great Chief Gray Wolf that anything he chose to do was not wise! It would be showing disrespect for the chief!

"But today? I must," Strong Hawk grumbled to himself.

He began to run in the direction of the sweat lodge, his bare feet cooling as the dew-dampened grass spread out beneath them. As he breathed he sucked the cool morning air into his lungs, invigorating him, and the rush of the wind on his face was even more welcome and refreshing. The heavier smell of wood burning suggested that some of the Indians were already awake in their wigwams, readying themselves for the day ahead of them. In the distance a dog barked, a horse whinnied, a baby softly cried. They were all familiar sounds to Strong Hawk—the peaceful sounds of his father's Chippewa village.

Something tugged at Strong Hawk's heart, realizing that his father could be taken from him and his people so quickly. Hadn't it happened to Chief Yellow Feather? Hadn't it also happened to Chief Wind Whisper?

"He just can't die," Strong Hawk whispered, choking as a fast-growing lump rose into his throat. "I must do everything within my power to see that he lives on, for many moons to come."

As Strong Hawk grew closer to the sweat lodge he caught sight of the low fire burning before it and he knew that Thunder-In-The Sky had already heated the stones that were used in the healing ceremony. Realizing this, Strong Hawk knew the dangers of entering the sweat lodge without having been invited. No air was ever allowed to enter once the stones were heated and placed inside the sweat lodge, and lifting the deerskin flap at the entrance could be the cause of such an untimely entrance of air.

"Hopefully I can move as quickly and as soundlessly as my father boasts so often I do," he said aloud, now only a few footsteps away from the lodge. "I will move as a spirit does. I will be soundless."

116

Once he reached the lodge, Strong Hawk stopped outside it long enough to catch his breath. He frowned as he looked at the small dwelling built with the smallest dimensions possible for the ceremonial curing of illnesses. The lodge consisted of a framework of bent poles closely covered with blankets, yet in the shadow of the fire it appeared menacing, because many men had been known to suffocate in such a sweat lodge when too overcome by heat and the lack of proper air.

Sniffing, Strong Hawk recognized the sweet and clean aroma of the cedar. It was emanating through the blankets of the lodge, and Strong Hawk knew that not only were the heated stones being used in an effort to cure his father, but also cedar boughs, as well. Cedar was known to purify, and when the boughs were boiled in water they would also serve as an antidote to sorcery.

Having procrastinated long enough, Strong Hawk bent his back, lifted the entrance flap, and stealthily moved on inside the lodge. He was quickly blinded by the darkness of the dwelling. He dropped to his haunches and stayed there, silent, letting his eyes adjust so that he could see beyond the soft glow of the candle burning in the center of the sweat lodge.

The heat in the small space was almost suffocating. It seemed to hammer away at his chest and temples the longer he sat there, but he could not disturb his father just yet. Though he had told his mother that he would not be afraid to interfere with the shaman's rites, he now knew that he had spoken out of turn. For now, he would just continue to watch. Chief Gray Wolf's belief in the shaman was strong. To disturb such a shaman at work would be to cause Strong Hawk's father possibly even more harm, by causing his rage to enflame so. *Ay-uh*, for now, Strong Hawk would just continue to observe.

Slowly objects became identifiable to him. First he saw the implements used for healing in the sweat lodge. There were four stones in the center of the floor, a pail of water, and a bunch of grass that would be used for sprinkling water on the stones. The three smaller stones were flat on some surfaces so as to support the larger stone, which was as nearly spherical as could be procured. This larger stone was regarded as the Chippewas' messenger to the great spirit Wenebojo.

Strong Hawk knew enough about this spiritual ceremony to know that the stones had been heated in the small fire outside the lodge. The three smaller stones were always heated first and placed in position in the middle of the lodge.

It was often at this point that the men who would be a part of the ceremony would enter the lodge. The larger stone was then heated as nearly red-hot as possible and brought in and placed in position with great care on the other three rocks, and the ceremony would then begin. Strong Hawk knew that he had arrived just prior to the beginning of the ceremony, because Thunder-In-The-Sky had not yet dipped the bunch of grass into the spiritual water.

His eyes were fully adjusted now, and Strong Hawk focused them on his father. Chief Gray Wolf sat straight-backed before the hot rocks with his eyes closed and lifted to the ceiling and his arms locked across his bare chest. He was clothed in only a loincloth, even his headband had been discarded, so that his coarse black hair hung loose and down his back. His copper skin was already shining with perspiration and his face was flushed, his skin drawn taut across his high cheekbones.

Letting his gaze move to the opposite side of the rocks, Strong Hawk now saw Thunder-In-The-Sky. He also sat quietly, his eyes closed in his own silent meditation. The shaman was stark naked, except for a rattlesnake bag worn over his shoulder, made of the skin of a rattlesnake and mounted on red flannel. The body of the snake hung down the shaman's back, with the head projecting over his shoulder. Inside this bag could be found either of two powerful curative agents . . . perhaps *mi-nisino-wuck,* the most highly valued herb of the Chippewa. A piece of this dried root was believed to effect a happy outcome in any difficulties. Or perhaps the shaman preferred the *Lathyrus-Venosus-Muhl,* the wild pea, whose roots were used to cure the sick and to act as charms. The shaman's coarse gray hair hung in a pigtail down his thin back, and his face was a mass of wrinkles. He looked a hundred years old, and when he moved his bones popped, as though a limb from a tree were snapping in two.

Thunder-In-The-Sky laid the ceremonial water and bunch of grass out in front of him. Suddenly he picked up the grass and dipped it in the water, then sprinkled it on the larger, upper hot stone.

"*We-e-e-e, ho-ho-ho,*" Thunder-In-The-Sky chanted with the action. Sweat poured from his brow and beads of perspiration were popping up all over his thin, caved-in chest.

"We-e-e-e, ho-ho-ho," Thunder-In-The-Sky once more repeated. "Wenebojo, hear the message being transfered to the spiritual rock. Take pity on Chief Gray Wolf. Make him well again so that he may continue to lead his people."

Thunder-In-The-Sky sprinkled water on the upper stone a third time and once more chanted. *"We-e-e-e, ho-ho,"* he said shrilly, his eyes still closed, his head bobbing up and down.

Chief Gray Wolf then answered the shaman's call. *"Ho-ho-ho,"* he said, raising a hand above his head. *"We-e-e-e, ho-ho."*

Thunder-In-The-Sky dropped the grass to the floor of the dwelling and went to stand, stooped, over Chief Gray Wolf. He grasped onto the head of the rattlesnake bag that hung over his shoulder and began moving it in a circle. "The steam is rising from the stone messenger," he said. "It is evidence of response on the part of the stone. The message will be received by Wenebojo. Wenebojo will help us in our undertaking of curing you of your strange illness, Chief Gray Wolf."

Gray Wolf lowered his hand and opened his eyes, staring dazedly at the larger stone. As though in a trance, he extended his hand over the stone and began moving it slowly in a circle. "I desire this messenger to say to Wenebojo that I desire health and long life," he said hoarsely, sweat pouring in silver rivulets down his cheeks and bare, muscular chest.

Thunder-In-The-Sky stooped to his haunches next to Gray Wolf. He slowly wiped the sweat from his chief's brow, then urged Gray Wolf to stretch out on his back, away from the stones. Then Thunder-

In-The-Sky reached for his rattle, a small wooden cylinder with a sewn cover of hide, which contained small stones and was pierced by a stick that formed the handle. He began to shake the rattle above Gray Wolf.

"Oh, my spirits, come and help me. Take pity. Help Chief Gray Wolf," Thunder-In-The-Sky cried in a slurred voice. He dropped down on the floor, crouching on his knees, weaving from side to side. He reached for something else, holding two white sucking bones in one hand and the rattle in the other. He shook the rattle and chanted in a low drone.

Strong Hawk tensed, knowing what the next procedure would be, but he couldn't interfere now. He had waited too long. The only thing that he could do was watch over his father and be there if he should need him. Only after the complete ceremony was over could Strong Hawk speak of his presence there. If he had only come sooner. . . .

He slunk back into the dark corner, still only a silent observer.

As though in a trance, Thunder-In-The-Sky laid down his rattle and lifted one of his hollow-tubed sucking bones, about as long as his thumb, and swallowed it. He then leaned forward, resting his weight on his hands and knees, looking at Gray Wolf. Then he swallowed the second sucking bone and began to weave back and forth again. All at once he spit the bones out of his mouth, all slimy with spittle, into his shaking hands.

He reached for his rattle again and began shaking it, filling the small spaces of the steam lodge with the faint sound of *wish-ah-wish-ah, wish-ah-wish-ah*.

121

Putting one of his sucking bones in his mouth and holding it between his lips, he still shook the rattle with his free hand, while he bent down low over Chief Gray Wolf's chest and rested the bone there, against it, and began sucking vigorously on the bone.

Suddenly Thunder-In-The-Sky brandished his rattle robustly, signaling that he had succeeded at what he had been working so hard at. He leaned out away from Gray Wolf and began spitting over and over again, smiling broadly. He had succeeded. He had sucked the sickness from Gray Wolf's body, and the sickness now lay on the floor of the lodge.

"Mee-gee-kee-shee-tahd," Thunder-In-The-Sky said proudly, rising to his feet. "It is done. You soon will be well, Chief Gray Wolf. Go now. Rest in peace."

Strong Hawk rose to his feet and stepped out into the open, startling the shaman, causing him to let out a soft cry and flinch.

Gray Wolf opened his eyes, blinking them wildly when he heard the outcry. He leaned up on an elbow and squinted as he looked through the semidarkness toward his son. "Strong Hawk?" he gasped. "What are you doing here?"

"Thunder-In-The-Sky has his way of looking out for you," Strong Hawk grumbled. "So do I have my own ways, *gee-bah-bah*. I have come to make sure that you are all right."

"In the presence of our ancestral spirits and with the powers of Thunder-In-The-Sky, why would you even think that you were needed?" Gray Wolf said, rising to a sitting position. His fingers combed through his hair, straightening it. "Do you not have the same faith as your father, my son?"

Strong Hawk's eyes wavered. "You know that my idea of the way things are and should be sometimes differs from yours, *gee-bah-bah*," he said. He gave Thunder-In-The-Sky a half glance. "But I much prefer to discuss these differences in private. Will you return to your house with me? Will you . . . *now* . . . ?"

With the back of his hand Strong Hawk wiped the perspiration from his brow. It was becoming harder and harder to breathe in the close confines of the steam lodge, and he could see how his father was laboring for breath. It was as he had thought. The steam . . . the heat . . . was beginning to be just a bit too much for his already weakened father.

Thunder-In-The-Sky picked up his rattle and sucking bones and stopped to look from Gray Wolf to Strong Hawk, revealing his anger by the set of his jaw and the flashing of his dark eyes. *"Gee-mah-gi-on-ah-shig-wah,"* he growled, then hurriedly brushed on past Strong Hawk and left the sweat lodge in a huff.

Gray Wolf began rising shakily to his feet, wheezing with the effort. "I believe you have offended our shaman," he said, groaning as he placed a hand to the small of his back. "You should never reveal your lack of faith in his mystical powers in his presence. It isn't good. You will be the next chief. Thunder-In-The-Sky is surely threatened by this. He feels he will have no place anymore in our village."

"Thunder-In-The-Sky is not my concern," Strong Hawk said dryly. *"You* are, *gee-bah-bah.*"

"You worry too much about your father," Gray

123

Wolf grumbled.

"And should I not?" Strong Hawk dared to say. "You would not be here in a sweat lodge with a shaman if you weren't concerned, yourself."

"How did you even know where I was?" Gray Wolf asked, taking a shaky step toward Strong Hawk.

Strong Hawk's eyes humbly lowered. He didn't answer, not wanting to fuse his mother's fears with his own, thinking this might unduly upset his father.

"It's your mother, isn't it?" Gray Wolf sighed. "She told you, didn't she?"

Strong Hawk slowly looked up at his father and began to speak but didn't. Instead, he jumped with a start as Gray Wolf teetered and half fell against him. "Father!" he gasped, grabbing for his father's arm.

Gray Wolf laughed nervously. "It's the heat. That's all," he said. "Let's leave this place. What I came for has already been achieved. I now wish to go to your mother and show her that I am all right."

"But are you really?" Strong Hawk challenged, taking his father by an elbow, steadying him as he led him out into the cool splash of the morning air.

"My son, what can I say to make you understand that your worries are in vain?"

"There is something that you can agree to do that will make me worry less."

"And that is?"

"Let me ride to St. Paul and get a white man's doctor."

Gray Wolf jerked himself free of Strong Hawk. He glared at him, the soft rays of the morning sunrise now glowing orange on Strong Hawk's face etched with concern. "Your words are those of your mother," he said hoarsely.

"I agree with Mother," Strong Hawk said stubbornly. "I wholeheartedly agree. Give me permission, Father. This once? Let a white man's doctor come and check you over. What harm could it do?"

"The spirits will be offended and will leave our village. That's why I have never agreed to such a thing as that," Gray Wolf growled.

"But to please Mother? Won't you chance anything to please her?"

Gray Wolf lowered his eyes and kneaded his brow. "*Ay-uh.* Yes, there *is* your mother to think about," he murmured. "The burden on her has been great of late. Perhaps this one time I can agree to let the white man's doctor enter our village." His eyes rose quickly and he glowered toward Strong Hawk. "But only this once, Strong Hawk. Never again."

Strong Hawk's shoulder muscles relaxed. He let out a heavy sigh of relief. A broad smile curved his lips upward. He clasped his fingers onto his father's shoulders, beaming. "*Mee-gway-chee-wahn-dum,*" he said, smiling. "Thank you so very much, *gee-bah-bah. Gee-mah-mah* will be so pleased."

"Let's go to her. *Ah-szhee-gwah,*" Gray Wolf sighed. "I am sure she is eagerly waiting to see if you succeeded in your little scheme the two of you cooked up. *Gee-wee-do-kah-wahn-mah-shee-cheh-gayd.* Partners in crime. That's what you two have proven to be."

With arms locked, Strong Hawk and Gray Wolf walked to the large log house on the outer edges of the village. The fog was dissipating over the far reaches of the St. Croix River, and a mockingbird's song echoed through the forest. Lazy smoke spirals rose from the smoke holes of the wigwams, and the aroma of various foods being cooked floated tantalizingly through the air.

"Life is good," Gray Wolf said, squaring his shoulders. "Spring makes life even better."

"*Ay-uh*," Strong Hawk agreed, feeling a gentle warmth flow through his veins as he saw his mother's outline in her upstairs studio window, watching anxiously. And when she suddenly moved from the window, Strong Hawk knew that she had seen them and was most surely rushing down the staircase and to the front door to greet her husband and son.

"And you choose St. Paul over Duluth to ride to for a doctor?" Gray Wolf asked, now in the shadow of his house.

"*Ay-uh*. Though both cities are a night's ride away, St. Paul seems to me to be the closest," Strong Hawk said, smiling to his mother as she opened the door and waited at the threshold.

"And you will leave now?" Gray Wolf asked, giving Danette a pleasant smile.

"As soon as I dress more fully," Strong Hawk said. He warmed even more inside when his father stepped away from him to go and embrace his wife.

Danette clung to Gray Wolf but gave Strong Hawk a questioning look from the corner of her eyes.

Strong Hawk gave her a nod and a wink and walked away from his mother and father confident that he was no longer needed there. A slow, empty ache suddenly circled his heart, wondering if the future held for him the same sort of companionship and camaraderie that was shared between his parents. In Judith, couldn't he expect the same . . . ? Even more . . . ?

Judith. Even her name made a dizziness spiral through him. Oh, to touch her again . . . to kiss her. . . .

Judith looked over at Rory, guiltily noting
how his face was wild and unruly. His cheeks had
become red and loving him in these styles. And
she knew Judith face reminded of this
and her father at St. Paul

Chapter Ten

The two horses left a trail of dust behind them as Judith and Rory rode in a steady gallop along the dirt road. St. Paul had been left behind and an umbrella of elm limbs overhead shaded the riders from the heat of the sun.

And then the trees were behind them and freshly plowed, rich black earth stretched out on both sides of the road.

Judith lifted her face to the sky, enjoying the rush of the wind upon her cheeks. Her hair rose and fell atop her shoulders in golden rivulets, and her shirt caught the breeze and whipped it about the waistband of her jeans. She was enjoying these rare moments with her brother, wishing that they could do it more often. But his duties as a lawyer kept him too busy . . . so busy he had not even taken the time to find a wife. So how could Judith expect him to make more time for her *or* his father?

"Whoa! Wait up!" Rory shouted as he rode up next to Judith.

Judith looked over at Rory and softly laughed when she saw how wild and unruly his black hair had become and loving him in his cowboy shirt, boots, and jeans. He had been transformed into the brother she remembered from long ago, in Texas. And didn't he look so handsomely tall in the saddle . . . and didn't his green eyes have a bit of the old sparkle to them?

Somehow Judith had to believe that those times hadn't been so bad for him as he now talked of their being. Though father and son hadn't learned how to become friends, Rory had enjoyed the freedom of the range. He had never missed a day of riding out alone, or with Judith, on horseback.

"What's the matter, big brother?" Judith shouted, still riding quickly on. "Out of practice? Is this too much for you?"

Rory laughed into the wind. "So you think I'm out of practice, do you?" he shouted back at her. "Just let's see about that!"

He flicked his horse's reins, sank his knees into the side of the horse, and shouted, "Hahh!" and rode on away from Judith.

Giggling, glad to see her brother's livened spirit, Judith wrapped her reins more securely about her gloved hands. She also shouted at her horse and rode quickly onward, bouncing in the saddle, for the moment quite content.

"Come on, boy," Judith yelled to her gelding. "We can't let Rory's mare beat you, now can we? Come on! Put speed in your steps!"

The wind whipped her hair more fiercely about her shoulders and stung her cheeks, and the sun beat down on the top of her head. Perspiration rose on her brow and above her mouth. She licked her lips, tasting the saltiness of the sweat. She blinked her eyes as the dust from Rory's horse rose up and into her face.

Smiling, she finally overtook Rory and looked over at him, triumphant. "What were you saying, big brother?" she yelled.

"Damn," Rory said, then laughed as he drew his mare to a halt.

Judith drew her reins tight and spun her horse around, settling it down next to Rory's. "Would you care to challenge me in anything else this morning, Rory?" she teased, breathless from the hard ride. "Do you want to take target practice with me sometime? I hit the bull's-eye quite often now."

"Judith, since when did you learn to shoot a gun?" Rory said, wiping perspiration from his brow with the back of his left hand. "Father refused to let you even touch a gun when you were younger."

"He was wrong to do that," Judith said, readjusting her shirt, which had blown from the waist of her jeans. "I needed to know the skill then as badly as now. The rattlesnakes were as dangerous in Texas as the lumberjacks are in Duluth."

"I guess he didn't want you to blow off a toe," Rory chuckled.

"Oh, well," Judith shrugged. "I can shoot a gun now, and almost as well as Father. I bet I can shoot even better than you. Surely you've gotten out of practice by sitting behind a desk so much."

Rory leaned forward in his saddle, chuckling. "Now didn't I just prove you wrong about my skill at

130

riding a horse?" he said, amusement shining in his eyes.

"Well, yes . . ." Judith said, then quickly added, "But still I beat you, big brother."

"But who was beating who first?" he challenged. "Your horse was only able to overtake mine at the very last moment."

"Well, yes, I guess you're right," Judith sighed, then giggled again as she saw Rory's eyes twinkling even more as she continued not to give in to him so easily, even in words.

"It would be the same with guns, Judith," Rory laughed. "Perhaps . . . just perhaps . . . you would hit a few bull's-eyes. But I would hit more than you. Neither riding a horse nor shooting a gun are so easily forgotten by a man."

"Okay," Judith shrugged. "So I was wrong about those two things. But I'm not wrong about your feelings about Father. You still hold a grudge, don't you?"

"And why shouldn't I? He hasn't changed. Why should I?"

"He has, too, Rory. His ill health is changing him. But he'd be the last to admit to that change."

"So knowing that, what good would it do for me to return home? He wouldn't appreciate the time I would sacrifice to do so."

Anger rose inside Judith. She gave Rory an annoyed look. "Sacrifice?" she fumed. "That's how you would feel about a visit with me and Father in Duluth? That's a terrible way to feel, Rory."

Rory laughed nervously. "I guess I sound a mite crass, huh?" he murmured.

"Something like that," Judith said hotly. "And remember you said that. I didn't, though I was thinking it."

"What do you say we dismount, rest, and have that talk that you came to St. Paul for," Rory said. "I'm ready, if you are."

"I hope you're ready to do more than talk," Judith said, dismounting. "I hope you're ready to agree to go and see Father."

Judith looked about her, and seeing a small patch of land that wasn't plowed, but instead ripe with grass, protected by a square of white picket fence, she began to lead her horse toward it. Tying her horse to the fence, she noticed two stones rising from the ground, half hidden behind a tangle of weeds. She surveyed the plot of land more carefully and concluded that this was some sort of private cemetery plot, though it seemed out of place here, with the earth around it plowed, ready for spring planting.

"What have you found?" Rory asked, leading his horse up next to hers. He secured his reins, now seeing the gravestones.

"It's apparently two graves," Judith said, raising an eyebrow toward Rory.

"Shall we try and make out the names on the stones?" Rory asked, already moving toward the gate that hung loose on broken hinges.

"I feel as though we're intruders," Judith said softly, inching her way alongside Rory.

"I doubt if anyone could care," Rory shrugged. "It appears that the graves have been left untended for some time now. I'm surprised the farmer who owns this land didn't tear the fence down and use the land as he pleased."

Judith gasped. "But, Rory, everyone respects the graves of the dead," she said, now taking the step that led her directly before the two gravestones.

"Yes, I'm sure," Rory said. He dropped to his knees and began tearing the tangled weeds away from one of the stones.

Judith stooped to her knees and began clearing the other stone, and when she was finally able to read the inscription she read it aloud.

"This one says, 'Mavis Odell, 1814-1859, Rest In Peace,'" she said, then looked over at Rory as he began reading the one before him.

"Hmm," he said. "I can barely make it out. The weather has eaten away at the letters."

He raked his fingers through his thick crop of black hair. "Let's see. I believe it reads: 'Derrick.' Yes, 'Derrick Odell.' The years '1810-1859,' and then the words 'Rest in Peace.'"

His eyebrows arched as he let out a low gasp.

Judith's eyes widened. "What is it, Rory?" she softly questioned.

Rory gave her a quick, serious look. "Do you remember my telling you that the house that I purchased had at one time been a boardinghouse?"

"Yes . . . ?"

"Do you remember the name of the person who I said owned it?"

Judith placed a forefinger to her lower lip, then her eyes brightened in remembrance. "Rettie? Wasn't the name Rettie?"

"Yep. A Rettie Toliver," Rory said.

"So . . . ?"

"Well, the gossip is that her name was Odell at one time, and that her brother and his wife had been slaughtered by Indians." He kneaded his brow. "I just wonder . . ."

"You're wondering if this might be her brother's grave?" Judith blurted.

"And his wife's," Rory said studiously. "The name Odell isn't that common in these parts. Interesting, isn't it?"

"Do you know what became of Rettie?"

"Gossip is that she now makes residence with Indians."

Judith gasped. "With Indians? After her own brother was murdered by Indians?"

"That wasn't all the Indians did to her."

"Good Lord. What else?"

"I hear they kidnapped one of Rettie's nieces."

"And she still lives with the Indians?"

"Her other niece married an Indian chief."

Judith's face flamed. Strong Hawk! His mother . . . was . . . a . . . white woman! Yet his mother *couldn't* be Rettie's niece. The number of years that had passed since these graves had been dug were proof of that.

"Which Indians, Rory?" she suddenly blurted. "The Chippewa or the Sioux?"

"The Sioux did the slaying," he said matter-of-factly. "The Chippewa did the marrying."

Strong Hawk's face flashed handsomely before Judith's eyes. She tremored with ecstasy, feeling suddenly close to him. "I would have thought so," she finally murmured, smiling softly.

"What? What are you thinking of?" Rory questioned, rising to his feet, straightening his back.

Judith rose to stand beside him, still staring down at the graves. "That it wouldn't be the Chippewa who were responsible for killing these two innocent people," she murmured, then smiled up into Rory's face. "I knew it had to be the Sioux."

Rory kneaded his chin, deep in thought. Then he spoke. "You can talk so warmly of the Chippewa, knowing they are the ones causing Father the problem?"

"I think you have it wrong, Rory," Judith said, moving toward the gate.

"What the hell does that mean?" Rory asked, taking a step ahead of her to open the gate for her.

She swung around and boldly faced him. "I'm all for Father. You know that," she said. "I'll do anything for him. But I don't have to agree to everything he does."

"Like what, sis?"

"I think he's the one causing the Indians undue problems," she said firmly. "I feel somewhat guilty for being the first white people to interfere in their tranquil lives. They're gentle Indians and they deserve to be stubborn."

Rory took Judith by the elbow and led her from the fenced-in burial plot to her horse. "You're a hard one to figure out, sis," he laughed. "How come you have sudden divided loyalties? What have the Chippewa ever done for you?"

Judith's pulse raced. She lowered her lashes over her eyes, hiding the truth that lay in their blue depths. Then she placed her foot in the stirrup and swung her leg over the horse and settled into the saddle. She spied a thick stand of trees ahead that reached on into the beginnings of the forest.

"Rory, let's go where there's some shade," she said. "Let's have that talk before we forget why it's needed."

Rory gave her a lingering look, then mounted his own horse, and they rode in silence until they reached the trees and once more had their reins secured.

Leaning against a tree, Rory again gave Judith a studious stare.

Judith bent and plucked a dandelion, then went and also braced her back against the tree beside her brother. She felt Rory's eyes on her and became uneasy. "Rory, why on earth are you looking at me in that manner?" she finally blurted, setting her jaw firmly as she challenged him back with a steady stare. She nervously twirled the stem of the dandelion around and around between her fingers.

"It's your comments about the Chippewa," he said. "Somehow I felt there was more to what you said than you fully revealed."

Judith's lashes fluttered, embarrassed, having forgotten how the lawyer side of her brother's character made him so observant and tuned in to other people's feelings. He could almost read a lie on a person's face. He most definitely could read their eyes.

She looked quickly away from him, dropping the dandelion in her sudden awkwardness. "I don't know what you're getting at," she said softly.

Then she once more looked up at him, her eyes flashing. "I get it," she said bitterly. "It's just a ploy . . . to evade the subject of Father."

Rory unbuttoned the sleeves of his shirt and began rolling them up to his elbows. He laughed. "No. That's not my intention at all," he said, giving her a half glance. "In fact, sis, I've got quite a surprise for you."

Judith stepped out away from the tree, eyeing him quizzically. She spread her legs and placed her hands on her hips. "And? What sort of a surprise?" she asked, glad finally to leave the subject of the Chippewa behind them.

"I've decided to return to Duluth," he said, chuckling when he saw her eyes light up.

"Rory! You will?" she squealed. "As easy as that you've decided to go and see Father?"

"I couldn't disappoint my baby sister, could I?" Rory said, winking at Judith.

"How long have you known that you would go to Duluth?" Judith giggled, shaking her hair to make it ripple down her back.

"Oh, since yesterday," Rory said, chuckling.

"Rory, why didn't you tell me?"

"Because I thought you just might go right back to Father with the news before I had a chance to have this time alone with you."

"Oh, Rory," Judith sighed, then rushed into his arms and hugged him tightly to her. "I love you, big brother. Did I ever tell you just how much?"

"Never enough times, sis," Rory said, burying his nose into the depths of her hair.

"Just hold me tight, Rory," Judith sighed. "I always miss you so much."

Strong Hawk bent his back as his stallion led him beneath the low-hanging branches of an oak tree. He had ridden the full day and night without stopping and knew that St. Paul was only a few more miles ahead. Once he broke free of the forest he would travel the rest of the way on the dirt road that wound its way beside the graves of his great-great-grand-parents. Once more he would stop at the small burial plot and pay his respects, then he would hurry on into St. Paul and find a doctor who could be trusted to travel back with him into the village of his father's people. For many reasons it was never wise to guide any white man into the land of the Chippewa. But sometimes it was necessary.

Having the need to rest his stallion before venturing on, Strong Hawk drew it to a halt and dismounted. Caressing its soft mane, Strong Hawk looked slowly about him. Now that his horse's hooves had been silenced, he was able to hear voices. He tensed, listening even more closely. Then he relaxed. Surely he had been imagining things. It had only been the wind. No one was sharing this stretch of forest with him.

Shrugging, he decided to go on his way, but by foot, so that his stallion could get some more added relief from its travels. He pushed his way through the dense brush and then stopped when he caught sight of two figures embracing in the distance. He *had* heard voices earlier. He hadn't been imagining things. But . . . who . . . ?

Tying his stallion's reins to a limb, Strong Hawk moved stealthily closer to the couple. His insides did a strange rolling when he saw the long golden hair curving down the back of the woman. It was the color and length of Judith's!

His gaze moved slowly up and down the full figure of the woman, whose back was to him. With a pounding heart he recognized her, even though she was dressed in men's breeches!

His hands had memorized every dip and curve of her. His lips had tasted her petal-soft flesh . . . his eyes had feasted upon her even before he had had her.

Then he laughed to himself. "I am a fool," he whispered. "Judith has me so mesmerized, I see her in every woman whose hair is as blinding in its gold color. Judith would not be here. She is in Duluth."

Crouching behind a tree, he continued to watch, knowing that he could not travel onward until the man and woman left. They were in his path, and he did not wish to stop and converse with them.

Then, as the woman pulled free of the man's arms and her laughter filled the forest with its sweet softness, Strong Hawk quickly recognized the laugh. And when she turned her face so that he could see her full profile, he wasn't at all surprised to see that, yes, the woman with the golden hair was Judith, after all.

A bitterness rose up into his throat and his face reddened with rage as he watched the man possessively take Judith's hand as he led her to her horse and helped her onto it. Jealousy tore through Strong Hawk. He hung his face into his hands, growling. All the while Judith had made love with him, had she been thinking of the man with the short black hair and tanned face? Surely not! Judith didn't seem to be that sort of tease. And Strong Hawk had known that he was the first with her sexually. So, why was she with this white man now, and so happy about it?

Too humiliated . . . too angry . . . too hurt . . . to watch any further, Strong Hawk turned and began running in the other direction. How could he ever forgive himself for being so foolish over a woman?

Chapter Eleven

Though Rory had promised Judith that he would return to Duluth to meet with their father, he did not give her a set date as to when. Full of doubts, Judith returned home, already having decided not to tell her father of Rory's decision, fearing that Rory just might possibly change his mind and not come at all.

Climbing the staircase, removing the pins from her fancy hat adorned with various assorted colorful flowers on its straw brim, her eyes were drawn upward to the open door of her father's study. Cigar smoke was drifting in thick clouds from the room, and a low, hacking cough was cause for Judith's spine to stiffen. Her father apparently hadn't heeded her warning about his bad habit of indulging in cigar smoking, and she knew what usually accompanied a heavier use of tobacco. He was overworking himself at his desk.

Creeping on up the staircase, soundless in her movements, Judith then moved stealthily toward her father's door and peered inside the room to where he sat at his desk, pouring over his opened ledgers. Judith's hand went to her mouth and her heart sank. Her father looked as though he hadn't shaved since she had last seen him, and his thinning hair lay about his head, uncombed.

Almost panicking, Judith knew that she must do something—anything—to make things right for her father. And she couldn't wait for Rory's arrival. What good would it do, anyhow? Father and son would probably just get into bitter debates, as always.

Chief Gray Wolf! She had to go to Chief Gray Wolf to plead her father's case! Only in doing this could she feel that her father's future could be brighter and ease the pressures that were a burden to him.

Taking quiet steps backward, Judith decided to not make her presence known to her father. She would change clothes and go now to the Indian village. Her father would believe that she was still in St. Paul, safely with Rory. And she was of no help here, since her father would stubbornly not take her advice as to what was or was not good for his health. He would continue to puff on his damn cigars even if she were there, scolding him. He would continue to worry over his ledgers!

If she could only return from the Indian village with good news for him. Perhaps Strong Hawk could even assist her in reasoning with Chief Gray Wolf!

"I am stupid for believing that," she scoffed to herself as she jerked her hat from her head and hurried to her room. "Strong Hawk wants the same for me. He wants me to persuade my father to do as the Indians wish. It is solely up to me to convince Chief Gray Wolf of what he must do. I must tell him of my father's weakening condition. Surely he will listen!"

Quietly changing out of her travel suit and into her jeans and shirt with the fancy embroidery design and leather cowboy boots, Judith felt her heart was nervously pounding. She knew that what she was about to do was risky, yet this enhanced her excitement. And deep inside she knew that she wasn't traveling to Chippewa country only for her father, but also for herself. Thoughts of seeing Strong Hawk again made a drunken splendor course through her veins. His lips. His hands. His eyes.

"I mustn't let myself think about him in that way," Judith whispered, curling her hair up under her cowboy hat. "My mind must stay alert to argue my father's rights with Chief Gray Wolf. My father is the only person I am to consider. His life surely depends on it!"

Again as soundlessly as a feather drifting in the wind, Judith determinedly left her bedroom and stole down the full length of the hallway, past her father's study and then on down the staircase.

Sighing with relief of having thus far eluded him, she crept on through the remainder of the house, making sure no servants caught her in her act of deceit. And only when she was safely in the saddle on her horse's back and already riding toward the forest did she feel that she could truly breathe more easily and relax.

Her shoulder muscles loosened, her back became less rigid, and she let the reins ease around her gloved fingers. Though dangers were many in this adventure of hers, Judith would not let fear dissuade her

143

from what must be done.

Smiling, she moved a hand to the pistol holstered at her right hip. It was fully loaded. Just let any man try anything with her and he would quickly learn that he had chosen unwisely among women on the trail!

The only thing that plagued Judith's mind was the worry of having to sleep one full night alone in the forest. She would have to practice sleeping with one eye open!

Giggling, she flicked her reins, hurrying her brown mare into a faster trot, now having left all signs of her estate behind her. She had chosen not to travel the roads, but to try and take a shortcut through the forest. Perhaps, just perhaps by doing so she wouldn't have to sleep in the forest. Would Chief Gray Wolf invite her as a friendly gesture to spend the night in his village? Would Strong Hawk even want her to? She would never forget their last moments together. He had revealed too much to her. His reasons for having made love to her had been all wrong.

She wanted to hate him, but her heart just couldn't. In no way could she truly ever hate him. Their sensual moments together had been sheer bliss! He had spun a web of rapture around her heart, and nothing could penetrate or destroy it.

"Strong Hawk," she whispered, loving the sound of the name as it spilled across her lips. "I love you. . . ."

She almost choked on a sob, needing him, wanting him. The forest on all sides of her was such a reminder of him that she felt he should be there with her, and a torment so grievous she could hardly bear it tore through her.

Setting her jaw and straightening her back, she forced herself to realize the absurdity of her thoughts. Strong Hawk was her enemy now, only her enemy.

The sunshine streamed down in soft-spoked rays from the roof of the forest. The buds on the trees had, as though by magic, been transformed into beautifully formed leaves that sent off a fragrance that filled the air with an aroma of freshness and newness.

Just ahead of Judith on the trail a covey of partridges was feeding on pigeon berries that thrust through the carpet of pine needles on the forest floor. The birds had already filled their crops until their breasts looked lopsided. Suddenly alerted to the approach of Judith's horse, they arose from the ground with a great whirring of wings, taking off, fast and low, quickly disappearing into the limbs of the tall pines.

Laughing softly, Judith went on her way, making her way around first one tree then another, feeling more isolated from humanity with each hoofbeat of her horse. The sounds of the birds in the trees echoed around her . . . a rustling of the brush on the side of her cause for her to stiffen in the saddle.

Yet, nothing truly openly threatened her, making it easier for her to decide to travel onward. Danger lurked everywhere one traveled, even on a most populated road, didn't it? Even today, with the turn-of-the-century only the blink of an eye away, highway robberies were many.

She believed that this would continue to be so until more people owned the horseless carriages now being introduced into society. With the streets steep as ski slopes in the city of Duluth, not too many had yet spent money on the new vehicles. It was hard enough to keep a buggy or carriage from losing its footing being sent down a steep street into the waters of Lake Superior, much less to put trust in an unpredictable new invention that hadn't yet proven to be dependable on flat surfaces.

Losing momentary sight of the sun, Judith moved into an area of thicker trees and creeping vines. She tensed and slowed her horse's approach. Cautiously, she watched both sides of her for any sudden movement. She knew to be wary of bears, wolves, and coyote. But nothing would make her turn back. She had come too far.

The doctor had come and gone from Chief Gray Wolf's house. Strong Hawk clutched tightly to his horse's reins, still hearing the ringing of breaking glass in his ears after his father had angrily thrown the white man's bottle of liquid medicine against the wall.

Strong Hawk had understood quickly enough the reason for his father's rage and had just as quickly left on horseback, in the direction of Duluth. Chief Gray Wolf couldn't possibly put faith in medicine that came in a bottle that reeked of the same white man's evil fire water that stole the Indians' minds from them. No matter how the doctor had tried to explain to him that the bottle did not contain whiskey, but medicine that should be taken in moderate dosages to build strength in Chief Gray Wolf, Strong Hawk's father would not listen. He had ordered the doctor back to St. Paul and now seemed in even a worse state than before the doctor's arrival!

Ducking his head as he rode on horseback beneath some gray beards of moss trailing down from the low branches of an oak tree, Strong Hawk kept his eyes focused straight ahead. He would not stop until he reached Duluth. He would then search and find Judith's house and personally confront her stubborn father, to plead his *own* father's case. Surely the white man could find it in his heart to listen to reason, especially after hearing of the great Chief Gray Wolf's weakening condition. If Strong Hawk couldn't succeed in this, he doubted that he could ever hold his head proudly high enough to accept the title of chief when the day came for him to do so.

"I must convince the stubborn white man to listen," Strong Hawk grumbled. "I must!"

From somewhere in the distance a loon laughed in its strange, hysterical-sounding way. The tall pine forest bounced the eerie cry from tree to tree, echoing and re-echoing until it died in a soft quiver. The sun glowed through the tips of the trees onto Strong Hawk's face as he looked up to meet its warmth, his thoughts now heavy as he remembered his last trip through the forest, to St. Paul.

Jealousy fused with anger inside him, becoming a torment, when he remembered Judith and the tall white man embracing. Though their lips had never met, it was the intensity of the embrace that would forever plague Strong Hawk. How could Judith have made such passionate love with him, an Indian, then go right into the arms of another, a white man?

Strong Hawk had thought her to be an almost perfect woman, with only wholesome qualities. But she had proven herself to be perhaps even a guttersnipe, whose blue eyes and golden hair went about blinding all those who were caught up in her loveliness.

Wiping perspiration from the palm of his left hand onto the deerskin of his fringed leggings, and squaring his shoulders to cord his muscles tightly beneath his fringed shirt, he shouted at his horse and hurried on his way.

Yet he was wondering at the same time how he might be near Judith again when he was in Duluth and pretend to not love her. In truth, he knew he could never love another.

The sound of horse's hooves ahead caused Strong Hawk's heart to skip a beat. Though determined to get to Duluth as quickly as possible, he drew his reins tightly, to stop his stallion and see who the approaching stranger might be.

One could never be too cautious in the forest. More often than not the chances were no one could be considered a friend unless it was another Chippewa. Everyone else gave reason to be wary. Hadn't the recent arrival of the white man into the village of the Chippewa proven this to be true? Judith's father only had mischief on his mind. White man always spelled trouble. A move north by the St. Croix band of the Chippewa was the only answer. Up close to the Canadian border, a land no one had yet inhabited. It was ripe for the presence of man . . . the red man!

But Chief Gray Wolf still would not think to dislodge his people. His hope for a better future for his people still depended on the land and forests beside the St. Croix River. It was Strong Hawk's duty to do what he could to make his father's dreams become a reality, though it became even more doubtful as each day passed that these dreams could come true.

Inching his horse behind the wide and thick trunk of a towering elm tree, Strong Hawk quietly drew his rifle from its leather pouch at his horse's side. With his finger on the trigger, he crouched low, watching for the other horse to draw closer . . . closer . . . closer. . . .

Judith sensed a sudden silence above and around her as the birds' chatterings ceased. It was as though a presence larger than they had come into view, frightening them into hushing their merry play in the trees and brush. She drew her reins taut and drew her brown mare to a shuddering halt.

Pushing her hat back away from her brow, Judith squinted her eyes and surveyed the land and trees around her, watching for any sudden movements and listening for any foreign sounds.

Almost afraid to breathe, she removed her pistol from its holster, slowly cocked it, then crept down and out of her saddle, to the ground. The thick bed of pine needles beneath her boots muffled her footsteps as she took a few steps away from her horse.

Her heart did a flip-flop when she heard the whinny of a horse from somewhere ahead of her. She now knew that she wasn't alone—and where there was a horse, there was man!

She groaned when her horse answered the unseen horse with its own soft whinny as it stamped nervously at the ground.

Judith turned quickly on her heel to face her horse. "Shh!" she scolded, placing a forefinger to her lips. "You silly horse, do you want to give us both away?"

A sound behind her, the snapping of a twig, the crush of dried leaves, sent Judith spinning back around with a start. She gasped and quickly lowered her pistol when she found herself face-to-face with Strong Hawk.

"Strong Hawk!" Judith harshly whispered.

"Judith?" Strong Hawk questioned. He lowered the barrel of his rifle, looking at her in wonder.

"What are you doing here, Strong Hawk?" Judith questioned, wishing that her heart would be still. But with him so close, so handsome, so alone with her, it was hard to remember why she should hate him. She was once more becoming swallowed whole by sensuous feelings for him. Oh, why did the dark abyss of his eyes have to affect her so strangely?

But she knew the answer. She was lost in love, no matter how hard she fought her feelings.

"What are *you* doing here, alone in the forest, without an escort?" Strong Hawk hotly demanded, grasping more strongly onto his rifle, so his knuckles grew white. Images of her with the white man flashed before his eyes, causing his gut to twist unmercifully.

Yet, now, with her so close her loveliness was blinding him to the agonizing truth—that she didn't care solely for him. All he wanted was to draw her into his arms and drink the jasmine of her lips, savor her closeness.

"I asked you first," Judith said, stubbornly tilting her chin.

"It is usual for Strong Hawk to be in the forest," he growled. "So I do not see that any explanation is necessary. But, Judith, it is not usual for you to be in the forest, alone. Why are you? Don't you realize the dangers?"

Judith smartly twirled her pistol around on her forefinger, showing off her skill to Strong Hawk. "First, Strong Hawk, you do not own the forest," she spat. "Secondly, I am very capable of defending myself from anyone who gets in my way."

An amused twinkle rose in Strong Hawk's eyes as he watched her toy with her pistol, and then his gaze traveled over her, amazed at how she was dressed, having seen her in woman's attire the one other time.

"Yes, dressed as a man as you are, possibly you would be safe traveling alone," he chuckled. "What man would lust after a woman wearing a man's hat, shirt, and breeches?"

Judith's face and eyes grew hot with embarrassment. She flung her pistol into its holster, glaring at Strong Hawk. "Why, I never . . ." she gasped. "You are insulting!"

Strong Hawk's smile faded. "I didn't mean to speak in insults," he said, taking a step toward her.

"Then what did you mean?"

His gaze traveled over her again and then his eyes met her look of mellowing wonder. "It's just that I've never seen a woman dressed as you are," he said.

"I'm from Texas," Judith explained. "All women who live on ranches and ride the range become acquainted quite young with the wearing of jeans.

Moving to Duluth did not change this about me. At heart, I am still Texan!"

Strong Hawk's eyes grew cold, his jaw set. "As I am and always will be Chippewa at heart," he said dryly.

Judith sighed exasperatedly. Her shoulder muscles became less tense. "As if I didn't already know that," she said. She looked over his shoulder at his waiting black stallion, and then back up into Strong Hawk's eyes. "You never did say what has brought you this far from your village, or do I even have to ask?"

"What do you think my reason is?"

"Perhaps the same reason I have chosen to travel to your village."

"My . . . village . . . ?"

"Yes."

"Are your plans to go and have council with my father about your father, Judith?"

"Yes."

Strong Hawk clamped his mouth tightly closed and began storming away from her.

Judith's eyes widened and her lips parted, then she moved quickly after him. "Strong Hawk, wait!" she said, now half running because his long legs were carrying him much too quickly away from her.

"We have nothing else to say to each other," Strong Hawk shouted over his shoulder. "You have your idea of what is right. I have my own. This takes us in opposite directions!"

Judith panted as she continued to run after him, and as he mounted his black stallion she finally reached him. Breathing hard, she looked up at him as he slipped his rifle back into its leather pouch.

"Please, Strong Hawk, let's talk." she asked, now

feeling desperate at the thought of his going to Duluth to confront her father. She had to stop him. And didn't this even give her an excuse to be with him? Persuading him could have its rewards.

Strong Hawk didn't want to meet the challenge in her eyes or in her voice, but his dreams had been too troubled by her to so easily ride away from her. He was being pulled. He wanted to be loyal to the wishes of his father, yet his heart was finding loyalties elsewhere.

Slowly turning his eyes downward to meet the pleading in hers, the color of the sky and rivers, he felt himself losing control over how he wanted to behave in the very next moments. He wanted to laugh scornfully at her and ride away from her, to show her that she could not control his heart so easily. But the innocence in her soft look captured him heart and soul.

"Talk is cheap," he growled quietly.

"Not between friends," Judith said, smiling weakly up at him. Her voice shook as she added: "We are friends, aren't we, Strong Hawk?"

"Friends?" he said, his eyes wavering. "At one time I thought we were more than that."

"Me too," Judith said, lowering her eyes, blushing.

Seeing the color rising to her cheeks and hearing the sweet softness in her words made Strong Hawk's pulse race. No woman so sensitive could be a guttersnipe. Surely he had been wrong about her! But he could never question her about that other man. She would never know that he had been a silent witness to that embrace!

Quickly dismounting from his horse, Strong

Hawk placed his fingers to Judith's shoulders. *"Mee-goo-ga-yay-ay-nayn-da-man,"* he said.

When her eyes slowly rose to his and he saw the sparkling of tears in their corners, it ate away at his insides. With his finger he wiped her tears away, smoothing them into her flesh, then drew her lips slowly to his.

"Strong Hawk . . ." Judith whispered, consumed by her heartbeats. She wanted to fight him off, but her desire for him was stronger than any of her other emotions.

She tipped her head back, waiting to greet the warmth of his lips upon hers, and she didn't even protest when he brushed her hat from her head. A sensuous shiver ran through her as his fingers wove through her hair and loosened it to hang lustrously golden across her shoulders.

"I can't help but love you," he whispered huskily just before he kissed her.

Lips met in a melting kiss, and their bodies fused as Strong Hawk drew her even closer into his body. Judith's fingers went to the nape of his neck and clung to him. A soft moan rose up from inside her as he cupped her buttocks through the tightness of her jeans. His male strength, which had risen with need of her, pressed hard against her. Her head began a lethargic spinning, her tongue met his as he pushed it between her teeth.

All was lost to Judith except for the exquisite nearness of Strong Hawk. Even when he skillfully lowered her to the ground, she was willing. And even when his fingers became eager on the buttons of her shirt and snaps of her jeans, she was willing. She even

154

helped him lower his fringed leggings, in a drunken stupor, it seemed, eagerly wanting the thrill of the touch of his nudity against hers and the fulfillment that would be theirs, once more, together.

When he reached to remove her boots, she had to giggle, for even she had to struggle to do that.

Leaning up, she watched with love in her eyes as he finally freed her of her boots and then her jeans, and at the same time she slipped her shirt off.

"Mee-kah-wah-diz-ee," Strong Hawk said huskily as he fell to his haunches before her, exploring the nude silken curves of her body with the heated passion of his eyes. His hands reached and cupped each of her breasts, making circles around her hardened nipples with his thumbs.

Slowly, he bent his back and let his tongue replace his hand at her breast. Hotly . . . wetly . . . he consumed her breast as his hand traveled lower, to where the soft vee of her golden hair lay waiting between her thighs, covering the core of her womanhood, pulsing, eager.

A scorching flame shot through Judith as she felt Strong Hawk's fingers began a slow caress around the place where her whole being seemed to be surrounded by hungry need. She let him lower her back to the ground and she willingly spread her legs as his fingers continued to play and build the fires of desire inside her.

Almost frantic with her need of him, she let her fingers explore his body, touching the sleek smoothness of his copper skin where his narrow hips led her around to his sex resting against her thigh.

As he kissed her long and passionately, she let her

155

fingers circle his pulsating shaft, marveling at its velvet-soft skin, no longer fearing its size, only wanting it inside her. As though she was very experienced, she moved her hand up and down his hardness, feeling a sensual shudder shake him and hearing a soft groan in the depths of his throat.

His lips left hers and went to the slender curve of her throat and kissed her there, stiffening against her as her fingers continued skillfully to play with him. As she moved her fingers with more speed, so did his fingers move inside her. She was becoming breathless, her face flushed, her lips dry. And when she could bear it no longer, she moved her body so that she could guide his manhood inside her, then sighed as she felt the magnificence of how he so fully filled her, and began lifting her hips to his eager thrusts. Each thrust sent a message to her heart. She answered it in the only way known to her and clung more fiercely to him as her hips rose and fell in unison with his.

One of his hands kneaded her breast, while the other one wove into her hair, to guide her mouth to his. She felt the trembling of his lips as he once more kissed her, and she gave herself up to the rapture and was glad that his lips muffled her soft cry of passion as her peak was reached and then was quickly gone.

Strong Hawk smiled to himself, realizing that she had already met her full pleasure, then concentrated fully on his own. He buried his lips along the delicate line of her throat and began working more earnestly in and out of her. His heart was thundering like a wild bird's wings flapping inside his chest, his body was slick with perspiration, and he felt giddy from the euphoria of once more being with the woman he loved.

He closed his eyes and let the wondrous warmth of release splash through him. He clung to her, thrusting over and over again inside her. He quivered and shook, and then it was over, and he was left peaceful and relaxed, atop her.

"My love . . ." Judith whispered, kissing him softly on his cheek.

"My beautiful Judith," Strong Hawk said huskily, his hands once more absorbing the total softness of her breasts. Then he rolled away from her and onto the ground, not caring where they had chosen to make love, only that they had.

Judith rose up on her elbow and traced his jawline with her forefinger. "Strong Hawk, I didn't come all this way, alone, for this," she giggled.

"Nor I . . ." he chuckled.

"When we're together it's so easy to forget everything else, isn't it?" she murmured, lowering her eyes, now remembering her father.

Strong Hawk rose to his elbow and possessively placed his hand to her breast. "When we're together there *is* nothing else . . . there is no one else," he said. "We truly become as one."

"I know," Judith said, swallowing hard. "But, Strong Hawk, I do have to think of someone else. I must think of my father."

"And I mine," Strong Hawk said hoarsely. He looked over his shoulder in the direction from where he had just traveled, then ahead to where he had planned to travel, then into Judith's blue eyes.

"We both want the same thing," he said. "Let us

try to reach some sort of compromise, Judith."

"Like what?"

"Now that you are so far from your father's house and since my village was your destination anyway, why not go there with me and let me acquaint you with my people and their ways. And then you can decide who is right and wrong here."

Judith stiffened, her eyes wavered. "I already know what must be done," she softly argued. "What's best for my father, Strong Hawk."

Strong Hawk placed a hand gently over her mouth. "Don't argue," he said. *"Mah-bee-szhon.* Go with me to my village. Give my people, give *me* a chance before going to my father with more arguments for your father."

"I'm not sure if I have time," Judith said as he released his hand from her mouth.

"Make time," he grumbled. "If not for our fathers, Judith, then for us."

Judith looked up into his eyes, seeing such a devoted love for her in them. She was drawn into his arms. She hugged him tightly to her. "All right," she whispered. "For us."

Somehow, she felt the loyalties in her life were changing. . . .

Chapter Twelve

The sparkle of the St. Croix River was on the left side of Judith and Strong Hawk was on her right. With a nudge of her knee and the flick of her reins, she rode alongside Strong Hawk into his Indian village. The aroma of a deer roasting on the spit over the communal fire rose up into Judith's nose, causing her stomach to growl from hunger. But the giggling all around her was cause for Judith's attention to be drawn from her hunger, as she looked in wonder at the squaws who were poised in front of the wigwams. When she noticed that they were pointing at her, gazing intently at her attire, she realized that it was her jeans that were the object of the ridicule. That was understandable, seeing that they were all dressed in dainty, quite feminine dresses that were highly embroidered with colorful beads, though their dresses were made of deerskin and not of cloth or fancy silks. They had probably never before seen a woman dressed in man's breeches.

Amused at the squaws' reaction Judith smiled to

herself and turned her face away. She was now aware that this entrance into the Indian village the second time was much different than the first. With Strong Hawk at her side she didn't experience any fear, but, instead, pride. It seemed strangely normal to be with Strong Hawk in such a way, and it was at this moment that Judith could let herself envision a future of many such entrances with him.

If the differences between their fathers could be settled, Judith could even envision a full lifetime with Strong Hawk, as his *wife*. But the word marriage had not yet been spoken between them. There was even still the chance that he was only using her.

"We will go to my parents' house," Strong Hawk said, edging his stallion over closer to Judith's horse. "My father has been ailing. Hopefully he is resting."

"Ailing?" Judith asked, recalling thinking that Chief Gray Wolf had had the same weakened, ill appearance as her father. "In what way, Strong Hawk?"

"It is his heart," Strong Hawk grumbled. "He has recurring chest pains."

Judith's eyes widened. "*My* father is afflicted with the same ailment," she gasped. "That is why I so desperately want to do what I can to help him."

Strong Hawk's eyes narrowed as he gave Judith an icy stare. "Then you can understand the importance of why *I* must do what *I* can, to help *my* father," he said. "I fear for his life. No one can be allowed to upset him. My loyalties to my father are strong." He would not tell Judith that this loyalty had become a bit shaky, since he had met her. He wanted to do what made her happy, as well. Oh, the torment of being torn between loyalties . . . !

"As is mine, for my father," Judith softly argued. She would not tell Strong Hawk that this loyalty had become less, since she'd met him. Oh, what was she to do? She was now so torn!

"Today you will think only of my father," Strong Hawk said, glancing over at Judith, then focusing his eyes straight ahead, on his parents' house. "You will do this for me, Judith. Then tomorrow we will think of your father."

Judith's insides splashed cold. "It is so easy to instruct me to put my father from my thoughts?" she said bitterly. "You know he is why I am here."

Again Strong Hawk looked her way. "I would have hoped that your decision to come this far from Duluth, alone, would also have included your need to be with me," he said dryly. "Confess, Judith. Tell me that is so."

Frustrated, Judith refused to look his way. Instead, she watched the log house as it became closer. "Do not confuse me so, Strong Hawk," she said, her gaze now being pulled to him, as though commanded by the pull of his. She met his steady stare, once more caught up in the rapture of him and his Indian mystique. In his dark eyes she could read so much, and passion took precedence over all.

A slow smile lifted Strong Hawk's lips. "It is good to know that you are confessing to being confused," he chuckled. "That is proof that our night spent together meant the same to you as it did to me."

"And that is?" Judith said, not recognizing the strange hollowness of her voice. Oh! What a time to let him disturb her so! Chief Gray Wolf and Strong Hawk's mother were only a breath away, and Judith had the need to appear strong-willed, in order to persuade them to listen more seriously to what she had come to say.

"It made me realize many things," Strong Hawk said.

"Strong Hawk, you are talking in circles," Judith sighed, letting the reins in her hands go lax after drawing her horse to a halt in front of the large log house.

Strong Hawk dismounted and went and lifted his arms to Judith to assist her from her horse. "When I'm with you, my thoughts run in circles," he laughed, placing his hands to her waist as she swung her leg over the horse.

"I have to admit to the same when I'm with you," Judith giggled, melting where his hands pressed into her flesh as he lifted her on down to the ground.

Then her smile faded. "Please, Strong Hawk?" she softly murmured. "Let's get serious. We must place thoughts of each other from our minds. So much is at stake here. You know that, as well as I."

"*Ay-uh,*" Strong Hawk said, nodding. "As the next chief-in-line, I understand quite well what is at stake here. The future of my father's people. The future of my people."

Judith's eyes widened. She swallowed hard. "Strong Hawk, you can't mean that your people's future is dependent on the decision reached between your father and mine," she gasped. "Surely you don't mean that."

"In my father's eyes, this is so," Strong Hawk grumbled.

"And in yours?" Judith softly questioned.

Strong Hawk's jaw became tight, his lashes heavy over his eyes. He could not reveal his true feelings about his need to move the St. Croix Band of the Chippewa north. Perhaps later, but not now. It was not appropriate . . . not while he was still fighting his father's battles.

"*Mah-bee-szhon,*" he said, placing his hand at her elbow. "This day you will not only meet my father again, but you will become acquainted with my mother and my Aunt Rettie. Afterwards, I will show you the village and take you to the privacy of my dwelling. Later this night you will even witness one of the most celebrated feasts of our people. The Spring Feast. I would not have been able to partake in the celebration this year had I gone on to Duluth. So finding you on the trail and returning to the village with you has many advantages."

Judith walked alongside him, her heart racing from the anticipation of coming face-to-face with Chief Gray Wolf again and meeting Strong Hawk's mother. Then all of his words were fully absorbed. Her head jerked around as she questioned him with her eyes.

"Did you say something about an Aunt Rettie?" she gasped, recalling whose house Rory now lived in and the gravestones she had seen while horseback riding with Rory. The names on the gravestones became visible in her mind's eye: Mavis and Derrick Odell . . . and their possible relationship with Rettie

Toliver and the fact that Rettie now lived with Indians. Surely there weren't many women with the name Rettie. It was such an unique, different name. And surely, there was only one Rettie who made residence with Indians!

The dates on the gravestones now also flashed before Judith's eyes. Why, Rettie, if it was the same Rettie, would have to be elderly, to say the least!

Strong Hawk heard the surprise in Judith's voice. "And why do you react so, when hearing of my Aunt Rettie?" he asked, stopping Judith as they reached the front door. "You act as though you may have heard the name Rettie before."

Judith looked up into his eyes. "I have," she said softly. "And only recently."

"What did you hear?"

"That she makes her residence with Indians and that her one niece was abducted by Indians while her other niece married an Indian."

"We are speaking of the same Rettie," Strong Hawk chuckled. "Did you hear that her other niece, Amanda, also married an Indian and bore a child from that union?"

"No, I didn't," Judith said, now truly marveling at the relationships of all these white women with the Indians. Yet hadn't she, too, become enraptured by one?

"Amanda is no longer alive," Strong Hawk growled. "She was slain by a Chippewa warrior who had hate in his heart for my father, Gray Wolf."

"No. How horrible," Judith gasped, covering her mouth with a hand.

"But her daughter lives on," Strong Hawk said, his

mood lightening. "North Star. She now makes residence in my mother's ancestral home in Duluth. She was sent there, to attend the white man's school. She is one we are all proud of."

"This Aunt Rettie," Judith said. "My brother makes his residence in her . . ."

Her words were cut off when the door swung open before her, revealing a woman shorter than she, older, but as lovely as she surely had been as a young woman and in love with the Indian brave Gray Wolf. This day she was dressed casually in a pale blue high-necked cotton dress, which displayed a splash of white polka-dots on its foreground.

Her black hair had been swept up into a coil at the back of her head, with a feathering of curls about her forehead and ears, evidence of the natural curl in her hair.

Tiny silver-plated earrings in the shape of squash blossoms dangled from her ears. Her cheeks were a healthy pink and her lips cherry-colored. Her blue eyes were friendly, her smile warm.

"*Gee-mah-mah*," Strong Hawk said, beaming as he took a step forward and fondly embraced his mother. "I've brought a guest."

"Strong Hawk, how nice," Danette said, smiling over at Judith as Strong Hawk moved back away from her. "And who is this lovely lady, my son?"

Strong Hawk hesitated, almost afraid to reveal Judith's name to his mother, knowing that his mother surely blamed Judith's father for Gray Wolf's most recent bout of ill health. Yet he had no choice. Names had to be spoken if a compromise was to be made possible. And he was proud to introduce Judith to his mother. Hopefully, she would one day bear his name, a part of the Chippewa culture herself.

"This is Judith," he said thickly. "Judith McMahon."

He turned and faced Judith. "And, Judith, this is my mother. I'm sure you would prefer to call her Danette, though she was given the Indian name Sweet Butterfly by my father many moons ago."

Danette's smile faded. Her eyes questioned Strong Hawk. Yet she didn't openly question him. He was wise. Behind all of his actions were good reasonings. Now having to force herself, she reached a hand toward Judith.

"I'm very pleased to meet you, Judith," she said in a strained voice. "Please come in. Perhaps you'd like some tea? Or maybe coffee? Or are you hungry? I've just made a batch of oatmeal cookies."

Judith could see how Danette's mood had changed at the mention of her name, and she suspected that the subject of Travis and Judith McMahon had been a frequent one in this household since they had made their first visit to the village. As was the name Chief Gray Wolf a bitter one on Judith's father's tongue. She knew that her name and her father's had to have the same effect on Chief Gray Wolf and his wife.

It made Judith uneasy, knowing that friendship was having to be pretended toward her and was not sincere. But she would play the game. She really had no other choice.

Accepting Danette's hand in hers, she shook it, but, like Danette, only halfheartedly. "I'm also pleased to meet you," Judith murmured. "And, yes, tea and cookies sound quite good."

Judith gave Strong Hawk a sideways glance, lowering her eyes as he met her look of remembrance. "Seems it's been a while since we've last eaten. We . . . uh . . . concentrated on our travels, more than . . . uh . . . food," she quietly added.

Danette caught the exchanged looks and her insides quivered, recognizing the look. From memories of the past and of her shared times with Gray Wolf in the forest when their love was young . . . when their love was filled with more kindled passion than now . . . she knew why her son and this woman hadn't taken the time to eat. They had taken advantage of that time alone. They were in love. Danette could see it in their eyes. She could almost feel the heat of their passion radiating between them.

This troubled Danette, yet, it was easy to understand, this passion that could become such a magical thing between two people of two opposite cultures. She would not interfere, no matter that Judith's father meant only ugly things for the Chippewa. She couldn't interfere, remembering the interference of her own Uncle Dwight those many years ago. It was only right that her son and his newfound love find their own answers to this thing that was now pulling them sensually together.

Danette eased her hand away from Judith's. She gestured toward the open door. "Then come on inside," she urged.

"Father? How is he?" Strong Hawk asked, guiding Judith on into the parlor with his arm possessively about her waist.

"He thinks he's better," Danette said, scowling, closing the door behind them.

"What do you mean, *gee-mah-mah?*" Strong Hawk asked, stepping away from Judith. He went to the staircase at the far end of the room and looked up, toward the second floor. "He is resting in bed, isn't he?"

Danette fussed with a cushion of the sofa, fluffing it. "No. He isn't," she said. "He's at the council house, helping to prepare for the celebration tonight."

She clasped her hands tightly behind her as she nodded toward the sofa. "Judith, won't you please sit down while I go and get the tea and cookies?"

"Why, thank you, ma'am," Judith said, lifting her hat from her head, causing her hair to fall in gold rivulets down upon her shoulders. She stared at Strong Hawk and at the worry suddenly in his eyes. As she settled down onto the couch she watched him hurry toward the door.

"I must go and see what I can do to help," Strong Hawk grumbled, taking wide, anxious steps. Then he stopped and swung around to face Judith. "Please relax with Mother. Perhaps between the two of you my father won't have to be included in any more worries of what your father has planned."

Judith half rose from the sofa, her mouth open, ready to argue this point with him, but she found herself suddenly alone as Strong Hawk hurried on outside and Danette left the room to go to the kitchen.

"Well!" Judith gasped, inching back down on the sofa. She felt awkward. She felt desperately alone in such unfamiliar surroundings. She hadn't thought to consider Strong Hawk's leaving her alone. With

168

him by her side, anything would be easier. Yet she couldn't grow used to depending on his nearness. It was hard to understand him and what was motivating him as far as she was concerned.

Trying to relax, settling back against the sofa, Judith placed her hat beside her and looked around at the furnishings of the spacious parlor. At first glance she had known that it had been furnished by Danette without the assistance of her Indian husband. Everything spoke of the white man's culture, and it appeared as though Danette had kept up with the latest styles of a modern house.

At the wide windows the drapes were of an elegant beige brocade. The walls were elegantly covered with wallpaper with a design of beige leaf patterns. Along the walls were many beautiful paintings framed in gold, and there were more on the wall of the staircase.

The upholstered parlor suite consisted of a matching large sofa, arm chair, rocker, and two large parlor chairs of a stylish appearance, the colors of each piece harmonizing with the others, also in beige tones to match the drapes and wallpaper. Each piece of furniture was overstuffed, handsomely decorated, and finished with deep fringe, fancy bindings, cords and tassels, and ornamented with rococo brass gimp ornamentation.

Several new-styled banquet lamps with ten-inch globes and nine-inch bowls, handsomely decorated in beautiful free-hand colorings and with gold-plated bases and mountings, sat on oak-finished tables about the room.

Judith's gaze stopped when she saw a gramophone on another table. Seeing this and a home cabinet organ in a far corner made Judith's eyebrows raise. Only the more affluent segment of the populace spent money on such luxuries. Perhaps Danette had once been from such an affluent family. Strong Hawk had referred to his mother's ancestral home in Duluth. This made Judith now eager to know more about Danette and who she really was.

She squirmed on the sofa, glancing over at the large stone fireplace that filled much of the space on the one outside wall. Beneath its grate, gray ashes lay, dead, and on its mantel was another sign of prosperity. It was a mantel clock made of black marble, ornamented with gold-plated scrolls. It stood on four beautiful metal feet that matched the scrollwork.

The dial of the clock was designed in a fancy rococo embossed pattern, the very latest fashion. The numerals were Arabic, and the hands were very fine hand-sawed blue steel in a fleur-de-lis pattern. As Judith looked at it, the clock struck the hour of three with the sound of a cathedral gong.

Judith cleared her throat and placed her hands politely on her lap as she heard Danette's soft footsteps moving back into the room on the highly waxed oak floor. She gave Danette a half smile as Danette placed a silver serving tray on a table beside the sofa.

"I think this should do it," Danette said, pouring tea into a teacup whose edges were daintily trimmed in gold. "This should tide you over until the feast."

She gave Judith a guarded look. "You will join us this evening, to celebrate the Spring Feast, won't you? You do plan to spend the night here?"

"Are you offering me an invitation to stay?" Judith tested, quietly thanking Danette when she handed her the teacup and saucer, and then a cookie.

"I hadn't wanted Strong Hawk to miss the celebration when he determinedly left for Duluth earlier," Danette said, settling down opposite Judith with her own cup of tea. "Now that he has returned before the feast, I hope that he will stay."

"It is not for me to say whether or not Strong Hawk will stay or leave," Judith said softly.

"You are here. He is here," Danette softly argued. "That tells me much, Judith."

"We just happened to cross paths on the trail," Judith tried to explain.

"Oh?" Danette said, raising an eyebrow. "Is that truly how it is that you two are together? You just accidentally met in the forest?"

Judith's face blushed pink. "And how else do you think it happened?" she challenged.

Danette took a sip of tea, looking over the cup rim at Judith, seeing so much of herself in her. She was beginning to like her. They seemed to have been made from the same mold. They had the same fiery spirit. Judith even dared to wear a man's jeans!

Yes, Danette could truly like Judith!

Danette lowered the cup, ran her tongue across her lips, then smiled. "Tell me. Why were you traveling in the forest alone?" she asked, setting her cup and saucer on the table. She settled back in the parlor chair, crossed her legs, and decided to enjoy this rare visit from another white lady. Idle chatter would be a nice change. But she had to remember Gray Wolf and his dislike of this lady's father. It would not be wise to

171

become too friendly.

"Why was I?" Judith said, after consuming the last bites of her cookie. "I'm sure you've already guessed."

"Your purpose was to come and talk further to my husband of your father's wishes," Danette said dryly. "I must warn you. You have wasted your time. What your father has said that he plans to do is wrong. My husband will never agree to cooperate with him."

Judith brushed some cookie crumbs from her lap, placed her teacup and saucer on the table beside Danette's, then scooted to the edge of the sofa. "I must have council with Chief Gray Wolf," she said, smoothing some strands of hair back from her brow. "Not you, Danette. I hope you understand."

"I do not want you to disturb my husband with this any further."

"I must."

"My husband is not a well man. I insist that I must protect him from stress."

"My father is also ailing. I only come here because he *is* sick."

"Do you agree with what he plans, Judith?"

Judith lowered her eyes, "Not really," she murmured.

"I thought not," Danette said softly. She rose and went to Judith and placed her hand gently on her shoulder. "Let's forget our troubles for the moment. A celebration is being planned. Be a part of the celebration. See the beauty of the Chippewa. Then decide what you must do."

Judith looked up into eyes the same color as her own. "I already know. Why delay it?"

"A few hours should not make that much difference," Danette said. She reached for Judith's hand and softly grasped onto it. "Come. Let me introduce you to Aunt Rettie. She will be glad to see that we have a visitor from Duluth. Though originally from St. Paul, she has chosen a doctor from Duluth. She will even be traveling to Duluth soon, to make residence in my house, with her niece North Star. It is imperative that she be closer to her doctor. She has not been at all well of late."

Judith rose to her feet, anxious to meet the elderly woman with the colorful past. And as she walked with Danette toward the closed bedroom door near the foot of the staircase, the framed paintings on the walls once more drew her attention.

"The paintings," she said. "There are so many. And they're beautiful. Is there someone in your family who paints as a hobby?"

Danette's eyes lit up and her heart warmed. "It is I," she said, smiling proudly. "These paintings are mine. I've been painting for years. Would you like to see more?"

"I'd love to," Judith said eagerly.

"I wouldn't want to bore you, Judith."

"Never. You couldn't. I admire anyone who can use their hands so skillfully. My father has stifled all my hopes and dreams every time I decided on something that I'd like to do."

Danette sighed heavily. "At one time I had that same problem," she said. "When I was younger, before I met Gray Wolf, my Uncle Dwight caused me many problems over my love of painting. But nothing could stop me. Painting was my life." Her eyes took on a dreamy, faraway look. "Until Gray Wolf, that is."

"But you still paint?"

"Always. *Ah-pah-nay!*"

Judith couldn't suppress a giggle. "And what did you just say in Chippewa?"

"I tend to forget that not everyone speaks in Chippewa," Danette laughed. *"Ah-pah-nay? That means 'forever' in Chippewa."*

"Ah-pah-nay . . ." Judith tested it on her tongue. "I'll remember that."

Danette went to the closed bedroom door and slowly began turning its knob. "We'll look in on Aunt Rettie first," she whispered. "And then I'll take you to my studio upstairs. I'll show you what I'm painting now."

Judith followed Danette into a room darkened by a pulled shade at the one window. Shadows of rifted light shone from the sides of the shade, leaving just enough light to see the elderly woman stretched out on the bed with a lacy shawl spread out over her.

The sweet aroma of lily of the valley perfume was almost overpowering in the room, the same aroma that Judith had faintly smelled on Danette. Judith now understood why the aroma would cling to Danette's attire. It emanated profusely from the elderly woman.

"She's asleep," Danette whispered. "This is the way she spends most of her days now. I dread the day she won't wake up. She's such a special person. At one time, she was quite a character—spunky and so full of life."

Something tugged at Judith's heart as she looked

down at Rettie, seeing sparse gray hair circled in a bun atop her head and a thin, gaunt face of a shallow gray color. Spread out on the shawl, Rettie's hands were mostly bone, the skin drawn taut over them. Her narrow line of lips suddenly quivered in her sleep and her cheek twitched. Judith hoped that the elderly lady was dreaming of the days of her youth. Oh, to have been witness to those days with this lady who now so heartily still clung to life! Judith would have loved to have known her.

"She soon will reach her hundredth birthday," Danette sighed. "I only hope that she does." She placed an arm through Judith's. "We must leave her to her dreams. Come. I'll show you my studio."

Together they crept out of the room, closed the door behind them and began ascending the stairs. At the top of the stairs Danette guided Judith into a large room bright with sunshine and a low gasp rose from Judith.

Her gaze swept around the room, seeing the hundreds of paintings. What wasn't stacked on the floor was on the walls. Then she melted inside when she saw the painting in progress on the easel beside a window. As the sun shone brightly onto it, Judith went to it and looked upon the handsome face of Strong Hawk. It was as though the painting might come to life, so expertly had it been created on canvas.

In the dark eyes, jawline, and lips she saw his usual strength. His headband and yellow feather were prominent, and the portrait ended at his squared, muscular shoulders.

"Do you like it?" Danette asked, going to stand beside Judith. She tipped her head and scrutinizingly surveyed what she felt was one of her best works of art. And, oh, how easily it had come for her. To paint her son had almost been the same as painting Gray Wolf those many years ago.

"I love it!" Judith sighed, daring a touch to the dried oils. She ached to have the portrait. It was so much Strong Hawk! His mother had captured him and his personality to perfection!

"It was time for the portrait to be painted," Danette said. "He is now a man, the future leader of the St. Croix Band of Chippewa."

Judith spun around on her heel, gesturing with her hand. "You've such talent," she exclaimed. "Such talent should be displayed. Have your paintings ever been displayed at an art show?"

"*Ay-uh*," Danette said, laughing softly. "They were. Many moons ago, at the Minnesota State Bank building in Duluth. But not recently. I keep a low profile. I'm sure that pleases my husband more than having a wife who craves an audience."

"But it is a shame to keep everyone from seeing your talent," Judith said, walking around the room, surveying the paintings within reach of her eyes.

"There are many that are on display in Duluth," Danette said matter-of-factly.

Judith spun around, eyes wide. "But I thought that you just said . . ."

"In my house," Danette interrupted, smiling softly toward Judith. "My earlier works are on the walls in my house, the Thomas mansion, in Duluth."

"The Thomas mansion?" Judith queried, though having already heard of Danette's house in Duluth from Strong Hawk. A mansion? Yes, it would have to be, to be Danette's.

"It was willed to me upon the death of my uncle," Danette said, getting a faraway look in her eyes. "At one time I thought I would sell it. But I thought better of it later. It was a place to have for my children, if they so desired to make residence there."

"I'd love to see those paintings," Judith said eagerly. "Could I?"

"You really want to?"

"Oh, yes!"

"All right. I believe that can be arranged. I'll write the address of the Thomas mansion down for you. And when you go there, just explain to North Star who you are and why you are there."

"I shall go there immediately upon my return to Duluth."

"Also, when you are there, you will, perhaps, meet my other son, Giles."

"Your other son?"

Strong Hawk stepped suddenly into the room. "So this is where I find you?" he chuckled. He gave his mother an amused, appraising look. "My *gee-mah-mah*'s retreat."

"Strong Hawk, have you seen?" Judith blurted, moving toward his portrait.

Danette quickly blocked her way. "*Gah-ween*, no, he hasn't," she said quickly.

"Seen what?" Strong Hawk asked, questioning Judith, then Danette with a raised eyebrow.

"Later, son," Danette said, already ushering him from the room. She wanted to be alone with Strong Hawk when she revealed his portrait to him. She knew that the time was fast approaching when she wouldn't have any more private, shared moments with him. Another woman was now there, filling the empty spaces in his heart.

Judith stopped, stunned, watching Danette and Strong Hawk leaving the room ahead of her. She felt strangely, suddenly alone. It was obvious that Strong Hawk's mother was purposely stealing him away from the room, but for what reason? In doing so, she was also stealing him away from Judith.

With lips and jaw set she hurried out after them and took her place at Strong Hawk's other side as they began descending the stairs.

"I've come for Judith, to show her our village and my personal dwelling, *gee-mah-mah*," Strong Hawk said. He circled an arm about Judith's waist.

"Your father? How was he?" Danette asked, trying to ignore his reference to taking Judith to his personal wigwam. She knew what might happen between her son and his chosen woman and she didn't want to disapprove. Hadn't she herself been as free in her love with Gray Wolf? Somehow it did seem right, now, even for Judith.

"He is at his height of glory," Strong Hawk chuckled. "He is ordering everyone around to be assured that tonight's celebration will be the best ever."

"I'm sure he's enjoying himself immensely," Danette said, laughing. "I only hope he doesn't overdo it."

"He will do what he wishes, no matter what we say or do," Strong Hawk said, shrugging. "I've almost resigned myself to that fact. You should also, *gee-mah-mah*."

"I'll try," Danette sighed.

They reached the lower floor and Strong Hawk placed a gentle kiss on his mother's cheek. "I will now take Judith away from you," he chuckled.

"I've enjoyed talking with her," Danette said, returning Strong Hawk's kiss.

"I'm sure you will have the opportunity again," Strong Hawk said, giving Judith a warm glance. Then he went to her and began walking her toward the door, again placing an arm about her waist.

"Danette, thank you for the tea and cookies," Judith said from across her shoulder.

"Anytime," Danette answered back.

"Did you truly enjoy meeting my mother?" Strong Hawk softly questioned as he leaned down closer to Judith's ear.

"Yes. Quite."

"Did you argue?"

"Some. At first."

"But not so much later?"

"No."

"Then my heart is full of happiness and hope. . . ."

Chapter Thirteen

Strong Hawk manned the paddles and pulled the low-riding birchbark canoe away from the shore. With strong strokes he dipped the paddle tips quietly into the water, sending the canoe shooting forth with each stroke. He had already shown Judith the village and now was ready to show her the wild rice, which grew in the more shallow waters of the St. Croix River.

The sun pulsed and glowed overhead, and the damp breeze welcomed them as they challenged a bend in the river. Judith was seated in front of Strong Hawk. Soft furs covered the floor where she sat. As the canoe slipped smoothly along she clung to its sides, watching as tall, swaying green plants appeared in a shallow inlet ahead. This must be the wild rice of which Strong Hawk had been speaking.

Strong Hawk guided his canoe into the shallows until it was lost in the jungle of greenish-yellow grass that towered above their heads, then laid his paddles aside.

Judith turned questioning eyes to him. The canoe was now only drifting.

"You are now seeing the staple food of the Chippewa," Strong Hawk said, gesturing with a sweep of his hand toward the long green plants that swayed with the lapping of the water. "It is called *manomin*, which in the Chippewa language means 'good berry.'"

Judith then turned her eyes to the rice. "I've never even heard of wild rice," she murmured. "It's hard to believe that it's anyone's staple food. I always thought the Indian's survival would depend on the killing of game or on fishing."

Strong Hawk reached and captured several stalks of the rice and cradled an armful of the heads, studying them closely. He then plucked one of the top grain-bearing husks from the stem.

"*Ay-uh*, our existence does depend on all these things," he said. "But the wild rice is the easiest stored, to last us through the severe winters, when game can no longer be found and the river hides its fish beneath its thick cloak of ice."

He turned the rest of the bunch of rice loose, and as a breeze caught it the bundle swayed momentarily alone, then joined the sea of green, showing no traces of ever having been disturbed.

"Without manomin, the Chippewa would perish," Strong Hawk growled, stripping the protective green husk away, leaving a kernel of rice lying on the palm of his hand. "And the years have taken their toll on this bed of *manomin*. There is no longer enough to go around, enough for each family to share equally. In time, some will starve, unless new rice beds

181

are found."

Judith rose from her seat and went and sat down beside Strong Hawk. She was remembering Danette's apparent riches. Surely no Chippewa would die, with her wealth to share with the tribe!

"Strong Hawk, your mother is from an affluent family," she murmured. "Wouldn't she have enough money . . ."

Strong Hawk glowered toward her. "The Chippewa are a proud Indian," he said dryly. "No handouts from any white man or woman will ever be acceptable. The Chippewa make their own way in the world. That's the way it has always been. That's the way it shall be."

Judith blanched. "Strong Hawk, that doesn't make sense," she dared to argue. "Your pride would stand in the way of lives?"

"We do not look at it in that way," he grumbled.

"Then what? This white woman you refuse help from is your mother. Doesn't that make any difference?"

"Though she is my mother, she is white, and for centuries the white man has been the Indian's enemy, though blood has rarely been spilled between the Chippewa and the white man," he said, plucking another rice husk, turning it from side to side, inspecting it. "The Chippewa must survive without assistance, for once we agree to accepting handouts, we will no longer be a free people."

Judith placed a hand to Strong Hawk's copper cheek. "Strong Hawk, you speak of the white man as being your enemy," she said softly. "You do not see *me* as an enemy, or as a threat. Do you?"

182

Strong Hawk's eyes wavered. He reached his hand to cover hers. "Do you not see me as an enemy because of our fathers' differences?" he said hoarsely.

Judith swallowed hard, her lashes momentarily lowered. Then she once more gazed intently into his questioning eyes. "At times, yes, I have felt as though we were enemies," she said. "But I don't want to. My feelings for you are so . . . are . . . so . . ."

Strong Hawk let the rice husk fall to the floor of the canoe. He swept his arms about Judith and drew her to him, crushing his lips to hers, kissing her in total demand.

Judith's breath was drawn quickly from her, feeling the fierceness with which he kissed her. Enemies? No. Never. How could they be, when such ecstasy continued to flare between them?

Wrapping her arms about his neck, she clung to him and returned his kiss, thrilling as his hands moved seductively down her back and then between them, then gingerly cupping and softly kneading both her breasts.

Strong Hawk drew his lips away from hers. He devoured her with his passion-dark eyes, lifting his hands to her face, to softly frame it. "My dearest Judith," he said huskily. "No matter what, you know that what we share is not what enemies share. You make my heart go wild . . . my head to spin. My love for you is strong. One day . . . one day . . ."

Judith's pulse raced, her face was hot. "One . . . day . . . ?" she quietly questioned.

Strong Hawk dropped his hands away from her and once more ran his fingers through the wild rice grasses. "Enemies take on many shapes and forms," he said thickly, obviously ignoring her question. *"Manomin* has many such enemies. During its period of germination and growth the Chippewa have seen such enemies that take the wild rice away from our people. The pan fish pick the seeds from the bottom of the lake, water fowl become hungry and eat it, and beaver dams ruin the stands of rice by raising the water level. When the water becomes too low, or too warm from lack of rain, the stalks wither and die. Also, higher water from too much rain will drown out the tender shoots."

Judith sighed exasperatedly, realizing she was being purposely ignored. But she wouldn't let Strong Hawk's doing this ruin her moments with him. Being with him, alone, had its own rewards. Soon they would once more be saying their good-byes. . . .

"The parched, winnowed and tanned wild rice becomes one of the most delectable of foods, the perfect complement to a roast duck dinner," Strong Hawk continued. He gave Judith a hazed faraway look as a soft smile touched his lips. "Nothing can equal the aroma of ricing camp with the wood fires burning, the rice drying, and the dewy fresh air drifting in from the river. It gives one a contented feeling of well-being as the first grain of the season is offered for a blessing from the Great Spirit."

"When is this done?" Judith asked, herself now caught up in the wonders of the rice.

"The time of the *manomin-gisiss,* the Wild Rice Moon, is September of the year," Strong Hawk said. "I hope that somehow you can share this special celebration with me some day."

"Speaking of celebrations," Judith giggled. "Don't

you think we should return to the village, to ready ourselves for your Spring Feast? I'm excited and eager to participate."

"*Ay-uh,*" Strong Hawk said, nodding. "You will experience the merriment of my people and you will return to your father with a heart full of love and respect for all Chippewa."

The mention of her father made Judith once more aware of her purpose in being so far from Duluth. She silently went back to her seat and clasped onto the sides of the canoe as Strong Hawk once more took command of the paddles and soon had the canoe moving soundlessly through the clear blue of the St. Croix River.

Along the shore mud hens and other water fowl swooped down to settle in little clusters, waiting for unwary fish. Moss agate, translucent, silvery, and gray rolled up and down with the water, and fragrant wintergreen and bright little carnelians lined the shoreline.

And then the village came into view, with its large circle of wigwams built into the dense growth of pines and hemlocks, a perfect shelter from the north and west winds. The Chippewa were timber people, and their wigwams were made of birchbark and grass mats. The air pulsed with life, an insectlike hum, as Judith and Strong Hawk beached their canoe and began making their way through the village.

Strong Hawk had earlier explained that the Indian girls were taught to stay at home, to convert the fruits of the hunter and fisherman into food and clothing. They were taught how to make wigwams and other furnishings, to chop wood and gather berries and rice and medicinal herbs, to make birchbark vessels and maple sugar. They also dressed skins, sewing them into clothes. These were the roles of the women; also they were the bearers of children and the cooks.

The boys were taught to occupy themselves outside the home, to become brave warriors and successful woodsmen by mastering the bow and arrow, spear, traps, and snares and the ways of the forest and its creatures. Boys early acquired an appetite for praise. Village-wide feasts celebrated their first successes at killing an animal and catching a fish, and the independence of following lonely winter traplines for weeks at a time.

Judith silently marveled at how hard all the Indians did work at surviving, and admired them, feeling drawn into this mystique that surrounded them, strangely wanting, somehow, to become a part of them. Was this how Danette had felt when faced with the decision to leave her culture behind her and live with the Indians? Danette had, and she still seemed happy for having reached that decision!

Smelling a strong aroma of fire and the stench of what smelled like flesh burning drew Judith's gaze in the direction of the council house grounds. Since she and Strong Hawk had been away from the village, something had been added. Fires in long trenches filled with coals, over which the carcasses of animals were roasting, had been built in front of the council house. Indian squaws were crouched over these, turning spits on which various wild beasts were being roasted whole, their claws, eyes, everything left on them, some of them still even in their skins.

Judith recognized a beaver, rabbit, coon, and a young bear.

Covering her mouth with her hand, she paled and turned her eyes quickly away, gulping hard.

Strong Hawk saw her reaction and chuckled. "It is in accordance with ancient tribal customs that the animals be cooked in such a way on the day of the Spring Feast, the day our tribe celebrates the return of the sun from the south," he explained, circling an arm about her waist, to pull her next to him. "Is it so distasteful to you, Judith, this ancient custom of my people?"

Judith laughed nervously and gave him a half glance. "Strange that you would put it in such a way," she giggled, having felt a bitterness rising into her throat when she had seen the animals.

"What do you mean?"

"By using the word 'distasteful,'" she said, smiling up at him. "Do you actually expect me to eat any meat from one of those things? The thought of tasting it turns my stomach."

Strong Hawk's eyes gleamed. "There will be other foods offered," he said. "But one usually shares something of all that is prepared for the feast."

Judith visibly shuddered. "But the animals are being cooked with their teeth and . . . ?"

"Cannibalistic, you think?" Strong Hawk teased.

Judith laughed throatily. "You said that," she said. "I didn't."

Strong Hawk smiled to himself as he directed Judith on through the village and to his wigwam, which sat away from the others, at the outer edges of the forest. When they reached his wigwam he raised

187

the entrance flap and nodded toward it.

"My dwelling," he said. "Please step inside. Up to this day my wigwam has been empty without you."

Judith took a step backward, trying to hide her surprise. Strong Hawk had been raised in a normal house, and now he had chosen to live in a wigwam?

Her gaze swept over it. It was a somber, peaked lodge, with sloping sides of smoke-blackened bark meeting at the top, where blue smoke billowed from the smoke hole, swirling away into the forest.

She stepped inside with Strong Hawk. Deerskins and blankets were rolled up neatly to the side of the lodge, there were rush mats on the floor, which had been recently swept, and a hand drum was hanging on the wall. Strips of meat and little bundles of aromatic herbs and roots dangled from a pole over the fire in the firespace outlined by rocks in the center of the room. Light was shining through the chinks of the bark wall, and in the semidarkness Judith could see a bright blanket bundled next to the fire.

Strong Hawk yanked down a sliver of dried meat hanging by the entrance and jerked off a piece to chew. Then he hesitated and offered it to Judith.

"Canoeing makes me hungry," he said. "Did it have the same effect on you, Judith? If so, this meat could momentarily fill the emptiness in your stomach."

Still remembering the gory sight of the cooking animals over the fiery trenches, Judith turned her head away from Strong Hawk. "No, thank you," she murmured. "I'm fine. Just fine."

Laughing lightly, Strong Hawk thrust the piece of meat into his mouth and quickly consumed it, watching Judith as she stood so quiet in the dark shadows of his wigwam. He knew that she was filled with many questions. He understood. He took one of her hands and guided her down onto the rush mat flooring beside the fire.

Settling down beside her, he picked up a twig and stirred the glowing coals in the firespace. "You seem silently filled with wonder," he said. "Want to talk about it?"

Judith ran her fingers nervously over the material of her jeans, which was tightly stretched over her leg. "Why have you chosen to live like this?" she asked, her gaze once more taking in the crude dwelling. "Why a wigwam? Your parents, even your father who is chief, have chosen a much more, uh, comfortable dwelling."

"Privacy, Judith," Strong Hawk said. "A man my age needs to live away from his mother and father."

He looked toward her. "A man my age needs privacy for many reasons," he said huskily, reaching his hand to trace the sensual fullness of her lips. "Can you understand this, Judith? This need of a man to have such privacy?"

Judith moved her eyes slowly to his and became locked there, held by the command of his dark, fathomless eyes. "Are you saying what I think you're saying?" she softly questioned, jealousy rising inside her at the thought of his having possibly brought other women there, to be alone with them. There was only one reason to want to be alone with a woman where there were more blankets, than furniture!

"*Ay-uh*," he said, smiling coyly at her.

"But you only moments ago said that your

dwelling had been empty without me," she murmured. "But, of course, saying that didn't mean that you've never had women here before me."

"Don't you understand the compliment I paid you by saying that?" Strong Hawk asked, dropping his fingers, to now trace the outline of her breast through the cotton of her shirt. "No other woman has meant anything to me before you. They were only used to fill my needs, Judith."

The feel of his fingers on her breast and this talk of sensual, private things was causing Judith's heart to race and her to become breathless. She momentarily closed her eyes, trying to block out all thoughts of other women being there, making love with Strong Hawk. He had said that they had meant nothing to him. She had to believe him. She wanted to be special . . . to be the only one he cared about.

But she was still haunted by how easy it would be for him to be lying to her. Hadn't he just confessed to using women? There could be many assorted reasons to use women. One obvious one could still be to help his father!

Suddenly Strong Hawk's lips were on Judith's lips, warm, wet, his tongue now working through her teeth, to touch her tongue in a sensual dance.

Moaning, Judith returned his kiss, welcoming his tongue inside her mouth, letting him steal her momentary doubts of him this quickly from her mind. She let him lower her to the rush mats, where he stretched out over her, pinioning her to the floor. His fingers twined through her hair, his knee nudged her legs apart. Though there were two layers of clothes as shields between them, Strong Hawk's swollen strength of manhood was there, hard against her thigh.

Judith was becoming wild as his fingers slowly worked their way up inside her blouse, setting fires on her flesh where he touched anew. And then he was fully cupping a breast, his thumb pressing hard into the taut knob of her throbbing nipple.

"My Judith . . ." Strong Hawk whispered huskily as he drew his lips away from her. He leaned up, watching as his fingers loosened her shirt buttons, slowly revealing the pink satin of her flesh to him with the release of each one. And as the shirt was gaped fully open, he swept it away from her and feasted his eyes upon her breasts.

Slowly he lowered his mouth to one of the stiff peaks and consumed a nipple between his teeth while his hands now worked at loosening her jeans.

Judith's heart was beating so hard she could swear that it was echoing from wall to wall of the wigwam. Her eyes seemed to have a veil over them she was so lost in rising passion. She licked her lips nervously as she reached her hands to her jeans and squirmed out of them. There was no shame, no worry about whom he had possessed on this same spot before her. It didn't matter even that so far he had been the victor in this, her time to fight her father's battles successfully for him.

She smiled to herself. Though Strong Hawk was thus far the victor, didn't she share in the victory? When she was with him, she could never feel the loser.

Surrendering fully to him, she spread herself out on the rush mat flooring, her clothes and her boots tossed aside, letting Strong Hawk's tongue and hands send her into a sweet, lethargic mindlessness.

Kneeling down over her, Strong Hawk kissed the hollow of her throat, then moved lower to first one breast and then the other, lower still, circling his tongue around and inside her navel.

Judith barely breathed as she felt his hot breath on her flesh as his head went lower and he let his tongue graze the flesh of her thighs.

Feverish with desire, Judith dared to watch as Strong Hawk's fingers spread the soft curls of gold hair that guarded the core of her womanhood. With an even greater thumping wildness of her heart, she watched his head lower and his tongue reach down to touch her pulsing love mound. Spirals of pleasure soared through her as the wetness of his tongue touched her and caressed her where all her sensual feelings seemed to be centered.

Shivers ran up and down Judith's spine as Strong Hawk's lips kissed her long and hard there, pulling from her a soft cry, when suddenly she couldn't control the complete release from fully engulfing her. The colors of the rainbow flashed inside her brain as she exploded with rapture. She wove her fingers through the coarseness of his hair as his tongue lunged up inside her, over and over again, until she was left breathless, spent and gasping for breath as he finally drew gently away from her.

Smiling devilishly, Strong Hawk scooted up to lie next to her, his hands still exploring every sensitive pleasure point of her body, watching her face screw up in torment, then pleasure, then torment, then pleasure.

Judith's eyes lethargically opened. She looked as though through a dreamy haze toward Strong Hawk. "Strong Hawk, please . . ." she whispered, smiling sheepishly over at him. She tried to brush his hands away, without succeeding. "What are you trying to do to me? I may never be the same again."

Strong Hawk chuckled as he rose to lean over her. "I want you always to want me," he said huskily. "This technique that I choose to use. Is it working?"

Judith giggled, so throatily she hardly recognized herself. "My love, I am completely at your mercy," she said. "I am your prisoner. Is that what you want me to say?"

"*Ay-uh*," he said. "But now, my darling, make me your prisoner. Show me your skills."

"I am not as skilled. . . ."

"Just do to me what I did to you. Then you will be as skilled."

Judith's eyebrows raised. "How can I do what you just did?" she marveled. "Strong Hawk, that's quite impossible."

"I see that I must be a teacher as well as lover," Strong Hawk said, smiling down at her. Then his smile faded. "First you must undress me, Judith." He leaned away from her and let her move to her knees before him.

With trembling fingers, Judith removed his headband and feather and laid them aside. She then slowly drew his buckskin shirt up and over his head and tossed it aside. Smiling up at him, she splayed her fingers across his beautiful copper chest. It was tight with corded muscles, and the thunderous pounding of his heart was evident in the hollow of his throat.

He sucked in his breath when Judith lowered her lips to one of his firm nipples and swirled her tongue around and over its rubbery darkness, then sank her teeth into it and softly chewed.

Strong Hawk closed his eyes and set his jaw hard as he groaned. He placed his hands to the nape of her neck and guided her lips lower. "You know what you must do next," he whispered huskily.

Judith's knees grew weak, only half guessing what he could mean. She placed her thumbs over the waistband of his fringed leggings and began lowering them over his hips, watchful as the powerful part of him became visible in its full, throbbing glory.

"*Ay-uh*, that," Strong Hawk said, as he lowered her head closer to himself. His loins ached, his heart beat like a thousand drums inside him. And when he knew that she understood her next move, he eased his leggings on down, completely away from him. Then he stretched out on his back, watching her golden hair fall down over his abdomen as her lips moved lower and lower.

Not quite sure what to do, Judith hardly breathed as she kissed the tip of his hardness. She then placed her hands on him and began moving them as her tongue discovered the joy of touching him there. Lowering herself down closer to him, she placed her mouth more fully over him, hearing his gasp of pleasure as she did so.

Almost blinded by passion, she continued pleasing him in this new way until he reached and grabbed her by the waist and spun her around to face him.

"Ride me," he said hoarsely. "I want to reach my

peak inside you."

Judith crept up and straddled him, letting him fit himself fully inside her. She closed her eyes and held her head back, sighing, feeling the pleasure build once more.

Strong Hawk's fingers were digging into the flesh of her legs, his groans filling the small spaces of the dwelling. And suddenly Judith felt his thrusts become more wild, and his warmth fill her as he cried out with intense, joyful release.

Knowing the feelings that he was experiencing spurred the same joy inside Judith, and for the second time in only a matter of moments she was once more catapulted to paradise.

Afterward, Judith collapsed on the bulrush mats next to Strong Hawk, breathing hard, completely spent. She smiled as she looked over at him and saw how hard he was laboring for breath, knowing that he was just as tired as she.

"My energies are all used up," she softly laughed. "I'm not sure if I can even go to the celebration. My knees surely wouldn't hold me up, Strong Hawk."

"Ay-uh, I feel the same, though we must go," he laughed.

He turned to lean on his elbow, facing her. "But it was good, wasn't it, Judith?" he asked, lowering a soft kiss to her lips.

"Yes," she murmured, swallowed whole by his handsome nearness. "It was good. Never better. I love you so, Strong Hawk."

"My Judith," he said, then swept her up in his arms and tightly held her.

Judith clung, completely at peace now with herself

and the world. "Strong Hawk, why do you continue to call me Judith?" she softly questioned.

He inhaled the sweet jasmine scent of her flesh as he buried his nose into the gentle curve of her throat. "That is your name," he said. "This is why. Why do you ask?"

"Chief Gray Wolf gave the white woman he fell in love with an Indian name," she murmured. "Is that only done after a white woman becomes the wife of an Indian?"

Strong Hawk drew away from her, his eyes warm with love. "No. That is not why or how it was done," he explained. "My father preferred that the woman he loved be given an Indian name only because he is of the old school of Chippewa."

"Oh? And you're not? This is why you've never suggested I be called by name other than Judith?"

"I am not of the old school of the Chippewa," he grumbled. "My beliefs are much different from my father's and his father's before him."

Judith lowered her eyes. "I am glad to hear that is the reason you've not chosen to call me by another name," she said softly. "I thought it was because you didn't love me enough—or respect me enough."

Once more Strong Hawk drew her into his arms. "Judith is a lovely, gentle name," he said thickly. "I love it as I do the woman who bears the name. I love you. I respect you. Always remember that."

"Will you love me *ah-pah-nay*, no matter what, Strong Hawk?"

Strong Hawk's eyes widened as he looked down at her. He saw her soft smile. "How do you know the word 'forever' in Chippewa?" he chuckled.

"Your mother," Judith laughed.

"*Ay-uh*," Strong Hawk nodded. "She is also a skilled teacher." Then he laughed hoarsely. "But of course, she teaches you different things than I."

"*Ay-uh*. Quite," Judith murmured.

"*I do*," Strong Hawk said, framing his face between his hands.

"You do what?" Judith asked, reveling in the warmth of his hands on her cheeks.

"Love you. *Ah-pah-nay.* . . ."

Chapter Fourteen

The pulsating of the steady drum beats in the distance caused Strong Hawk to stir quickly to his feet. He offered Judith his hand and she rose to stand into his embrace as he once more gave her a lingering, passionate kiss. Their naked bodies fused, Judith's breasts pressing hard into Strong Hawk's chest, her fingers traveling over his sleek buttocks. She could never get enough of him. Could she even leave him when the time arrived to do so?

But she must. She had to return to her father. She only hoped that she wasn't taking too much time before doing so. What if he had worsened in her absence? What if he had discovered that she wasn't in St. Paul with Rory?

Strong Hawk drew gently away from her. "We must prepare ourselves for the celebration," he said huskily. His eyes appraised her, his lips slowly lifting into a smile. "Though I would prefer to continue our own private ceremony. How am I supposed to keep my hands off you, Judith, with you so beautiful . . . so much a woman?"

Judith cupped his chin in her hand and let her thumb run up and down the firm line of his jaw. "And I you?" she said quietly, aglow with a sensitized warmth that continued to be awake inside her. "Surely there has never been such a handsome Indian brave as you."

Strong Hawk chuckled. *"Ay-uh,* there has," he said, stepping on away from her. "My father and his father before him, my Grandfather Yellow Feather. My mother tells me that we all were poured from the same mold."

He gave Judith an amused look. "Handsome?" he laughed. "You truly think me handsome?"

"The most," Judith giggled, going to him to hug him tightly to her.

Strong Hawk burrowed his nose into the soft gold of her hair. "I've a gift for you," he said. "Something for the celebration."

Judith's eyes widened as she stepped away from him. "Oh? What is it?" she asked, anxious.

Strong Hawk went to a dark corner of the wigwam, stooped, picked something up from a low shelf along the wall, and went back to Judith. "A deerskin dress," he said. "Mother brought it and placed it here for you while we were canoeing. Will you wear it? Will you be Indian for the evening?"

"You want me to be Indian?" Judith murmured, accepting the dress. She held it out before her and let it ripple down to be fully revealed to her appreciative eyes. Though only made of deerskin, of a muted beige color, it was exquisitely beautiful, with beads of all colors sewn onto the front in the shapes of the

199

forest wildflowers, and with delicate fringe around the hem of the skirt. It was so lightweight and soft that it was almost as though she had nothing outspread between her hands.

"It's absolutely beautiful," she sighed.

"Will you please me by wearing it?" Strong Hawk asked hoarsely.

Judith's thick lashes grew heavy over her eyes as she looked up into Strong Hawk's dark, fathomless eyes. "I'd be proud to," she said. "I do love it, Strong Hawk."

"It is yours to keep," he said, reaching a hand to touch her cheek. "Take it with you when you return to Duluth, to remind you of our times together."

Judith's eyes closed and she leaned her face more into his hand, sighing. "Do you think I need a dress to remind me of you?" she said. "Strong Hawk, I don't believe you even know the hold you have on my heart."

"I would hope that I have some idea," he chuckled. "But you haven't said. Will you accept the dress as yours? Will you take it with you to Duluth?"

"*Ay-uh . . .*" she said.

Strong Hawk stepped away from her, looking down at her with amusement in his eyes. "You please me even more this evening," he said. "You have spoken in Chippewa more than once to me today. That is *o-nee-shee-shin*."

"And what does *o-nee-shee-shin* mean?" she asked, raising an eyebrow.

"Good. It is good that you know some words in Chippewa. You are an apt pupil, my Judith."

"I have the best teacher."

200

"I would like to teach you all the ways of the Chippewa," he said, swinging away from her. He once more walked over to the darker corner of the wigwam, and when he showed himself by the light of the fire again he wore a brief loincloth.

Judith's eyes widened and her mouth went partially agape as she absorbed what he was wearing and how the briefness of it outlined the magnificence of his manhood.

Then she rose questioning eyes to him. "That is what you choose to wear to the celebration?" she softly asked, blushing.

"*Ay-uh*," he said matter-of-factly, now braiding his hair. "It is the Spring Feast. All braves must celebrate the return of the sun from the south in their briefest attire, to capture the wind on their bare flesh, to give thanks for the warmer breezes and the promise of what spring brings to our people."

"All the braves will be dressed . . . in . . . such a manner?" Judith gasped, clutching the deerskin dress to her bosom.

"This will displease you?"

Judith laughed nervously. "It isn't that," she said, lowering her eyes.

"Then what is it?"

"It will just be a bit unnerving," she said, then giggled as Strong Hawk came to her and placed his forefinger to her chin, to lift her eyes to meet his.

"Seeing so many braves in such a way will stir your insides to lusting after them?" he teased, his eyes twinkling.

"Strong Hawk!" Judith gasped, once more feeling her cheeks flame with color.

"Oh, I see," he further teased. "It will only be me that you will be watching with an anxious heart."

"*Ay-uh . . .*" Judith said, shaking her head up and down. "Only you. And, Strong Hawk, it will be disturbing. So much of you is revealed."

Then her lashes lowered. "And I won't be the only one witnessing you dressed in such a way. As you know, the whole village of Indian women will also be observing you."

Strong Hawk stepped away from her, laughing heartily. "My Judith," he said. "My Judith is *gah-way.*"

Judith sighed heavily. "Strong Hawk, please speak in English," she said. "What are you accusing me of in Chippewa?"

He moved to his haunches and placed several clay pots before him. "Jealous," he chuckled. "I do believe you are jealous."

"And shouldn't I be?"

"*Gah-ween.*"

"Oh!" she said, softly stomping a bare foot. "What did you just say? Please stop teasing me so by speaking in Chippewa!"

Strong Hawk placed his fingers into one of the clay pots and covered their tips with a bright red paint, then began decorating his chest with it. "I said no, you have no need to be jealous," he laughed. "For years I have had my choice of Chippewa maidens. You do not see any I have chosen to be my wife, do you?"

"No . . ."

"Then rest your mind," he said. "It is no different now."

Judith watched Strong Hawk, stunned at how he was now spreading different colors of paint across his body in contrasting designs. "Is it required to paint yourself so?" she softly questioned. "And in so many vivid colors?"

"These paints made of squeezed berries and vegetables represent many things to my people," Strong Hawk said. "Yellow is to give thanks for the abundance of sunshine. Green is for the grass and leaves of the trees. Blue is for the blessings of the river and loveliness of the clear, cloud-free sky. White is for the full moon at night, which leads our braves to the midnight hunt. Red is for extreme happiness."

The final strokes of zigzagged streaks of white were placed on Strong Hawk's cheeks, and his body was finally completed in its designs of many colors. He looked up at Judith, who still watched. He softly laughed as he rose to his feet.

"Now don't you think it is time for you to slip into your dress?" he asked, going to her to take it from her. "I will even help—and then I will braid your hair."

Raising her arms over her head, Judith welcomed the soft dress being pulled down over her. When Strong Hawk's fingers grazed her flesh, she trembled, then looked down at the dress and how it clung to her. The nipples of her breasts were outlined beneath the buckskin, her waistline was tiny, and her hips softly flared.

"*Mee-kah-wah-diz-ee*," Strong Hawk said huskily, lifting her hair from her shoulders, then letting it ripple back down to hang lazily down her back. "*Ay-uh*, you will be the most beautiful woman at the celebration. I will proudly sit with you at my side.

203

And when we dance to the music of the drums and flute, all braves will be jealous of me."

With deft fingers Strong Hawk silently braided Judith's hair, loving the touch of its softness, unlike his or that of the Indian maidens who had shared his blankets. It was almost the same as a rare silken fabric, and it shone lustrous in the two braids that now lay down her back.

Judith's hands went to the braids. She lifted the end of one and looked at it. "Well? How do they look?" she asked, never having before braided her hair. A ponytail, yes. But never braids.

Strong Hawk stepped away from her. He kneaded his chin contemplatingly and raised an eyebrow. "Hmm. I just don't know," he teased.

Judith paled. She brushed the braid back and over her shoulder. "You don't like them?" she whispered.

Strong Hawk tore into a fit of laughter, then sobered. "My Judith, you have never looked lovelier," he said, embracing her. "I like you as part Indian . . . part white."

Judith sighed heavily. "Why do you tease me so?" she said. "For a moment there . . ."

"Hush," Strong Hawk said, stopping her further words as he sealed her lips with a finger. "You are lovely. You are always lovely. And now is the time for me to share you with my father's people. *Mah-bee-zhon*. Let's go and be a part of the celebration."

Judith wriggled her toes, suddenly aware of her bare feet. "My boots will look funny with this beautiful dress," she worried. "But I have no other shoes with me."

"You are to go barefoot," he said, looking down

into her eyes. "All maidens will go barefoot this night. It is required."

"At least I don't have to attend the celebration in only a loincloth," Judith said, giving him a coy look.

"Now that could be arranged," Strong Hawk teased. "But I'm afraid no one's mind would be on the celebration. You would be the center of all attraction. You would become the celebration."

"I'm sure," Judith said, unable to suppress a tremor.

Placing an arm about her waist, Strong Hawk chuckled as he guided her from the wigwam.

The day had turned into night, yet the sky shimmered in pale orange as bonfires burned throughout the village and reflected up onto the low-hanging clouds. The night had a mystical quality about it, filled with vibrations of the incessant drumbeats and chants from Indians already filled with merriment at the celebration already in its first stages.

Clinging to Strong Hawk's waist, Judith walked alongside him to the grounds that spread out before the council house. A larger fire had been built there, and Chief Gray Wolf and Danette were seated together upon a raised platform upon which were strewn thick, glossy bear hides.

Judith was quickly captivated by Danette's beauty. Her midnight-black hair was drawn back and woven into two thick pigtails, and her own highly decorated buckskin dress was worn with grace. Her eyes showed her contentment; her lips were set into a soft smile. The only thing different about her was the single white streak painted across her brow, to match the one drawn on her husband's brow.

Once Judith's attention became centered on Chief Gray Wolf, she felt her insides do a strange flip-flop. He was so much Strong Hawk! How could a son and father resemble each other so? Her heart warmed when she saw that this night Gray Wolf didn't have the caste of illness on his handsome face. He sat proudly tall, his chiseled features unmarred by worry lines, as though magically wiped away by his own silent contentment, which lay soft in the green of his eyes.

Judith avoided looking down at his loincloth, embarrassed even to let herself wonder about how he might compare with Strong Hawk there!

Strong Hawk guided Judith on around the mass of Indians who were quickly settling down in a wide circle about the fire. "We will sit beside Mother and Father, on their right side," he whispered.

He smiled to himself seeing that Judith was being watched and approved of, if the eyes of his people spoke truth. He knew that she was affecting them as she had him. There was a graciousness about her, a friendliness that could only draw kindness, in return, to her.

"I see you've finally arrived," Chief Gray Wolf said, nodding toward Judith and Strong Hawk. He gave them a faint smile, then let his gaze sweep over Judith, approving of what he saw. He could understand his son's becoming enraptured by her. Gray Wolf again saw resemblances in her to his Sweet Butterfly, his wife of many moons. It was the spirit that sparked in both their eyes, and the daring quality that led them to separate themselves from the way most white women were expected to behave by the white community.

And hadn't they both learned to appreciate the ways of the Chippewa quite quickly? This made them both unique, in a very special way. Gray Wolf would not dissuade his son from having the need to be with this lady with hair the color of the midday sun.

Judith spoke a quiet hello to Gray Wolf and then to Danette as Strong Hawk urged her down onto a colorful blanket beside him.

Strong Hawk folded his legs before him. "This is a special night," he said hoarsely. "But first we will eat, drink, and dance."

Glancing quickly over at Strong Hawk, Judith was remembering his earlier mention of dancing. He had included her, as if she would also be dancing. "You don't expect me to dance, do you?" she asked, curling her feet up beneath her.

"*Ay-uh*," Strong Hawk said, eyeing her questioningly. "Why do you sound as though you are surprised?"

Judith looked almost shyly about the group of Indians, then back into Strong Hawk's eyes. "Because I won't know how, Strong Hawk," she blurted. "Surely you only expect me to watch, not participate."

"You will want to," he chuckled. "You will get caught up in the celebrating and will forget who you even are. Just be patient. Enjoy the food and drink. Then you will see."

"I doubt that," Judith said beneath her breath, and then tried to force herself to relax as she let the activity around her sweep her up in wonder.

The Indians were now all seated on colorful blankets, the braves adorned by their decorations of paint and attired only in loincloths as Strong Hawk had earlier warned her they would be. The squaws were all in their most highly decorated buckskin dresses, and barefoot.

But there was one thing missing. Children! There were none in eye range here at the council grounds, nor any running and playing in the village. Judith couldn't help but wonder why.

Bowls of food were now being passed around, heaped with parched corn, crunched maple sugar, roasted pumpkin seeds, and the various meats that had been cooked prior to the feast. Along with the bowls of food were passed cups of a pale yellow liquid.

Judith accepted both a bowl and cup, trying to blot from her mind the way in which the meat had been prepared. She followed Strong Hawk's lead and ate the food with her fingers and took eager drinks from the cup to wash the greasy taste of the meat down her throat.

After a few drinks of the yellow liquid, Judith felt a strange lightheadedness, a kind of spinning. She stared down into the cup and then over at Strong Hawk. "What is this?" she said. Her tongue even felt heavy, wide, and hard to control.

"Do you like it?" Strong Hawk asked, smiling devilishly down at her.

"I can't decide," Judith said, giggling. She watched as an elderly Indian squaw refilled her cup.

"Drink. Enjoy," Strong Hawk encouraged, shrugging.

The pulsating beats of the drum in the distance and the haunting wail from a flute seemed louder, more emphasized to Judith. She raised her eyebrow quizzically to Strong Hawk, then took another deep swallow from her cup.

She giggled again. "More," she said, holding the cup out before her. "I can't seem to get my thirst quenched."

She drank another cup empty, then another, feeling deliciously warm inside. Her face was flushed, her heart pounding, her eyes hazy and hot. She turned her eyes to the circle of Indians and watched as many began rising and dancing around the fire, the braves quickly joined by the women.

Judith's pulse raced as she recognized the sensual quality of the dances as the bodies swayed and brushed against each other. There was no denying the arousal of the braves, with only loincloths briefly over their male strength. And as the women danced against the braves in a slow, grinding motion, it created a stormy reaction inside Judith. Never had she had such a tortured pain between her thighs, her own arousal was so intense.

Not understanding how she could let watching the display of erotic behavior cause her to become so shamefully aroused, she turned her eyes away, not able to control the pounding at her temples.

Out of the corner of her eye she saw Strong Hawk rise to his feet and join in the dance. Slowly Judith let her gaze move to capture the whole of him. She dropped the cup to the ground and licked her lips seductively as she saw the slow, gyrating movements of Strong Hawk's hips as he began motioning with outstretched arms for her to join him before the fire.

The drums were pounding their boom-boom sounds with furious accents on the first stroke. Judith watched Strong Hawk pick up the rhythm of the drum and begin to chant.

"Hi-ya-ya-ya, Hi-ya-ya-ya," he chanted as his feet continued to beat out the rhythm of the drums. His body swayed and his arms now tossed first right, then left. Round and round Strong Hawk now went, in a rising frenzy of excitement.

Then once more his eyes, heavy and dark with heated passion, looked down at Judith. His hands beckoned her upward, his gyrating hips and flapping loincloth driving her almost wild.

"Mah-bee-szhon," he said huskily. *"Nee-mee-win."*

Judith noticed how quickly the crowd of Indians was thinning as couples left, clinging, moving away into the darkness.

Strong Hawk leaned down and took Judith by the hands. "It is *zeegwun.* Spring. It is the time for thoughts of new life . . . of young love," he said huskily. "Now do you see the importance of this feast? It is a new beginning. Nine months from this date our village will be rewarded by many new offspring."

Judith was hardly absorbing his words she was so caught up in the magic of the moment. Strong Hawk's eyes were magnets, drawing her to him, her senses reeling in drunken pleasure. A scorching flame shot through her as his lips momentarily possessed her. And then he held her away from him and once more began swaying with the music.

"Move your hips," he said huskily. "Let your feet move in rhythm with the drumbeats."

Filled with a wild, unleashed passion, Judith didn't say anything; instead she let her mind become more intoxicated by Strong Hawk's nearness and his continued suggestive movements. Then she spun around with him and into his embrace. When she felt the hard outline of his sex grinding against her, her breath caught in her throat. Slowly he moved against her, his fingers on her buttocks, pulling her closer and closer.

Mindless, her heart racing and her mouth dry, Judith began her own body movements against him, her inhibitions cast aside after having drunk from that first cup of pale yellow liquid. She had been drugged, but she was oblivious of that now, or of any other worries. She was surrendering herself fully to this thrilling, floating sensation stealing her mind from her. And when Strong Hawk drew her up and into his arms and began carrying her away with him, Judith clung about his neck, and her eyes rapturously closed, enjoying the warmth of his breath on her face, stirring shivers throughout her.

"My love . . ." she whispered, sounding to herself as though her voice had come from a deep well, echoing over and over again in her mind. She was aware only of the thunderous pounding of Strong Hawk's heart against her cheek as he ran with her away from the now subdued celebration. And when he carried her into the darkness of what appeared to be some sort of tunnel, even then she did not have the wits to question him about where he was now taking her. Only to be with him, *wholly* with him, seemed to be the importance of the moment.

A muted light appeared in the distance. Water, dripping on all sides of Judith, sounded like loud crashes, so intensified were her senses from the drug in her bloodstream. She batted her lashes nervously, able now to make out the flickering of a campfire, and as Strong Hawk approached it, lighting everything about her, Judith realized that she had just been taken inside a cave.

Strong Hawk's mouth upon hers once more stole her senses from her. Her lips trembled as she returned his kiss, her eyes closed with ecstasy. She felt herself being lowered onto a soft blanket, and she welcomed his eager hands on her breasts through her dress and on her bare thigh as he began easing the dress up and then quickly away from her.

Sighing lethargically, Judith watched Strong Hawk step out of his loincloth, splendidly nude and ready to fill her with the great strength of his swollen manhood.

"Love me, Strong Hawk," she whispered, reaching her arms out to him. "Love me now or I may just explode from my need of you."

Settling down on his knees, Strong Hawk bent his back and began worshipping her satiny flesh first with his lips and then his tongue. Judith writhed in response, becoming feverish with building desire.

With his hands on each of her breasts, gently kneading them, Strong Hawk's lips kissed and teased her between her thighs, then left a trail of fire as he

212

moved them upward to flick his tongue around the sharp peak of her breasts, whose tips were swollen buds of pleasure.

And then he entered her from below, his thrusts hard and demanding. Judith lifted her hips to aid in their pursuit of momentary bliss, and in her drugged state a few brief strokes were all that were required to give her a mind-shattering release.

Strong Hawk felt her shudder and heard her soft cry of passion, then worked more energetically, the torment building, heating up to a crescendo in his loins.

And then his own passion exploded and spilled over inside her, leaving him winded, but peacefully so, as he scooted to lie beside her on the blanket.

Judith curled up next to Strong Hawk, still in a drunken haze. She giggled softly as she draped her arm loosely over his chest. "What was in that cup I drank?" she asked softly. "I don't believe I've ever felt so strangely giddy."

"It was a potion made from many herbs and roots taken from the forest," he said, leaning up on his elbow to look down at her. His fingers went to her hair and smoothed several damp strands back from her eyes. "It was used to urge copulation. It is essential for our tribe of Chippewa."

"Now I understand why no children were present at the feast," Judith said, once more loosely giggling.

"*Ay-uh*, the celebration was only for the adults of the community," Strong Hawk said, lowering a kiss to her exquisite lips.

Judith sighed, loving the taste of him . . . the smell of him. She reached her hand to his sleek, muscular chest and stroked it. "I was out of place at the celebration," she pouted.

"Why do you say that?"

"The reason for the feast made it wrong for me to be there."

"Why, Judith?"

"It was to increase the population of the Chippewa, wasn't it?"

"*Ay-uh.*"

"I am not of the Chippewa," Judith said, and then she quickly sobered, realizing where her mind had taken her. Copulation? Babies? *She* could even be pregnant! Why hadn't she thought to worry earlier about this? Though she dearly loved Strong Hawk, she did not wish to become pregnant out of wedlock. Such women were scorned, were looked upon as whores!

Moving shakily to her feet, she searched desperately around her for the buckskin dress. Somehow, things had gotten out of hand. And she alone was truly responsible for anything and everything that had happened and would happen to her.

Strong Hawk rose hurriedly from the blanket. He placed his hands to Judith's waist and forced her around to face him. "What do you think you're doing?" he growled.

"I've got to get out of here," Judith softly cried, wiping at her eyes, trying to remove the film of haze that persisted.

Blinking her eyes, she looked around her and gestured. "Where am I?" she blurted. "Why did you bring me here?"

Strong Hawk's fingers dug into her flesh. "You are

214

in the sacred cave," he grumbled. "My grandfather was directed here by the giant owl of the forest while he was experiencing his childhood vision. My grandfather led his people here, and here we have since made our residence. The sacred cave is the symbol of many things to the St. Croix Band of the Chippewa. Among these is shared love. It is said that my father was even conceived in the sacred cave."

"As perhaps your son or daughter may have just been conceived?" Judith sobbed, frantic at the thought. She jerked angrily away from him. "Is that what you want, Strong Hawk? To get me with child? By doing so you would have complete control over my destiny, and then my father's. Isn't that so, Strong Hawk?"

"*Gah-ween,*" he said, fiercely denying her accusation. "That is not so."

"Then why?" Judith insisted.

"Judith, I believe the love potion is affecting your logic," Strong Hawk said, glowering. With set jaw and corded shoulder muscles he bent and grabbed her dress from the floor. He thrust it angrily into her arms. "Here. Get dressed. We shall return to my dwelling."

"That suits me just fine," Judith said dryly, already slipping the dress over her head. With a torturous hurt circling her heart, she watched Strong Hawk secure his loincloth about his body. She could see hurt in his eyes, fused with anger. Had she spoken out of turn? She never wanted to inflict hurt upon the man she loved. But hadn't he caused her hurt? He would try anything to get his way where his father was concerned!

Yet, wasn't she guilty of the same? Even now she thought of another approach to winning their conflict. She wouldn't demand council with Gray Wolf, after all, as she had originally planned. She would go to Danette's mansion in Duluth and make friends with North Star, perhaps even Strong Hawk's brother. Danette had mentioned a brother. Anything to remove herself from this hold that Strong Hawk had on her.

"Yes," she said, smiling smugly. "Let's return to your wigwam. I'm very tired, Strong Hawk."

"Ay-uh" Strong Hawk grumbled, circling an arm about her waist. "Rest. Rest will soothe away our anger. Tomorrow is a new day, a new beginning, my Judith."

Judith tremored with ecstasy as he drew her against him in guiding her away from the fire, still battling her feelings for him. She gave him a half glance, knowing that she would be gone early the next morning before Strong Hawk awakened. He wouldn't have the chance to use his powers of persuasion again so soon. She had her own plans for success. Yes, North Star. Strong Hawk's brother. What had Danette called him? Giles. Yes, Giles.

Chapter Fifteen

On Judith's return to Duluth she had found her father neither better nor worse. And no word had yet been received from Rory.

Determined, Judith flicked the reins of her horse, sending her mare at a faster clip, the wheels of the buggy squeaking ominously as they challenged the steep street it was traveling along, up and away from Saint Louis Bay.

Judith had decided to make a good impression when she introduced herself at the Thomas mansion. She had purposely dressed in a stylish waist and skirt and a Gainesboro hat. Her waistshirt was a pale turquoise, made of the very best taffeta silk. It was tucked all around, with a taffeta silk bow in front and a high-standing collar, and flaring cuffs lined throughout with a good quality of cambric. The skirt was of a matching color, made from twilled cloth, with three rolls of satin piping on either side of the front, and three inverted plaits, interlined with crinoline. Her hat was made of a turquoise-blue silk-finished velvet and had five bias folds of contrasting colors, turquoise and black, around the crown. In front it sported two handsome birds, fancy sweeping aigrettes, and was finished with knots of velvet drawn through a handsome rhinestone and jet buckle.

She was dressed in the latest fashion, down to the new French corset made with quality French sateen, heavy satin strips, lace, and baby ribbon trim, boned with the dreaded celluloid-tipped steels, which dug unmercifully into her flesh.

She forgot the discomfort of her fancy attire, instead remembering the smile that seeing her so dressed had brought to her father's usually sullen face. It was a fact that she did wear jeans much too often. She would have been the first to admit it. But who was there to dress differently for? Only with Strong Hawk did she become aware of wanting to be as beautiful as humanly possible.

Shaking her head fitfully from side to side, she forced herself to brush thoughts of Strong Hawk from her mind. She had a purpose this day, and he was no part of it. Other members of his family perhaps, but not him.

In her mind's eye she let the address of the Thomas mansion materialize, then directed her buggy to the left, finally on a straight plane of street. Judith was impressed when she recognized the street as one of the most affluent ones in Duluth. Two- and three-story mansions with manicured green yards lined the well-groomed street.

Her destination soon came into view. It was a rectangular shaped two-story house with a wide porch, stained glass windows, and a mansard roof.

Judith led her horse up a gravel drive, then drew it to a halt beside a reined stately horse and carriage. Tying her horse's reins onto a hitching post, Judith went to the front steps of the austere Victorian house. Made of granite, the steps were solid and somewhat intimidating, and the granite sills of the windows were pale gray against the warm brick facade of the house.

Now on the porch, Judith raised the solid brass knocker on the heavy oak door and let it bang heavily as she knocked twice. Patiently she waited, clutching her velvet purse, hoping to be accepted without too many questions. She had to be cautious, she couldn't quickly disclose her true reason for being there. She would only gain North Star's friendship with sincerity, even though she knew she was using this friendship for her own personal gain. And there was Giles, Strong Hawk's brother, to consider. Would he have white or red skin?

The door swung suddenly open. Judith was taken aback and her eyes were riveted to a beautiful woman of her age whose skin was copper, like an Indian's, but whose hair was as gold as Judith's and whose eyes were as blue. It was a contrasting combination, unnervingly so.

And she looked so daintily lovely in her petiteness! She wore only a pink cotton dress, but its lace at her plunging neckline and at the hem made it delicately pretty.

"Yes . . . ?" North Star asked, clinging to the edge of the door. Her eyes swept over Judith, admiring her smart, very stylish attire. Judith looked like she had just stepped out of a fashion magazine.

"Are you North Star?" Judith asked softly.

"*Ay-uh*," North Star said, her brows arching. "And you? What is your name and your purpose for being here?"

"My name is Judith. Judith McMahon," Judith said, shifting nervously from foot to foot, under the woman's close scrutiny. The mere fact that North Star had spoken in Indian made Judith even more nervous. But she was now recalling who North Star's parents had been. One had been white, the other had been Indian.

"I recently made the acquaintance of Danette . . . Chief Gray Wolf's wife," Judith quickly added. "She gave me permission to come here, to see her paintings. Have I come at an inconvenient time?"

North Star's face became full of shadows, revealing her mistrust. "How could you have become acquainted with Danette?" she asked quietly. "She hasn't been in Duluth for some time now. She is with her husband, Chief Gray Wolf."

"Yes," Judith said, nodding. "I know. That is where I was introduced to Danette and where I saw her paintings."

She tilted her head and looked past North Star, into the house. "May I come in?" she urged. "I assure you that I was given permission."

North Star stood her ground. "No one ventures to the village of the Chippewa without a purpose," she said cautiously. "What was your purpose for being there?"

Judith's smile faded. She suddenly felt trapped. If she told the full truth, she would be just as quickly banned from the premises. A half truth would have to do.

"My father had council with Chief Gray Wolf," she said, trying her hardest to suppress the tremor in her voice. "But I am not sure why. You know how it is. Men rarely discuss business with women, especially a mere daughter. It was while they were in council that I met Danette."

"Oh, I see," North Star said, breathing more easily, no longer feeling threatened.

"So? May I?"

"Pardon?"

"May I see Danette's paintings?" Judith asked, laughing softly. "She has a rare talent, you know. Quite unique in her choice of color and designs. It's a shame they aren't on display, for everyone to see and admire."

North Star stepped aside, also laughing softly. "*Ay-uh.* Yes. Do come on in," she said, gesturing with the sweep of a hand. "And I hope you will overlook and forgive my rude mistrust of you. Being part Indian, I cannot be too cautious. I've been a target of unjust gossip and . . . even some ridicule."

Judith blanched, her eyes grew wide. "No," she gasped. "How could anyone?"

"I seem to be an easy target," North Star murmured. "Perhaps people like to take advantage."

Judith's eyes lowered, guilt awash inside her for perpetrating an act of deceit like those of whom North Star was already scornful. But she couldn't let these guilts dissuade her. Her father's feelings were more important here!

Moving past North Star, Judith stepped into a wide entrance hall that opened to three spacious parlors and a dining room. The portraits lining the walls grabbed Judith's attention. She gulped hard, her eyes wide, the light from a hand-blown glass chandelier that resembled large concoctions of delicately spun sugar reflecting enchantingly on one portrait in particular.

At first glance, Judith thought that she was looking at Strong Hawk's portrait, but as she inched closer to it and was afforded a better look, she recognized the differences between son and father, and knew that this was a portrait of Chief Gray Wolf, as a young man. His piercing green eyes stared alive back at her, almost, and a slight tinge of red in his hair made Judith's eyebrows raise in question.

"That's one of Danette's most prized in her whole collection," North Star said, stepping up next to Judith.

"Why is it there and not with her, in her house back in the Chippewa village?" Judith softly queried.

"She has her reasons," North Star said softly. "Something about proving something to her Uncle Dwight. I never questioned her about her reasons any more than that. All I know is that her Uncle Dwight caused Danette many heartaches where Gray Wolf was concerned. Somehow, it even seems right to me that Gray Wolf's portrait should hang where Dwight's once hung."

Judith let her gaze move slowly to North Star, realizing that some very troubled times lay in this family's past. "This Uncle Dwight," she dared to question. "What happened to him?"

North Star lifted her shoulder in a gesture of indifference. "He died in a fire many moons ago," she said. "It was at the time of the great forest fire that burned a good portion of Duluth. Dwight escaped a train as it was traveling in reverse away from the fire, but he couldn't escape the fire itself. He died in the flames."

Judith placed a hand to her mouth. She was recalling recently being on the train on her way to St. Paul and how thoughts of the fire had even then entered her mind. Such a fire haunted humanity for years to come, for in its path, many had died.

But it was strange that North Star didn't seem mournful of this one man's death. Had this Uncle Dwight been such an unlikable person that his death would even have been welcomed?

North Star saw Judith's reaction. She reached her hand to her arm. "I have upset you in some way," she murmured. "I'm sorry. Perhaps some tea would make you feel better?"

Judith shook her head. "Yes. That would be fine," she murmured.

"Please go on into the parlor and make yourself comfortable," North Star said, nodding to one of the three parlors that was the closest. "I won't be long."

"Thank you," Judith said, sighing as she was left alone in the hallway. Before going into the parlor, she studied the other paintings. The ones that she now was admiring were mostly of nature settings, many being of Lake Superior and the great ships with open sails that had at one time been such a common sight in Duluth's great port. Steamships had now replaced them, and much else had so much changed as well, at this time so near the turn of the century.

Then, hesitant to climb the stairs to see the rest of the paintings, Judith decided, instead, to go on into the parlor as North Star had suggested.

She gasped at the loveliness of the room as she entered it. Dramatic red-glazed walls set off a beautiful fireplace with a mantel and over-mantel, refinished in antique Chinese red and carved with pagodas and figures of Chinese men. A bronze French Dore crystal chandelier sent an inviting glow from its gaslights, settling on elegant walls and ceiling frescoes, quarter-sawn oak woodwork, and European carpeting. The Chippendale chairs and sofas were covered in the finest imported silk, and drop leaf and lamp tables were arranged generously around the room.

It was a room that spoke of good taste, careful choosing, and much wealth, though it was evident that most of the furnishings had aged from many years of use.

Footsteps from the hallway caused Judith to spin around and look in that direction, expecting to see North Star returning with the tea. Judith jumped with a start when she saw that it wasn't North Star at all, but, instead . . .

Her heart thundered inside her, her hands went to her throat. "Strong Hawk?" she gasped, yet then shook her head slowly back and forth as her eyes crept up and down the full figure of the man who was now across the threshold and moving toward her.

How could it be Strong Hawk, dressed in such a way? This man wore a suit and vest of a dark gray double diagonal all wool worsted cloth, a white silk shirt with a detachable collar, and a bow tie. His pants were of the latest double-ribbed hairline cassimere, impeccably pressed and so tight the muscles of his thighs could be seen through the material.

Judith took a step backwards, still in a state of semishock, now carefully studying his facial features and the way in which he wore his hair. His features were handsomely identical to Strong Hawk's, except that in this man's dark eyes there was a coldness. And his hair. It was of the same coarse, black texture, but he wore it clipped neatly to lie against his collar, and it was stylishly parted in the middle and combed to perfection.

"Did I hear you speak my brother's name?" Giles said, now circling Judith, his eyes closely studying her. "Why is that? How is it that you happen to know Strong Hawk? It can't be that he's come to Duluth without stopping by to see his twin brother."

Judith spun around on her heel, her eyes wide. "Twin? You, you are Strong Hawk's twin?"

"None other," Giles said in a cool, casual tone. He walked away from her and went to a desk to remove a cigar from a solid oak cigar chest. "Giles to most, but Silver Fox to some."

Judith laughed nervously. "Now I understand why I thought at first you were Strong Hawk," she said, still watching his every movement, comparing each with Strong Hawk's. If Giles were dressed in Indian attire and his hair were long, there would hardly be any way to tell him and Strong Hawk apart.

Yet, there was this coldness about him. It was in his eyes and his manner. And why had the two brothers chosen such different ways of life?

"And you? Aren't you going to introduce yourself?" Giles said, wetting the tip of his cigar as he circled it between his lips.

"Judith. Judith McMahon. I've come to see your mother's paintings," she said clumsily, wishing he would direct his eyes elsewhere. When Strong Hawk looked at her in such a way, it turned her insides to warm mush. With Giles, it was different. Judith felt his indifference, his continuing coldness, transferring to her.

"And why is that?" Giles asked, lighting his cigar. He went and settled down into a deep wing chair, crossed his legs, and placed his fingertips together before him. One dark wedge of an eyebrow was lifted as he puffed leisurely on his cigar.

Judith was now becoming annoyed. Though he was dressed like a gentleman, he was not one. He had not offered her a chair but instead had comfortably seated himself and had put her in a position of feeling as though on display and at odds with herself.

"I have already fully explained my reason for being here once," she said dryly, stubbornly tilting her chin. "North Star will return soon with tea. If you must know every minute detail, ask her."

Giles rose quickly from his chair. He tossed his cigar into the fireplace, then moved to stand over Judith to glower down at her. "It is for me to decide who will have tea here in my house," he said hotly. "Not North Star."

Judith paled, humiliated. "Why, I . . ." she exclaimed. With a hand holding her hat in place she began storming from the room. As she made a quick turn to move out into the hallway she collided with North Star, knocking a silver serving tray from North Star's grasp.

Judith teetered sideways, dropping her purse and watching tea splashing all over the front of her skirt and hearing the clatter and crash of the teacups and saucers as they broke and scattered in all directions across the carpet.

"Oh, no," North Star groaned, steadying herself against the wall.

Judith finally steadied herself, her gaze seeing the full damage not only to her person, but also to the carpet and the front of North Star's dress. Brown blotches of tea were everywhere and broken fragments of glass twinkled beneath the light.

"I'm so sorry," Judith gasped, stooping to try and collect the silver tea service and tray up into her trembling fingers.

Then her eyes narrowed and anger flashed hotly inside her as Giles came out to survey the damage. "You're the one truly to blame here," Judith snapped at him. "I've never met such a rude man. You're nothing like your brother."

Giles lifted a shoulder in a gesture of indifference. "Yes. Most say that," he said icily.

"Oh!" Judith stormed, straightening her back as she handed North Star the tray.

North Star's eyes wavered as she looked from Giles to Judith, then her gaze settled on Judith's soiled skirt. "Your skirt," she softly cried. "I'm afraid that it is ruined."

"Don't make such a fuss," Giles scolded, kicking his highly polished shoes at the broken glass at his feet. "From appearances, this lady is from a family who can readily afford to buy her another skirt."

"Giles, we should replace it," North Star softly argued, giving Judith a weak smile.

"Ha!" he laughed. "Such an unladylike show of temper on her part is the reason for this catastrophe. She shall replace her own skirt."

"Giles!" North Star gasped, paling.

Judith's jaw tightened. She had never before had the urge to hit a man. This was the first. She knew that she must take her leave and fast, or she wouldn't be responsible for what she did do!

"North Star, thank you for your kindness, but I must now leave," she said, giving Giles a sour glance. She picked her purse up from the floor and made the front door her hurried destination.

"Judith, I'm sorry." North Star murmured, walking along with her to the door.

"Don't be," Judith said, giving Giles another glance across her shoulder. "I'm sorry. For you. For having to make residence with him."

The sudden crash of the knocker on the door drew Judith and North Star to a startled halt. They gave each other silent glances, then North Star set the serving tray on a table and went on to the door and opened it.

Judith looked around North Star and saw an Indian dressed in a fringed buckskin shirt and leggings standing on the porch. Her heart was reminded of Strong Hawk, even more now at the sight of the familiar attire than when she had looked at Giles, who in every handsome feature was Strong Hawk's double.

Then her eyebrows rose, wondering if the Indians frequented the Thomas mansion. But, of course, they would. The house was fully inhabited by a family of Indians, though their way of dress was of the white world. But the color of their skin could never be denied.

"Flying Eagle!" North Star gasped. "What is it? Why have you come?"

"I bring news to you and Silver Fox," Flying Eagle said, his voice shallow, his dark eyes sad.

Giles stepped around Judith to North Star's side. He reached a hand to Flying Eagle and clasped it onto Flying Eagle's shoulder. "What is it?" he asked thickly. "Why do you wear the look of woe? What has happened to bring you to the city of the white man?"

Flying Eagle looked from North Star to Giles, ignoring Judith's presence. "It is Chief Gray Wolf," he said solemnly. "He was not witness to this morning's sunrise. His spirit is now hovering somewhere between his lifeless body and its long voyage to the land of eternal bliss."

"*Gah-ween . . . !*" Giles shouted, his hands dropping, to circle into tight fists at his side. "Not *gee-bah-bah*. He can't be . . ."

"*Ay-uh. Mee-suh-ay-oo,*" Flying Eagle said, humbly lowering his eyes. "*Nee-mah-gah-ah-shig-mah.*"

Tears shone in North Star's eyes. She fell into Giles's arms. "*Un-bay-gee-way-dah,*" she sobbed.

Judith was numb from the news and the sorrowful scene being enacted before her. Her heart ached, remembering with warmth her feelings for Chief Gray Wolf. He had been a kind man, though a stubborn one, his motives always arising from his

229

loyalty to his people. It was hard to imagine that such vitality, such strength, such kindness had been snuffed out as a flickering candle might be.

Her thoughts went quickly to Strong Hawk. Oh, how he must be mourning the death of his father. Strong Hawk had so faithfully fought to make things more serene, so that his father would not be disturbed with stress. She had a need to go to Strong Hawk, to comfort him.

Yet might he be partially blaming her for his father's death?

Giles's eyes seemed to bore through Judith as he looked her way, over North Star's shoulder. *"Gee-mah-gi-ung-ah-shig-wah,"* he grumbled, placing emphasis on the way in which he spoke in Chippewa. It was as though his father's death had reminded him that he was Indian, though he had appeared to mock the Indians by having chosen to dress as a white man.

Judith inched her way toward the door. "I don't know what you just said," she faintly said. "But I am going." She stopped and placed a hand on North Star's shoulder. "I'm sorry, North Star." She challenged Giles's somber stare. "Giles, I'm very sorry to hear of your father's death."

"Ki-kijewadis," he said hoarsely. *"Nin-mamoi-awe."*

Judith stepped away from Giles and North Star, torn by her own feelings. She couldn't help but wonder what this death could mean about her own father's health.

Then guilt splashed through her for thinking such selfish thoughts when it was Strong Hawk who was the one in need of her thoughts . . . her kind thoughts.

Hurrying down the steps to her buggy, Judith made a quick, perhaps rash decision.

"I must go to him," she whispered. "Strong Hawk needs me. Surely he can't hold me to blame."

Boarding her buggy and heading away from the Thomas mansion, she was now wondering how she could explain to her father her reason for being away from him for several more days.

"I'll find a way," she said determinedly. "I must."

Her insides tremored as a thought struck her. "Good Lord . . ." she said aloud. "Strong Hawk is now *chief!*"

Then her face shadowed. "But wait," she murmured. "There is Giles to consider. He is Strong Hawk's twin."

Chapter Sixteen

Rushing into her house, Judith removed her hat, all afluster, now having concocted a story to use for her escape to Strong Hawk's village. Her pulse raced, hoping her father wouldn't recognize the lie when looking her squarely in the eye. But it was a chance she had to take.

Voices bouncing from the drawing room on her left stopped Judith dead in her tracks. Her ears perked up when she recognized the succinct way of speaking that belonged to her brother Rory, and then the low, lazy Texas drawl of her father.

"Rory!" she whispered excitedly. "He's come. Thank God, he did as he promised."

Her cheeks warmed with color and her heart raced, thinking the timing grand! It would not only benefit her father, but herself, as well! Her father and brother needed time alone, to discuss business and personal matters, and Judith wouldn't even be missed.

Tossing her hat onto a chair, Judith almost ran into the drawing room, the rustling of her skirt and rush of her feet causing all attention to be drawn quickly her way.

"Rory!" Judith sighed, falling into his arms as he rose from his chair to welcome her. She inhaled the fragrance of a man's rich cologne on the lapel of his wool jacket. This mingled with a touch of whiskey and cigars on his breath, both of which were being shared with his father.

"A promise made is a promise kept, sis," Rory said, affectionately hugging her.

Stepping back away from him, Judith beamed. "How long can you stay?" she dared to ask, giving her father a half glance. She was happy to see his face splashed with color and a mellowness of sorts in his faded eyes as he smiled up at her from a plush leather chair.

It was evident that, so far, father and son had only exchanged pleasant words. Hopefully, they wouldn't turn bitter while Judith was away. That was her only reason for being hesitant about leaving.

But nothing would keep her away from Strong Hawk. With their differences cast aside, their love for each other was strong. She would forget that he had possibly tricked her to get her with child. She had been foolish even to accuse him of that. Strong Hawk was not a deceitful man.

Yet, for his father?

"I plan to be around for a few days," Rory said, his green eyes shadowed by thick lashes as an uneasy look marred his dark face, which seemed to place more emphasis on his long nose and his square jaw.

"Oh?" Judith said, not wanting to appear too anxious. "A few days? Exactly how long is that?"

"And is that so important?" Rory asked, arching his eyebrow. "Isn't it enough that I'm here?" Then his eyes shifted downward. He reached his hand to Judith's skirt and touched the spots of the deep tea stain. "What happened to you? Your skirt is one hell of a mess."

Judith took in a deep breath, glancing quickly down at her skirt. In her worries about Strong Hawk and how she could succeed in going to him, and in her happiness at finding Rory talking with her father, she had completely forgotten about the accident at the Thomas mansion. Her face turned many shades of red as she recalled her confrontation with Giles and how he had riled her.

But this was no longer any concern of hers. She hadn't told her father that she had gone to the Thomas mansion, but only to a friend's house. This was the reason for concern. How could she get herself out of this dilemma?

Her face suddenly brightened with a smile. Wasn't it just too perfect? This so-called friend would be the same friend whose house she would be visiting for the next several days.

"I've just recently made a new acquaintance," Judith said. "When we were having tea today, I clumsily spilled mine onto my lap."

"A new acquaintance?" Travis asked, pouring himself a cup of coffee, then tipping a whiskey bottle so that he added some whiskey to his hot brew. "I knew that you had said that you were visiting a friend today, but you didn't mention her being someone you only recently met."

He screwed the cap on the whiskey bottle. "Who is

this friend, Pug, and where does she make her residence? Have I ever met her father?"

Judith went to her father and leaned down to hug him, not taking her eyes off the whiskey bottle now standing on the table beside his coffee cup. He still refused to listen and even so boldly showed her that he now drank his alcoholic beverage with his coffee! She had to force herself to be congenial.

"Father," she said, patting his balding head as she stood over him, "which of all those questions do I answer first?"

"Who is she and where does she live?" Travis growled, annoyed, sensing something amiss but not able to put his finger on just what.

Judith swung her skirt around and went to lock her arm through Rory's, hating to leave him now that he had managed to find the time to return home. But Strong Hawk was the most important man in her life now. Even before Strong Hawk, Rory had been second in line. Judith's father had always been first. Strange now, how things had changed.

"Her name is Martha Hubbard," Judith blurted, keeping her eyes focused somewhere just above her father's head so as not to have to make eye contact with him. Lies did not come easily to her, and her father would be the one able to catch her in such a deceit.

"She lives several miles from the city," she quickly added. "And she has invited me to stay a few days with her, to teach her how to shoot a pistol. You see, it's only her and her mother. They feel quite defenseless out there all alone."

She felt a weakness in her knees, wondering how

on earth she could have conjured up such a tale. And was it convincing enough?

She now dared a look at her father, seeing only his eyes peering up at her over the rim of his coffee cup as he sipped leisurely from it.

"You don't mean you are thinking of visiting her while I am here, do you, sis?" Rory asked, looking down at her from his lanky height.

Judith felt imprisoned between these two sets of eyes, as though a wall was closing in on her. She inched herself away from Rory, clearing her throat nervously.

Tilting her chin, she looked from her brother to her father. "Yes, in fact, I did agree to visit her again quite soon," she said dryly. She lowered her lashes. "Even today. I came home to change into my jeans, get my pistol, and return to her house."

Her lashes shot upward. "Don't you see? If I don't teach her how to shoot and then something happened to her, I'd forever feel responsible. And now that you are here, Rory, to be with Father, I can even stay away from home these few days with a clear conscience. I won't have to worry about Father's being alone. It's as though it was all planned."

"Ha!" Rory scoffed, tossing his head. "Sounds planned, all right. And sure as hell makes little sense." He shrugged. "But do what you must, sis. Don't let my being here stand in your way."

Rory's words were filled with hurt. She went and wriggled into his embrace, placing her cheek on his solid chest. "Please try and understand," she murmured. "And please take care of Father."

She looked up at him. "And, Rory, try and do

236

something about his drinking so much. Don't encourage it by drinking with him."

"Just go on your way, sis," Rory said shortly. "You take care of whatever it is pulling you from this house and I'll take care of things here."

"I really must go," Judith said in a soft whisper, swallowing hard. "Some day I'll tell you all about it, Rory. Just don't be hurt and don't wonder about it. We mustn't put doubts in Father's head. He has enough to worry about."

"Whatever you say, sis," Rory whispered back. "I knew there was more to this than a friend needing to be taught how to shoot."

He kissed her cheek, gave her a long, studious gaze, then said, "Whatever you've got up that pretty sleeve of yours, be careful, huh?"

"I can take care of myself," she said.

"I'm sure you can," he chuckled.

"And you try to not lose your temper with Father," Judith urged. "He needs you, Rory. He needs a son this time. Not a daughter."

"I'll believe it when I see it," he growled.

"Open your eyes," she said solemnly. "You'll see plenty."

"What's all the whisperin' about?" Travis asked, pouring more whiskey into his coffee cup. "Do you think I'm too old and senile to be included in your conversations?"

Judith swept away from Rory, her hands clasped nervously together before her. "I was just saying good-bye to Rory," she said. "I would like to prepare to leave now, Father. Is that all right with you?"

He nodded toward the door. "Go on. Get yourself

outta here and show that newcomer a thing or two with your six-shooter, Pug!''

Judith laughed. "I'll try," she said, then turned and hurried from the room, emitting a heavy sigh of relief at finally being free and able to do what her heart was leading her to do.

She laughed to herself when she heard her father bragging about her to Rory. She stopped momentarily, to listen.

"Damnest thing, Rory," Travis said, chuckling. "Pug can hit a bull's-eye almost every time now. She even outshoots me."

Judith heard a pause, then her father's further words. "And how's it with you, Rory? Can you still shoot a gun? Can you even ride a horse? Or do you still insist on riding a sissy buggy everywhere you go?"

Judith's breath caught in her throat and a chill coursed through her veins. It was going to be no different this time between father and son, and she had only fooled herself in thinking it could ever be any other way. Now she felt pulled in two directions. Should she stay home and play referee, or should she hurry on to Strong Hawk? Perhaps Strong Hawk wouldn't even welcome her.

"Oh! Why is life filled with so many uncertainties?" she softly uttered.

She took the steps of the staircase at a fast clip, already feeling the rush of air on her face she would feel when she rode her horse in the direction of the Chippewa village. She had made her decision about what must be done the moment she had heard of Chief Gray Wolf's death, and nothing would

238

dissuade her from going to Strong Hawk, the man who was now her reason for being.

Fatigued, hot, and sweaty, Judith reined her horse beside a meandering stream, to refresh herself before tackling the denseness of the forest again. Knocking her hat aside, uncaring that it fell to the ground, she let her hair tumble loosely around her shoulders, then eased to her knees before the water. Sinking her hands down into its cool depths, she cupped them full of water and splashed it onto her face.

"Ah . . ." she sighed, letting it soak into her pores and trickle down her neck. "That feels so good."

When a few drops sneaked beneath the collar of her shirt and teased the lobes of her breasts, she began releasing the buttons of her shirt.

She slipped the shirt off, then leaned over, capturing her reflection in the mirror of the water and seeing how her breasts hung sensually away from her body. Her insides heated up, remembering how Strong Hawk's hands and tongue on this part of her anatomy could set her heart to racing and her mind to do a crazy reeling.

Frowning, she shook her head to clear her thoughts, then splashed water across her bosom. She shivered with the intense coolness, then grew stiff when she heard the snapping of a twig from somewhere close behind her.

Another sound, this time of crushing leaves, sent panic racing through Judith. She grabbed for her shirt and held it to her bosom just as Strong Hawk's reflection became visible in the water beside hers.

"Strong Hawk . . . ?" Judith softly whispered.

She let her eyes move slowly to him as he stood beside her, sure this time that it was Strong Hawk, and not his twin. Strong Hawk was dressed in only his brief loincloth, without even his headband this day. Zigzags of black had been painted on his high cheekbones and brow. His eyes were not friendly and his lips were set hard in a narrow line. When he spoke, he folded his arms tightly across his chest.

"Once more I find you in the forest so far from your home in Duluth?" he growled. *"Gah-ween-nee-nee-sis-eh-tos-say-non.* Why are you here? When we were last together you even sneaked from my wigwam, like a thief in the night. First you come, then you go. Why is this, Judith?"

His eyes glazed over as he looked at the swells of her breasts that Judith could not so readily hide beneath the folds of her shirt. His loins became tight, his insides awash with desire for her.

But this was not the time. His thoughts should be filled with his father's burial, and then the duties that awaited him as chief.

Judith moved awkwardly to her feet. She still clutched tightly to the shirt, feeling the heat of his eyes on her, arousing in her the same passion as always when she was with him.

Then she felt ashamed, realizing that his thoughts were on anything but her. His father had just died. But, then, why was Strong Hawk here? Why not with his people? He was now chief, wasn't he? Or had Giles arrived at the Indian village and challenged his right to be chief?

"Strong Hawk, I've come to be with you," she said softly. "I know of your father's death. I felt that perhaps you would want me with you. Please, let's put all of our differences behind us for now. Let me help you in any way that I can."

Strong Hawk's eyes darkened. "How could you know of my father's death?" he challenged.

"I was at your mother's Duluth mansion," she murmured. "She gave me permission to go and see her paintings. While I was there, word of your father's passing arrived. I'm so sorry, Strong Hawk."

"Are you truly?" he said in a low grumble.

"What do you mean?" she softly gasped.

"You and your father are in part responsible for my father's death," he harshly accused. "Had you not come and placed an added burden on my father, he might have lived on, even for many moons into the future. He would still be reigning chief, not I."

Judith fitfully shook her head, unable to comprehend his words, though she had feared something like this when she had decided to come to be with him.

"No," she murmured. "You are wrong. Surely you can't mean what you've just said." She bit her lower lip, and tears flooded her eyes at the thought that he could hold her in any way responsible.

Something grabbed at Strong Hawk's insides when he saw the hurt he had caused Judith, the woman who haunted his every waking hour. It was easy to cast blame, wanting, by doing this, to dispel all the guilt he felt for having been inadequate in what he had done for his father. Now that his father

241

was dead, he could think of so many unspoken words and unaccomplished deeds. Though steadfastly loyal to his father, Strong Hawk couldn't help but feel that he should have been even more readily available, to prove his devotion, his love.

And now he was showing the same failings to the woman he loved. In life, one never learned.

With a heart-wrenching sob, Strong Hawk reached for Judith and pulled her into his arms, easing the shirt from her clutches. Now he fully embraced her, feeling the heat, the thrust of her breasts against his bare chest. His fingers twined through her hair, his lips searched and found hers.

Before kissing her, he whispered, "I'm sorry, my Judith. Forgive this Indian whose heart is torn with grief."

Judith tremored, her arms laced about his neck. "Strong Hawk, please . . ." she whispered. "Just kiss me. I've already forgotten what you are even asking forgiveness for."

His lips were soft, his tongue a sensual probe as it wove its way inside her mouth. A knot of desire coiled inside Judith, her knees becoming weak and her heart racing out of control. Her breath caught in her throat as Strong Hawk began creeping his fingers between them, causing goose pimples to rise on her flesh wherever he touched it.

And then a soft moan rose from somewhere inside Judith as she felt his fingers gently circle a breast.

Almost wild with wanting him, she wrapped her leg about one of his, enabling her to fit even more into the curve of his body. When she felt his manhood swell against her through the cotton of her jeans, she let her hand drop, to touch him, to even search inside his loincloth.

She felt him stiffen as her fingers made contact, and her eyes widened in wonder as he eased her hand away and stepped quickly away from her, placing his back to her.

"Gah-ween," Strong Hawk mumbled, shaking his head back and forth, the sun streaming down upon his back, making his skin glow with a copper sheen. "Please put your shirt on, Judith. The temptation is too great, and for now I must keep my mind clear for my duties ahead."

Embarrassed, feeling as though he thought she had been a seductress luring him into a deadly trap, Judith slipped soundlessly into her shirt. Tucking it into the waist of her jeans, she walked over to Strong Hawk and stepped around to face him.

Grief fused with torment was etched onto his handsome face, causing Judith's thoughts of herself to fade away into nothingness. She had come to help Strong Hawk in his time of trouble, and now was proof that he, indeed, did need her, but in a way other than sensual.

"Strong Hawk?" she softly said, reaching her hand to his cheek. "I'm here. Tell me what I can do."

"No one can replace my father," he said hoarsely. "That is the only thing now that could ease the pain in my heart."

"One must learn to accept one's losses," Judith urged quietly.

Strong Hawk's eyes rose to gaze at her. "And you?

If it was your father who had taken his last breath, would you be able to accept his death without grieving?''

"I didn't say that you shouldn't grieve."

"What did you mean, then?"

"That you must look ahead, to the future, and never look back. No one can replace your father. You mustn't even wish for it to happen. He now lives on, in you, Strong Hawk. Surely you know that."

Strong Hawk's eyes softened. A slow smile lifted his lips. "*Ay-uh.* I said before how wise you are. Again you prove this to me," he proudly stated. "And the spirits have guided you to me this day, to share my duties as son and chief with me. Come. Let us go on to my village. I've many things left undone."

"Why are you here, now, in the forest, Strong Hawk?"

"The burial ceremony for Father has been delayed until the arrival of Silver Fox and North Star. And now that they have arrived, I needed time alone with the spirits of the forest before the burial ceremony began. The spirits are wise. They guided my way to you," he said.

Strong Hawk stooped to pick up Judith's hat and handed it to her. "Let us now go. We shall enter my village together," he added.

Pinpricks of apprehension arose on Judith's flesh. She gave Strong Hawk a guarded look as she slapped her hat against her knee to knock the dirt from it. "Your people," she questioned. "Will they look at me as an intruder at such a time as this?"

Strong Hawk's shoulders squared, his jaw tightened. "It is not for anyone to judge me for what I now do," he grumbled. "I am now chief. I am now Chief Strong Hawk."

Judith's heart thrilled with the thought, but then she was reminded of Giles and wondered why it was that he was not the one chosen to be chief. And, also, now that Strong Hawk was, wouldn't it be he who would be faced with the decision about the land— and the trees . . . ?

Chapter Seventeen

A heron crying from across the lake warned that the day was ending. Shadows pointing eastward were lengthening over the forest. The tips of the trees were ablaze as the sunset painted them with their dusky splendor, and everything was mutely quiet in the village of the Chippewa, except for the haunting beat of a lone drum that struck its steady beat from somewhere afar, outside the council house.

Chief Gray Wolf lay peacefully at rest on a platform before his people, dressed in the most official costume that had been his as reigning chief. He wore a white doeskin tunic and leggings beautifully embroidered in beads and porcupine quills laid on in colorful symbolic designs. He was crowned with two large eagle feathers, which distinguished him as chief, and his hair had been meticulously braided and shone with grease.

Chief Gray Wolf's face, moccasins and blanket were painted with brown fungus and vermillion as was the custom of the Chippewa. A round spot of brown had been placed on each cheek, and over it had been painted a horizontal line of vermilion.

The council house resembled a sweat lodge. Steam rose from a pile of hot stones in the center of the lodge upon which had been sprinkled a liquid concocted from boiled bark and evergreen boughs. The miraculous mists were to relieve mental stress, as well as to purify the air.

All around the sides of the lodge were tied-up packages and mysterious bulging containers hanging from the ribs of the wigwam, suspended by basswood twine. Soft fires were lighted in all four firespaces of the lodge, casting shadows on the mournful faces of Chief Gray Wolf's people who sat obediently in clusters, looking humbly up at the quiet figure of their chief.

The family of Chief Gray Wolf sat isolated from the other mass of Indians on a platform behind Chief Gray Wolf's body. Attired in his new chief's attire of highly decorated white doeskin and fancy headdress that hung with many colorful feathers down to the small of his back, Chief Strong Hawk sat proudly tall, his chin high, his jaw set, and his arms locked across his chest.

Judith had hesitantly taken the place at his right side, while his mother sat to his left, then next to her Giles, dressed in a full Indian outfit, and then North Star.

Judith hadn't yet received any explanation as to why Strong Hawk was now chief and not Giles. But the fact that she was sitting at such a prominent place during this important ceremony of the Chippewa had given her cause to forget Giles and everything else, except the occasional looks of wonder from an Indian who might look her way. Judith figured that she had been seated where a wife usually would have been, and she understood the questioning in the Indians' eyes. In a delicate, white doeskin dress, with her hair braided, dressed as Danette was, Judith almost felt as though she had been transformed into an Indian.

Shaman Thunder-In-The-Sky suddenly entered the lodge with a blanket hanging loosely from his thin frame. His gray hair was wild and his face was blackened, and to give him power he wore a shriveled bird's claw about his neck, next to his chest, curved and fragile with age. Tied to the end of the claw was a short strip of buckskin decorated with a row of beads and two small gray feathers. In one hand he carried his buckshot rattle and in the other he clutched onto a medicine bag filled with herbs, roots, feathers, and wooden images. In life such a bag was carried with these charms inside it to protect one who carried it against bullets, whereas in death it was placed with the deceased to protect against evil and to assure that the spirit would not be made to wander aimlessly in the darkness, exposed to the ravages of wolves, bears, and other flesh eaters. The mystical bag could assure that a spirit would be guided west, to a camping ground of eternal bliss.

Thunder-In-The-Sky went and stood over Chief Gray Wolf and began a low drone of chants as he tied the medicine bag about the fallen chief's neck. After this was done, the shaman began to shake his rattle in rhythm with the drum that still thumped outside the council house.

248

Holding the rattle low over Chief Gray Wolf's body, he continued to shake it, its *hush-ah-hush* sound accompanied by vibrato, throaty songs now being sung by other Indians. Their songs lacked a definite system of nostalgia and standard of exactness. Melody and rhythm conveyed a central idea rather than reflecting individual words. Only one or two words occurred in a piece, for the singers derived supernatural power from rhythmic repetition.

Judith watched and listened, feeling strangely detached. She gave Strong Hawk a sideways glance, seeing a dark scowl on his handsome face. Before the ceremony he had spoken briefly of his dislike for the Shaman Thunder-In-The-Sky and had only agreed to let him perform the rites because it had been the request of his father that the shaman be allowed to do so.

Strong Hawk had wanted the full honor of presiding over his father's burial. He had said that he felt cheated, having to sit by and watch, not perform.

Not sure if it was proper at such a time, Judith hesitated before inching her hand over to Strong Hawk and taking his hand in hers now that he no longer had his arms crossing his chest.

Warming inside, Judith felt Strong Hawk's hand circle hers to squeeze it affectionately, though his eyes were riveted coldly straight ahead.

Judith let her gaze move back to the silent, yet still handsome form of Chief Gray Wolf. Tears scalded her eyes, a knot formed in her throat. She wiped a fallen tear from her cheek, feeling the loss, though she had never truly been given the opportunity of knowing him well. And, somehow, she felt the loss of that even more.

The more she looked at the handsome features of Gray Wolf, the more she realized just how much Strong Hawk did look like him. It was as though she was looking at her beloved Strong Hawk, and the thought tore fragments of her heart away.

Unable to bear it any longer, she turned her eyes away, now capturing the full profile of Danette as she looked Danette's way. Danette had a serene look on her beautiful face, yet there were sparkles of tears in the corners of her eyes, and Judith knew the torment of this wife's being forced to share her husband with his people when she surely ached to be alone with him. Judith hoped that the time would never come when she would be witness to Strong Hawk's death. To lose him would be to lose herself. . . .

Danette felt Judith's eyes on her, yet she forced herself to look straight ahead. The emptiness grew broader inside her, her heart an ache so severe it threatened to fully engulf her. She wet her dry lips with her tongue, then suppressed a soft moan when she realized that Gray Wolf's lips would never kiss her again. How could it be that her husband could be taken from her when they still had so much to share?

Her mind wandered back to the day of their first meeting and to how Gray Wolf had grabbed her from her runaway buggy, saving her from an assured death in the cold abyss of Saint Louis Bay, in Duluth.

Blinking her eyes nervously, she let herself recall his first kiss on the bluff overlooking the great blue expanse of Lake Superior. She had stopped him from taking her fully that day, and now she regretted that decision. At least, that would have been one more shared intimate, sensual embrace with him that could not have been taken from them. One more memory. Oh, to have the chance to be in his embrace again, to savor his closeness, his intense love for her.

But it was gone. All gone. Lost to her, *ah-pah-nay. Ay-uh*, forever. . . .

Thunder-In-The-Sky let out a sudden high, cry, outstretched his arms over his head and looked skyward. "Oh, Spirit Wenebojo, aid and protect our fallen chief while his spirit travels on the road of souls to the land of eternal bliss," he chanted. "Help him to avoid the wrong turns in the road. Send the spirits of his ancestors to meet and assist him. Let them join together in a celebration of togetherness!"

The shaman lowered his eyes and arms and once more began to shake his rattle as he began to dance in choppy circles. His head bobbed up and down to the rhythm of the distant drum. He chanted loudly in his high-pitched voice.

"Hai-Ay! Hai! Ay! Ay!" he cried. *"Hai-Ay! Hai! Ay! Ay!"*

Then he came to an abrupt halt, silencing not only his moving feet but also his rattle. He laid his rattle aside, went and stood before the largest of the four fires in the dwelling, coughed hoarsely, then spat in to the fire. There was a sudden awed silence weighted with sorrow as a great hush fell over the many Indians, all eyes watching the magical powers of the shaman.

Once more Thunder-In-The-Sky cleared his throat, spat again into the flames of the fire, then began to speak with extreme rapidity, punctuating his words in unison with the sharp beats from

251

the drum.

He reached his hand over his head and stared blankly into the fire as he spoke. "The trail will be long and dusty, my chief," he said. "But once there you will find the great Dancing Lodge where all people are waiting for you. In the land of eternal bliss there is day and night. During the day there is absolute silence. When night comes, the drums will be beaten and the spirits assemble from all directions and dance during the entire night, dispersing at daylight. My chief . . . my brother . . . you will be happy. You will be rewarded for your generous ways in leading your people. This is our last farewell, Chief Gray Wolf."

Low chants and wails now erupted from the crowd of Indians. The shaman moved ceremoniously from the council house. One by one the Indians rose to their feet and began filing by Chief Gray Wolf to take a last look, and soon only the family was left, to ready Gray Wolf's body for the last of the burial rites.

Judith welcomed Danette at her one side as North Star crept to the other side where Strong Hawk had just been sitting. The three women sat somberly quiet as Strong Hawk and Giles began wrapping Chief Gray Wolf's body with a very heavy birch bark, then tied it with basswood cord.

And when this was done, Judith followed behind Strong Hawk as he and Giles carried Gray Wolf's secured body from the council house, out into the waning hours of the afternoon and on in the direction of the sacred cave, where a grave had been prepared earlier, beside the many other mounds of earth already there.

Judith glanced over at Danette, who walked beside her husband's body, keeping her hand pressed tightly to it. Judith admired Danette for her composure at such a time, but worried that later, when Danette returned to the silence of her house and the emptiness of her bed, her husband's absence would be even more pronounced.

Fires burned in many trenches, pulsating orange against the darkening sky, but it was the sunset that cast the most powerful surge of orange as it lighted the sky from its half disc on the horizon.

The drum's steady beat mingled with the wails of the women and the chants of the men who trailed along behind their chief and his mourning family. When they finally reached the gravesite, which lay in the dark shadows of the sacred cave, Danette released her hold on her husband. She stifled a sob behind her hand as she stepped back to let Gray Wolf's body be lowered into the shallow grave, which faced west, the direction for the spirit's journey. And with weak knees and a quickly constricting throat she watched Strong Hawk place his father's beautifully decorated bark quiver, filled with arrows plumed with gaily colored feathers, into the grave, along with his father's hunting knife, one of his traps, and his rifle.

"You will never be without thoughts of home and family, *gee-dah-dah*, with your personal possessions to carry always with you," Strong Hawk said, almost choking, he had such a need to cry. He felt as though his right arm had been severed, his love for his father had been so fierce.

With trembling fingers, he, along with Giles, began spreading sheets of birch bark and rush mats into Gray Wolf's grave, with stones at the side to hold them down. Then came the dirt, until a swollen mound was all that could be seen, causing an awkward hush to fall over the onlooking Indians.

Strong Hawk turned on his heel, searching for the sticks and wood with which to set fire to light his father's way. After much preparation Strong Hawk struck a match to the kindling material and watched as a great fire took hold and sent its own quivering light into the heavens.

"Go now, my father!" Strong Hawk cried. "Begin your long journey. I have started the fire to light your way. Peace and joy and undying love accompanies you!"

He swallowed hard, turned to face the grave, then spoke even more softly. "*Gee-bah-bah*, I already miss you," he said hoarsely.

Judith placed a hand to her throat and turned her eyes away from Strong Hawk, feeling his pain. But she couldn't go to him. He was, it seemed, on display, for all eyes were upon him, the now reigning chief of the St. Croix band of the Chippewa.

One by one the Indians walked past the grave and silently observed it, then went to Strong Hawk and embraced him, their eyes revealing trust, hope, and exceeding loyalty in their depths. It was apparent that Strong Hawk had been accepted, and even now, so soon, Chief Gray Wolf was being forgotten. The Chippewa lived for the future . . . not the past. A leader had just been born, and they were showing their support and faith in him. . . .

Chapter Eighteen

Finally alone in the privacy of Strong Hawk's wigwam, Judith slipped the soft moccasins from her feet and began unbraiding her hair, all the while watching Strong Hawk pacing the length of his home in his lingering somber mood.

Judith felt that she should leave, now that she had paid her respects and had given Strong Hawk at least a fraction of support, though he appeared not to even know that she was there. He was like an animal, stalking his prey.

Then his eyes were suddenly upon her as he came to an abrupt halt. *"Weh-go-nen-dush-wi-szhis-chee-gay-yen?"* he asked hoarsely, seeing Judith's loosened hair as it now lay in golden waves across her shoulders. "What are you doing? Why have you unbraided your hair?"

Judith now avoided his eyes, knowing what the command of them could do to her. "I must go, now that the ceremony is over," she said softly. "You need time to be alone. You need time to be with your family. I don't want to be in the way. This is a sad time for all concerned.''

Strong Hawk swept his fancy headdress from his head and placed it carefully on a rolled up bundle of blankets in a corner, then went to Judith and clasped his hands on her shoulders. "You mustn't go," he grumbled. "Don't you see? I need you now, as never before. Your presence will help me forget my sorrow. You fill my heart with joy, Judith. Surely you know this."

Judith shook her hair from her shoulders, looked up into his eyes, catapulted into the world of him, only him. Her lips trembled as she spoke. "How can you say that when only moments ago you were pacing the floor, with no awareness, I am sure, that I was here, watching you in your tormented grief?" she softly accused. "Why is it different now?"

"I have hurt you in my moment of shadowed thoughts," he said sadly. "I am sorry, Judith."

Judith gently framed his face between her hands. "No. Don't," she crooned. "It is I who should apologize. I am being selfish, wanting you to think solely of me, in this, your time of grief. I don't know what I was thinking, accusing you so unjustly."

Strong Hawk laughed softly, releasing his hands from her shoulders to hug her to him. "We both are too quick to accuse the other," he said. "We must just be grateful to be together. At this moment in time, life is not so generous to others. My poor *gee-mah-mah*. How lonely my mother must be."

He drew Judith closer, burying his nose into the thickness of her hair. "Let's not waste time," he said huskily. "Love me now. Fill my heart and soul with the sweetness of you."

"Are . . . you . . . sure . . . ?" Judith tested, kissing him softly on his cheek. "It's not too soon after . . . ?"

A rush of feet into the wigwam was cause for Judith and Strong Hawk to break quickly away from one another. Judith's face reddened and her pulse raced when she found herself face-to-face with Giles and his dark, accusing eyes.

Strong Hawk stepped between Judith and Giles. He placed his hands on his hips and glared at Giles. "What is the meaning of this, my brother?" he growled. "You make it a habit to rudely enter one's dwelling, unannounced?"

"My lack of manners is the last thing I have on my mind," Giles growled back. "I've many questions that need answers, Strong Hawk." He gave Strong Hawk a shove, knocking him sideways. "And let's start with why *she* was here to participate in father's burial rites. Why is she here at all?"

Strong Hawk caught himself before falling. His eyes narrowed and his hands circled into two tight fists as he once more stepped between Judith and Giles. "First you force yourself into my dwelling, you manhandle me, now the chief of our people, and then you dare to question me about my woman? My brother, it seems you've learned nothing by living the way of the white man."

Giles leaned into Strong Hawk's face. "Just because you now are proclaimed chief, that doesn't give you any power over me," he hissed. "Remember, my brother, I could challenge you for the title if I chose to do so. We were born only seconds apart. You just happened to be the first."

257

"I was chosen many moons ago to become next chief-in-line," Strong Hawk grumbled. "Even Grandfather felt that I was best suited for this honor. Do you forget to whom he gave his prized yellow feather?"

"Only because I chose to move to live the life of the white man did Grandfather do that. That is also why Father chose you over me to become the next chief-in-line," Giles argued. "Until then, it was questionable."

"Ha! You can fool yourself by thinking that," Strong Hawk said, stepping away from Giles to go and settle to his haunches before the fire in his firespace. "It seems that you've not only become caught up in greed, loving the feel of the American dollar between your thumb and forefinger, but also in ignorance, as well."

Giles went and settled on his haunches opposite the fire from Strong Hawk. It was now brother against brother, their profiles exact in the light of the fire, their Indian attire only different in its coloring. Judith stood in the shadows, watching and listening.

"You can try your best to humiliate me in front of this woman who you claim as yours, but it won't work," Giles said dryly. "For, you see, I've more on my mind than idly tossed banterings. I've come to demand that you agree to allow me to bring my lumberjacks to this rich land filled with trees. It's only fair, Strong Hawk. You owe this to me, since it is you who have gained all the rights and privileges of being a powerful chief over a great people, leaving me virtually nothing. A few seconds earlier, those many moons ago when we were born, and *I* would have been the one now in a position to ridicule *you*."

Judith's thoughts became muddled, finding it hard to grasp Giles's words, let alone understand them. Giles had spoken of lumberjacks. His lumberjacks. He had spoken of land. Of trees. Why . . . ? Who was he, really . . . ? Did she now have to feel that she would not have to bargain with one Indian for her father's rights, but two?

She placed her hand to her brow, slowly shaking her head. Nothing inside her brain would seem to click into place. It seemed to be scrambling even worse, the more she listened to the two brothers still arguing.

"*Anim-osh!*" Strong Hawk shouted. "How can you talk of business and personal hurts at such a time? Our father's spirit hasn't even made its full journey yet to the land of eternal bliss. Father's spirit must be looking down upon you with shame because you are too full of 'self,' instead of Father."

Giles rose quickly to his feet, his eyes flashing with increased anger. "You call me *dog?* The worst thing a Chippewa can call anyone?" he said hoarsely.

"You shame yourself as a dog might by your thoughtlessness at this time," Strong Hawk said, hanging his face in his hands. "You deserve to be called nothing better. Now please leave me, Silver Fox." He lifted his eyes to glare up at Giles. "The name Silver Fox. Have you cast it aside, as well as your manners?"

Giles circled the fire and stood fuming over Strong Hawk. "I didn't come to your dwelling to be insulted," he said dryly. "I came to argue for what is mine. This land is due me, as payment for loss of leadership and for being robbed of the chance of being chief."

Strong Hawk pushed himself up from his haunches and stood eye-to-eye with Giles. "Your argument is still not a valid one," he said icily. "When you chose to go and live in our mother's fancy house in Duluth and wear fancy clothes, even clip your braids to look like a white man, and then take over the management of mother's lumber company, you *then* lost all rights and claim to everything that could have been yours had you not chosen the white man's lifestyle over the Indian's."

"Someone had to run the Thomas Lumber Company," Giles argued. "I did it for Mother."

Strong Hawk tore into a fit of laughter, then sobered. "I'm sure you did it for *gee-mah-mah*," he said scornfully. "Your art of jesting needs improvement, Silver Fox."

Strong Hawk went to take Judith's hand, to lead her out of the dark shadows and draw him next to her as he walked her to stand before the fire beside Giles. "Silver Fox, it is time that you meet my woman," he said thickly. "I'm sure you've had dealings with the McMahon Land and Lumber Company in Duluth, haven't you?"

Giles kneaded his chin contemplatively. "Yes . . ." he murmured. "They happen to be a rival lumber company. Why do you ask?"

Chuckling, Strong Hawk gestured with his free hand in a sweep toward Judith. "My brother, this is Judith McMahon. Her father is the owner of the professed rival of the Thomas Lumber Company. The land and trees of the Chippewa have also caught *their* fancy, it seems."

Judith was dying a slow death inside, now realizing just who Giles was and whose was the company he represented. And it was not amusing for Strong Hawk to be putting her in such a position now, an inanimate object to be discussed as though she had no wits about her to join in the conversation.

"What . . . ?" Giles gasped, taking a step backwards.

"*Ay-uh*," Strong Hawk said, chuckling. He drew Judith even closer. "And she is my woman, Silver Fox."

"You plan to marry her?" Giles asked, his voice strained. "You would give her the trees and the land, to hand over to her father?"

Judith's mouth dropped open. She blanched. Then she looked up into Strong Hawk's eyes and saw the amused twinkle fade away. He had been caught in his own trap of words. She soundlessly listened, to see how he would further handle this situation.

Breaking away from Judith, Strong Hawk went to the entrance flap and lifted it. He nodded his head toward it. "Go," he said. "For a moment there I let myself also become a part of your shame this night. I said too much. This is not the time to be discussing serious issues. Do you forget? We just buried our *gee-bah-bah*. Go on your way, Silver Fox. Take North Star and return to Duluth. And I do not want to hear talk of land and trees again. *Mee-suh-ay-oo. Mah-szhon.*"

Giles stormed from the wigwam, then turned and glared one more time at Strong Hawk. "Being chief has already gone to your head," he growled. "Soon you will forget that you even have a brother."

261

"That would not be so hard to do," Strong Hawk sighed. "You make it easy, Silver Fox."

Dropping the flap closed, Strong Hawk turned to face the questioning in Judith's eyes.

"Why didn't you tell me?" she softly questioned. "The name Thomas. I made no connection whatsoever to your mother's maiden name and the lumber company in Duluth."

"It wasn't important before," he said, going to her to cup her chin in his hand. "As it is of no importance now."

"How can you say that, Strong Hawk?"

"Because nothing has changed with the knowing."

"Much has changed!"

"Not as I see it."

"But your brother also wants the trees."

Strong Hawk placed a forefinger to Judith's lips, sealing them. "As you heard me tell Silver Fox," he said sullenly, "this is not the time to discuss anything. I refuse to speak of trees with you, as I do my brother."

Heat rose into Judith's cheeks as anger flamed inside her. She jerked away from Strong Hawk and hurriedly slipped the Indian dress from over her head. She reached for her jeans but clumsily dropped them as Strong Hawk grabbed her by her wrist and jerked her around and fully into his embrace. His lips scorched hers as he kissed her hard and long, his fingers digging into the flesh of her naked buttocks.

Judith struggled, pushing against his chest, but his lips held her bondage, as did his hands now at the nape of her neck, holding her solidly there. Her struggles waned as his lips began to drug her, so demanding, so filled with need. She wanted to fight her wild and wanton feelings, but his fingers now stroking the supple lines of her body were making that passion that lay smoldering inside her rise quickly to the surface, bursting like claps of thunder as her heart pounded against her ribs.

"I need you so badly tonight," Strong Hawk said gruffly as he inched his lips from hers. "Forget your anger . . . your frustrations. I am even witness to the wildness of your heartbeat. It lies there for me to feel beneath your silken flesh. Let's forget all sadness. Comfort me, my Judith, in the ways you know best."

"Strong Hawk, I'm so confused about so many things," she murmured. "How can I—how can we—at such a time as this?"

"The magic of love was created for such a time," he said huskily, his thumb teasing the taut tip of her breast, loosening a passion-filled moan from somewhere deep inside her.

"Do not deny me this moment," he said huskily. "Do not deny yourself."

"Oh, yes," Judith sighed, closing her eyes in ecstasy as Strong Hawk's lips lowered to her breast and his teeth nibbled at her swollen nipple. His hand traveled downward and began stroking the satiny curve of her inner thigh, purposely only occasionally grazing her throbbing womanhood.

"Now . . ." Judith whispered, urging him downward onto the rush mat flooring. "Strong Hawk, I do love you. I could never love another."

His eyes were glazed, two hot coals, searing her as he looked down at her while he stood on his knees to remove his clothes. He tossed them aside, a piece at a time, then, once splendidly nude, he teasingly ran his hands up and down her smoldering flesh.

Judith writhed, her fingers digging into his shoulders as his lips sent feathery kisses where his hands had just explored.

"Strong Hawk, you are torturing me," Judith said, writhing against his lips pressed into her navel. He stole her breath away when he drove the strength of his manhood suddenly inside her and began his eager thrusts. She coiled her hands around his neck, locked her legs about his hips, and let the euphoria take hold.

Her lips sensually parted as his tongue was there entering her mouth. She was drowning in this river of rapture, her insides splashing warm as his hands kneaded her breasts.

Flushed, Judith closed her eyes, welcoming a soft kiss at the hollow of her throat after Strong Hawk freed her mouth of the burning kiss. She clung, she sighed when she reached the wondrous, momentary release. And when she felt his wilder thrusts and quiverings, she knew that he had also reached that most-desired pinnacle of mind-boggling rapture.

Strong Hawk's warm breath sent shivers along her flesh as he rested his head against her shoulder. His fingers claimed her fully as he let them attempt to raise her once more to a peak of passion. He again began his slow thrust, in time with the play of his fingers on her love mound.

Judith's heart began its furious pounding again. She bit her lower lip, already feeling the rapture once more mounting. With gentleness, she framed his face between her hands and urged his lips to hers.

Weaving her fingers through his hair, she became lost in his meltingly hot kiss. She lifted her hips to meet his each thrust and welcomed their second quiet, joint explosion of love as they shuddered into each other's bodies, the wigwam filled with the sound of Strong Hawk's thick, husky groan.

Once their passion was spent, they lay locked together, breathing hard against the other's shoulder. Then Strong Hawk drew away from Judith, gazing intently down upon her, his dark eyes even more fathomless.

"My love for you swells inside me," he said. He placed a doubled fist to his chest, against his throbbing heart. "My heart is so filled with you."

Judith urged him back down upon her. She hugged him tightly, savoring his closeness, so aware of his muscular chest, arms, and thighs pressing into her. "I could never say in words my true feelings for you," she whispered. "Just hold me, Strong Hawk. Hold me."

He wrapped his arms about her and raised her even closer, shivering delightfully when he felt the crush of her breasts against his chest. "You have eased my sorrows," he murmured. "Thank you, Judith. Thank you for coming to be with me."

"How could I have not?" she said, giving him a soft kiss on his lips. "My heart guided me here. I had worried, though, that I would not be welcome."

"You are always welcome," he said huskily.

"Always?"

"Always."

Judith would not argue that statement with him. She knew that once she returned, later, to discuss business with him now that he was chief, he would not so readily welcome her.

But she would not worry herself at this time, their private moments of pleasure. She let her mood stay light and welcomed his scalding mouth once more giving her a fevered kiss. The night had just begun. . . .

Chapter Nineteen

The music of distant birds and the rays of the morning's sunrise shimmering through the smoke hole in the wigwam's ceiling gently awakened Judith. Stretched out comfortably on the blankets beside a soft glow of coals in the firespace, she fluttered her eyelashes and flexed her arms above her head. A soft snore fluttered through Strong Hawk's lips, his face a mask of contentment as he still hovered somewhere between dreams and his first stirrings of awakening.

Judith watched him sleep, full of remembrance of the lengthening hours of the night and how they had shared one sensual interlude after the other. Even now she didn't feel satiated. If Strong Hawk should even dare to touch her again in the same passionate way now, she surely would melt into the blankets like butter beneath the heated fingers of the sun.

Even a look from Strong Hawk to her could cause a sensual ripple to course through her veins. There was no doubting that what she felt for Strong Hawk was true love. But, oh, the complications that could forever tear them apart! And now that he was chief, the gap would surely become wider, for she still had to place her father's best interest before her feelings for Strong Hawk. Hadn't Strong Hawk's father just been buried, and hadn't he had the same affliction as her father? She could very easily have been attending her father's funeral instead of Chief Gray Wolf's. She even still could—nothing had changed as far as her own father was concerned.

"I must return home and see how he is," she whispered to herself. "What if Rory has already returned to St. Paul and left Father alone with only the servants? And this new development, the fact that Giles owns the rival lumber company and is also going to fight for this land and trees is something I must talk over with father!"

With a heavy heart, already missing Strong Hawk, she knew that it was best to leave without first alerting him. He had spoken aloud as he slept, of her staying with him and becoming his wife.

Her mind had spun with happiness at such a thought. But with things left undone in her life, she had quickly saddened, knowing what her answer would have to be should he ask her. It was best for them both if she didn't have to refuse him anything at this time. They had shared too much for her to deny him anything.

Yes, she would leave now before he awakened, and she only hoped that he would understand and eventually forgive her. This was not the first time she had left him in such a way. His reasons for being angry with her would now be doubled!

With a frown of worry she looked toward his muscled arm, which still pinned her at his side. How could she move it without his knowing it? It was as though he had purposely placed it there. As a protection against her escaping from him a second time? Somehow, had he known?

Barely breathing, watching Strong Hawk's face for signs of stirring, Judith placed her hands to his arm and began inching it away from her. She flinched when he smacked his lips and grumbled something inaudible beneath his breath, then took it upon himself to swing his arm up and away from her as he flopped his body over on his other side, facing away from her.

Judith sighed with relief and stole quietly to her feet. With her muscles tensed, and half-crouching, she went about the wigwam, scooping her clothes up from the floor and into her arms. With a racing pulse she began to slip hurriedly into her jeans and shirt, and then came the hard struggle with her boots. She finally got them on. When she stooped to pick up her hat she felt a strong hand suddenly grasp her leg, causing her to tumble down next to Strong Hawk.

Momentarily stunned from the surprise of his having discovered her in her escape, Judith wet her lips with her tongue and cleared her throat nervously.

"You were planning another silent departure from my village?" Strong Hawk accused, leaning down over her. He placed a hand on either side of her as she lay on her back looking up at him. "Why is this, Judith?"

Seeing the anger in the narrowing of his eyes and

the splash of color on his high cheekbones was evidence enough to Judith just how much her planned escape had upset him. "It's my father," she gulped. "I must return to Duluth and see to his welfare. He is not a well man, just as your father wasn't. I've been already gone for too long. Please understand, Strong Hawk."

"I understand this bond between father and daughter," he grumbled. "It was such a bond that I had with my father. Such bonds make for a devoted loyalty."

"Then you do understand why I must go to my father?"

"Ay-uh," he said. "But why did you see the need to leave me without even a good-bye? Didn't our time together mean anything to you?"

"Yes. It meant the world to me," Judith sighed, reaching her finger to trace the outline of his handsome copper face. "That is why I chose to leave without awakening you. Good-byes are hard between lovers."

"Ay-uh," Strong Hawk said throatily. He curled his arms about Judith and drew her to him, capturing her lips with his. He gently kissed her, then released her, hesitatingly so.

"Go. But soon we must meet again," he said. "I have much to say to you that is not proper to say, since my father's spirit has not yet completed its lonely journey. Soon. Soon we must talk."

Judith rose to her feet. She accepted her hat as Strong Hawk handed it to her, then felt a thickening in her throat from the need to cry when he came to tower over her. Departures were not only hard, they were sad!

Strong Hawk's lashes were heavy over his dark eyes as he stood there studying her features as though to memorize them, then turned his back to her and slipped his loincloth on.

"I will see to it that many braves accompany you on your journey back to Duluth," he said. "I would go, but my people await decisions from me, their new chief. As a new chief is welcomed, so must his ways be, and I have not yet voiced any of these aloud. I am sure the elders of the tribe are anxious to see how my beliefs differ with those of my father."

"I don't need anyone to make this journey with me," Judith scoffed, plopping her hat on her head. "I am quite capable of fending for myself." She began searching the wigwam for her discarded gun and holster.

Strong Hawk went and got her gun and holster from a far corner. He took them to Judith and fastened the gunbelt about her narrow waist. *"Neen swaygideed-wayquay,"* he chuckled, his eyes gleaming.

Judith placed her hand on her pistol. "And what did you just say?" she laughed. "You keep forgetting that I only am familiar with two of your Chippewa words."

"I called you my 'lady unafraid,'" he said. "But I still insist that my braves ride at your side. I will not let anything happen to my *ee-quay*, my *woman*."

Tears burned at the corner of Judith's eyes. She hated to leave Strong Hawk. She suddenly wrapped her arms about him, swallowed whole by the ecstasy of him as he embraced her.

271

"I'll miss you," she softly cried.

"The nights will be long without you," he said huskily.

Judith forced herself away from him and lifted her chin. "I really must go," she said, choking back a sob. "My horse? Will you direct me to it, Strong Hawk?"

They stepped out into the sparkling, dewy mist of morning. The wind through the trees sounded like dreamy whispers as Judith and Strong Hawk exchanged one last lingering look, their eyes soundlessly speaking what their hearts were feeling.

In the downstairs study, a room darkly paneled, with thick oak beams running across the high ceiling, a scattering of fancy leather chairs and a huge oak desk placed before a wall filled with books, Judith waited for her father's outburst to cease. She had just told him about Giles and his untimely intentions.

In a yellow cotton dress, with full gathers at its waist and a broad white collar at the high neck, Judith gave Rory a troubled glance, glad, at least, that he was still there to be witness to why her concerns ran so deep over their father. Now she wished that she hadn't told her father anything about Giles and had instead figured out a way to settle this new problem herself.

But knowing that her father would eventually have found out, she had thought it best that it come from her. At least she would be present just in case his newest tirade brought on another spell.

"Now we have two damn Indians to contend

with," Travis shouted, slamming his doubled fist into the palm of his other hand. His face was flaming red, his eyes wild. In his loose-fitting pressed wool trousers and silk shirt, the fact that he had shed some pounds was clearly evidence. This alone was cause for Judith's alarm. His body seemed to have wasted away so quickly of late.

Travis swung around, rubbing the stubble of a new growth of whiskers on his chin. His eyebrows lifted. "How did you say you came about this news?" he snarled toward Judith.

Judith's insides knotted. She was like a captured moth fluttering in a spider's web, getting more enmeshed by the moment as she now floundered for words. She went to her father's desk and picked up a silver letter opener and ran her forefinger down its sleek flat surface, avoiding her father's eyes.

"My friend Martha," she murmured, never at ease when put in the position of telling a nontruth. "Her uncle works for Giles. He's a lumberjack. He told Martha's mother in my presence."

"Well, then, there's only one thing left to do," Travis roared, flailing his arms into the air. "I must return to the Indian village and talk with Chief Gray Wolf."

A coldness splashed through Judith. She blanched. She had forgotten that her father wouldn't know of Chief Gray Wolf's death. No one knew quite yet, except for the Chippewa. And if she told her father, he would question her until she would have to tell him how she knew. She couldn't let this happen. She couldn't let him discover her true feelings for Strong Hawk and that she had been secretly going to him.

"No. You mustn't," she quickly blurted, placing the letter opener back on the desk, for holding it revealed the trembling of her hands.

Travis stopped his pacing and looked at Judith with a deep questioning in his eyes. "Oh?" he said shallowly, his eyebrows arched. "And may I ask why not?"

Judith went to Rory and gave him a look of pleading. Rory had shown signs of guessing that she had not for the past several nights been where she had said she was going. Rory had seemed to sense that a man was involved in her little game of deceit.

Rory stood stiffly quiet, his mood already dark from the strain of having spent several days with his father. In one breath his father had said that Rory should take more interest in the family business, while, on the other hand, in almost the same breath, he had scornfully poked fun at Rory, saying he would never have the backbone to run such a challenging business, that Rory seemed best suited for his desk job in St. Paul. Rory had been on the verge of leaving just as Judith had returned home.

Feeling alone in her private struggle, since Rory didn't appear to want to further involve himself in this family matter, Judith spun around on her heel and boldly faced her father.

"Why must you travel to the village of the Chippewa?" she said in a rush of words. "Father, it is not in your best interest, healthwise, to do so."

Travis coughed into a cupped hand. He went to his liquor cabinet and poured himself a shot of whiskey. He tipped the glass to his lips and swallowed the liquid in one gulp.

He ambled over to his desk and slammed the empty glass down onto it. Easing down into his plush leather chair behind the desk, he groaned ominously. "Yes, Pug," he sighed. "I'm doubtin' if these weary ol' bones'll ever fit into a saddle again."

He gave Rory a guarded glance, then Judith. "This'd be a good time for your brother here to prove his worth," he grumbled at Judith, nodding his head as he leaned forward in his chair, now looking directly at Rory. "Yep, Rory, let's see if you've got the stuff that's required of you to call yourself a true man. Prove you can even stay in the saddle as long as your sister here can."

Rory's face flamed with anger. He went to the desk and placed the palm of his hands down onto it, leaning down into his father's face. "Ol' man, I'd like to make you eat those words," he growled. "Not only those words, but each and every one you've said these last several days. I come home to check on your welfare and what do I get for a thanks? A steady diet of verbal abuse."

"Then go with Judith and take care of this Indian mess once and for all for me," Travis challenged. "Talk to Chief Gray Wolf before his son makes full claim on the trees and land. Now's the time to show your stuff, Rory. If not now . . . never."

Judith was near panicking. Neither her father nor brother could go to Strong Hawk's village! It was not wise, for many reasons, one of which was the state of mind that Strong Hawk was in.

Yet, how could she stop this challenge now begun between father and son? If she discouraged Rory's going, Rory would be the loser here!

She had no choice but to play along and, hopefully, if she could accompany Rory, find a way to tell him about her and Strong Hawk. Somehow she would even get him to turn back and not go to the Indian village. This was not the time. That had to come later. Between her and Rory, surely they could come up with the right answers to this building family crisis.

Then her eyes lighted up with a thought. She rushed to the desk and stood beside Rory. "Father, I believe I may have a much simpler plan than going to the Indian village," she said, breathless.

"And what might that be?" Travis asked, easing his back against the cushion of the chair. "Or is this a ploy to protect Rory from my challenge?"

Judith gave Rory a sideways glance, smiling nervously up at him, then once more gazed intently down at her father. "No. This is no ploy," she said dryly. "What I propose may be a quicker solution."

"Well, Pug, spit it out," Travis sighed. "I'm feelin' a mite tired. The thought of a bed sounds mighty good to me."

"Why not just meet with Giles?" Judith said cautiously, realizing as she said it that even this was a threat to her. Should Giles open up and tell all about her to her father, her father would surely disown her. But it was a chance she had to take. She had to think of Strong Hawk at this time.

"Giles?" Travis questioned.

"Yes. Surely you can talk things over with him, uh, tell him that you were the first to speak to Chief Gray Wolf about the trees."

"Never!" Travis shouted, slamming his fist on the

desk. He rose shakily to his feet and made his way toward the door, his head half hung.

"Leave as soon as you can," he said from across his shoulder. "This needs taking care of and soon."

Judith rushed to her father's side. "Father, will you be all right?" she asked, taking him by an elbow. "Rory and I will be gone for several days."

Travis's eyes were now mellow as he looked down at Judith. "Pug, there you go again babyin' me," he chuckled. "When are you goin' to meet a man, have kids, and rightfully have someone to baby?"

Judith smiled, only smiled. . . .

Chapter Twenty

It was an unusually hot day for early May. Judith's legs seemed glued to her jeans and her jeans stuck to her saddle. She took her cowboy hat from her head and fanned herself as her horse made its way through the forest. Though they were in the shade of the thickened leaves of the trees, there was a mugginess as the dampness from the undergrowth mingled with the breeze of the day.

Rory drew his horse up next to Judith's, perspiration making his dark face take on a glossy sheen. He unbuttoned his shirt, revealing a thick crop of kinky black hairs on his chest.

Wiping his brow, hatless, he looked incredulously over at Judith. "We've already ridden a full day," he said. "I've been almost afraid to ask before, but just how much farther must we travel before reaching the Indian village?"

"Gettin' blisters on your sitter, big brother?" Judith teased, having noticed how he had begun running his hand between the saddle and his buttocks.

"Don't tell me *you're* going to start in on me," Rory groaned. "Father's constant ribbings almost got the best of me this time, sis."

Judith's playful smile faded. "I didn't mean to imply anything of the kind, Rory," she said, placing her hat back on her head. "Do you forget? I'm the one who goes horseback riding with you. I know you haven't forgotten your skills."

"That's more like it," Rory chuckled. He peered through the dense forest ahead. "Surely there's water somewhere in this cemetery of trees. The horses need watering, and I could stand for a refreshing myself."

"There's a stream just ahead," Judith assured him.

Rory's eyebrows raised as he once more directed his full attention on Judith. "You certainly know your way around," he said, questioning thick in his words. "Why is that? As far as I know, you've only been to the Indian village once, and that was with father. Do you have a perfect memory, or what?"

Judith turned her eyes away from him. She had yet to gain the nerve to tell Rory what she must. She had already waited too long. There were many miles behind them, with even less before them. But each time she had begun to speak, her tongue had become thick and her knees had taken on a bizarre weakness. Though it shouldn't be, it was going to be hard to tell her brother that she was in love with an Indian, and not only with an Indian, but one who was now chief, one who was the enemy of their father.

"Well? How do you know so much about these parts?" Rory persisted.

Judith's head jerked around, startled into answering. "Rory, we've got to talk before going any farther," she blurted. "Let's find that stream, refresh ourselves, and then have a heart-to-heart."

Rory raked his fingers through his hair. "You've taken on a sudden seriousness," he said hoarsely. "Why is that, sis? What haven't you told me?"

Judith slowly shook her head. "I'm afraid you're not going to understand," she murmured. "That's why I've waited so long to tell you."

"Waited so long? For what?"

Judith let the reins go lax in her hand and slumped somewhat over her saddle. Why did life continue to be so difficult!? "We've traveled much farther than we should have," she said, giving Rory a nervous smile.

Rory threw his head back in annoyance. "God!" he exploded. "You continue to talk in circles. How am I expected to make any sense of this conversation? How could we have traveled too far? There's no Indian village even in sight."

"And there won't be," Judith said quietly, glad to see the sparkle of water ahead. Somehow it would be easier telling her fears . . . her dreams . . . her secrets to her brother in a more relaxed atmosphere. Oh, if only he could understand and become her ally in this battle of the heart that kept being sidetracked by her need to protect her father.

Yet she did have hope. Rory was here with her. Only a few weeks ago, Judith wouldn't have thought this would be at all possible. Rory had almost completely severed his ties with the family. Hopefully for a while longer he would forget that he had even desired to do that. Perhaps he would even return, fully, to the fold.

But Judith couldn't fool herself into believing that Rory would turn his life completely around for his father or her.

Rory grabbed for Judith's reins and stopped her horse as his own came to a halt. "Now you explain what you're talking about," he said hoarsely. "Aren't we hot and sweaty on these horses because we're on our way to the Indian village?"

"Well, yes . . ."

"Aren't we going to meet with Chief Gray Wolf?"

Judith swallowed hard and her eyes wavered. "Well, no . . ." she said, shaking her head slowly back and forth.

"No?" Rory gasped. "Why not?"

"Chief Gray Wolf is dead," Judith exhaled, lowering her eyes, waiting for Rory's explosion and his outburst of angry, confused words.

"Dead?" Rory once more gasped, clumsily dropping Judith's reins.

"Rory?" Judith said, reaching to touch his hand. "Let's go on to the stream. It's just up ahead. Let's have that talk."

"Damn it, sis," he said hoarsely. "I think we'd better."

The wind rushed against Strong Hawk's face and bare chest as his black stallion plunged through the forest. He had wrestled with his decision to make this journey to Duluth over and over again in his mind. Until he had this thing settled with Judith, he couldn't lead his people with a clear head. She was always there, in his mind's eye, crowding everything else out, muddying his logic. He now knew that she must be at his side for him to reign successfully as chief. Somehow he would steal her away from her father!

Hot, restless, and in dire need of stretching his legs, Strong Hawk directed his stallion over to the stream that wound its way through the forest in its still and tranquil way. His horse could get a drink, he could get refreshed, then go on his way. It had been wrong even to let Judith leave without having told her of his full intentions toward her. Their destiny was to be together!

Blackbirds perched and fluttered their feathers overhead in the trees as Strong Hawk now dismounted before the diamond-glistening water. Standing in the shade of a towering oak tree, he watched yellow perch swim along the beams of the sun in the water. His horse drank thirstily, swooshing its tail as a bee buzzed annoyingly about its flank.

Chuckling, Strong Hawk lowered to his knees and splashed water onto his face and then his chest, savoring its coolness. Then he cupped his hand and took a drink, swallowing the water eagerly down his parched throat.

Then, feeling refreshed enough, he pushed himself to his feet, stretched lazily, and grabbed the reins of his horse, ready to proceed onward, with lovely visions of Judith dancing around inside his head. If his mother and his grandmother had adjusted to the Indians' way of life, so could Judith. Thus far, she had shown no distaste for anything while visiting his village.

"Except the animals being cooked whole over the

fire," he laughed. "And even I have never taken a liking to such a sight."

Swinging his leg over his horse and into his saddle, Strong Hawk followed the stream. Even it brought memories of Judith to his mind. It was almost a torment not to be with her. They had spent time in this place; he had first observed her in this very stream.

It stirred his loins, recalling the soft splash of the moon on her pink, silken curves. Tonight! Surely he would have her fully again tonight!

Ducking his head beneath low branches of trees and winding his horse around ground tangle and stubble, he determinedly traveled on through the forest. He was aware of the sun lowering in the sky, its rivulets now only warm against his face as they laced through the branches of the trees.

Chipmunks scampered away from the horse's hooves, blue jays squawked overhead, and a deer broke through the brush, its dark eyes fearful and wild.

Patting his stallion's mane, Strong Hawk continued on his way. Then he tensed as he caught a movement ahead, and in one glance realized that it was not made by forest wildlife, but by humans.

With a jerk of his reins, he brought his horse to a sudden halt. Dismounting, he secured his horse, then moved stealthily, creeping from tree to tree, until he was able to see the two full figures beside the stream. His insides grew numb when he found himself looking into the loveliness of Judith's face. But no! It couldn't be! Not again. This was not her father! And now . . . again . . . embracing?

Emitting a low growl, Strong Hawk tore his eyes away. Blinded with rage and a wounded sort of hurt, he turned and began running back toward his horse. His eyes blurred with tears; his heart was tearing into shreds. Judith was not his alone. She had never been. How could he ever have let himself forget the other time he had seen her with the tall, thin white man with the clipped coal-black hair and tanned face? How could she profess to love one man and then embrace another?

Jumping onto his horse, he grabbed his reins and swung the horse around and back in the direction of his village.

"I now know what I must do," he growled. "And it will be done without her!"

Judith eased out of Rory's arms. She looked up at him, still apprehensive. "Do you really understand?" she asked. "I've just opened my heart to you. You now know of my love for Strong Hawk. You said you understand. But do you?"

Rory stooped down beside the water and began tossing pebbles into it. "What is hard to understand is why your first infatuation has to be with an Indian," he scoffed. "I would've never believed it if I'd heard it from someone other than you."

"Infatuation?" Judith gasped.

"Sis, I have to believe that's all this is."

"It is not—I love him."

Rory gave her a half glance. "Why, sis?" he asked. "And why *that* Indian?"

Judith settled down on the ground beside Rory.

She pulled her knees up and hugged them to her. "How does one deny the feeling of one's heart?" she sighed. "The first time I saw Strong Hawk, my heart was lost to him. And each time with him since, my feelings for him strengthen."

"But you know that it can never work out," Rory argued. "Father will never allow it. And do you forget so easily the feelings between Father and the Chippewa?"

"Right now things are complicated," Judith said, stretching her legs out before her, running her hands over the tightness of her jeans. "But they have to work out. I must be with Strong Hawk. Somehow!"

"God!" Rory said, hanging his face into his hands. "An Indian. My sister and an Indian."

Judith's back stiffened. She glared over at Rory. "Not just any Indian," she argued. "He is now a chief."

Rory rose his eyes to hers. "And that's supposed to mean something?" he scoffed. "Are you ready to give up the life you have? The comforts? To live in an Indian wigwam? I can't see you do that, sis. Not for any man, let alone an Indian."

"Other women have done it," Judith said softly, scooting to stare down into the mirroring reflection of the water, remembering the time when Strong Hawk's reflection was suddenly there, beside hers, in his utter handsomeness.

"Yes, so I've heard," Rory said dryly, tossing his head.

Judith's head swung around to face him. "The house in which you now make your residence?" she quickly blurted. "You remember who owned it at one time?"

"Yes. A Rettie Toliver."

"Well, Rory, she is Strong Hawk's distant aunt," she said. "In fact, she lives in Strong Hawk's village, with Strong Hawk's mother. And, as you already know because of having found out about Giles, Strong Hawk's mother is quite white . . . as was his grandmother."

"And knowing that is supposed to make me feel better about your relationship with an Indian?"

"These women lived just as comfortably in houses as we do in Duluth," she continued to argue. "It would be the same for me." Her eyes wavered. "Rory, you said that you understood earlier. You even gave me a big hug for reassurance. Have you changed your mind?"

Rory raked his fingers nervously through his hair. "It's just that everything at once is just a bit too much," he scowled. "And you know that I didn't wish to become involved in any of Father's business problems. When did he even give me the time of day, sis? And now I've you to worry about. When will I be free to return to St. Paul and my law practice?"

"My problems are mine alone," Judith snapped. "I don't need you or anyone to worry about me. All I ask for is your understanding."

"And what about Father? What will we tell him when we return to Duluth after not going to the Indian village as he wanted us to do?"

Judith hung her head. "We'll think of something before we arrive back in Duluth," she murmured. "All I know is that this isn't the time to go and discuss business with Strong Hawk. He's still too troubled over the loss of his father. And he has to settle into the duties of being chief. We'll have to talk to him later. That's the way it must be.''

"Later could be too late," Rory said, rising, stretching. "From what you said about Strong Hawk's brother, Giles, *he* won't waste time moving his crew to the forest beside the Indian village. Once he's there, you might as well forget trying to help Father.''

"I also said that Strong Hawk is dead set against his brother doing that," Judith corrected. She stood up and brushed dried grass and leaves from her jeans. "That gives us an edge. I do believe that, Rory.''

"We'll lose that edge the minute Father hears that we didn't meet with the Indian Chief Gray Wolf.''

"That's it!" Judith suddenly exclaimed.

"That's what?" Rory asked, his eyebrows forked.

"When we return to Duluth we have the perfect answer for Father!''

"Answer to what?''

"As to why we didn't get anything settled with the Chippewa.''

"And that is?''

Judith clutched onto Rory's arm. "Father asked us to go and talk to Chief Gray Wolf, didn't he?''

"Well, yes.''

"Chief Gray Wolf is dead. We will return home with that news.''

"You knew that before we even left Duluth," Rory argued. "You could have told him then.''

"No, I couldn't have," Judith argued back. "There was no way that I could have known, unless I confessed to having been with Strong Hawk. Surely you see that, Rory."

"Yes, I guess so," Rory said. "But now there is another chief, sis. Father will wonder why we didn't have council with him."

"Grieving chiefs do not discuss business, especially with the white man," Judith said. "We will tell father that Chief Strong Hawk was too troubled to discuss trees and land."

Rory kneaded his chin. "Yes, I suppose so."

Judith went to her horse and swung herself up into the saddle. "Come on, Rory," she urged. "Let's head back. Things don't look so bleak after all."

"But when will we get this cleared up for Father?" Rory grumbled, mounting his horse. "I can't stay in Duluth forever. Yet now that I see the trouble Father's company is in, I'd be a heel to turn my back on him."

"In time I have to believe Strong Hawk will listen to reason," Judith said, snapping her horse's reins. "I'm hoping that his feelings for me will help in the persuasion."

The horses unsaddled and secured in the stables, Judith and Rory walked arm-in-arm toward the spreading ranch-style house, allies now, brother and sister together at heart, as never before. They exchanged warm smiles as they rushed up the front steps and onto the wide porch, then gasped in unison when they saw the huge black wreath hanging on the oak front door.

Judith and Rory broke away from each other, startled into speechlessness. Then Rory was the first to break the silence.

"What the . . . ?" he gasped.

"Rory, a black wreath means only one thing!" Judith said in a whisper.

"Father . . . ?" Rory said, his voice fading, as was the color in his face.

"Father!" Judith cried. She broke into a run, rushed on into the house, fearing the discovery of the meaning behind the wreath. Then her stomach lurched and a bitterness rose into her throat as she spied the open casket in the parlor, at the far end of the room.

"Oh, no . . ." she cried, covering her mouth with her hands. Her head began to spin, her knees were quickly weakening. She felt Rory's arms grab her as she sank away into unconsciousness.

Chapter Twenty-One

The funeral was over. The house was as quiet as though it was itself a tomb. Judith and Rory sat in the downstairs study, their eyes glued on a Mr. Armistead, the lawyer sitting at their father's great oak desk.

Dressed in full black, with black lace gathered about the delicate line of her neck, Judith fought against the growing lump in her throat. She couldn't cry at such a time as this. She had to prove just how strong she was. She had caught Rory watching her, as though he was expecting her to fall to pieces at any moment.

Judith's hair was drawn into a severe bun atop her head, and her cheeks were pale. She clasped and unclasped her hands on her lap, wishing the lawyer would get on with it instead of sitting rigidly in her father's chair, poring over the paper that he had just taken from an envelope. The man attired in a black suit, tie, and white shirt with detachable collar looked quite proper, with his short-cropped gray hair parted neatly in the middle and a thin gray mustache to match. His face was narrow, as was the set of his eyes. He was all business—cool and aloof.

Squirming uneasily, Judith acutely missed her father's presence in the room. She ached to hear her father speaking her name, calling her Pug. Never again would she hear or see him. The void was deep, so very, very deep. . . .

Adjusting his spectacles on the wide bridge of his nose, the lawyer lifted his slate-gray eyes to look from Judith to Rory. "What I have here is legal and binding," he said, folding and placing the paper back inside the envelope. "Though it is not my idea of how a will should be written, I complied to the wishes of Travis McMahon and agreed that his will be handled in this way."

Rory cleared his throat and nervously straightened his tie, his navy blue pinstriped woolen suit accentuating his trim figure and the dark coloring of his face and hands. His thick lashes were heavy over his green eyes, his lips were slightly trembling. He had feared hearing the terms of the will for so long. Yes, Judith had been assured the family business, but there was much more to the estate than the lumber and land company.

"Just tell it like it is," he blurted, scooting to the edge of his chair. "No need in delaying any further."

"Yes," Judith said softly, placing her fingertips to her temples, feeling a slow throbbing of a headache beginning. "Let's get this behind us. It doesn't even seem right that we should have to deal with such matters so soon after our father's burial."

Rory reached and took her hand and softly

squeezed it. "Are you all right, sis?" he asked hoarsely. "Do you need a glass of water? What can I do to make this easier for you?"

"Nothing," she murmured. "I'm fine. Just fine."

She eased her hand from his and gave him a weak smile, afraid that it would soon be he needing the comforting, if the will reflected Travis McMahon's true, heartfelt wishes. Her father had told her many times that if things didn't improve between him and Rory, Judith would be the sole heir of the McMahon riches. Though Rory had recently shown devotion to his father, it had probably come much too late.

Yet Judith had often wondered if this reason of her father's had been the true one, or if he had been hiding another reason for his uneasiness over his one and only son. There had been an obvious strain between them for as far back as Judith could remember.

The lawyer leaned over the desk, handing the envelope toward Judith. "This is solely for your eyes to see," he said, giving Rory a cautious glance. "You read it, and then you will have decisions of your own to reach."

With trembling fingers and mouth agape, Judith accepted the envelope, avoiding Rory's eyes, which now were upon her. "Thank you, sir," she said in a near whisper. She stared down at the envelope, anxious and apprehensive. Her fears had been well founded. It seemed that Rory had been neglected by his father, even up to the end.

Judith was filled with dread, and she now wondered if she would ever understand her father and his motives, which seemed so unfair to her where

Rory was concerned.

The lawyer pushed himself away from the desk and out of the chair. He placed a black satchel under his left arm and headed across the room. "I've done all that was required of me here," he said. "I'll see myself out." He stopped and gave Judith a wavering stare. "You know where to reach me after you've reached your decision."

He gave Rory a half glance, then rushed from the room, leaving a strained hush behind him between brother and sister.

Rory left his chair and lumbered over to the liquor cabinet and poured himself a shot of whiskey. "Well, that's that," he said dryly. "So much for the reading of a will."

He gave Judith a somber look. "If you want to call that damn thing a will," he growled, nodding to the envelope that Judith now had clutched to her chest. He emptied the whiskey from the glass in one fast gulp.

Wiping the wetness from his lips with the back of his hand, he once more stared at the envelope. "Well, sis? What are you waiting for? Aren't you going to read it?"

Judith's lashes lowered. "I'm so sorry, Rory," she said in a low sob. Then she looked imploringly up at him. "But you and I are both being premature in our assessments, I am sure, of what is written here."

Rory slammed the glass down and stormed across the room. "On second thought, you can read it alone," he growled.

Judith scrambled to her feet and followed Rory from the room and out into the hallway. "Rory, where are you going?" she asked, watching him take the steps of the staircase two at a time.

"To my room. To pack. Where else?" he said from across his shoulder.

"You can't leave me, Rory. Not now. Please?"

Rory stopped and slowly turned and looked down at her. He saw Judith's vulnerability and cursed his father for the games he played, even in death. "You'll be all right, sis," he softly reassured her.

"Please wait a few days?" Judith begged. She gestured with a sweep of her hand toward the many rooms which lined the hallway. "I'll be so alone here without Father—or you. . . ."

In her heart she knew that she needed Strong Hawk, not her brother, to help ease the burden of sadness from inside her. If she could only talk Rory into staying a while longer, to make sure that he saw that all legal rights were protected for the family business, she could take the time to flee to Strong Hawk, to seek the comfort only *he* knew how to bestow upon her.

Rory loosened his tie and yanked it from his collar. "For you, sis," he said. "But for only a while longer. Things can be left hanging just so long in St. Paul."

"Thank you, Rory. Big brother, I love you."

He gave her a slow smile. "I love you too, sis," he said. "Now, do what you must. Read the contents of that will. I'm sure Father won't rest in his grave until you do."

Judith bit her lower lip, seeing the shadow of hurt in his eyes and hearing the bitterness in his voice. Her heart ached as she watched him go on up the stairs. Then, as though a hot coal was burning her fingers, the envelope lured her eyes downward. Tapping it contemplatingly on the palm of her left hand, she went back into the study. She would feel closer to her father there. She settled down into his great leather chair, which still reeked of cigars, and emitted a heavy, nervous sigh as she slowly removed the paper from the envelope.

Spreading it out between her hands, she saw the familiar handwriting of her father. This caused a soft sob to rise from her throat, and her eyes momentarily to blur with tears. Wiping the tears from her eyes with the palm of her left hand, she began reading the will, which was, in a fact, a letter from her father. She grew more numb by the second.

. . . and, Pug, this is the time for truth, now that you are left without my supervision and I am sure wondering what your next move might be. First, let's clear the air about Rory and why the stipulations of this will demand that he never read this. You see, Pug, Rory is not my son. Yes, I know you are shocked to find this out. Imagine my shock when I found out. I had already had seven years with him as my son. How did I find out? It was during one of your mother's sick spells she was so prone to having. She had a high fever at the time and was talking out of her head. While listening to her and bathing her fevered brow with a dampened cloth, I heard her call out another man's name and then her confession that Rory was this man's son, not mine.

Yes, Pug, your delicate, sweet mother was

also a whore. While I slaved and built our ranch to what it became in Texas, she had men on the side, but one man in particular when she got pregnant with Rory. This man, who will forever remain nameless, was a shiftless drifter, one who worked only a while on the ranch as a servant. He was Mexican. He had the dark skin and hair, but oddly enough, emerald-colored eyes.

Did I just describe Rory? In doing so, I described his father.

This man had drifted on long before I knew the truth, and he's never been heard of since. I was ready to kill your mother as I would have most certainly killed the man, but your mother had a way about her. I loved her still, no matter that she was guilty of weaknesses of the flesh. . . .

Judith shook her head and looked away from the will, long enough to get her breath. All of this was just about too much for her. Her brother was only her half-brother. Her mother had been some sort of tramp.

"Good Lord," she whispered. "Now I understand so many things . . . The reason for Father to almost hate Rory, and the reason Father never remarried after Mother died. His trust! Oh, how had he ever been able to trust anyone again?"

Guilt became an ache in her gut. Even *she* had deceived him. But, sometimes, wasn't deceit necessary?

She lowered her eyes and continued to read. Her

father wrote more of his feelings, and then his attention turned to his estate. She was given full control of everything. The business, the house, the grounds.

But he was giving her the choice of sharing it with Rory. Whatever she wished, it was to be. It was her decision to make. He couldn't handle making that decision himself, not wanting to hurt Rory if it had narrowed down to his having to do it, to make a choice between his daughter and a son . . . who wasn't really a son.

Judith was to make her choice, but only if she understood that Rory was never to read the will nor be told the truth about his real father. A tear splashed down on the written words, smearing the ink. Judith dabbed it dry with her thumb, then read her father's closing words.

> I tried, Pug. I tried to accept Rory as my son. Remember that I had several years with him, to love, to teach him the skills of horses and guns, before I found out that he wasn't mine. Forgive me, Pug, if I failed you in any way. I love you, daughter. You were the only real thing that I ever had in my lifetime."

Judith touched his scrawled signature, all choked up with tears.

"Sis?"

Rory's voice across the room, at the door, drew Judith's head quickly up. She found herself in awe of this brother whom she now knew to have a different father. Strange how the knowing affected her in the way she now looked at him. Did he have his true father's features? Whose traits had he inherited? Whose intelligence had he inherited? His father had only been a drifter.

Now Judith understood more as things came to her in flashes. Her father's always ridiculing Rory over using a buggy instead of a horse and his worrying about Rory's losing his skill at shooting and horseback riding stemmed from the fact that Rory's father surely could do none of those things with skill. Travis had worried that Rory would inherit his true father's ways and realize, somehow, that he wasn't a McMahon after all.

Rory, having changed into comfortable jeans and a cotton shirt left unbuttoned halfway down the front, came into the room. "I was worried about you," he said hoarsely. "I wasn't sure if you should be left alone reading the will, after all."

Judith tore herself from her momentary trance, now seeing Rory as she had always seen him, as her beloved brother, someone she had even worshipped as a child. She dropped the will to the desk and hurried to strongly embrace him. Knowing the truth had changed nothing between them. Their feelings for each other had been instilled in them as children, and at this moment Judith couldn't love Rory more.

Her tears wetting his shirt, Judith clung to Rory. "Rory, hold me," she cried. "Just hold me."

A look of alarm passed across Rory's face. He had not expected the will to cause this reaction in Judith. Remorse, perhaps. But not fear, which seemed to be a component of her strange mood. His gaze fell upon the will, his heart nervously pounding. "What is it, sis?" he finally asked, urging her away from him. "Why are you this distressed?"

She wiped her nose with the back of her hand, sniffling. "It's just everything," she murmured. "Nothing specific."

"Well? Aren't you going to tell me?" Rory asked, still looking toward the will, afraid to go and read it for himself.

"Oh, the will," Judith said, laughing awkwardly. She went cautiously to the desk and folded the will in thirds and placed it back inside the envelope.

"Well? What about it?" Rory asked. "And can't I read it? Now that you already have?"

"There's no need," Judith said softly, clutching tightly to the envelope.

"Why not? What does it say?"

"That everything is to be divided in half between us," Judith said, giving him a soft smile. "Everything, Rory. Even the business. You will help me now? Won't you? I can't do it alone, Rory."

"Damn," Rory said, chuckling. "Half? The ol' man did love me after all, huh?"

"More than you'll ever know," Judith said. "Always remember that, Rory. He did love you."

"Let me see that thing," Rory said, taking two wide steps toward Judith.

"What thing?" Judith asked her eyes innocently wide. She slipped the envelope behind her and held on to it with even more strength.

"The will, you silly," Rory chuckled. "I think you've momentarily forgotten my profession. The lawyer in me won't let me rest until I read the will."

He stepped up to Judith. "Come on, sis," he urged,

playfully reaching behind her. "You're treating that thing like a damn treasure map."

Judith's insides rolled with fear. He meant to read the will, no matter what! Surely her father had known when he composed it that the lawyer in Rory would cause him to demand to read it. Then why had her father inserted the stipulation that the will only remained valid if Rory didn't read it?

A sudden realization grabbed Judith with a start. Her father had written the will in that way *knowing* that Rory would read it, in the end leaving everything to her, after all. Had her father done this subconsciously or deliberately? She would never know.

"Sis, give me that damn thing," Rory growled. "This is no kid game of keep-away."

He grabbed the envelope away from her, full of wonder at the fear in her eyes and how she had suddenly paled, her hands now covering her mouth to suppress a gasp. There was more here than met the eye, and Judith's fear was quickly transferring to him.

"Rory—no!" Judith whispered. "Give it back to me, Rory. Don't read it."

"The hell I won't," he growled. His temples were pounding, his fingers trembling. With determination he slipped the will from the envelope and began unfolding it.

Judith hurried to him and anxiously jerked on his arm. "Rory, you're a lawyer," she cried. "You know the terms of the will. Remember what Mr. Armistead said? I, alone, was to read it. If you do, it will become invalid."

"Knowing that alone is reason for me to have to read it," Rory grumbled. "No one would expect me to react in any other way."

Judith turned on her heel, placing her back to him as he began to read. Even before she had turned her eyes from him his eyes had registered shock and his jaw had tightened.

"My God . . ." Rory softly exclaimed. "Holy Father . . ."

When Judith heard paper crumbling she spun around to face Rory once more. She could see the humiliated rage masking his face and then her gaze fell and saw the wadded-up will crushed into the tight circle of his fingers.

"How could she—" Rory hissed, throwing the will across the room. "All these years . . ."

Judith was frozen to the spot. She had no idea of how Rory could be feeling at this moment, finding out that his life had all been a lie, a mockery.

Tears rolled down Rory's cheeks, his eyes becoming quickly inflamed and bloodshot. Then he rushed to Judith and drew her quickly to him, desperately hugging her to him. "Sis, oh, sis . . ." he sobbed. "Why didn't he tell me? I thought he hated me, because of *me*."

Also crying, Judith caressed his back. "I'm sorry, Rory," she whispered. "Please don't cry. I'm here. I'll always be here for you, big brother."

"At this moment I have found out many truths," Rory said, holding her away from him now, at arm's length. "One is how you truly feel about me." He looked momentarily away from her and cleared his throat, then once more looked down at her. "In the will, father gave you a choice. You were to share or not to share his wealth with me. You chose to share equally. That tells me much, little sister."

A tear wove its way down Judith's cheek. She swallowed hard. "Of all the things you should be feeling now, you place me ahead of the rest?" she murmured.

"Yes," Rory said thickly. "What you did, your choice, makes me realize how right I've been about you all along. You're damn special, sis. Damn special."

Once more he hugged her to him. "And, sis, knowing how much you've always loved me and still do helps to eliminate all my other torn emotions at this time. I will do anything for you, to make things in life right for you. Just you name it."

"Rory, what about you?"

"The will and what it has disclosed to me doesn't change anything in my life. I'll go on as before."

"Half is still yours, Rory, no matter what the will stated. No one will ever know the difference. No one but you and I will know that you read it."

He broke away from her and went and rescued the wadded-up will from the floor. He began unfolding its wrinkles, chuckling. "It's only a piece of paper," he said. "I handle such papers every day in St. Paul." He was trying his damnedest to not show his inner turmoil to Judith. In a sense, he was a bastard. His true father had been a nobody, a drifting nobody. His mother had been a tramp. Yes, the knowledge was cutting his heart into tiny shreds, possibly unrepairable. But Judith would never know. Nothing had changed the fact that they were still brother and sister.

"You *will* accept half, won't you, Rory?" Judith tested. "You know that I don't want full control of this estate." Her eyes lowered. "I've things in life that I wish to do besides see about land and trees."

"I tell you what I'll do," Rory said, once more scanning the spread-out page. "I'll see to things here for you, get things cleared up with Giles, hire you the best damn comptroller, then head back to St. Paul and do what I want in life. I don't want any part of Father's business or estate. I'm doing quite well on my own. And you must correct me when I persist at calling him Father. We now know different, don't we?"

Judith ignored his last statement about who his true father was. Instead, she stubbornly stated, "No matter what you say, half will always be yours. You can't stop me from placing half in the bank, in your name."

"Whatever." Rory shrugged. Then he turned serious eyes toward Judith. "Now what was this thing you needed to do for yourself?"

Judith swept the bottom of her dress around and strolled to a window to look toward the forest. "My needs lie far away, beside the St. Croix River," she murmured. "Strong Hawk. I need him so badly, Rory. I want to go to him. When his father died I was there, to comfort him." She spun around, eyes sad. "I need such comforting myself, Rory."

"Sis, you don't mean that you wish to travel that far, just for comforting. Can't I give you what you need at this time?"

"A brother's love, a brother's arms, can console only a part of me," she said, once more lowering her eyes.

"I see." Rory said, understanding, yet hating the understanding. An Indian? How could it have happened? Yet he knew that he could not dissuade her. Her eyes spoke what she dared not say.

"Today, Rory. I mean to leave today."

"Not alone, sis."

"*Ay-uh*. Alone."

Rory was taken aback by her use of an Indian word. He paled. This day much had been revealed to him. Too much, it seemed. He had already the same as lost his sister, leaving him almost totally alone in the world. He cursed the day his mother had slept with that Mexican. . . .

Chapter Twenty-Two

Judith had pushed her horse hard on the trail, her eyes always alert for danger on all sides of her, not even stopping to sleep for fear of possibly being eaten whole by a bear in the middle of the night. Thus far when traveling alone in the forest, she had been lucky. But after tempting fate so many times, luck would surely eventually elude her.

The horse snorted, jerking its head and continued on its way, bouncing Judith in the saddle. Placing a hand to the small of her back, she groaned. She wasn't sure if she had the strength to go on. Her legs itched against her jeans, which were completely wet from the mixture of perspiration and the heavy dew that had settled on her in the wee hours of morning traveling. She tugged at the gunbelt fastened about her waist. Even it was an annoyance, its weight and dampness digging into her flesh through the cotton of her clothes.

With her forefinger she pushed her hat farther from her brow and peered intently through the denseness of the trees. Where there weren't cedar and pine there were birch, oak, maple, ash, poplar, willow and hickory. The air was heavy with the smell of pine and damp earth, and the rustle of wild life beginning their new day guided by one basic need . . . that of survival. If one's eye could move quickly enough, one might see a reindeer darting from the thicket, a rabbit leaving its burrow, and squirrels and chipmunks competing for acorns that had fallen in the autumn and were now buried beneath the rotting leaves spread across the ground.

But Judith's concern was for her own survival, urging her to watch for only one thing—the shine of the St. Croix River, which would mean that once more she had been led by some unseen force to the man she loved. She had tried to blot from her mind the facts that her father's will had disclosed. Rory? Her half-brother? None of it seemed real, and she would treat it as just that—as something that was only a myth.

Sighing heavily, weary of the saddle and of her thoughts, Judith snapped her horse's reins and sent it into a gallop as they finally reached an open meadow. The sparkle of the river was in the distance, past this weaving scenario of wild daisies and buzzing bees. If Judith looked hard enough, she could see the sacred cave. Sadness was once more a burden, as she remembered Chief Gray Wolf's burial rites.

Then she slowed the horse's approach, now noticing something strange. There were no smoke spirals rising into the sky—there should have been many visible by now. No matter the heat of the day,

Indians had to have fire to prepare their meals.

"Hay-ai!" she yelled to her horse, sending it now into a frenzied gallop.

Her eyes squinted beneath the harsh-pulsating rays of the sun, now close enough to the village to see that there was not only the absence of smoke, but also no *wigwams!*

"No!" Judith cried. "Strong Hawk!"

Feeling faint, she clung to her horse's reins and thrust her knees harder into the horse's sides to hold herself steadily in the saddle.

Confused and fearful, she crossed the river, staring blankly ahead until she reached and passed the sacred cave. Even more stunned, Judith wove her horse in and around a graveyard of sapling poles in the ground that had been left behind by the Indians. She felt as though she was looking at skeletons where wigwams had at one time stood, now stripped of their bulrush mats and deerskin coverings. There wasn't even anything salvageable left in the village. It had been stripped as clean as the sapling poles had been of their coverings.

"It just can't be," Judith choked, numbness engulfing her.

A ray of hope flashed inside her brain. "Danette and Aunt Rettie . . ." she blurted, looking in the direction of the two-story log house. "Surely they didn't leave their house. It is filled with too many valuables. It would be too hard a task to move everything so quickly."

With a pounding heart, Judith rode her horse to the house, dismounted, and went and rapped her knuckles against the front door. Her lungs ached from her anxious breaths and her mouth had gone completely dry.

The ensuing silence gave Judith the answer she did not want to accept. There was no one here, either. Danette and Aunt Rettie had left with the others.

Judith ran her fingers desperately across her face. "Why?" she cried. "Where? Strong Hawk never mentioned leaving. And why wouldn't he tell me? Was he just toying with me all along?"

Daringly Judith turned the doorknob, having the need to explore further, to try and secure answers about this sudden disappearance. How had they left the fresh grave beside the sacred cave so easily? Chief Gray Wolf had only been dead a few days.

Judith entered the house, half afraid. Her footsteps echoed ominously around her on the hardwood floor as she moved stealthily from room to room. It was obvious that they had abandoned the house in haste. But unlike the Indians' belongings, which had been taken down to the smallest item, everything was left intact inside this house. Even a pot of stew had been left half-cooked on the stove.

"I don't understand. . . ." Judith whispered.

The aroma of lily of the valley perfume led her to Rettie's downstairs bedroom. The bed covers were rumpled, another sign of a quick departure. . . .

"The paintings!" Judith said aloud, her eyes widening. "Surely Danette couldn't leave her paintings behind. They mean the world to her. Without Gray Wold and now the paintings, how would she even feel alive? How will I, without Strong Hawk? How could he do this to me? Why to his *people*?"

Taking quick steps, she went upstairs to Danette's

gallery, stunned to see that everything was in place—untouched, it seemed—since Judith had last seen it. She moved from painting to painting, admiring them anew. And then her heart felt pierced by many knives as she saw the handsome portrait of Strong Hawk on the easel. As before, the painting seemed to come to life as she looked at it. Strong Hawk's absence was now even more pronounced, and an aching hollow pit plagued her insides.

With her finger she traced the outline of his features, swallowed whole by memories. Then she jerked her eyes away, curled her hands into fists, and rushed from the room.

Downstairs again, she plopped wearily down in a deep wing chair and began softly weeping. "What am I to do?" she whispered, not once, but many times. She had come this far, to find him *gone*? In her wildest dreams she had never thought Strong Hawk capable of such deceit as he had shown her. He surely had never loved her! How could he have, to leave without even saying good-bye . . . ?

As though someone or something above had pulled strings attached to her, she rose quickly from the chair. "I can't let him get away with this," she fumed. "I'll go in search of him. I will find him. I *will*."

Not having any idea of what to expect on a further journey, and not even quite sure just yet how she would decide which way to travel, she scurried around the kitchen, gathering together ample food-stuffs to feed her for several days. The thought of such an adventure gave her cause for weakened knees, but follow him she must. She had a few words to say to him, if nothing else. That alone would be worth the hardships that she might face.

After she had filled a picnic basket with provisions and secured it by rope on the back of her horse, Judith walked around the village, seeking clues. Her eyes studied the footsteps and the various-sized horses's hooves, discouraged when finding them a massive scramble.

Then something else caught her eye. There were deep markings in the dirt, one adjacent to the other, and these markings were scattered along the ground, facing north. She began following these drag marks until she reached the edge of the village, where they continued into the forest.

"These marks must have been made by a travois," she decided aloud.

She had read about such a device in a novel. The travois was a form of drag. It consisted of two poles, a connecting net or platform lashed between them, and a harness for hitching the device to a horse or dog. They had no wheels. The ends of the shaft dragged on the ground, and when the poles were worn short new ones were put on. It was the most widely used instrument of transportation besides the horse used by Indians.

"And with a sharp eye, it is this that will lead me to you, Strong Hawk," Judith whispered.

Her gaze looked north, realizing that Canada's border was not that far. Wouldn't life be harder for the Indians where temperatures were colder and snows were deeper?

Judith's eyes then widened. She looked slowly around her, at the trees and the land that had just been abandoned. It suddenly came to her that what her father had so struggled to attain was now free to be taken. . . .

Disoriented, having lost the tracks of the travois long behind her, Judith sat slumped over in the saddle. For two days and two nights she had searched for Strong Hawk, and thus far all she had found was a vast wilderness. During her first night asleep, some wild scavenger had raided her food supply, leaving her nothing with which to assure her own survival. Judith had then wrestled with whether she should turn back, or go ahead.

She had concluded that it didn't truly matter. Now it was probably as far in either direction. And thinking this, she chose to continue north. Rarely did she ever stop something that she had started, especially in midstream.

The landscape was changing the farther north she traveled. The forest had been left behind for a while, to be replaced by a large meadow. Grass and sedge blanketed this meadow, while poppies, dandelions, wallflowers, daisies, and asters brightened the area with a patchwork of breathtaking color.

In the far distance, a herd of caribou could be seen migrating north across this vast stretch of land, and overhead, soaring with their wide wingspreads, shocking white against the blue sky, a flock of Canadian Geese were making their way north.

The breeze was cooler, the sun not as intense, but Judith was perspiring. It was the weakness of hunger taking hold. She closed her eyes, yet still experienced a strange spinning inside her head. There seemed now to even be a dull ringing in her ears, and she feared that she just might fall from her horse in an unconscious state at any moment.

Shaking her head to try to clear it of all these strange interferences with her sense of logic, she opened her eyes and focused them on a stretch of trees in the far distance. She must at least manage to get there. Perhaps she could find shelter and something to give her some nourishment. If not, surely she was doomed.

Her head bobbing, Judith clung to her reins and moved in the direction of the vast spread of trees ahead. Once there she slid, trembling, out of her saddle, falling awkwardly to the ground, which was covered by the weed thistle, with its prickly leaves and small pink flowers.

"Ouch!" Judith said, feeling the palm of her hands being pricked by the leaves of the thistle plants. The pain caused her to be less groggy. She held on to her horse as she pulled herself up from the ground, her knees threatening to buckle beneath her once she placed her full weight on her feet.

Clinging to the horse, she wiped a hand across her eyes in an attempt to clear her vision of its fuzziness. The shade of the towering oak trees was welcome to her, as was the sound of water splashing from somewhere close by. She licked her parched lips, then smacked them noisily together. Water. How long had it been since she had had a drink?

Food. Water. Would this nightmare ever end? How foolish she was to have thought she could find Strong Hawk in this vast wilderness that stretched out now

312

into the never-traveled land that divided Minnesota from Canada. She was the same as dead. No one would ever even find her body. . . .

Stifling a sob, Judith guided her horse beneath the umbrella of trees, shivering as a cooler gust of air rushed against her face. There were strange bird calls from above her head, from birds she knew she couldn't even identify should she see them. She had heard about the pine grosbeak, the waxwing and pheasant that could be found in these parts. The latter she could readily identify, and her stomach rolled at the thought of having a pheasant baked and placed on a plate before her feasting eyes. But it was pure torture, letting herself think of such a luxury, and she doubted if she would ever even sit at a dinner table again.

She forced herself onward, having to concentrate fully on each step she took, finding her head swimming if she let her mind wander to anything other than taking one step . . . two . . . and another . . . and another.

Water tumbling from a small waterfall from debris in a stream that had been dammed up by beavers caught Judith's attention. She laughed, sounding crazed or drunk, while stumbling away from her horse to the water's edge.

Her knees gave way just as she reached the water. She hung her head over the embankment and thirstily fed water to herself from her cupped hands. Sobbing, she tossed her hat aside and let her hair cascade from across her shoulders and down into the water.

Combing her fingers through her hair, she drew it

313

back out of the water, then, refreshed, let her eyes absorb her surroundings. It was a peaceful enough setting. Moss covered the ground in a soft green carpet and also climbed the trunks of the trees. Delicate ferns laced the ground, and clusters of wild grapes hung in deep purples from climbing vines.

Crawling, her eyes wide, Judith went to the grapes and plucked a hand full of them, hurriedly eating her fill. Then she fell to the ground, breathing hard, and covered her eyes with the back of her arm as she fought the urge to fall into a restful sleep. She couldn't sleep. Not yet. She had to manage to stay awake long enough to build a fire. Fire was her only protection against being an open prey for wolves and bears.

Once more on her feet, she began gathering dried twigs and placing them close to the stream on a moist bed of moss. With shaking fingers she searched her pockets and found only two remaining matches. She held them before her eyes. These matches were her last means of survival. Without fire, she would have nothing.

Holding her breath, Judith struck the first match and held it to some dried leaves that she had woven between the twigs. She watched the match burning along its wooden stem toward her fingers and away from the leaves, while the leaves showed no signs of catching. And then a sudden blast of air snuffed the fire from the match, making Judith jump, startled.

"Oh, no . . ." she groaned, staring blankly at the crumbling, black, charred tip of the match.

She tossed it aside, tears flooding her eyes. Then she reached for the other, her last match, and struck it as she held it into a thicker layer of leaves.

"Please . . ." she softly prayed.

Her shoulders relaxed and she emitted a soft sigh of relief when fire began spreading through the leaves. When the twigs began crackling and popping began burning, Judith dropped the burnt-out match onto the slowly burning mass before her. She huddled over the fire, mesmerized by the licking pale orange flames.

Then, unable to keep her eyes open any longer, she stretched out beside the fire in a fetal position and found herself now existing only in dreams, dreams that were muddled by flashes of Strong Hawk's handsome face. . . .

Chapter Twenty-Three

The blast of a gunshot drew Judith awake with a start. Afraid to move, she let her gaze drift slowly about her, then gasped when she found the lifeless body of a grizzly bear lying only a few feet from her.

Then her haze traveled past the giant heap of brown fur and she found several Indians staring back at her from horseback. One of them was Strong Hawk.

Rising shakily to her elbow, Judith blinked her eyes, fearing that in her weakened state of mind what she was seeing might be an apparition. "Strong Hawk?" she whispered. "Is that you?"

Her head began to reel and blackness became the only focus in her eyes as she fell into unconsciousness. When she awoke she found herself in a familiar setting and recognized it to be a wigwam, an exact replica of Strong Hawk's in the village beside the St. Croix River. Words spoken nearby warmed her insides, as she overheard that not only had Strong

Hawk found her and rescued her from the bear, he had also taken her to his new village.

Then the warm feeling inside her became replaced by a cold chill. New village! She was reminded of why she had been put in the position of almost being mauled by a bear. Strong Hawk had moved his people away from the St. Croix River and hadn't even thought enough of her to let her know. And in searching for him, she had almost lost her life.

Anger raged through Judith. She tried to rise from the blankets to lash out at Strong Hawk, but the intense weakness in her limbs and the continuing spinning inside her head warned her that, in a sense, she was now Strong Hawk's prisoner!

"Ah-neen-eh-szheh-yi-on-non-gum?" Strong Hawk said, moving into the line of Judith's vision. He settled down on his haunches, a bowl of steaming liquid held in his hands.

"Where am I?" Judith said, only barely able to whisper. "Strong Hawk, why did you move your village?" Her nose picked up the smell of the rich soup in the bowl Strong Hawk held, causing an even greater ache to gnaw at her stomach. Her mouth involuntarily watered, and her stomach emitted a low rumble.

Strong Hawk pushed the bowl toward her. "Eat now. Talk later," he grumbled.

Judith wanted to refuse him, to show him that she didn't need him or his soup, but her hunger took precedence over all other needs. She tried to push herself up into a sitting position, but found that her weakness was even worse than she had previously

317

thought, and she crumbled back down on the blankets, panting, her brow a sparkle of perspiration beads.

"I can't" she said, barely audible.

Strong Hawk's insides did a strange rolling, seeing her so pitifully weak. Had he found her even only a few hours later, would it have been too late? Had he not followed the bear in her direction, would she have starved?

He admired her fiery, adventurous spirit, never ceasing to marvel when discovering her in new situations. But this time? Her boldness may have been a bit too much for her. Had he known that she would try to follow him, would he even have left without first telling her, to save her from this traumatic experience? Or would his constant envisioning of her and the white man embracing cause him to not care, to let her suffer in her misadventures, as he even now was suffering for knowing that she was a deceitful, conniving woman? He rebelled inwardly, still unable to accept her as anything but sweet, gentle, and his.

"Strong Hawk," Judith whispered, coughing. "I feel so strange. So out of touch—as though I may slip into oblivion. . . ."

These words spurred Strong Hawk into action. He placed the bowl of soup on the floor beside him, then sat down and eased Judith up against him.

"You must get some nourishment," he said hoarsely.

"I don't know," Judith said, breathing hard. "I'm too weak."

"I will feed you," Strong Hawk grumbled. "Just you rest yourself against me. Soon your stomach will be warm with soup."

He sank a wooden spoon into the soup, which was wild turkey broth, with many herbs and roots added. With a slight tremble in his fingers he placed the spoon to Judith's lips and watched as she eagerly ate, until not a drop was left in the bowl.

"How do you feel now?" Strong Hawk asked, helping her back down onto the blankets. His gaze traveled over her. Her golden hair tumbled over her soiled shirt in a mass of knots and dried leaves.

Her face, which usually had a shining pink glow to it, was now a gray color with smudges of dirt dotting her cheeks. The man's breeches that she wore were ripped at the knees and cuffs and were filth-laden. Strong Hawk hadn't yet attempted to remove her boots, for fear of disturbing her while she slept peacefully.

Judith smacked her lips noisily, looking up at Strong Hawk, able to focus more clearly now that some of her weakness had gone away. He wore his fringed shirt and leggings, and his hair was pulled into one long braid down his back. His headband displayed the yellow feather that Judith remembered his having worn from the first moment they met. In his fathomless eyes she could see a hidden anger, and she wondered what it was all about.

"The soup was good," she finally managed to say. "I feel as though I may now survive."

Strong Hawk refilled her bowl with soup, then once more moved to his haunches and stared into the flames in the firespace. She began to feed herself. He wanted to question her about the white man, but his pride would not allow it. With her again in his wigwam, Strong Hawk was fast dispelling the memories of her embracing that man. When he was with her, his world was her. It was a weakness that he could not shake—this desire for this woman with the gentle name, Judith.

"How could you be so foolish?" he suddenly grumbled, flashing her an anger-filled look. "You knew the dangers, yet you followed me? Why, Judith?"

She placed the empty bowl aside and managed to get herself propped up on her elbow. She challenged him with her own angry stare. "Why did you give me *cause* to have to follow you in such a way?" she hissed. "Not even a warning that you would be moving your village north."

Her eyes finally wavered. She forced herself to suppress a miserable sob. "And not even a good-bye, Strong Hawk? How am I to understand any of this?"

"I told no one but my people," he growled. "This thing I do, I do it for my people. Do you forget that I am now chief? It is my duty to lead, not to follow."

"But why? It's hard to believe that you left your father's grave behind, with it being so new."

"For years it has been my plan to lead my people north, where the wild rice is more plentiful and where the deer are in abundance. This land where our village is now planted is land yet untouched by man. My people will thrive here. There will be no threats of starvation for many moons to come. My father's spirit has made its long journey. He is no longer a part of the grave beside the spiritual cave. He has made his journey—so have his *people*."

"But knowing this, you still refused to share the forest that lies by the St. Croix River with my father?"

Judith said, almost choking on the words as she remembered how her father had died, with his dream unfulfilled. "Explain this, Strong Hawk," she said icily.

"It was in my father's best interest that I comply with his wishes while he was still chief of our people," Strong Hawk answered. "Now that I am chief, I do what I think is best."

"But your brother asked for the land and trees after your father's burial."

"That was too soon."

"And now . . . ?"

"The land and the trees beside the St. Croix are not any longer my concern," he shrugged.

"As simple as that?" Judith groaned. "If my father could have outlasted your father, he now would have his wishes fulfilled? Ironic isn't it, that both our fathers are dead?"

Strong Hawk was jolted by the news. "Your father? He is dead?" he gasped.

A knot formed in Judith's throat. "Yes. The same as yours. It was, it seemed, his heart."

"I am sorry, Judith."

"No sorrier than I," she choked.

"Life. It is full of many surprises and heartaches," Strong Hawk said, rising to tower over her. "But one learns to accept what life hands one's way and take from each day what one can."

"And you just decided to give me one of the biggest surprises of my life by moving your village north without telling me?" Judith said scornfully.

Strong Hawk chuckled as he gazed down at her. "It seems your strength is returning with speed," he said.

"Your words are heated."

His eyes traveled over her. "Perhaps a bath would cool you down." His lips raised into a half smile. "Would that please you? You do appear to need a cleansing. I even believe I smell something akin to *zee-gag* on your clothes."

Color rose to Judith's cheeks, having forgotten how terrible she must look and smell after her many days of travel without a bath. She had even lost her hairbrush somewhere along the trail, and she could tell by the tangles in her hair that she had probably taken on the appearance of a golden-haired witch.

"*Zee-gag?*" she murmured. "What are you comparing me to, Strong Hawk?"

"Skunk," he shuckled. "Surely a skunk has sprayed its perfume in your direction."

Judith's eyes widened. She emitted a loud gasp and tried to rise to her feet to give Strong Hawk a much needed sock in the ribs from her doubled fist, but still her knees would not hold her up. She crumpled back down onto the blanket, wheezing.

"How . . . dare . . . you . . ." she said throatily. "A skunk? Strong Hawk, I know that I smell unpleasant but, skunk? Good Lord!"

"Soon you will have the fragrance of roses," he said, moving toward the entrance flap.

"Where are you going? What do you have planned for me?"

He gave her no response. Instead he fled from the wigwam, leaving Judith totally alone, still full of wonder and unanswered questions. She felt helpless . . . totally helpless. It would take much time and food to return her strength fully to her. In the

322

meantime, she was at the mercy of Strong Hawk. Before, she would even have wantonly wanted this. But now? He gave her cause to doubt his love for her. She feared his need to place his worries about his people before his love for her. Such devotion from a chief most surely would leave little in return for the woman in his life.

Yet, hadn't Danette appeared to have been kept content by *her* chief husband?

"Danette . . ." Judith said in a questioning whisper. "Is she here also? Did she so willingly leave all that she so dearly loved behind her?"

These questions made Judith determined that she would not continue to lie there like a helpless newborn baby. She would get to her feet, or die trying!

Groaning, feeling the extreme shakiness of her knees as she struggled to them, she felt a sudden sweep of dizziness surge through her head and just as quickly cause her to fall back to the floor. She was still lying there, breathing hard, when Strong Hawk returned, carrying a basin of water and a deerskin cloth.

Judith gave Strong Hawk a weak glance, then once more turned away from him, feeling defeated. When he placed the wooden basin of water beside her, an aroma similar to that of roses floated up into her nostrils, almost tantalizing her.

"I will bathe you now," Strong Hawk said matter-of-factly.

Judith's eyes opened widely. She turned to face him. "You?" she gasped.

"Would you rather I send a couple of squaws in

here, to do it for me?" Strong Hawk chuckled, already wrestling with removing one of her boots.

Again Judith blushed. "No. I would not prefer that," she said sourly. "I wish to bathe myself."

He gave her an arched-eyebrow look. "Oh? You have recovered that quickly?" he said, finally able to yank the boot from her foot. He began struggling with the other boot, amusement bright in his eyes.

"Well, perhaps with a bit more soup?" Judith softly argued.

"We will share a feast later," Strong Hawk said, tossing her second boot aside. "Much is being prepared over the open fire. I will fill your stomach so full of delicacies that you will not be able to move from the blankets."

He began unbuttoning her shirt, his pulse racing as her breasts were slowly revealed to his feasting eyes. He gathered the required will-power into his brain to keep his lips and hands from speaking to her as words never could. His thoughts clouded, wondering if the white man with the clipped hair had tasted the jasmine of her flesh, or if their feelings had not yet taken them beyond embraces. It was true that Strong Hawk hadn't seen them kissing. Yet the embrace was branded into his memory as a leaf is sometimes fossilized into stone!

Judith's breath caught in her throat as his fingers grazed her flesh as he removed her shirt. She felt the heat of his eyes on her breasts, and it gave her a sensual thrill to imagine his lips there, possessing the tautness of her nipple. A sweet ache awakened between her thighs as his fingers now began lowering her jeans down and away from her. And when she was splendidly nude she became encased by tremors, enjoying the sweet pressure of his hands as they wandered slowly, even meditatingly, down the supple lines of her body.

"You are so *mee-kah-wah-diz-ee*," he said huskily. Then he smiled teasingly down at her. "Even smelling like a *zee-gag*, you are beautiful."

Fully understanding the meaning of the Indian word this time, Judith's eyes blazed with fury. She found the strength to rise to a sitting position and began plummeting her fists against his muscled chest. "You are impossible!" she cried. "I may smell badly, but I insist that I do not smell as badly as a skunk."

"Ah, so she comes fully back to life," Strong Hawk laughed. He grabbed her flailing wrists and held them in midair, sobering as he searched her face, reveling in its loveliness and drawn into the blue pool of her eyes. Then he jerked her to him and kissed her hard and long, feeling her surrender in the way her body lost its stiffness and slinked against him, soft and inviting.

Almost crazed with wanting her, Strong Hawk lowered her to the blankets and crept down over her, his clothes a hated barrier between them. He began to weave his fingers through her hair, but was rudely reminded of what was yet to be done when the tangles also became a sort of barrier to his further approach.

Drawing away from her, he gave her a quick sweep with his eyes, then reached for the deerskin cloth that he had dropped into the scented water. "First, let me ready you for our sensual moments together," he said softly.

"Do I taste as badly as you say that I smell?" Judith pouted. "Was my kiss so unbearable, Strong Hawk?"

"*Gah-ween.* No," he grumbled. "I only do this because it will enhance our time together. The water is not only treated with the dried petals of roses but also a special elixir that will make your skin tingle. It will make your senses come fully to life."

"I welcome anything that will give me more life," Judith said, worried. "But I'm not sure if I need that sort of stirring, Strong Hawk. You do understand my total weakness."

"Do you fear me?"

"Fear you?"

"Do you think I'm capable of taking advantage of you because of your weakened state? Are you ready to accuse me of this?"

"I didn't accuse."

"No. You only insinuated."

"I didn't mean to."

"Then just relax and *enjoy,*" he growled. "I would never do this for any other woman. Instead, it would be the woman treating me with such a sensual bath."

Jealousy struck a chord at Judith's heart. "How many have . . . ?" she asked, shivering as Strong Hawk wrung the deerskin cloth out over her abdomen, releasing several drops of cool liquid onto her flesh.

"Have what?" Strong Hawk teased, now rubbing the cloth over Judith. He began at her toes, slowly moving upward.

"How many have bathed you while you just lay there, being controlled by their wily ways?"

"Controlled?" Strong Hawk asked, his eyes narrowing. "Wily ways? Judith, you are talking in circles."

She was finding herself drifting in sensuality. Strong Hawk had found her most sensitive pleasure point and was circling it lightly with the cloth. He had been right to warn her of the tingling sensation that could be caused by this application. It was causing an erotic throbbing between her thighs, and it was almost becoming unbearable as he applied more pressure.

"Please," Judith said, flushed. She pushed his hand away. "I can't stand much more of that. If a bath is required, just continue. Don't tarry there, Strong Hawk. You must know what effect it has on me."

Chuckling, Strong Hawk continued with the bath, intermingling some manipulations of her body with his fingers, until he saw that her eyes were closed with pleasure. *Ay-uh*, she was more alive in this way than she would be if she rose to her feet. He knew the powers of the drugs he had just fed to her flesh. He knew how her nerve endings would be screaming for his lips and his fingers. He and his Judith would make love as never before, and afterwards her mind would not even recall the white man who apparently knew only the skills of a mere embrace.

Quickly disrobing, Strong Hawk carried Judith to his blankets and then lowered himself over her. His lips sent soft butterfly kisses along the soft planes of her face, only minutely grazing her mouth. He fluttered his lips across the slender whiteness of her neck, the hollow of her throat, and then her breast.

His loins ached miserably and his insides were fired by the drug he swallowed with each added touch

327

of his lips to her wet flesh. His heart pounded wildly; his cheeks flamed. He sank his teeth lightly into her nipple and chewed on it until a pleasured moan rose from somewhere deep inside Judith.

Opening her eyes, she gazed down at Strong Hawk, who now looked at her with drugged passion. She laced her fingers about his neck, feeling as though she were on a marvelous soft cloud, soaring. "What have you done to me . . . ?" she giggled. "You always seem to possess so many . . . ways . . . to bring out the ecstasy in me."

"Just being with you is all that I need to be placed in such a state," he whispered huskily.

"But, Strong Hawk, you . . . you left me so easily," she pouted. "How could you have, if you love me so?"

"You shouldn't be worrying about anything now," he scolded. "Your mind should be filled only with desire. Now confess. Desire. Fulfillment. Those are the main things in your mind, are they not?"

Judith sighed headily, closing her eyes. "Need you even ask?" she whispered. She tremored as his lips possessed hers in a hot, demanding kiss. His fingers felt like flames kindling her breasts, and the hardness of his manhood was like a velvet shaft pulsating against her inner thigh as he pressed it there, waiting for the moment of entry.

In her euphoria, Judith raised her leg and wrapped it about Strong Hawk's waist, her hands wildly exploring the wide expanse of his sleekly muscled back, then lower to the smooth expanse of his buttocks. Now creeping them along, she dared to

328

reach around to where his manhood patiently lay, waiting.

Her barely touching him there drew a guttural moan from between Strong Hawk's lips, and he leaned away from her and let her hand fully enwrap his hardness.

Strong Hawk's mind became filled with something like many shooting stars at night as Judith moved her hands over him. His hands went to her love mound and toyed momentarily with her there, but, unable to stand much more of these preliminaries, he placed his hand over hers and together they guided him inside her, filling her.

Judith wrapped her arms about his neck. She lifted her hips to his eager thrusts, tremoring as his hands once more traveled over her, touching her, fondling her. Their kisses were like honey, sweet and clinging, their bodies like hot molten lava, ready to explode.

And once their pinnacles were reached, they shared splendor in marvelous splashes inside their minds and bodies still clinging together, their hearts one.

"Though you could have been killed, I am so glad that you followed me," Strong Hawk said, speaking against the soft curve of her neck. "It has proven much to me."

"Not that I was foolish?" Judith teased.

"No," he said hoarsely. "Much more than that."

"What then?"

Strong Hawk still refused to make mention of the white man. Surely it had been an innocent encounter! Yet could two encounters be innocent? "Of your sincere love for me," he said, drawing away

329

from her, to look down into her eyes, trying to read the truth in them.

"I needed you so much after my father's passing," Judith murmured. "That was my reason for coming to you. When I found you gone, I felt betrayed."

Betrayed! He had thought the same about her! But still, he would never voice this aloud to her!

"And now?" he said, framing her face gently between his hands. "Do you now?"

"I doubt if I shall ever understand why you made your move so suddenly," she said, leaning her face more fully into his hands. "But, no, I no longer feel betrayed. I feel loved. Fully loved."

"And needed?"

"*Ay-uh*," she said in Indian. "And needed."

"Then there is no need for you to return to Duluth."

"*Ay-uh*. There is. I've my father's estate to see to," she said. Then her eyes widened as she remembered something. "Your mother, Strong Hawk. Where is she? Where is your Aunt Rettie? Your mother's house was abandoned, yet her belongings were still there. Why, Strong Hawk? Why?"

"I gave my mother and aunt their choices," Strong Hawk said, slipping away from her to stretch out on his back. He stared up into space, as though pondering. "They both chose to travel with me and my people."

"But Danette's paintings? Her personal items?"

"My braves were going to collect them later and bring them to our new village once a proper house had been built."

"Do you mean that Danette and your elderly aunt

are living in a wigwam, not a house?"

"*Gah-ween*. No," he said gruffly, directing his eyes to her. "They are not. They are now on their way to Duluth. Aunt Rettie grew sick our first full night here. When I found you, I was on my way back to this village after traveling halfway to Duluth with them. My braves now continue this journey with them. In two days my mother and aunt should be sleeping on soft beds in my mother's fancy house. Aunt Rettie will be seen to by a white man's doctor."

"Is she very ill?"

"Her age is against her. But she is a stubborn one. She is not ready to part from this earth just quite yet."

"Will Danette stay in Duluth, do you think?"

"I fear that she may. Without *gee-dah-dah*, she has no reason to stay with the Chippewa. Her heart has longed for the white man's world long enough."

"Do you understand her longings?"

"*Ay-uh*. It would be the same for me had I lived away from my people for so many years. I would hunger to experience my old life again."

"Do you understand why I must return also, Strong Hawk?" Judith dared to ask. She saw no need to explain about Rory. She expected that Rory would return to his own way of life when she got back. In many ways it seemed that Rory was to her as Giles was to Strong Hawk. They were bound by blood ties and heartfelt feelings from their youth, but their ideas of how things must be differed greatly. This caused Judith grief. What was she to do with her father's estate if Rory decided not to assist her? Though he had pledged to help, he had broken such pledges many times before.

"You will return to me in time, won't you, Judith?"

"Do you truly want me?"

"You will make a beautiful *wah-dee-gayd-ee-quay, ay-uh,* a most lovely bride," he said hoarsely. "In doeskin and with your hair brushed and braided, you will charm all who will look upon you as you reign by my side."

"The thought makes such a thrill course through my veins," Judith sighed. "But I fear that it shan't happen. There seems always to be an obstacle in the way of our love. If not the land and trees, surely there will be something else."

"It is meant that we should grow old together," Strong Hawk growled. He rose abruptly from the blankets and slipped his leggings on. "We are already as one. Nothing can break such a bond. *Gah-ween-geh-goo!*"

Without moccasins or shirt he stormed over and jerked the entrance flap aside.

"Strong Hawk, where are you going?" Judith said, gathering a blanket around her as she moved to a sitting position.

"To get us the feast I promised," he said from across his shoulder. Then he turned and gave her a half smile, his eyes agleam. "And to get you a buckskin dress. We must burn your clothes that smell of . . ."

Judith interrupted, nodding her head up and down. "Yes, I know. *Zee-gag.* We must rid ourselves of clothes that smell of skunk." She covered her mouth with her hand, softly giggling.

"Ay-uh," Strong Hawk barely said, marveling

over her remembering so well the way to say skunk in Chippewa.

"Don't be long," Judith then said. "Strong Hawk, I'm ravenous. I believe I could even eat a *zee-gag*."

"*Mee-goo-ga-yay-ay-nayn-da-man*," Strong Hawk chuckled.

"What . . . ?" Judith asked, raising an eyebrow.

"I just said that I think the same way," he explained. "Skunk. I could make a feast of many *zee-gags!*"

"Oh, you!" Judith said, then lay pleasantly down on the blankets, facing the fire, watching the flames dancing, listening to their hypnotic hiss. All of her hungerings were being fed this day. . . .

Chapter Twenty-Four

With a full night of shared contentment behind them Judith moved with renewed strength and vigor alongside Strong Hawk, enjoying being shown his new village. She wore a buckskin dress, soft and clinging, and moccasins cheerfully designed with porcupine quills. She had been delighted when Strong Hawk's deft fingers braided her hair, and it now hung down her back in one long, single plait.

Her need for food and love had been fulfilled with Strong Hawk, and their happy future together seemed assured. But too much unfinished business awaited her in Duluth. Though her father was dead, she still had to make things right for him. His dreams couldn't be cast aside just because he was no longer there to reap the benefit of his many hard years of labor. Somehow Judith had to be sure that her father's company prospered. This *had* to be done, in the memory of her father.

"See how my people work?" Strong Hawk said, gesturing, his loincloth lifting daringly as the breeze met his approach. "Already many wigwams are scattered along the lakeshore."

"It's as though you've always been here," Judith said, amazed at how quickly the village had taken shape. Even now the Indians continued to work. The men were busy placing peeled ironwood saplings up in the ground in elliptical patterns, and then bringing the saplings together in arches while the women bound the frameworks with green basswood fiber. Judith carefully noted that bark strips were being draped over the structure and secured by poles and more weighted basswood cords. A hide was then placed at the doorway to cover it, and bulrush mats were carried into the dwellings to be used as flooring and tables at mealtimes.

Craftsmen were busy creating their dental pictographs to display inside their wigwams by folding thin sheets of birchbark in two and biting designs into them with their canine teeth. Some women were gathering and hauling wood to stoke the open firespaces that heated and lighted the wigwams, dwellings that could comfortably house a family of eight, while other women were busy either washing their dishes and clothes in a lye solution made from hardwood ashes or airing the clothes and bedding.

Through the night Strong Hawk had talked of his people and how they lived, in an effort to make Judith understand his way of life, after having just talked in length about marriage.

He had said that wigwam life was particularly intimate when frosty winter weather drove the household indoors. When not out on the hunt, menfolk passed the daylight hours making and repairing snowshoes, traps and other wooden implements. The youngsters were made to play in the center of the bark lodge so that the adults could supervise their constant comings and goings. The wives wove fishnets and mats, or fashioned birchbark containers, *makuks,* used each spring for collecting maple sap.

But Judith had been promised a grand house, one similar to the one in which Danette and Gray Wolf had made their residence. It would be Strong Hawk's perfect gift to a perfect bride.

"We were lucky to find this lake with its abundance of fish and wild rice," Strong Hawk said, guiding Judith down a slope of thick grass toward the pearl shine of a massive body of water.

"We have named this lake Rice Lake, though it should perhaps have been named Water of Mystical Powers," Strong Hawk chuckled.

"Why Waters of Mystical Powers?" Judith queried.

"Because it is not fed by any larger body of water," Strong Hawk said, helping Judith down the embankment of loose gravel. "The water seems to bubble up from nowhere. But I will not argue that. It is a lake of pure riches for my people."

He helped Judith into a canoe. "I showed you the wild rice in the St. Croix River," he said. "I shall now show you the rice of Rice Lake. You will soon see the difference and why the lake received its name."

Judith settled down on a seat covered by a thick assortment of different skins. Her moccasins pressed into bearskins at her feet and she clasped onto the side of the canoe.

She watched Strong Hawk's muscles cord as he

sank the paddles into the water and with long strokes sent the canoe away from the shore shooting forth through the soft foam of blue water. The wind caressed Judith's face and the sun was a soft glow on her pink cheeks. She savored these things as she marveled at the beautiful setting that soon would be her home. A dense growth of pines and hemlocks bordered the lake, their bright greens reflecting in the clear water like a perfect painting. Fish swam away from the rapidly moving canoe in blue and yellow streaks, and an eagle soared overheard, its wingspread a shadow of gray in the water, beautiful in its exquisite form. In the far distance a mountain range rose splendidly in the sky, trees dark along its ridges and clouds crowning it in billowy whites against the brilliant backdrop of blue sky.

It seemed that Strong Hawk had led his people to paradise. Surely nothing could disturb the peace and tranquility that seemed to pulsate from the very pores of the land, the trees, and the lake.

And then the wild rice came into view in many shallow inlets. The morning sun was a golden treasure on the rim of the world, casting a rich light over the long green plants of rice, their heavy tops bending low, swaying with the lapping of the water. Strong Hawk guided his canoe into the shallows until the canoe was lost in the jungle of greenish-yellow plants that towered above their heads.

"It is the blessing of Wenebojo who has led my people to such riches as this," Strong Hawk said hoarsely, placing his paddles on the floor of the canoe. "Such an abundance of rice never even entered my dreams. It will feed my people for many moons

337

to come."

Strong Hawk bent the heads of the swaying stalks low, hefting the shaggy tops in his hands. Again and again he cradled an armful of the wild rice, studying it closely. He plucked one of the top grain-bearing husks from the stem and turned the rest loose. As a breeze caught at it, the bundle swayed momentarily alone, then joined the sea of green, king of this land that lay not far from Canada's southern border.

As he had done so often in the past, Strong Hawk stripped the protective green husk away, leaving the kernel of rice lying on the palm of his hand. It looked very much like a thin bead, greenish in color, from which protruded a sharp, hairlike tail.

"There will be much to celebrate beneath the *Manomin-Gisis*, the wild rice moon, this year," he said proudly. "My people will give much thanks to Wenebojo. It will be a feast of feasts—a celebration of celebrations."

Strong Hawk let the wind capture the seed from his hand and flutter away into the water. "And we will sit together, reigning as man and wife over the *Manomin* ritual," he said, giving Judith a soft smile. "Tell me that it will be so, Judith."

He placed a doubled fist to his chest, where his heart beat erratically. "My heart suffers so when I am not with you," he said huskily.

"After I get things settled in Duluth," she murmured.

Strong Hawk's pulse raced even more as he saw how the filtered sun's rays through the rice plants cast a sort of mesmerizing glow on Judith's heaving bosom, where the buckskin clung so sensually, and gave an opulent radiance to her gentle features.

"My heart wishes for you now," he said thickly. "But I understand loyalties and duties to fathers, in death as well as in life. Your loyalty to your father is to be admired, and I will not keep you from it."

"I must return to Duluth soon," Judith said, looking toward the beckoning forest. "Even, perhaps, tomorrow."

"Your strength will be fully returned to you for such a travel?"

"I plan to rest this afternoon while you see to your duties."

"*Ay-uh*. There is to be council held in my new council house with all my braves. I will instruct them as to what our future will be here in this new land. Some still seem not to have accepted the move. Some are too young to be so set in their ways."

"The world is now full of changes," Judith sighed, watching as Strong Hawk lifted the paddles and began sending the canoe out of the sea of wild rice plants. "It is nearing the turn of the century. So much waits to be explored and discovered in this new century. Your people *should* be prepared for the changes. The government is even a threat to you, Strong Hawk. So many Indians are now on reservations."

Strong Hawk's muscles flexed as he wove the paddles gracefully in and out of the water. "I do not fear the white man in Washington," he growled. "My enemy has always been and still remains the Nadoeus-Sioux."

"Why do you mention them now, Strong Hawk?" Judith asked, wondering why he was guiding his canoe to land that was now far from the village, a small island in the middle of the lake. Evergreens towered above the small body of land, almost black they were so dense in growth.

"I do not want to frighten you, but this move of my people has brought us closer to the Sioux," he said. He raised his hand and pointed toward the mountains. "My scout discovered a camp farther north from where we now make our village."

Judith's insides splashed cold. "Sioux?" she barely said. "Is there any danger?"

Strong Hawk beached the canoe onto a sandy slope. "The Sioux realize that the Chippewa, the Ojibway, are the largest and most important tribe of the Algonquin family who live here in the northern United States," he grumbled. "We were the *a-nicina-be*, the original, the first men in these parts, and they forever have been jealous. They are never a true threat."

"But perhaps they will challenge your right to be here on this lake, since you only recently arrived?" Judith cautiously said.

Strong Hawk shrugged. "They will test us," he said matter-of-factly. "That is all."

"How?" Judith gulped.

"That is not for you to worry about," Strong Hawk said, placing his paddles to the floor of the canoe. "They have failed all tests in the past. So shall they now."

"But I thought you had said earlier that this land was land never before touched by man. Any man."

"That was so, until we arrived, and the Sioux, who most surely have also fled their village farther south, or perhaps west. When I speak of our people being the first in these parts, I mainly speak of the land from which we just traveled. The Chippewa *are* the land, the mountains, the lake, and the rivers. The Sioux are out of place here. We will meet their challenge soon, and they will have to retreat. You will see. Please do not worry so, Judith. You seem to forget the strength of the man who loves you and who will always protect you."

Stepping out of the canoe into knee deep-water, Strong Hawk went to Judith and placed his hands to her waist, easing her to her feet. "I've more on my mind than the Nadoues-Sioux," he said huskily. "I've a need to be with you, Judith, away from interferences of my people and yours. Let us share this time alone before I return to my duties as chief."

"Your duty to me comes first?" Judith teased, tremoring as he lifted her fully into his arms and began carrying her to shore.

"*Ay-uh*," Strong Hawk said, stepping onto solid land, and on into the outer edges of the forest.

A cool breeze caught at the skirt of Judith's dress as Strong Hawk placed her to the ground. She shivered and looked slowly about her, feeling as though eyes were on her from somewhere in the blackness of the wide stretch of evergreen trees.

"I don't feel alone here," she whispered, working herself into Strong Hawk's embrace.

Strong Hawk chuckled. He placed his finger to Judith's chin and tilted her head so their eyes could meet. "No. In a sense, we are not alone," he said. "The forest is a great storehouse of power, life, and strength. Even on this isolated island the woods are a dim, sacred place full of shadows and unseen spirits. But they are nothing to fear."

"Whatever you say," Judith said, laughing softly.

A heron suddenly came flapping with its big wings from the woods toward Judith and Strong Hawk. Strong Hawk grabbed Judith and they fell together onto a bed of moss that lay in the shadows of the trees. Judith tensed when she saw the troubled expression masking Strong Hawk's handsome face.

"Strong Hawk, what is it?" she dared to ask, rising to a sitting position.

"Sometimes when one comes across an unexpected bird or animal in the woods it has a special meaning," he grumbled, looking about him, frowning.

"Special meaning?"

"An omen. Perhaps an omen."

Judith was glad when he swept her suddenly into his arms and urged her onto her back on the soft bed of moss as he leaned down over her.

"A good or bad omen?" she asked, looking innocently up into his dark pools of eyes.

"It surely is good," he said huskily, tracing the outline of her breast through the buckskin with his finger, then fulling cupping it. "The future only holds good things for my people and you, who will soon become one of us."

His lips lowered to hers, his tongue sensually probing inside the warm sweetness of her mouth.

Judith ran her fingers over the sleekness of his back and lower to where his loincloth reached around his waist. She slipped her hands beneath this and gently caressed the smooth hardness of his powerful buttocks, letting herself envision that which lay only a few butterfly touches away. She felt so brazen, letting such thoughts so often occupy her mind. But never with another man before Strong Hawk—and he was soon to be her husband. It was right, this hunger for the man whose future was also hers.

"We will share many births of spring, maturities of summer, and icy hands of winter," Strong Hawk said, easing up on his haunches over her. His hands were lifting her dress up, past her thighs, her hips, her waist, her breasts and then over her head. He tossed the dress aside and bent down and swept his tongue around the stiff peak of her nipple, while his hands explored her most sensitive pleasure points.

Judith quickly became breathless. She closed her eyes and arched her hips up from the mossy ground, inviting his fingers lower, where her heart seemed to be beating. When he finally touched her there her body sent off a rapturous tremor, and she worked herself in movement with the deftness of his fingers.

Sighing, now seeing Strong Hawk through a drunken sort of haze, Judith reached her hands to his loincloth and began slowly pulling it down. A drugged passion rippled through her when she saw his readiness. She was glad when he finished freeing himself of his skimpy garment and lowered his throbbing hardness deeply, wholly inside her.

A soft moan rose from inside Judith as Strong Hawk began his thrusts, slow yet determined. She had never felt so filled with him. Each stroke inside her was greater than the last. She sought his lips, guiding his mouth down to experience a burning, searing kiss.

Their bodies worked, their hands worshipped, their kiss was sweet, then frenzied, then sweet. Judith felt as though she were on a seesaw, first up, then down.

She clung about his neck with her arms, about his waist with her legs. She couldn't seem to get close enough, her passion was so strong. She wanted to be a part of him, never to have to let go again.

A swimming sensation was engulfing her; her heart beat in unison with his rapid strokes. "Strong Hawk, make it last forever," she gasped as he freed her lips. "Don't ever stop!"

"Oneegishin. Oneegishin," Strong Hawk said throatily. "If it were only possible that I grant you such a wish." He buried his lips into the delicate line of her throat. *"Ay-uh.* What we share is good."

"Love me. Just love me," Judith sighed, still floating, clinging.

"Ah-pah-nay," Strong Hawk said huskily. "Forever."

He felt the fire burning higher in his loins. "Now," he softly cried. "My Judith, now . . ."

He closed his eyes in rapture as she opened herself more fully to him, and he felt her tremors of ecstasy as he released his warm liquid into her womb. *"Gee-zah-gi-ee-nah?"* he murmured as his quiverings ceased. He burrowed his nose into the hollow of her throat, descending from his plane of wondrous pleasure.

Judith's breathing was shallow, her nerve endings raw from the intensity with which she had enjoyed her moment of heaven with him. She smiled to herself when she felt the fierceness of his heartbeat as it pounded against her breast, which was pressed firmly to him. Together, it seemed, they could conquer the world, so much energy was passed between them!

"My love, you must take time with me soon to again be my teacher," she whispered, tracing his handsome profile with her finger.

He chuckled. "Oh? You need to know more ways to make love?" he teased.

"Well, that too," Judith giggled. "But what I was referring to was the need to know your language. The words 'yes' and 'forever' are not sufficient to carry on a conversation in Chippewa, do you think?"

"It will be a pleasure, teaching you," Strong Hawk said, drawing away from her. He reached for his loincloth and slipped it on, then helped her into her dress. "First I will teach you a word, then we will make love, then I will teach you another word, then we will make more love."

"Strong Hawk, it seems you've truly only one thing on your mind," Judith laughed, straightening the lines of her dress along her shapely figure.

"When I'm with you. *Ay-uh!*"

"And if that is true, won't I be a threat to your, shall I say sanity, if I am at your side while you reign as chief?"

He drew her roughly into his arms and placed his hand between her braid and the nape of her neck, holding her head in place. "Without you there, I would be mindless for another reason," he said, his eyes dark coals of renewed passion. "I would be full of worry as to where you were, what you were doing, and with whom."

He urged her lips closer to his. "I would be *gah-way* of anyone who even looks your way," he said in a husky whisper.

"*Gah-way . . . ?*" Judith questioned, although she thought she had heard the word before.

"Jealous. My mind, my heart, would be filled with jealousy," he said, then crushed his lips scaldingly down upon hers.

Judith pressed herself into the hard frame of his body, her senses again reeling. Love, ah, how she was consumed by its fiery embers. . . .

Chapter Twenty-Five

Unable to rest, Judith walked beside Rice Lake, fretting over the long trip back to Duluth. She would never forget the trauma of having been lost in the forest, making the distance seem even greater. And it wasn't only this one trip that she dreaded. It was the many in the future that would be required for her to travel between Strong Hawk's village and Duluth, once she became his wife. Unless things took a quick turn for the better, she would have to return to Duluth often to see to her business and estate. Something deep inside her forbade her to think of selling the land and the lumber company. Perhaps it was her father's soul hovering close by, reminding her of how hard he had worked for it all.

Though the earth was still warm beneath her bare feet from the afternoon's sun, the breeze had taken on a nippiness. The skirt of Judith's buckskin dress whipped about her bare legs and her hair lifted from her shoulders. Stopping to stare across the tranquil body of water, she looked toward the far mountain range, seeing how the sunset appeared to be tipping it in sheer, red lace. Purple and orange streaks decorated the sky, blending in with the velvet sheen of darkness as it slowly ebbed its way across the horizon.

Trembling with the chill, Judith looked over her shoulder, capturing the last sight of the village before the cloak of night settled over it. Fires from outdoor firespaces glowed orange, and Indian women turned animals slowly on spits. Children ran, playing in and around the wigwams, dogs barked and horses neighed. Slow spirals of smoke rose lazily from the smoke holes, emitting a pleasant fragrance.

Judith sighed. Everything was so serene, a sort of paradise. But she felt too alone, having walked much farther than she had originally planned. Though Strong Hawk was still conferring with his braves, she thought he continued to linger this long away from her only because he thought she was resting and didn't want to disturb her.

"But he'll return to the wigwam soon, for the evening meal," she whispered. "It's best he finds me when he arrives there. My absence could give him a fright."

Smiling at the thought of his arms later possessing her, when all fires in the village were dimmed to dying embers, she began to walk toward the village. Now that was the true paradise. To be in his arms, to be wrapped up in the rapture of being with him sent a sensuous thrill through her. They had finally settled all their differences and now nothing lay as a threat between them. The strength of their love for each other was like a shield that would forever protect them from all future misunderstandings and unhappiness.

Hugging herself in an effort to ward off the penetrating chill from the fog that now began creeping in from the lake, Judith hurried her steps. The dew-laden grass had become cold and slippery beneath her bare feet, and the fires in the village were now only a shimmering haze.

The fog had seemed to materialize suddenly from nowhere, forming a blanket of white that engulfed her. Judith squinted her eyes and felt her way through its denseness, tremoring in fear as a screech owl emitted its scream from overhead.

The snapping of a twig from somewhere close by drew a shaky gasp from between Judith's lips. Stopping abruptly, she turned and looked cautiously around her. The low limbs of the trees looked like ghostly skeletons dancing as the wind whipped them around in the murky, swirling, foggy setting.

Peering intently, slowly scanning the space around her, Judith felt a cold numbness settling over her. But when she didn't see or hear anything with a human shape, she laughed nervously to herself.

"It's only my imagination," she whispered. She placed the back of her hand against her brow and softly kneaded her clammy, cold flesh, her fingers circled into a tight fist. "I'd best hurry on. My nerves are about to get the best of me. And why? What have I to fear so close to Strong Hawk's village?"

In her mind's eye she saw a flash of a Sioux Indian hovering close by with a knife poised, ready to swoop it down on her. The thought made her hair rise at the nape of her neck and her footsteps quicken. Oh, what a time to remember Strong Hawk's mention of the Sioux! They surely wouldn't 'test' Strong Hawk's people. Surely they knew who was the strongest.

She watched the fires grow closer, not quickly enough as far as she was concerned. The security of Strong Hawk's wigwam seemed an eternity away, yet again she felt foolish to be afraid. But she did know that she would feel much more sure about things if she had only brought her pistol with her on this isolated walk.

The sound of movement at her right side, where the forest stretched toward the Canadian border, made Judith stop with a start once more. With a thumping heart she slowly turned around. "Strong Hawk, it's you, isn't it?" she said, laughing nervously. "Darling, tell me it's you. Did you return to the wigwam and find me gone? Did you come in search of me?"

When there was no response, Judith's fears mounted. She knew that she was no longer alone and that she was not in the presence of a friend, or this friend would speak up to reassure her.

"God . . ." she whispered, fighting against the weakness in her knees. She must get to safety. She must!

Pulling strength from her realization that the village was no longer all that far away, she began to run through the shreds of fog in the direction of the fire's glow, the sounds of the dogs, the horses, the voices. . . .

Then she was stopped by a strong, solid arm grabbing her around the waist and a hand clasping her hard about her mouth. Fear made her heart plunge, her throat constrict icily. When she felt herself being dragged into the woods she began fighting back. She clawed desperately at the arm still holding her back pinioned against a body of steel. She kicked at the unseen assailant, only sending sharp pains through her bare heels, which had made contact with the bony, bare leg behind her.

On his fingers she smelled a strong aroma of tobacco, and she could hear his heaving breaths as he continued to hold her against her struggles, now almost carrying her as he made his way toward a sleek-maned brown steed. When they reached his horse her assailant released her from around her waist, only to spin her around to face him.

Though the forest was dark and the fog heavy, her assailant was close enough for Judith to see his face and his pure Indian profile. Was he Chippewa or Sioux? There was no way to distinguish between the two. This Indian wore only a loincloth, headband, and eagle feather. His dark eyes bore holes through her as she met his steady stare, but the darkness of night kept her from studying his eyes as she would like, to see if he were the threat that she feared he was.

"Who are you?" she hissed, forcing strength into her voice, though she felt anything but brave. She leaned up, closer to his face. "What do you mean by stealing me away like this? What do you want with me?"

"My name is Red Bear," the Indian brave said, in perfect English. "And you? You are not of Chief Strong Hawk's people, yet you are here. You are Strong Hawk's woman? Am I right, beautiful white woman with hair of spun gold?"

Judith took a step backward, now uneasy under his closer scrutiny. As the fog lifted, she could see how he was openly admiring her, his gaze moving approvingly over her. When his fingers reached to touch her hair, she flinched and slapped his hand away.

"It's none of your business who I am or why I am here," she murmured, looking past him, over his shoulder. If she took off running, could she . . . ?

No. It was useless. Even her screams would not reach the village. They would be swallowed by the denseness of the forest.

Red Bear lifted his shoulder in a shrug. "It matters not," he said dryly. "Should you be Strong Hawk's woman, that would enhance this test between the Sioux and Chippewa. But should you not be, that matters not. What I needed was a prisoner from Strong Hawk's village, and in you I have one."

"Test? Sioux?" Judith whispered, her eyes wide, her fears of who this was confirmed. And what Strong Hawk had predicted had become a reality. Her carelessness, being so far from the village, had made her a prime target for the Sioux, to be used as a pawn between the two warring Indian tribes, though Strong Hawk would be the last to wish for such a thing.

Red Bear grabbed Judith by the wrist and forced her to his horse. "You will now travel with me to my camp," he growled. "Then we shall see how long it takes for Strong Hawk to come and fight for you."

Judith blanched. She could envision an Indian war—blood, scalps being taken, and her possibly tied to a stake in the middle of the fight, helplessly watching. Her carelessness had gotten not only herself into mortal danger, but also Strong Hawk and his people.

But she knew that if the Sioux hadn't captured her, it would have been someone else. This thing to be settled between the Indians was something to be fought and won, and the victor would stay in this new land of plenty. So Judith's guilt lessened, though her fear was growing by leaps and bounds.

She clawed at Red Bear as he placed his hands to her waist and lifted her onto the blankets spread across the horse's back. "Let me go. . . ." she screamed. "Strong Hawk will kill you. I am his woman. I am soon to be his wife."

Eluding her fingernails, Red Bear chuckled. "Your confession makes my heart beat like a hundred drums," he said. "It is good that I have chosen my prisoner so wisely. Strong Hawk will not fight with a clear head when fighting for you. He will be blinded by worry over you. A Chippewa cannot bear to think of a Sioux with his woman in ʼany way. The Chippewa women are untouchable by my Braves. They even call my braves snakes."

He mounted the horse behind Judith, circling her waist with his arm, jerking her hard against him. "I will show Strong Hawk that even snakes know how to treat a woman," he grumbled. "You may not even wish to return to your man. Your time with me will prove which Indian is the gentlest."

Judith grew cold inside, fearing what the next several hours would offer her. She knew to expect him to take her sexually. Could she bear it? Even now she could feel the hard outline of his sex pressed against her buttocks. And when the horse began a gallop through the forest, the feel of his manhood moving even more into her made her fear him even more. Surely he was being stimulated by her closeness. He had even let his thumb graze her breast through her buckskin dress, drawing a low gasp of horror from between her lips.

But, surprising to her, Red Bear didn't pursue these touches, and he didn't take undue advantage of her pressed hips against him. He seemed to have only one thing on his mind, and that victory for his people was apparently to be his main goal.

Looking over her shoulder, Judith wondered if Strong Hawk had yet discovered her gone. When he did, would he understand what had happened to her?

They left the forest behind, traveled across a meadow and then entered another forest. And then there suddenly appeared the first signs of a mountainous region, and they climbed rocky slopes and traveled through gorges.

Judith's bones ached. Her legs were stiff from straddling the horse's back for so long. Her cheeks were stinging from the cold of the night and her eyes burned as the wind rushed against them. After several hours of travel she caught her first sight of campfires on a hillside in the distance. She felt Red Bear's arm relax around her waist and saw his knees sink deeply into the horse's sides. The horse raced onward and soon entered a circle of teepees.

Though it was dark, Judith was able to observe that these dwellings differed from those of the Chippewa. Their tops were cone-shaped and had colorful designs painted on and around their circular buckskin bases.

The camp seemed empty of women and children; perhaps they had retired for the evening. Only mongrel dogs raced about sniffing and yapping.

Poised stiff-backed on horses on the outskirts of the camp were many braves, rifles ready. Red Bear nodded to each one that he passed and worked his way on to one of the larger outdoor fires. There he dismounted and lifted his arms to Judith.

"I will now show you to my teepee," he said. "You will take nourishment, then rest. Tomorrow the Chippewa will come for you. We must be ready."

"I take it you plan to rest in your dwelling with me," Judith said haughtily, her eyes snapping with anger.

"Would you expect me to rest anywhere else?" he growled. "I rest in my own dwelling. Nowhere else."

"How is it that you speak English so well?" Judith asked as he began guiding her by the elbow toward the larger of the teepees of the camp. "Strong Hawk speaks in English, but also in Chippewa. You've not spoken in Sioux at all to me. Why is that?" Her gaze traveled over him. "It's obvious you are all Indian."

"For a time I was a part of the white man's culture," Red Bear grumbled, raising the buckskin entrance flap. "But when my father's spirit was beckoned from him it was my duty to return to my people, to lead them."

Judith edged on inside the teepee, staring disbelievingly at Red Bear. "You aren't the chief of this band of Indians, are you?" she gulped.

"Is that so hard to believe?"

"No. I should have realized that it would be the

355

chief who would choose which prisoner would be taken from the Chippewa."

"And so you are right."

Judith's gaze left him and began sweeping the interior of the teepee, seeing that it was hardly any different from Strong Hawk's wigwam. There was an abundance of blankets and skins where the bulrush mat flooring wasn't already seen. A slow fire sizzled in the firespace, over which hung a black kettle, steaming and emitting a tantalizing aroma that resembled that of beef stew. A large bow and a quiver of arrows hung from a sapling pole, also a drum, dried herbs, and smoked meats. The smoke hole sucked the smoke straight up from the fire, and a gentle, cool breeze was cut off as Red Bear dropped the entrance flap back into place.

"Sit," Red Bear ordered, gesturing toward a thick bearskin placed before the fire.

"And what if I'd rather not?" Judith snapped, stubbornly folding her arms across her chest.

Red Bear raised his shoulder with an air of indifference. "Then *stand*," he said dryly. "But I plan to sit *and* eat. It was a long ride to and from the Chippewa village. My hunger must be fed."

Judith watched as Red Bear sat down opposite the fire from her, crossing his legs. He reached for a wooden bowl and spoon and dipped some food from the kettle and began hungrily eating. Judith felt hunger pangs gnawing at her insides. She eased down onto the bearskin, loving the warmth and softness against her bare feet and legs. Clasping her hands onto her lap, she watched Red Bear eat, and when he filled another bowl and handed it and a spoon to her, she eagerly accepted.

Not even looking at what lay in the dish, afraid that she just might be dissaded from eating once she saw its ingredients, she began eating. She quickly recognized the taste of wild onion and carrots and she wasn't sure about the kind of meat of which she was finding bits and pieces. And she didn't dare ask. Getting her strength revitalized was the main thing to be concerned with. Should she have the chance to escape . . .

Red Bear placed his dish and spoon aside and poured a liquid from a wooden vase into a cup and offered it to Judith. Again she accepted his generosity, questioning him with her eyes about what he might expect of her in return.

"Your name is?" Red Bear suddenly asked. He reached for a long-stemmed, black stone pipe, filled it with tobacco, and after lighting it leisurely smoked from it. His shoulder muscles were relaxed, and his dark eyes showed no signs of being less than friendly. If Judith could have seen him as anything but an enemy to Strong Hawk, she would have had to recognize his handsomeness. His nose was long and straight, his jawline curved gently, and his lips were softly shaped.

But he was not only Strong Hawk's enemy, but hers as well, and she felt only mistrust and dislike of him.

"Judith. My name is Judith," she finally said, placing the cup aside, as well as the dish, after emptying the cool, pleasant-tasting liquid from the cup. She was afraid to let herself relax. To be caught off guard could possibly mean to be raped by this

Indian who had taken her captive.

"Your last name?" he insisted. His eyes became locked on her hair. He hungered to run his fingers through it, to touch its softness. He would never forget his times with North Star in Duluth. Their cultures had separated them, but not before love between them had been awakened. The call to be chief had been stronger than the call to be her husband. North Star having been born into the family of the Chippewa, even related to Chief Strong Hawk himself, forbade the union of North Star and Red Bear. The Sioux and the Chippewa had always been and always would be enemies. Unless . . .

"What does it matter to you what my last name is?" Judith said scornfully.

"I knew many white families in Duluth," Red Bear said, his eyes taking on shadowed memories.

"Duluth?" Judith gasped. "It was Duluth where you made your residence?"

"I worked there as a lumberjack for a spell."

"You? For whom?" She tensed, recalling the many Indians under her father's employ.

"Travis McMahon was the man who paid my wages, meager as they were."

Judith's mouth went dry. "My father?" she gasped.

Red Bear eased the pipe from between his lips, his eyebrows forked. "Your father?"

"Yes."

"Your father. My employer."

"Damn," Judith said, eyeing him even more speculatively.

Red Bear chuckled. "Such a word I heard often working side-by-side with the white man," he said.

Then his mood grew somber, wanting to ask Judith if she knew of North Star and if so, how she was. But this was the wrong time. The words between himself and his prisoner had become too friendly. That could be dangerous. He had to be prepared for tomorrow, for the coming of the Chippewa.

Judith's eyes wavered with her next question. "Did you know my father well?" she blurted, suddenly having the need to speak of her father, somehow by doing so drawing him closer to her. She missed him. She needed him. For too long he had been her sole protector.

"Time for talk has passed," Red Bear grumbled, knocking ashes from his pipe into the firespace.

Judith recoiled as he rose and stepped around the firespace and toward her. "What do you plan to do now?" she cautiously asked, watching him grab a rolled-up blanket.

"Here. Spread this on the bearskins," he ordered, thrusting the blanket into Judith's unwilling arms. "It is time to rest. Not talk."

Judith moved to her knees and began clumsily spreading the blanket, all the while watching him out of the corner of her eye as he began spreading a blanket alongside hers. She mutely watched as he removed his headband and feather and stretched out on the blanket on his back. She felt his eyes follow her movements as she then smoothed the corners back on her blanket. And when this was done she had no other choice but to stretch out, herself, on the blanket, very wary of his closeness. She could hear his easy breathing, smell his strong aroma of tobacco, and she was quite aware of his body only a few inches from hers. Should he wish, one grab would be all that was required to fully possess her. Her pulse raced, afraid to close her eyes, yet her eyelids were growing heavier and heavier.

"Don't get any foolish ideas of trying to escape," Red Bear suddenly grumbled. "As you saw, my men watch the camp. No movements escape their eyes."

Judith gave him an ugly stare. "I wasn't born yesterday," she snapped. "I know I can't escape. But Strong Hawk will rescue me. You'll be sorry you ever laid eyes on me."

"I doubt that," Red Bear chuckled. "Though you are my enemy's woman, I cannot ever forget the gold of your hair nor the blue of your eyes."

"Just as long as you look. Not touch," Judith warned, inching away from him. She pulled the corner of the blanket up and over her, hiding as much of herself as she could beneath it.

"You speak bravely," Red Bear said, turning on his side to face her. "But, yes, only a woman with a fiery spirit would capture Strong Hawk's heart. If my heart didn't already belong to another, I would challenge Strong Hawk for more than the right to be on this land of plenty. I would challenge him for you. But as it is, my dreams are already occupied by another woman with such eyes and hair as you possess. You have nothing to fear from me."

Judith breathed easier, full of wonder about this woman Red Bear had just spoken about. "Red Bear, you just made mention of a woman," she dared to say. "Are you confessing to being in love with a white woman? Such hair and eyes you described . . ."

He interrupted her. "Though her hair is gold and

her eyes are blue, she has the beautiful copper skin of the Indian," he said, his words drifting off as he flopped over and placed his back to her.

"What?" Judith gasped. In her mind's eye she was suddenly seeing North Star. "You've just described . . ."

"Enough words have been spoken tonight," Red Bear growled, once more interrupting her. "Too many words have been spoken. Sleep. Get to sleep, white woman."

The eyelids on Judith's eyes were no longer heavy. Her discovery had drawn her wide awake. Surely there was no other woman like North Star, with eyes and hair of the white race and the bronze of the Indian. Judith had to wonder how this might change the outcome of tomorrow's challenge between these two factions of Indians.

Yet, surely Strong Hawk didn't know about North Star and Red Bear. Was Strong Hawk in for more than one rude awakening where this Sioux chief was concerned?

Judith rolled up into a fetal position, facing Red Bear, whose back was still to her. She stared at him, thinking he just might be even more complex than Strong Hawk. She even found herself liking him.

But her love and her loyalty to Strong Hawk were fierce, and she fell into a soft sleep, praying for his victory, not letting herself even think of that ugly word "defeat."

Chapter Twenty-Six

Drums pounded and turtle-shells rattled as Strong Hawk stepped up to his circle of men. Having discovered Judith gone, he had decided there could be only one answer to her untimely absence. The Sioux! Judith would not have left on her own this time. She had no reason to—they had settled all of their differences. Their future was as bright as the face on the wild yellow daisy!

Attired in full buckskin, his face painted with black streaks across his nose and his cheeks, Strong Hawk shouted out orders to his braves, who now circled even more closely about him. The huge outdoor fire was reflected against the black sky of night and in the highly polished rifles held by each man. Their faces were dark with paint and anger; their hunger for a fight with the Sioux was finally being fed. But Strong Hawk's instructions as to how this battle was to be fought was causing a rippling of low grumblings among his chosen followers.

"There is to be no bloodshed," Strong Hawk

shouted, his eyes sharp in their hate of the Sioux. He folded his arms across his chest. "There are many reasons for this! We must remember that the Sioux have my woman. We cannot endanger her life. This challenge will be met by other means. We will test the Sioux by peaceful combat."

More grumblings bounced from man to man. Strong Hawk understood. His men wanted blood. They wanted scalps. But he had to prove to them that that was the way of the old school of the Chippewa. Today, as well as on all days in the future, peaceful means had to be found to settle differences.

"Try to understand my ways, my braves," he continued. "Though my heart is full of hate for the Sioux, it is best to not kill. The Indian people—the entire population of Indians—is already threatened too much. A bloody encounter would only quicken the complete fall of all Indians."

"You say this, that you want no bloodshed, though your woman was stolen from you?" one man dared to shout.

"No harm will come to her. She is a part of the test of the Sioux," Strong Hawk reassured him.

"Then why are rifles required if we are not to fight?" another scornfully shouted.

"No Chippewa ever enters a Sioux camp un-armed," Strong Hawk growled. "Being snakelike as they are, one can never fully trust them."

"Do we not share the dog's head feast before we travel to their camp?" another shouted. "Is it no longer a way to make our final pledge of our readiness to meet the Sioux challenge?"

"The dog's head feast was a way to pledge

readiness to face *death*," Strong Hawk said. "Since none of us are going to do such battle, that feast is not required."

He raised a doubled fist into the air. "I am now your leader," he shouted. "I am wise in all ways. Those who question my authority step aside and on my return I had best not find you here. You will no longer be a part of the St. Croix Band of the Chippewa! You will be shamed, to wander forever without a people!"

A dead hush followed Strong Hawk's threats. His eyes blazed as he gazed from man to man, studying each face at length before moving to the next. He was bothered today by two tests, it seemed! His test of leadership and his test by the Sioux! But better now than later. Strong Hawk understood very well that his reputation was at stake here—his reputation for wisdom, skill, and bravery, his ability to attract followers.

He knew that in the past bloody killings and the capturing of enemy warriors was, in part, a psychological release for the pent-up bitterness and frustrations of dealing with not-so-benign medicine men. Men also waged war to avenge the combat deaths of fathers, brothers, and uncles, or to annex new hunting grounds.

This night, their reason for revenge was twofold! The snakelike Sioux had kidnapped his woman! It would be easy to kill and maim. But this was the time to prove that the peaceful way was the way not just for now, but also for the future. . . .

Again Strong Hawk challenged each man with a set stare, pleased that none chose to step aside. They were one body now, giving him the support that he needed to be a successful leader. Had even one stepped from the crowd, it would have been the same as a corner of his heart's being ripped away. It had been instilled in Strong Hawk from childhood that to be a leader one had to feel a part of each and every one of his faithful followers. To lose face with even one could mean the beginnings of losing face with them all.

His chest swelled with pride. He had the same as wrestled with a bear and won, having fully won the trust and faith of every one of his braves.

"Oneegishin! Oneegishin!" Strong Hawk shouted. *"Gee-mah-gi-ung-ah-shig-wah!"*

"Hai-ay!" the braves answered in a ringing shout. *"Kitchiogema!"*

The women of the village, who had been hovering in their wigwams, now slowly emerged and watched the men mount their horses. Then, as the horses began leaving the village, the anxious women escorted the war party to the village outskirts, singing songs of farewell.

The moon waxed and waned like a huge winking eye as the horses traveled beneath the towering trees, the horses' hooves like thunder against the dew-dampened ground. Strong Hawk led the way, his thoughts on Judith. Should she be harmed in any way, all his words to his braves would have been for naught. His knife would move swiftly, his scalp-pole would display his prize. The peace that he so sincerely sought would once more be delayed. . . .

*   *   *

Judith wasn't sure what she was being readied for, but she highly disapproved of the manner in which it was being done! With his face painted in bright red zigzags, Red Bear sat across the firespace from Judith, unsmilingly watching the Sioux squaw grooming her. He had even boldly watched as she had been forced to sit nude before him while the squaw had bathed Judith in perfumed oils! Lust had been heavy in Red Bear's eyes, and Judith had seen the pulsebeat grow in intensity in a corded vein in his neck. But he hadn't moved to touch her, except for his eyes.

Now she sat fully dressed in a clean buckskin dress that reached below her ankles, and in soft white moccasins. Many layers of colorful beads had been placed about her neck, and wildflowers were being braided into her hair. Her face was flushed pink, her lips red from an application of a sweet-tasting foreign substance, perhaps the thickened juice of some wild berry.

The squaw stepped away from Judith and said something in Sioux beneath her breath, staring with appreciation toward her.

Judith tossed a questioning look in the squaw's direction, hoping that Red Bear would translate the squaw's words for her. Instead he rose to his feet and stood over Judith, offering her a hand.

"What am I to expect now?" Judith sighed, placing her hand in his, easing to her feet.

Still Red Bear didn't answer her. He guided her from the teepee into the brightness of early morning. Only wafts of fog remained, but the sun quickly melted them away to nothingness. Judith quickly became aware of the long, straight line of Indians on horses, their faces painted the same as Red Bear's, and dressed as neatly, in full buckskin attire. Each held a rifle, the gleam from the barrels reflecting ominously in Judith's eyes.

Then she noticed two horses being held steady by their reins by the same Indian squaw who had dressed her.

"Are we going somewhere?" Judith asked, giving Red Bear an ugly glance. "What are your plans for me, Red Bear? I have a right to know."

He returned her stare, his eyes cold and unfeeling, nothing like the night before when they had sat before the fire eating and talking. She had begun to like him. Now she was beginning to fear him once more.

It unnerved her when again he didn't answer her. It was as though he had lost his ability to speak during the night! Oh! The frustration of it all!

Slipping on the damp grass, Judith felt Red Bear's strong arm grab her about the waist to steady her as he led her to the horse. He helped her to straddle it, the only saddle being a colorful blanket with a red, yellow, and green zigzag pattern.

"Now what?" Judith whispered harshly beneath her breath, accepting the reins that were handed her by the squaw.

Red Bear mounted his stately black steed beside Judith. He took the horse's reins and let them lie lax between his fingers, staring straight ahead, but not urging his horse onward. Facing south, he seemed to be watching the forest, his jaw set, his eyes a cold glaze.

Swallowing hard in an effort to erase the constriction in her throat, Judith slowly looked about her, hearing the muted silence of all the Indians, who still sat on their horses, in a straight line behind her. No Indian squaws were in sight; neither were there children or dogs. The tension in the Indian camp seemed so tight that Judith feared that soon there might even be a loud, audible snap if the horses didn't move. Just how long could the Indians sit so quietly on their horses, not even moving a muscle? And why weren't they moving? Why mount a horse with no intention of traveling anywhere? It was as though the Indians were waiting.

Judith's eyes widened with partial understanding. Waiting! The Indians were waiting for Strong Hawk's arrival! Strong Hawk would be entering a trap! The rifles were proof of that!

Closing her eyes, shaking her head, she dared not think of the possibilities of what lay ahead. Was she experiencing her last moments of life? There would be no reason for her to be spared. She meant nothing to Red Bear. She was only bait, luring Strong Hawk and his men away from their peaceful Chippewa village.

Growing frantic at the wild thoughts inside her head, Judith fluttered her eyes open, thinking, "Escape!"

Cautiously, she once more surveyed the stoical faces of the Indians, and then she looked for a route of escape. Forward! That was her only choice! Yet too many guns were loaded and ready for firing! She couldn't get to the protective cover of the forest quickly enough. Already she could hear the explosion of gunfire. She even winced, somehow able to imagine the sting of the bullets as they pierced her flesh!

Understanding that escape was impossible, she straightened her back and lifted her chin, at least trying to appear to be brave, though her insides quaked unmercifully with a tortured fear. She feared for herself, Strong Hawk, and his many kind braves who so faithfully would follow him into possible massacre.

The sun rose higher in the sky, beating down on Judith's face, scorching it into a flaming inferno. Perspiration beaded her brow; the palms of her hands were clammy. With a parched throat and dry lips she looked toward Red Bear. He didn't appear to have budged an inch. He seemed to have turned into a stone statue, still staring south, contemplation etched on his powerful Indian face.

Judith stubbornly refused to ask him just how long he intended to stay there on the horses, though she was growing mindless from it all!

I must focus my thoughts elsewhere, she thought desperately to herself. I'll go insane if I keep watching and waiting.

Her gaze blocked out the Indians and their teepees. She looked on past them, to the dappled canvas of green that stretched out before her, and then upward to where the sun was alternating with billowing clouds in dominating the sky. Looking farther, to the west of her, she saw the mystical touch of God in the breathtaking cones of mountains and their masses of rugged rock that rose from another sea of green. The sounds were those of a living forest, the aroma sweet and fresh.

Then another sound became a reality—the neighing of horses other than those behind Judith, and the muffled sound of horses' hooves emanating from the thick green stretches of the forest.

Judith's heart flip-flopped. Her hands began to tremble. Strong Hawk! He was coming, and was making no effort to silence his approach. Surely he knew better!

Desperation seized her. She had to go and warn Strong Hawk. She couldn't just sit idly by and watch the massacre. Even the thought of bullets slicing through her wouldn't dissuade her from making a mad dash to escape. Strong Hawk was more important to her than even her own life!

Circling her fingers tightly around her horse's reins, she suddenly slapped them against its flesh and sank her knees deeply into its sides. "Hahh!" she shouted, ducking low, welcoming the feel of the rush of the air on her face as the horse carried her quickly forward.

Out of the corner of her eye she saw a flash of horse and flesh and let out a loud cry as she was grabbed from her horse and yanked onto Red Bear's, where he firmly held her in place against the steel of his chest.

Judith's head jerked hard as Red Bear drew his horse to a quick halt, then spun it around and led it back to the very same spot where it had been standing before Judith's attempt to escape. Trembling from the anger and fear fusing inside her, Judith began plummeting her fists against Red Bear's chest. "Let me go!" she screamed.

"So Strong Hawk would get you so easily, without first facing me, his enemy?" Red Bear growled. He watched as Judith's horse was positioned back in place alongside his. "Now you will once more wait patiently on the steed assigned to you. You will wait with me for Strong Hawk's arrival."

Judith's eyes flamed as she looked up at him. "Wait?" she hissed. "You mean for Strong Hawk's massacre, don't you?"

"In time you will see how I choose to challenge Strong Hawk. I will not tell you now only because your eyes are aflame with anger. Your blue eyes do affect me, white woman. But this is so only because they are the eyes of my woman."

"Oh!" Judith spat, yanking herself fully free of him as he loosened his grip from around her waist. Knowing she had no other choice, she jumped from his horse and swung her leg up over hers and once more was forced to wait and watch the forest. The sound of hoofbeats was closer, the silence in the village deafening.

And then Strong Hawk was fully there, directing his black stallion out of the dense, dark fingers of the forest, with his many braves. Judith's heart raced. She bit her lower lip, itching to go to him, but now knowing that all decisions of what must be done next were Strong Hawk's. He was the epitome of a leader, sitting so handsomely tall in his fancy leather saddle, in his full buckskin attire, his hair braided meticulously down his back. Judith's eyes narrowed when she saw the black stripes of paint marring his chiseled features. War paint. The same as Red Bear's, except for the color.

Her heart leaped as Strong Hawk's gaze met hers and their eyes locked. Her insides melted, seeing that in the depths of his eyes he showed no traces of fear. His confidence transferred to her, and she somehow understood that nothing was going to happen to him or her.

A half smile lifted Strong Hawk's lips as she smiled toward him, but just as quickly his face became etched in a hard, cold mask as he challenged Red Bear with a stare. And then Strong Hawk began urging his stallion forward, while his braves formed a silent, straight line behind him, their rifles a threat to anyone who dared to place their chief in danger.

Strong Hawk stopped his stallion only a few feet from Red Bear's. *"Ah-nish-min-eh-wah?"* he growled, leaning forward, his eyes daring, his jaw set.

Red Bear emitted a low, mocking chuckle. "Strong Hawk, you know that I do not converse in Chippewa with you," he said in English. "Do you forget that I had schooling in the white man's community? I speak English as well as the Indian whose mother was white." He gave Judith a half glance. "I speak as well as an Indian whose chosen woman is white."

Judith's mouth went agape. Red Bear had mentioned working in Duluth, but never that he had attended school. That had to be how he had met North Star.

Strong Hawk chuckled. "You prove your strength, your knowledge, by stealing a woman?" he taunted. Then he growled. "A woman who is soon to be my wife, Red Bear. Does this prove that you are more worthy to live in this land of promise?"

"It lured you to my camp, did it not?" Red Bear laughed, lifting his chin proudly. "My prowess was proved by stealing her away from beneath your very nose. You and your braves are blind, it seems."

"You are a lucky Indian for not having harmed her," Strong Hawk argued.

"You knew that I would not."

"*Ay-uh.* I have to believe that you are not of the old school of Sioux, as was your father. I have also placed the warring, bloody days behind me."

"It is the only way to guarantee the further existence of my people," Red Bear said icily.

"As it is also for mine," Strong Hawk said dryly.

"So now we meet, face-to-face, as chiefs, our fathers now a part of the land of bliss," Red Bear said. "What are we to now do between us to make things more bearable for our people, now that we have become the leaders?"

"You know the answer, Red Bear, though I can never like you, the Nadoues-Sioux that you are."

"Name throwing doesn't become you, Strong Hawk."

"Women stealing becomes you less, Red Bear."

"This gets us nowhere, Strong Hawk. Bantering is for children."

"You understand what is required of us, do you not, Red Bear?"

"We must find it in ourselves to share."

"Land. Only land, Red Bear. My woman is not a part of the bargain."

"She was a part of the test," Red Bear growled.

"Test?" Strong Hawk said, lifting a brow. "This is a test?" he scoffed.

"If you had arrived firing rifles upon my people and taking scalps, you would have failed my test.

You would have died," Red Bear said in a low snarl.

Strong Hawk gestured with a swing of his arm toward his men. "You are the one who is blind," he bragged. "My braves, my rifles outnumber you. Had I chosen to attack, as my ancestors did in the past, as my Grandfather Chief Yellow Feather did when he rescued my cousin Amanda from your grandfather's Sioux camp those many moons ago, you would be as dead now as your grandfather."

The mention of Amanda, North Star's mother who had been dead for many moons now, reminded Red Bear of his other purpose for this meeting with Strong Hawk. It had been too long now since he had held North Star in his arms and kissed her lips. Now was the time to speak out loud of his intentions. Now was the time to assure a peaceful coexistence between the Chippewa and the Sioux. Red Bear had to have North Star with him. He had waited long enough.

"A woman *is* a part of this sharing between us," Red Bear said thickly, his eyes wavering. The reins grew lax in his hands as he repositioned himself on his blankets.

"I have already said that she is not," Strong Hawk growled, placing his hand on his rifle as it lay in its leather pouch at the side of his stallion. "Let Judith come to me now, to prove that your words and intentions are honorable."

Red Bear's face lighted up in a smile. He nodded to Judith, who was looking breathlessly toward him. "Go to him," he softly ordered. "Go to your man." He then spoke to Judith, so that only she could hear. "Strong Hawk is a lucky Indian. You are not only a woman of spirit, but you are lovely, as well. The

374

combination is one rarely found, white woman. Be happy, white woman."

Red Bear's gentle words and the sincere look in his dark eyes stirred Judith. She felt an intense liking of him. She now knew that Strong Hawk had never had anything to fear from this particular Indian. Red Bear was anything but snakelike.

"Thank you," she murmured, almost humble beneath his steady, friendly stare.

"Go," he said again, softly, waving his rifle in the air. "Now. Ride beside your man. He is to be one of the greatest chiefs of the Chippewa. It is written in the wind. I understand and respect this."

Judith swallowed hard, gave Red Bear a quivering smile, then sank her knees into her horse and directed it to stand alongside Strong Hawk's. Tears came to her eyes as Strong Hawk reached his hand to take one of hers in his. She noticed a tremble in his lips as he smiled reassuringly at her, then released her hand and once more challenged Red Bear with a stare.

"So you willingly let my woman come to me," Strong Hawk said. "Then what was this mention of sharing a woman?"

"It is another woman close to your heart of whom I make mention," Red Bear said flatly.

"Stop speaking in riddles," Strong Hawk said, squirming uneasily in his saddle, never trusting the Sioux, though this Sioux was of his mind, wishing for peace as badly as he.

"I speak of North Star," Red Bear said, squaring his shoulders.

"North Star?" Strong Hawk gasped, color suffusing his face as anger rose in hot splashes through him. "Why do you speak the name of North Star in the same breath as you speak of sharing?"

Red Bear eased his horse forward, stopping beside Strong Hawk's on the opposite side of where Judith sat on her assigned steed.

"Strong Hawk, North Star has been my chosen woman for many moons now," Red Bear said hoarsely. "The differences between our people separated us, though. From our first embrace we knew the futility of our feelings for each other. But now? I see a future of togetherness. You and I have chosen a peaceful means to settle our differences, and it is this that gives me hope that you will let North Star come to me so that we may join not only our hearts, but also our hands."

"You and North Star?" Strong Hawk said, still numb from the discovery.

"We met while attending the same school in Duluth."

"She never mentioned . . ."

"She knew that it would not please you."

"Should it now?"

"No. I understand that it cannot. But should that matter?"

"Should it not?"

"Let her come to me. Let me go to her and bring her back with me."

"I cannot give you my blessing. Nothing changes the fact that you are Sioux and she is Chippewa."

"She is only part Chippewa," Red Bear argued. "Do you forget that her mother was white?"

Strong Hawk leaned toward Red Bear, glowering. "Do you forget it was your very own grandfather who stole her mother *from* her white family—after slaying them?"

Red Bear leaned toward Strong Hawk, glowering back. "Do you forget it was *your* grandfather who stole into *my* grandfather's village like a thief in the night and spilled much blood of many fine Sioux warriors, took scalps, and killed even my grandfather while rescuing North Star's mother?" His eyes lowered. "It seems we are now even, Strong Hawk. One dark deed begat the other. Now is the time to forget, to place grudges behind us."

"The land? Seems we've forgot this land that has beckoned us here, with its abundance of rice, its deer, and its purple mountains," Strong Hawk said, his eyes taking in the beautiful setting, which seemed at this moment to have turned into a temptress seducing the two tribes of Indians with its heady beauty.

"There is enough to share equally," Red Bear said, following Strong Hawk's gaze, seeing and feeling the same as he.

"Can we?" Strong Hawk challenged, now looking intently into Red Bear's eyes. "Never in the past has it been possible."

"Never in the past were *we* the leaders of our people, Strong Hawk."

"*Ay-uh*, you are right."

Strong Hawk slowly lifted a hand of friendship toward Red Bear and as he did so heard the low whisper of a breeze pass from the forest and felt it brushing against him, cooling, then warming his flesh. A tremble coursed through him, hoping the spirits had just given approval instead of a warning.

But no matter! What he was doing was right. Peace was the only way to ensure a future for his people—the Ojibway—the St. Croix Band of the Chippewa—the greatest Indian who had ever walked the face of the earth!

Red Bear's flesh tingled with excitement as he reached his hand and clasped it to Strong Hawk's. How many moons had Red Bear dreamed of such a union! No more wars! No more fear of war!

"We can never be as one, Red Bear," Strong Hawk said hoarsely, feeling the strong grip in his. "But, we can hunt and we can travel this land without forever looking over our shoulders."

"It is a beginning."

"And now, about North Star."

"Yes? Your decision?"

"If I were to say no, could you take that decision of mine in a peaceful way? You would forget her?"

Red Bear's insides coiled, his eyes narrowed. Perhaps he had been too hasty to agree to friendship. He eased his hand away from Strong Hawk's. Then he realized a "test" when he saw one, and understood. Only one answer could be spoken, or his prior words up till then would be called lies.

"Though I love North Star with all my heart, yes, in peace, I would accept your decision," Red Bear said, almost choking on the words.

Strong Hawk relaxed his shoulder muscles. He smiled coyly toward Red Bear. *"Oneegishin!"* he exclaimed. "Your answer makes me happy."

"Then? What is it to be?" Red Bear said, becoming annoyed by the waiting.

"Red Bear, don't you know North Star well

enough to know that the decision is hers to make?" Strong Hawk said, chuckling. "All you need to do is to ask her."

Strong Hawk gave Judith a soft smile. *"Wee-mah-gi-ung-ah-shig-wah,"* he said. "Didn't you say you had to go to Duluth to settle things there before becoming my wife?"

"Ay-uh . . ."

"Then let us go. I will deliver you safely there."

"Now?"

"I am growing impatient, Judith," Strong Hawk growled. He gave Red Bear a scornful glance. "Seems too many things continue to stand in our way of being man and wife."

"Ay-uh . . ." Judith said, then gave Red Bear a friendly smile, always remembering his kindness, though he had taken her prisoner. She was glad when he returned her smile of friendship. Somehow this smile formed a bond between them, though never one to be spoken about to Strong Hawk. North Star and Red Bear together! Yes, it seemed only right. . . .

Chapter Twenty-Seven

The golden light of the afternoon was quickly fleeing as the day was deepened into sunset, the shadows of the forest gaining confidence. Judith and Strong Hawk huddled by a low fire, their journey now having lengthened into several days. They had left Strong Hawk's braves behind at the Chippewa village and now were sharing their last night alone on the trail before reaching Duluth.

Judith sipped coffee from her tin cup and Strong Hawk took his last bite of meat from the bone he held, the last remains of the rabbit that had served them well as their evening meal.

"I think I could go on forever like this," Judith sighed, closing her eyes. "Why must there be anything in the world but you and me, Strong Hawk?"

Her lashes fluttered open. "Have you enjoyed these days and nights as much as I?" she murmured dreamily.

Strong Hawk tossed the bone across his shoulder,

wiped his mouth clean of grease with the back of a hand, then scooted closer to Judith. He eased the tin cup from her hands and sat it on the ground, then gently kissed the palms of each of her hands.

"My Judith . . ." he said huskily, his fingers now caressing her bare arms. "My heart soars like an eagle. My thoughts are filled with kindled flames of desire for you. There aren't enough nights or days left in my lifetime for me to have the time to tell you of my feelings for you."

"Thank you for coming for me at the Sioux camp," she murmured, reveling in the touch of his breath now on her throat as he pressed his lips fleetingly there, then on up to her ear to tease and torment her almost to mindlessness.

"You've thanked me many times already for that," Strong Hawk grumbled, now unbraiding her hair with nimble fingers.

"Doing so again gives me reason to show my thanks, over and over again," Judith said dreamily as she felt his fingers now loosening her hair over her shoulders.

"In the red splash of the sun's setting, your hair takes on the color of the wild poppy," he said, placing a sweet kiss on her brow. "Its red shades set my heart afire."

"Kiss me, Strong Hawk," Judith whispered, twining her arms about his neck. "Darling, make love to me the entire night. Tomorrow will come too soon, and we must say another good-bye."

"But for only a short while, Judith."

"*Ay-uh.* For only a short while." They hadn't discussed at length what it was she was to do. She hadn't even yet mentioned Rory. Somehow his name just hadn't come up. Even now she had no need to mention her brother. She only hoped that he was still in Duluth, overseeing the affairs of the estate. Surely, by now, he was even worrying about her. She hadn't planned to be gone so long.

Strong Hawk lowered her to the ground as his lips fully possessed hers, his hands gently brushing her hair back. Then he let his fingers roam lower, stroking her breasts through the thin layer of buckskin.

A moan surfaced from inside Judith as she felt her breasts responding, her nipples tightening, hot beneath the pressure of his hands. She pressed herself harder against him, raising her hips to find the firmness of his manhood beneath his own buckskin apparel. She let her hand travel around to touch him, to let the feel of him send her head into a sensuous spinning.

Strong Hawk drew away from her, his dark eyes passion-filled. He placed his fingers to the hem of her dress and began slowly lifting it up and over her body. Where his hands momentarily grazed her flesh, fires were set, and Judith tremored in ecstasy as he let his lips now follow the trail already heated by his hands.

Softly he kissed her ankles, higher to her thighs. The dress was quickly slipped over her head and tossed aside. Strong Hawk splayed his fingers across her abdomen, ready to worship her softness where her love mound lay with its golden hair between her thighs. He lifted her legs to let them rest on his shoulders, then set his lips against her.

He felt the quivering in her body and heard her low gasp when his kiss became longer, drawing the feelings from her, to be a part of him, it seemed, as her love bud rose larger between his lips.

One, then two flicks of his tongue and he let his lips make a path of rapture upward until he reached her breasts. Cupping each one in his hands, he buried his face between them, the ache in his loins a hellish torment.

"Strong Hawk, your clothes . . ." Judith whispered, hoarse with passion. "Please . . ."

Strong Hawk rose slowly to his feet to tower over her. His face was a mask of desire as he began to undress. He couldn't take his eyes from her silken, perfect body, now splashed in color by the golden flames of the fire. Night had fallen, the night sounds of the forest were faint, the smell of freshness keen as it filtered upward through the fallen leaves, the twisted vines, and the never ending ground tangle.

Judith's gaze raked over Strong Hawk as he stepped out of his final piece of clothing. He stood there looking powerful, his skin a beautiful copper sheen as the shadows of the fire danced across it.

His readiness was intoxicating to her, and she eagerly accepted it inside her as he lowered himself over her, filled her, and began his sweet and gentle strokes. She clung to him as Strong Hawk sent butterfly kisses across her face to the hollow of her throat and to her breasts.

Breathless now, Judith raked her fingers through her hair, then clung to him again as he gave her a long, rapturous kiss. She wrapped her legs round his waist and let her hips become consumed by him. Her heart pounded, it leaped, it soared. Her pulse was erratic. A sob broke through their kiss as she felt the peak of her desire rising.

The wild tremors captured her fully, the thrill of completion sweeping her insides with a sensual, splendid glow. And when Strong Hawk's body also became a mass of wild quakes, Judith clung more fiercely to him and welcomed his splash of warmth inside her tremoring cocoon of love.

Strong Hawk relaxed his body against her, breathing hard. He pressed his nose into the depths of her hair as it lay goldenly against her neck. "You are my heart. You are my soul," he whispered. "You are the meaning in my life. I need you, Judith. Don't wait too long to return to me."

Judith brushed some loose strands of his coarse, black hair back from his eyes. She kissed him gently on the cheek. "I shan't," she murmured. "Soon, Strong Hawk. We will be together. And when we are, it will be until the end of time."

He drew away from her and framed her face between his hands, his eyes devouring her perfect features. "You *wah-wee-duh-nah-gay-win?*" he said huskily.

"Strong Hawk, you forget," Judith giggled. "I cannot understand the Chippewa way of speaking except for two—no three—words."

Strong Hawk chuckled, his eyes now taking on a softer mood. "I said do you promise all that you just said to me?"

"*Ay-uh*, my love. I do. *Ah-pah-nay.*"

Placing his hands beneath her head, he drew her lips to his. He kissed her ardently, then once more embraced her, dreading having to say good-bye, though their future tomorrows were the same as guaranteed.

Though hating to separate from Strong Hawk, Judith couldn't suppress her delight when she saw the first busy outskirts of the city of Duluth as her horse moved toward it. Then she worried about this glee, knowing that one day soon she would be leaving Duluth forever, to make residence with Strong Hawk in his village of Indians. Would it be all that easy to uproot herself so completely, to move into a different environment and culture? Her feelings for Strong Hawk had blinded her to all such thoughts. And now was not the time to let them begin plaguing her! Strong Hawk was going to be her life! He was already! Only a few minor details to iron out, and then their dream would begin.

"When I return to my village I will instruct my most skilled braves to begin your house," Strong Hawk said, seeming almost to have read her troubled thoughts. "We will fill it with what pleasures you, Judith. You won't want for a thing, just as my mother never wanted for anything."

"You are what pleasures me," Judith murmured, reaching over to stroke Strong Hawk's hand as it rested on his thigh. "I can never want for more than having you."

Strong Hawk chuckled, his eyes beaming. "You say that now," he said. "But you are used to luxury. You would soon grow to miss it."

"Yes, perhaps," Judith sighed, once more grasping her reins with both hands. Her hair lay unbraided across her shoulders, her cheeks were pink with contented excitement. With the passing of time and all that had transpired since she had left Duluth, the burden of her father's passing had almost been completely lifted from her shoulders. She was not going to dwell on the past. Hope for the future was too bright. Now to go to Rory and see what he had managed to arrange in her absence.

Judith and Strong Hawk traveled side-by-side on their proud steeds up the steep streets of Duluth. Carriages, buggies, and men on horseback were scrambling up and down the thoroughfare. Judith became aware that she and Strong Hawk were the objects of much scrutiny. That was understandable, and even cause for silent amusement for Judith, who realized how she must look in her Indian attire and in the company of an Indian.

Oh, the reaction of all these people should they know that she soon would marry this handsome Indian! They all would have just cause for staring and wonder then!

They reached the street that led to the McMahon estate and traveled along it until the wide, spreading ranch house came into view. Judith edged her horse closer to Strong Hawk's, sadness strong in her eyes.

"I already miss you," she said. "I'm not sure I can stand saying good-bye."

"The sooner you see to your business affairs, the sooner we shall be together," Strong Hawk said flatly.

"Strong Hawk, are you always so practical?"

"Don't tempt me, Judith."

"How?"

"By giving me cause to abduct you now and sweep you away with me and back to my village without giving you the chance to even enter your house."

"You would do that?"

"Would you fight me for release?"

"I doubt it," Judith laughed.

Strong Hawk rose his shoulder in a shrug. "Then I won't bother," he chuckled. "The fight is what I like so much about you. You have the spirit of a wild mustang."

"I'll remember to put up a fight occasionally once we are man and wife," Judith giggled. "The struggle could be fun. Perhaps it would light both our fires."

"You'd best not start talking about lighted fires," Strong Hawk chuckled. "I may consume you right here on the street, for everyone to witness."

"I'm sure we'd teach all the onlookers a thing or two," Judith teased back. "Your ways of making love are unique, my darling."

As they reached the wide, winding gravel drive that led to Judith's house, Strong Hawk drew his stallion to a shuddering halt. He stared toward the lowspread house and its squat second story, then back to Judith. "I will say my good-byes here," he said hoarsely.

"You do not wish to go inside my house?"

"It does not concern me."

"But you say you will build me one. Don't you want to see . . . ?"

"Judith, when yours is built, everything inside it will be of *your* choosing, not your father's," he said. "Do you understand my meaning?"

"I hadn't thought of it in that way," Judith said,

cocking her head to one side. "Yes. I understand."

"And, Judith, you must not delay any longer. I must not delay you. It only lengthens the time that separates us from being wholly together."

Judith leaned over and let him kiss her, brief though it was. "I shall join you soon," she murmured.

"Do not travel that distance alone again," he grumbled. "Go to Silver Fox. He will see to it that you will be accompanied by those who can be trusted."

"Silver Fox?"

"I will go to my brother now and explain to him. He will understand."

A flush rose to Judith's cheeks, already dreading any sort of confrontation with Silver Fox—Giles. On the other hand, didn't she have to speak with him quite soon about other matters? The land . . . the trees!

"Keep your heart free of anything but me," Strong Hawk said, then spun his horse around and guided it in a soft trot away from her.

Judith watched him for only a moment, then recalling him urging her to get everything settled as quickly as possible, hurried on toward the house.

Anxious to see how things were going, Judith didn't take her horse to the stable. Instead she quickly dismounted and slung the reins about a hitching rail. A slamming door followed by a rush of feet down the front steps drew her quickly around, and she was quickly engulfed by a set of arms.

"Sis. My God," Rory exclaimed, hugging her tightly to him. "A posse is being formed in town. We

388

were going to head out real soon, in search of you. I had begun to think that possibly you hadn't made it to the Indian village, that you had run into foul play. Why have you been gone so damn long?''

Judith warmed up to his embrace and hugged him back, relieved that he hadn't returned to St. Paul. "It's a long story," she sighed. "Let's go inside and I'll tell you all about it."

Strong Hawk had to take one more look at Judith, and then he would hurry on to talk with Silver Fox. And he had to check and see if his mother and aunt were all right, after their long journey.

With a jerk of his head, Strong Hawk looked over his shoulder. His gut twisted into a tight knot, and jealousy raged through him as he saw Judith in the embrace of that same man as the two other times. His eyes were glued to them. How tightly they held each other! How could she? Was Judith a woman of no morals? Did she divide her heart and love between two men? Did she enjoy toying with men, lying to them, cheating on them? It was obvious that she cared for this man with the clipped hair and fancy white man's clothes. And after promising that all tomorrows would be Strong Hawk's and hers? Had this white man been in her house all this time, waiting for her return? Would they now share intimate embraces in a bed?

A low growl rumbled from somewhere deep inside Strong Hawk. He was seeing Judith now with hate, his eyes two narrow slits.

"She has made a fool of me for the last time," he

hissed. "The white man can have her. She is nothing but dirt beneath my feet! Love! Ha! Who needs it?"

With an ache in his heart, he felt the strong need to return to his people. Though his mother was near, he could not see her now. She would read the sadness in his eyes. He would return and see her later.

Full of tormented frustration, he rode hurriedly away, his head held high, his eyes stinging with suppressed, hot tears.

Judith locked her arm through Rory's and moved up the front steps. "Rory, tell me. Have you accomplished anything in my absence?"

"You will be surprised to see just what has transpired in your absence," Rory chuckled, his green eyes agleam.

"Rory, what have you been up to? Did that legal mind of yours come up with a solution to our problems?"

"I was temporarily sidetracked, sis."

Judith groaned. "No, Rory," she sighed. "I'd hoped that everything would be settled, so I could get on with my future."

"I said temporarily. Just you wait. You'll see," Rory said, smiling mischievously down at her.

Then his face shadowed in a frown as his eyes swept over her, seeing her disarray and the buckskin dress. "Sis, tell me what happened out there," he said. He stopped on the porch and clasped his fingers onto her shoulders. "Why were you gone for so long?"

Judith placed her hand to his cheek. "Rory, I'm

here. I'm all right," she murmured. "Shouldn't that be enough for now? There are things that need talking about other than myself. Surely you know my need to know what you've done about things here in Duluth."

"I was so damn worried."

"I'm sorry."

"You weren't harmed in any way?"

"None whatsoever," Judith said, smiling warmly up at him. "Now, Rory, don't you think it's about time for you to reveal to me just what you were talking about a moment ago? What have you done in my absence? Come on. Tell me."

Rory chuckled beneath his breath. He placed an arm about her waist and swept her on toward the door, which stood ajar. "Better yet, I'll show you," he said. "But prepare yourself for quite a surprise. You won't even believe it, Sis. I still don't, hardly. Things have a way of happening fast." Again he released a low, pleased chuckle.

Judith's eyebrows raised, becoming more confused by the moment. She stepped into the house, then let Rory guide her into the parlor. Judith stopped and emitted a low gasp when she saw a lady standing before the fireplace, staring down onto a fireless grate with her back to Judith. The lady was dressed expensively, in a satin dress, with a fully gathered, billowing skirt and long sleeves.

But it was the gold of her waist-length hair that drew Judith's attention. Judith recognized the hair, the fragile shape of the lady. Was it . . . ? But it couldn't be North Star. Why would she be here, in the McMahon ranch house?

Rory stepped away from Judith and began walking toward North Star. "North Star, Judith has returned," he said, going to North Star to take her hand in his, to guide her fully around to face Judith.

Judith felt her knees weaken, her heart flutter strangely, and her face become pale. "North Star?" she said, placing her hands to her cheeks in dismay. "It *is* you."

"Hello, Judith," North Star said, her copper face lovely with its dainty features. "It's so good to have you home again. We've been so worried about you, haven't we, Rory?"

"*We've* been worried?" Judith said in a near whisper, taking a step closer. "North Star, I have to ask, why were you concerned, along with my brother? Why are you here?"

Rory lifted North Star's left hand and showed off a gold wedding band. "This is the reason," he said hoarsely. "Sis, you are now in the presence of my wife."

Judith once more gasped. "Married?" she said, breathless, remembering Red Bear and his hopes and dreams of a future with North Star. If this wasn't possible, would he forget his peaceful intentions and once more war with Strong Hawk and his people?

Had North Star forgotten all her feelings for Red Bear? So much depended on their marriage. Now it was something that could never be. And Rory? Married? And to North Star, a woman who was part Indian, when he had scoffed about Judith's own feelings for an Indian? What had happened to change his mind? Oh! None of this made any sense whatsoever!

Judith went to stand before Rory and North Star. "When did this take place?" she asked dryly. "Rory, you hadn't even met North Star before I left. You haven't ever talked favorably of marriage." She shook her head, placing her fingertips to her temple. "Please forgive me, but you must understand my shock. This has happened so quickly."

Rory drew Judith into his arms. "Ah, sis, I shouldn't have broken the news to you in such a way," he said, hugging her to him. "I should have waited at least until you were rested from the trip."

Judith eased out of his arms and looked from North Star to Rory. "But married? So soon?" she asked, still thinking about all that Red Bear had said. Surely North Star couldn't forget such a love so quickly.

"I couldn't see any reason to postpone the inevitable," Rory chuckled, placing his arm about North Star's waist. Judith saw North Star tense at his gesture of ownership. Judith wondered about that. Newlyweds were thought never to get enough of each other, if true love was the reason for the marriage.

"Giles approved," Rory continued to say. "He even gave North Star away at the wedding."

"Giles?" Judith said, now remembering things other than her worries of Red Bear and what his discovery of this marriage could mean to the Chippewa. She hadn't even thought to be happy for her brother, seeing how pleased he was with himself at his victory, having won a woman, to be his wife. But Judith's thoughts were still with Strong Hawk and her undying loyalty to him. Strong Hawk's future was hers.

"Yes. Giles," Rory said, breaking away from both women to go to the liquor cabinet. He withdrew three tall-stemmed crystal glasses and a bottle of vintage champagne. "We have many reasons to celebrate, sis."

"Celebrate?" Judith said, taking small steps toward him. "Oh, you mean your marriage? My coming home?"

"And the merging of two companies," Rory said, his eyes twinkling almost as much as the champagne that he poured into the three glasses.

Judith accepted the glass into her trembling fingers, stunned almost numb by this added piece of news. "Merging of two companies?" she said weakly. "Whose? What are you talking about, Rory?"

Rory went to North Star and gave her a glass of champagne. Then he swung around and faced Judith. "Giles and I came to a mutual agreement," he said, taking a sip of his champagne, watching Judith over the rim of his glass.

Once more Judith felt the color draining from her face. Her fingers clutched more tightly to the stem of the glass, hardly believing anything that was transpiring here. In her absence, all of this had happened? Unbelievable!

"You and Giles?" she said in a near whisper. "What are you saying, Rory?"

"There is no reason to rival Giles's company any longer," Rory chuckled. "We've merged. We're one company now."

Judith's head was spinning at the added news. "Merged? Rory, how did you?" she gasped.

Rory placed his glass on a table and went to Judith,

taking her free hand in his. "Sis, don't you see? That was the answer we were seeking," he said. "There is no need for our loggers to move north, to the land by the St. Croix River. Between both our companies, we now have enough trees here in this area to work for several more years. Don't you see? Don't you agree?"

"But, Father?" she whispered. "Would he have approved?"

"Strangely enough, yes," Rory said, shrugging. He took his glass and refilled it and settled down onto a chair as North Star eased down onto the sofa opposite him. Judith followed their lead, sitting down beside North Star.

"What do you mean, Rory? How would you know how Father would react to this decision of yours?"

"While pouring over Father's ledgers in your absence, I found notes referring to Giles and a possible merger, if worse came to worst," Rory said matter-of-factly. "It's all in black and white for you to see, should you feel the need."

"But he hated any rival company," Judith said, glancing cautiously over at North Star, not wanting to offend her new sister-in-law, though that title, "sister-in-law," was still so hard for Judith to accept as reality.

"Yes. But to save his neck, Father was ready to do anything," Rory said, once more sipping on his champagne. "First he was going to try to settle things with the Chippewa, and if that didn't work he was going to do the next-best thing. He was going to go to the Chippewa who had turned white. He was going to wheel and deal with Giles."

Judith gave North Star another quick glance,

seeing how North Star's eyes were suddenly aflame with quelled anger. Rory hadn't yet learned, it seemed, to watch his reference to the Indians. Judith could see stormy waters ahead, should he not change.

Judith directed her attention back to Rory. "And Giles accepted? So easily?" she murmured, setting her half-emptied glass down on a table.

"I think the merger of families made his decision for him," Rory chuckled, seeming pleased with himself.

Judith tensed. Surely Rory hadn't used North Star and Giles to serve his own purposes. No. Her brother wasn't the type. Or was he? Judith had grown away from Rory these past years, after he had chosen to go his separate way from the family. Could he be devious?

"So Giles didn't agree until after the marriage?" she quietly tested.

"The very day. After the ceremony," Rory said, rising to go to North Star to urge her up next to him. He kissed her softly on the lips. "I've got the prettiest wife in these parts, don't I, Judith?" he said hoarsely. He traced North Star's features with his finger. "My little half-breed married to her own half-breed."

Judith's insides splashed cold, hearing her brother referring to himself as a half-breed. But, yes, he would have to be plagued by his past, the past that he now knew about. His father was Mexican. His mother was white. Had that made the marriage to North Star easier? Did he feel that they had more to share than names? Than companies? Was it their pasts? Yes, they had been born into the world of parents who had each been of different cultures. It gave them a camaraderie of sorts.

"I'm going to take North Star back to her roots,"
Rory continued. "She has never seen her aunt's house
in St. Paul. Strange, isn't it, that it now is to be her
home, after all these years? Her mother, Amanda, had
even made her residence there with her Aunt Rettie
after the death of her parents. Yes, North Star will be
returning to her true heritage."

"How soon do you plan to leave, to return to
St. Paul?" Judith cautiously asked, hoping that it
would be soon. She felt the need for North Star to put
many miles between her and Duluth should Red Bear
come for her. When Red Bear found out that she was
married, oh, what could be expected to happen? The
thought made spirals of fear course through her
veins.

"Now that you're home safe, North Star and I can
leave this very day," Rory said.

"The business, Rory?" Judith tested.

"Giles is going to take charge. He's going to run
them both. The problem is no longer yours, sis."

"It seems too easy, Rory," Judith said, rising,
pacing.

Rory went to her and grabbed her by her arm. "You
should be happy that it's finally settled," he growled.
"God, Sis, what more do you want of me? I've left my
business to God knows what. I've stayed here until
your return. Did you expect me to take full control of
things myself when you knew that I wanted to be in
St. Paul, with my law practice?"

Judith flinched, hearing the anger in his words. It
was obvious that he was still hurting inside from all
that their father's death had revealed to him. This

marriage with North Star could, perhaps, be the answer to his sadness, if he gave it a chance.

Yet, if he knew about Red Bear and the relationship between North Star and the Sioux, what would his feelings be then?

"I'm sorry, Rory," she murmured. "Yes. I'm glad that you have things settled." She glanced over at North Star. "And, yes, I believe that you should take North Star with you to St. Paul. And soon. It's time that you and your wife have time all to yourselves to get your house in order, as man and wife."

"Then you understand, sis?"

"Yes. And I appreciate what you've done to clear things up for me here," she said, hugging him. "I'm sorry if I caused you even one moment of grief."

She paused, then said, "When are you leaving, Rory? When are you going to St. Paul?"

Rory's eyebrows forked. "Hey, what is this?" he teased. "I get the distinct impression that you're trying to get rid of me."

Judith's face flushed. She looked away from him, getting a glimpse of North Star out of the corner of her eye, knowing that North Star would always be a reminder of, oh, so much. . . .

"No. It's nothing like that," she said, moving away from him, toying with a ceramic statue on the fireplace mantel.

"Then, sis, don't act so anxious," Rory said, laughing nervously.

A loud knock on the front door caused a hush in the parlor. Everyone exchanged looks, then Rory went to the door and opened it. He offered a handshake to Giles, who was standing there.

"Come on in, partner," he laughed teasingly. "I've got someone to show you. Judith. She's finally returned. There will be no need for a posse."

Giles, in an impeccably tailored suit and with neatly combed hair, stepped into the house, briefly shaking Rory's hand. Then he walked away from him and toward North Star, seemingly ignoring the reference to Judith, apparently with only concern for North Star on his mind. He looked down at North Star with heavy lashes. He took her hands in his and squeezed them.

"Hon, I've something to tell you," he said, avoiding looks of dismay from both Judith and Rory.

North Star blinked her eyes nervously, seeing the troubled expression etched onto Giles's handsome face. "What is it?" she asked, already feeling her stronger heartbeats, knowing that the news wasn't good. "What news have you brought to me? What has happened?"

"It's Aunt Rettie," Giles said, lowering his eyes. "She is no longer with the living. She took her last breaths of life a short while ago, North Star. Her heart had grown tired of beating."

North Star gasped. Her eyes flooded with tears. In a flash she was in Giles's arms, sobbing. "No . . ." she softly cried.

"*Ay-uh*," Giles said, caressing her back. "It is so. You are needed, North Star. The family awaits you."

Rory felt separated from his wife in a strange way, as though a wall had been suddenly placed between them. He went to North Star and eased her from Giles's embrace and drew her into his arms. He felt her tense. His insides grew cold, wondering why she would not—could not—accept his comforting. Yet he had felt the void between them at other times. He had begun to wonder if they could ever truly learn to love each other as a man and wife should. The marriage had been for all the wrong reasons, but he had hoped that, in time, they could learn to love each other.

But if that was not to be, he had, at least, saved the business for Judith by marrying North Star. If nothing else, he could return to St. Paul without that burden on his shoulders.

He watched as North Star went back into the arms of Giles. In her sorrow she had forgotten that she had a husband. And that wasn't the way of wives. Rory now fully doubted the worth of his marriage.

"Take me home, Giles," North Star softly cried. "Take me back to my family. We must be together. We must mourn as one."

Giles cast Rory a troubled glance. "North Star, what about Rory?" he whispered into her ear.

"Giles, please take me home," she whispered again. "My heart is full of pain. Please?"

Giles shook his head toward Rory, understanding what Rory must be going through. Giles had known for a long time of North Star's hidden feelings for Red Bear, but he had never let her know, for fear that she would have taken his knowing and ensuing silence as encouragement to pursue the subject of marriage to that Nadoues-Sioux! Had North Star married Rory for all the wrong reasons? Had she thought that marriage to the white man would make her forget the red man? It seemed to have proven wrong, or she would be taking comfort from her husband in her time of sadness.

"All right," Giles said. "Get your shawl. I will take you home."

Rory wanted to object, to tell North Star that *he* wanted to take her home—their home in St. Paul. But he kept his silence. Surely her grief was blinding her to what was real. He would give her time. But how much time would be required? Could a distant aunt's death truly cause such pain, such grief? Were there hidden reasons? Had she just needed something to hide behind so that she could cry? She had lain limp in his arms many times after making love. It had been as though she had been in mourning even then!

After North Star rushed from the room in a rustle of skirt and petticoats, Giles went to Rory and placed his hand firmly on his shoulder. "Come with Judith real soon. You are now part of the family," he said. "You must overlook North Star's behavior. At times like this, she has never been strong."

"I appreciate your explanation," Rory said hoarsely. "And, yes. We'll be there, to join in the mourning. Soon."

Judith eased up next to Rory, his pain suddenly hers, and she hated North Star for what she was doing. . . .

Chapter Twenty-Eight

The lights were dim in the parlor at the far end of which Rettie's open casket was being viewed. Danette had managed to find several sprays of bouquets with lily of the valley as the dominant flower and the room smelled strongly reminiscent of the perfume that Aunt Rettie had always worn.

Family mingled with neighbors in the spacious room. Everyone was talking in hushed tones of respect. Soft organ music drifted in from another parlor, where others stood, silently paying their respects.

Judith stood with Rory in this other parlor, both of them feeling like outsiders. North Star had seemed to have deserted her husband, and Strong Hawk had not yet arrived for the visitation rites.

Judith's heart went out to Rory, but he didn't seem all that disturbed by his wife's behavior. He seemed to be resigned to accept any and all traumas in his life with a backbone and nerves of steel. But Judith was wondering just how long Rory would continue to let his wife humiliate him, even if death seemed to be the cause.

The breeze from the front door's being opened drew Judith's eyes to the hallway. Her heart began to race when she saw the tall outline of Strong Hawk, dressed in his most sedate buckskin outfit. His headband was without its feather, his face etched with sadness.

Upon closer observation, Judith further noticed that something was wrong in the way Strong Hawk walked. His shoulders were not as powerfully squared as usual. She knew that it was not in Strong Hawk to let death make him appear weak. So what was the cause?

She ached to run to him, but remembered her place and the circumstances of his arrival. He would come to her when he felt it was right. Would he be surprised to find her there, in the Thomas mansion? What would his reaction be to the discovery that North Star was no longer free to marry Red Bear? Though Strong Hawk would never approve of North Star's marrying a Sioux—any Sioux—Judith knew that he felt that such a marriage would be good for his people.

For support, Judith worked her arm through the curve of Rory's and clung to him. She let her eyes follow Strong Hawk until he disappeared into the other parlor where Rettie lay. After some time passed, he once more came into view and walked into the parlor where Judith was. It was then that Judith's impulse to go to him almost made her forget the proper way in which this should be handled. She had to keep convincing herself that once he discovered her there he would come to her. He would want to be with her at such a time. Hadn't she been able to give him comfort after his father's death? Hadn't he comforted her as no one else could after her own father's death?

Breathlessly, she watched as Strong Hawk sank down into a chair and slowly began to scan the room with his eyes. When his gaze finally found her, Judith's insides froze at his reaction. It was nothing like what she would have expected from the man she was soon to marry! He was looking at her with a fierce hatred in the depths of his dark eyes. His face was even screwing up into a grimace so grotesque that she barely recognized his handsomeness at all.

Judith's temples pounded. Her thoughts screamed out why, over and over again. Her feet felt glued to the floor as he continued to glare at her with utter contempt, and then fixed Rory with the same look.

Judith took a step away from Rory, dropping her arm from his. "Strong Hawk?" she whispered, reaching out her hand toward him. "What's the . . . ?"

She didn't get to complete her question. Strong Hawk rose from the chair in a lunge and walked with brisk steps from the room, leaving Judith stunned, disbelieving what was happening. What had caused this change in him? What had she done to cause it?

Her lips trembling, she rushed after him, not caring when people began looking at her, silently scolding her for making the slightest bit of noise with the rustling of her feet. She sucked in her breath and ignored them, lifting the tail of her black crepe skirt up into her arms. She was now out in the hallway, and she saw Strong Hawk disappear into another

404

room at the far end.

Keeping her head half bowed, she worked her way through the traffic in the hallway, nothing stopping her now that she had begun this pursuit of the man she loved. She had to find out what was the matter with him, or the wondering would scramble her insides—she felt them already twisting and knotting from frustration.

The light from the rooms poured mutely out into the hallway, making a path for her to follow, and then she was finally there, outside the door that she had seen him enter.

Stopping, she tried to regain control of her senses and her thundering heartbeat. She took several deep breaths, brushed a stray lock of hair from her brow, then took the one quick, bold step required to lead her into the room. She found herself surrounded by walls of bound books and only Strong Hawk there, almost dwarfed by the many shelves that towered over him.

Inching her way into the room, which was dimly lighted by one lone gaslight on the wall, Judith trembled, almost afraid to question Strong Hawk.

Yet why should she be afraid? She had done nothing to warrant his callous behavior! If anyone was in the wrong, it was he. He had much to explain to her! He had many apologies to make.

With her jaw set and her head held high, her hair lying in golden streamers down her back, Judith made her presence known by clearing her throat. She watched Strong Hawk spin around on his heel to discover her there. His face still reflected disgust for her.

405

"Strong Hawk, what on earth is going on here?" she blurted. She rushed across the room and reached out her hand to touch his arm, but he flinched and drew it away from her as though she had shot him instead. She gasped and covered her mouth with her hand and took a step backwards, eyeing him incredulously.

"Strong Hawk" she once more said in a whisper.

"Go back to your lover," Strong Hawk growled, nodding toward the door. "You have some nerve coming and bringing him here to flaunt him in front of my family. How could you? You had to know that I was here. Was it because you decided not to keep him a secret any longer?"

Judith's thoughts began to be muddled. She couldn't understand what he was saying. She shook her head to clear herself of her confusion, but nothing would help. She looked blankly up into his eyes.

"What did you just say?" she asked, becoming pale. "Who are you talking about? What lover, Strong Hawk? Nothing you've just said makes any sense. None of it!"

"Don't you hold anything sacred? First you play with love. Then death? Who even asked you to come to my mother's house? Don't you feel that you are an intruder?" Strong Hawk accused, his face glaring down into hers, his teeth shining brightly back at her as he talked almost in a hiss.

Judith's mouth dropped open, her heart beginning to tear slowly apart. "Strong Hawk, this can't be you saying these things," she said with a soft sob. "You have no basis for anything that you are accusing me of. Please explain yourself!"

Strong Hawk waved his hand toward the door. "That man," he snarled. "In the parlor. The one you were hanging on to. I've seen you with him before. Each time I saw you, you were embracing. Do you love two men at once? Or am I the only one who is a fool?"

"The man in the parlor?" Judith gasped. Then she felt waves of relief washing her insides clean of hurt and wonder. Now she understood! And surely no one had yet taken the time yet to break the news to Strong Hawk of North Star's marriage to Rory. Perhaps the death of Rettie had made them forget to tell him. If they had, Strong Hawk's anger would have been dispelled long ago. He would now be shocked, hopefully relieved, to find that this man who was North Star's husband was Judith's brother. Judith saw her mistake in not having mentioned Rory before now to Strong Hawk. So much would have been spared the man she loved.

"*Ay-uh*, the man . . ." Strong Hawk grumbled. "He . . ."

Judith placed her forefinger over his lips, sealing them of further words. She smiled sweetly up at him, her lashes wetting with sudden splashes of tears from her eyes, now truly understanding why Strong Hawk had just treated her so miserably.

"Strong Hawk, that man is my brother, Rory," she said in a rush of words. "That man is not only my brother, but now he is also North Star's husband."

Strong Hawk jerked his head back, his eyes registering surprise and relief all in one. "Your brother?" he said thickly. "North Star's husband?

How can that be? Why wasn't I told?"

"I should have told you long ago that I had a brother," she said, lowering her lashes, flicking tears from them. "But I just never seemed to think about it, and when I did, we were not together at the time."

"And North Star? When? How? Why?"

"While I was away from Duluth this last time, my brother and North Star were married," Judith said cautiously, knowing that it wouldn't take long for Strong Hawk to think about Red Bear's words about the woman he loved and hoped to marry.

"But North Star had never spoken of him before."

"She hadn't met him before."

"They met and married so quickly?"

"*Ay-uh,* Strong Hawk."

Judith's way of saying yes in Chippewa brought a smile to Strong Hawk's lips. His face had a radiant glow in it, and his eyes were once more alive with love for her. He drew her roughly into his arms and kissed her long and hard, holding her so tightly to him she could barely breathe. But she welcomed this, having feared losing him when he had begun behaving so irrationally toward her. She had thought that perhaps he had never loved her at all, but only what her body could give him.

But now she knew that she was wrong and that she should never have doubted him. There had been misunderstandings building upon misunderstandings, and now everything appeared to be finally working out again.

Yet how could he have doubted her love for him so easily? Trust was a big part of love, was it not?

Strong Hawk eased his lips from hers and looked

down at her with his dark eyes, his face a mask of apology. "Will you forgive me, Judith?" he murmured. "Will you forget those moments that showed my insane jealousy of you?"

"I would—could never love another man," she said softly. "I had always thought you understood that, Strong Hawk. I have showed you in every way possible the depth of my love for you."

"*Ay-uh*. I know," he said, lowering his eyes.

"But, yes, I do forgive you," Judith whispered, slipping back into his gentle embrace, placing her cheek against his chest. "How could I not? Darling, you are my life. My very breath."

Once more he kissed her, but this time it was sweet and gentle. His lips quivered against hers, revealing the emotion he felt at the moment. His fingers laced through her hair, his heart pounding wildly against his ribs. But he quickly remembered his reason for being in his mother's house at this time and didn't want to bring shame to his family by acting like some crazed lover, so he released Judith and walked her toward the sofa and sat down with her.

"Now tell me about North Star's marriage to your brother," he said, once more frowning, as his worries were directed elsewhere. Red Bear. When Red Bear heard this news . . .

"Strong Hawk, I don't think it will last," Judith said, sad for her brother.

"Why then did they marry?"

"I believe for all the wrong reasons," Judith said, toying with the folds of her skirt.

"These reasons are?"

"I think North Star was lonely. She needed

companionship. She doubted that she would ever be free to marry Red Bear, so when Rory asked her she looked to him as an escape of sorts.''

"And your brother?"

"Perhaps he did it for me," Judith said, feeling a blush rise to her cheeks.

"You?"

"It's a long story. And perhaps not such a pretty one to tell, if I am right," Judith murmured. "Let's just wait and see how things work out."

Strong Hawk pushed himself up from the sofa and began a slow pacing, kneading his brow. "I don't want ever to think that I had *wanted* North Star to wed Red Bear," he growled. "But I now feel that it would have been best for all concerned."

"You fear Red Bear's wrath once he finds out about North Star's marrying my brother?"

Strong Hawk swung around and boldly faced her, frowning. *"Gah-ween!"* he said scornfully. "No! I have told you many times that the Chippewa are stronger than the Sioux. But I wish for a peaceful coexistence now. My people have had a taste of peace and they welcome more of the same. I do not wish to have to paint my body with war paint. I do not wish to have to take scalps to prove my strength as chief. In peace, these things can be avoided. They are not necessary."

"So you do fear what Red Bear might do?"

"Fear? No. I just feel a deep despair."

Judith went to him and hugged him tightly to her. "This is a bad time for you to have to worry about such things," she sighed. "Your aunt lies in the other room. Your thoughts should be only of her."

"When one is chief, one's brain must be capable of being filled with many things at once. That is the way it is with me," he said, placing his nose into her hair, reveling in its sweet aroma. "I am glad to be able to push all bitter thoughts of you from my mind. I will be able to function better now that I have you back."

"Darling, you never lost me," Judith whispered, trembling as his fingers grazed the outline of her breast.

"In my heart and mind I had lost you," he said thickly.

Judith lifted her lips to his and softly kissed him, then drew away from him, idolizing him with the blue of her eyes. "Never again shall I give you the cause to feel that way," she murmured. "I am free now to travel with you back to your village, to become your wife, Strong Hawk."

Strong Hawk's pulse began to race. "You are free? So soon? You can return to my village as I return?" he asked hoarsely.

"Yes. Rory saw to everything while I was gone. The business is no longer any concern of mine."

"How did he manage that?"

Judith lowered her eyes and swallowed hard. "Giles. He made arrangements with Giles."

Strong Hawk's insides twisted. He lifted Judith's chin and directed her eyes upward. "Does any of this have to do with North Star?" he growled.

"Just perhaps," Judith said in a bare whisper.

"Your brother. Is he a devious man? Or is it in his blood to treat North Star fairly now that he has taken her as a wife?"

"It is she who seems not to be treating him fairly," Judith murmured. "So don't think so harshly about my brother. It is he who is paying the price, it seems, if he did marry her for all the wrong reasons."

The sound of soft footsteps behind them drew them around in unison. Danette moved into the room. She wore a fully gathered black crepe dress with twisted ribbing decoratively trimming the waist, the high collar, and the cuffs of her long sleeves. The dress rustled crisply as she came and placed her hands on Judith's and Strong Hawk's arms and smiled weakly up at them. Her auburn hair was drawn into a severe bun at the back of her head, and graying curls lay across her brow and at her ears. Her fair complexion revealed minute wrinkles crinkling the corners of her eyes and the sides of her mouth, although her waistline was still that of a twenty-year-old.

"My children, you mustn't stay hidden away like this," she murmured. She singled Strong Hawk out with a warm gaze. "Strong Hawk, so many people are asking about you. You know how rare it is for you to be in Duluth. Please go back into the parlor."

"*Gee-mah-mah*, this is no social function," Strong Hawk growled, frowning. "It isn't respectable for people to stand around visiting amongst one another while Aunt Rettie lies in her death sleep."

Then he cast Judith a half glance, knowing that he was the most disrespectful of the lot for having left the parlor in such a huff when he saw her and shortly afterward accusing her so unjustly.

"I know that it seems this way to you, Strong Hawk," Danette said, patting his hand. "The

412

Indians' way is much different. But you must accept this different custom of the white man. Go into the parlor, my son. I'm proud of you. I want everyone to see your handsomeness."

"They have Giles to look at," Strong Hawk grumbled. "Isn't that enough?"

Danette ran her hand over the smoothness of Strong Hawk's buckskin attire, her eyes clouding with memories. Gray Wolf. Oh, how she missed her husband.

"Giles is not you," she said. "There is only one Strong Hawk. Please do as your mother asks?"

Judith choked up as she watched Strong Hawk suddenly draw his mother into his arms and hug her tightly to him. "This son does not want to disappoint his *gee-mah-mah. Ay-uh*, I will return to the parlor as you request," he said hoarsely. "But first tell me. How are you doing? Have you decided where you will be living? With Aunt Rettie gone, you are free now to return to our village if you so choose. Your house could be built alongside mine and Judith's."

Danette stepped out of Strong Hawk's embrace, her blue eyes wide. "You and Judith?" she murmured. "Then you are . . .?"

"As soon as we return to my village we will become man and wife," Strong Hawk said, placing an arm about Judith's waist to pull her next to him. "She has proven her love for me in many ways. She will make a good chief's wife, just as you did, Mother."

Danette's cheeks flushed crimson, her hands clasped tightly together into the folds of her skirt. "I am so happy for you both," she sighed.

413

"And now, knowing this, that there will be another white woman in the village, will you choose to return also, Mother?" Strong Hawk asked, already missing her should she choose to stay behind.

"Perhaps later," Danette said, lowering her eyes. "Right now I would like to get used to living without Gray Wolf." She raised her eyes and smiled with affection toward Judith. "And I believe our Chippewa people should have the opportunity to get to know Judith better before my return. They will discover quite soon how wise a chief they have. Your choice of a wife so pleases me, my son."

"I am proud of my choice," Strong Hawk said firmly.

"Have you viewed Rettie's body together?" Danette asked softly, looking from Judith to Strong Hawk.

Judith tensed. She had taken the one look required of her. She had always found it hard to look upon a face that was waxen in death. She had even written a request and placed it with her lawyer that upon her own death the casket would remain closed. She wanted no one viewing her body after death. It didn't seem right, somehow, that one should be placed on display in such a way. She had listened too often to people standing over a casket, pointing out the faults of the corpse.

"Have we . . . together . . . ?" Strong Hawk said uncertainly. "No. We haven't."

"Then you must," Danette said, working her way in between them. She placed an arm about each and began guiding them from the room, down the crowded hallway and into the dimly lighted parlor.

414

Judith's knees weakened and her throat grew dry as she was forced to stand over the casket. She was suffused by the scent of lily of the valley cologne and the aroma of the real flowers that lay like miniature bells among red roses on the closed half of the casket.

With wavering eyes she took her last look at Rettie, seeing sparse gray hair circling a face that showed strength even in the frailty of death. At age one hundred, she looked as though she were content with all that she had experienced, for there was a trace of a smile on the narrow line of her lips.

"She appears to be at peace," Danette whispered. "I'll miss her. She became such a part of my life."

"Ay-uh . . ." Strong Hawk said, a knot swelling in his throat. Though Aunt Rettie had been swallowed up by old age since he could remember, not able even to converse much because of her lengthy naps, he had always been quite attached to her. Yes, her death would leave quite a void in all their lives.

"She seems only asleep," North Star said, edging her way in between Judith and Strong Hawk to place her arm about Strong Hawk's waist. "I feel such a loss. I should have visited her more often. But I guess I just let my life here in Duluth become too important."

Strong Hawk took this as the opportunity to speak to her of what now lay heavily on his mind, though this was not the place or the time. But when was?

"North Star, you appear pale," he said, touching her cheek. "Let us step out onto the porch and get a breath of fresh air, shall we?"

Judith's pulse raced, seeing through his ploy. She understood and wouldn't interfere.

"Yes. Let's," North Star murmured. She accepted Strong Hawk's hand at her elbow and smiled an "excuse me" over her shoulder at Judith and Danette, then lowered her eyes as she was led through the house and onto the porch.

In her lace-trimmed black silk dress, with a high collar at her delicate neck and long sleeves covering her arms, North Star still felt a chill as a breeze whipped around the corner of the house. Her waist-length hair lifted in gold billows from around her, and the skirt of her dress rose above the slim tapers of her ankles.

North Star hugged herself as she found a corner of sunshine at the far edge of the porch and let it warm her insides as she turned and looked up at Strong Hawk, who now stood, somber-faced, over her.

"Judith just told me of your marriage to her brother, Rory," he said. "Are you happy?"

The suddenness of the question took North Star by surprise. She flinched as though hit, then composed herself as she nervously cleared her throat. "And why shouldn't I be?" she shallowly asked.

Strong Hawk clasped her shoulders with a tight grip of his fingers. "North Star, I know about Red Bear," he grumbled.

"How?" North Star gasped, her eyes suddenly wild. "When?"

"Only recently did I find out about your feelings for the Sioux who is now chief of his people," Strong Hawk said, almost in a hush.

"I ask you again, *how?*"

"When I recently met with Red Bear and made peace with him."

416

"Peace? Between the Sioux and the Chippewa?"

"*Ay-uh . . .*"

North Star covered her mouth with her hand, suppressing a tortured sob. She spun around, hiding her reaction from Strong Hawk's watchful eyes. She had long ago given up the hope of ever being able to be with Red Bear as his wife. Their people had hated each other for way too long ever to live in peaceful coexistence. It had been easy for her to marry Rory, believing she would never be able to be with Red Bear. And now to find out that she had married in haste? It was too ironic even to be real.

"North Star?" Strong Hawk said, placing a hand to her shoulder. He urged her around to face him. "What I've just revealed to you. How is it to affect your life?"

North Star sniffled, her eyes cloudy with tears. "It will not at all," she said stubbornly. "By marrying Rory, I have made a commitment. I live up to my commitments. You know that."

"But you don't love Rory."

"I will stand behind my commitment, Strong Hawk."

"*Ay-uh.* You would," Strong Hawk murmured. He drew her into his arms and gave her a comforting hug.

"I am glad you've made peace with Red Bear," North Star murmured, her heart aching more by the minute.

"Do not be too glad too quickly . . ." Strong Hawk grumbled.

North Star inched out of his arms and studied his face, which revealed tensions he had not admitted to.

417

"Why do you say that?" she asked, once more holding the skirt of her dress down as the wind whipped at it.

Strong Hawk glanced quickly away from her, knowing he could never tell her that she was a part of this peace. He could already see her hurt and confusion over this untimely decision of hers to marry a man who did not have her heart.

"The Chippewa and the Sioux? Peace? Ha!" he scoffed. "Knowing their snakelike ways, even tomorrow they will cause our people problems."

"Red Bear is a man of his word," North Star said hotly, her face flaming with color. "You will see. Now that he is chief, he will not cause our people any hardships."

Strong Hawk's eyes twinkled, seeing how North Star defended the man she loved. It was good to see the fire return to her eyes, even if it was a hated Sioux that had caused the change in her.

"We shall see. . . ." he said, suppressing a chuckle. Then he once more grew somber, wondering just how Red Bear would react when he heard that he had lost his woman *ah-pah-nay, ay-uh,* forever. . . .

Chapter Twenty-Nine

The funeral had been brief. Afterwards the good-
byes of the family had been strained and lengthy.
Rory and North Star had boarded a train for St. Paul,
Judith and Strong Hawk had left on horsebck back to
the Chippewa village on Rice Lake. Danette had
stayed behind, once more mistress of the Thomas
mansion, achingly alone, except for her son Giles,
who in no way gave her comfort, except that he
carried all the burden of the Thomas Lumber
Company.

Judith and Strong Hawk pushed their way north,
anxious to begin their new life as man and wife. The
previous night they had shared a feast of venison by a
campfire. Soft words of love had been spoken
between them, and Strong Hawk had surprisingly
revealed to Judith that they had just become man and
wife, with no ceremony whatsoever required other
than what just shared.

"Strong Hawk, you are always full of surprises,"
Judith now laughed, easing her horse up next to his.

"Why didn't you tell me before of the simplicity of the marriage ceremony of the Chippewa? In truth, we could say we've already been married. Many times. We've performed the same ritual together so often. Why was it different this one time?"

"Because I said that it was so," Strong Hawk said, giving her a warm smile. "The timing had to be right."

"And it was?"

"*Ay-uh.*"

Judith lifted her shoulder in a soft shrug. "No matter," she laughed. "Just as long as I can say I am your wife."

She giggled and felt a flush suffuse her face. "I wouldn't want to live with you in sin, my love," she teased.

"Never," Strong Hawk chuckled. His gaze now roamed about him, seeing how the forest was darkening with night, soon to shadow everything in velvety blackness. One more night alone in the forest was required before arriving at his village. This was good. Once there he would become swept up into his full duties as chief, only having Judith to himself at night.

But, ah, the long hours of waiting to be with her would enhance the pleasure of their nights!

"We will make camp here," he said, gesturing toward a small clearing where pine needles made a blanket of rusty brown along the ground. Oak and maple trees were crowded by cedars and pines. Flowers of purple, gold, and crimson were signs of autumn's approach, and goldenrod and asters filled the widespread meadows.

Strong Hawk knew that it was the time of the Blueberry Moon, when the wild rice was rich and ripening. Before long, the wild rice celebration would fill his village with much happiness. Ah, when the Turning of Leaves Moon shone brightly over his village, there would be much for which to give thanks!

"It seems that my life has become unending travel," Judith laughed, swinging her leg over her saddle and dismounting. "I can't believe the many times I've traveled the forest and slept on the ground instead of a bed these past weeks."

Strong Hawk dismounted and took Judith's reins with his and secured both horses for the night. "There will be no more need for that after this night," he said. "Your new home will keep you there. That is what you wish, isn't it, Judith?"

"Yes," she said, stretching the tired soreness from her back. "But I will have to return to Duluth occasionally to check on things."

"Giles is seeing to everything. You will have no need to bother with it."

"Giles can never get the feeling that I will become blasé about my father's business, which is now mine and my brother's," she snapped. "Yes, I'm grateful that the merger has taken place between our two companies. But a merger it is. Nothing more. Giles can never be allowed to fool himself into believing it is wholly his."

Strong Hawk went to Judith and smoothed her hair from across her shoulders, letting it ripple through his fingers and down her back. "Place thoughts of Duluth behind you," he said hoarsely.

"Your life is with me now. You must not let anythin[g] interfere in what we have waited so long to share.

"But, Strong Hawk," Judith softly argued, but he[r] words left her with her breath as Strong Hawk swep[t] her fiercely into his arms and crushed his lips dow[n] upon hers. Her heart became filled with a wondrou[s] joy, her mind aswirl with passion once more ignited[.] She twined her arms about his neck and let him eas[e] her to the ground no longer caring that it was not [a] bed, for rapture could flare between them at any tim[e] anywhere.

Strong Hawk's hands glided over the sensuou[s] curves of her body, her jeans and shirt tight an[d] revealing. His fingers crept to where her thighs cam[e] together and began a slow caress there through th[e] coarse material of her jeans, the friction causing [a] low, guttural moan to rise from deep inside Judith[.]

She wove her fingers through his shoulder-lengt[h] hair, wriggling as his hands and lips continue[d] to make her become mindless. Waves of pleasur[e] flooded her senses. And when he unbuttoned he[r] jeans and lowered them over her hips, she remove[d] her shirt and melted as his tongue was quickly ther[e] claiming a breast in soft, wet flicks.

Breathless, Judith began working with his shirt[,] scooting her hands beneath it to ease it up from hi[s] chest.

"Strong Hawk, you must also undress," she said i[n] a voice that did not sound like her own. "I want t[o] feel your body against mine. I want you to fill m[e] with your hardness."

"My gentle Judith becomes a tigress out here in th[e] wild?" Strong Hawk teased, slipping his shirt ove[r] his head.

"*Ay-uh . . .*" Judith giggled.

Strong Hawk rose to his feet. "Then you remove my leggings," he said thickly. "And after you do, show me the skills that only you, my woman, possess."

Feeling drugged in her moment of need of him, Judith moved to her knees before him and reached her hands to the waistband of his leggings. She gasped throatily when his hands reached down and cupped each of her breasts and circled his thumbs about her thickened nipples. And when he freed them and placed his hands to his hips, watching her, she began lowering his leggings, an inch at a time.

Leaning up, she kissed the flesh of his abdomen, flicking her tongue into his navel until she felt his sensual quiverings and could hear the increase in his breathing. She then proceeded in lowering his leggings even more, now revealing his throbbing, ready hardness.

Judith lowered her lips to this part of his anatomy, almost drowning in heartbeats in anticipation of this unforbidden fruit that she was to taste. Barely grazing the tip of his manhood with her lips, she felt the intoxication of the moment deepening, and his hands in her hair, guiding her mouth even closer, made her knees grow weak and her heart become even wilder in its beats. Remembering the pleasure he had given her in this way, Judith forgot all her inhibitions and returned the pleasure, splaying her hands against his hips, closing her eyes to the rapture once more weaving between them. She kissed him.

She let her tongue discover all of him. And then suddenly this wasn't enough for him. He stepped completely out of his leggings and lifted her up next to him.

Judith pressed her breasts into the copper sheen of his chest. He gyrated his hips, causing his manhood to tease her flesh. And then he lifted her from the ground.

"Place your legs about my waist," he said huskily.

"Yes," she said, drunk with ecstasy.

And as she did so, he skillfully entered her and held her in place as his hands dug into the flesh of her hips. In even strokes he began to give to and draw pleasure from her. She laced her arms about his neck. He gave her a look of rapture, then kissed her long and hard, all the while thrusting . . . thrusting. . . .

Their bodies began quaking, their sensual moans filled the air, sending echoes through the forest. And then it was over and their bodies became quiet, yet still fused.

Judith rested her flushed cheek against his solid chest. "Will it always be as beautiful?" she whispered, breathless still. "You take my mind momentarily from me, you know."

"Our love is strong. It will always be beautiful. Just let us never doubt each other again."

"I shan't."

"Nor shall I."

Strong Hawk gave her a soft kiss on her cheek, then placed her feet solidly on the ground. "We must make camp," he said. "You nor I are as familiar as we should be with this area. An animal might even now be stalking us for its evening meal."

Judith scooped her clothes up and dressed while Strong Hawk slipped into his clothes. "Perhaps even a Sioux could be a threat," she dared to say, looking guardedly toward Strong Hawk.

"Why would you say that, Judith?"

"Red Bear. What can we expect from him after he hears of North Star's marriage?"

"Only time will tell," Strong Hawk grumbled, now gathering firewood. "But that is something that I do not plan to lose sleep over. If Red Bear once more becomes a challenge, it is I who will accept the challenge, and be the victor."

"But . . . peace . . . ? You wanted peace."

"Hasn't man, since the beginning of time?"

"*Ay-uh . . .*"

"It is no different now than ever before."

"And if peace cannot be obtained?"

"Then there will be *war.*"

Judith shivered, feeling very, very far from civilization as she had always known it.

Shadows made by outdoor streetlights were playing along the ceiling above North Star's head. She watched them for a while, then looked toward the sleeping figure of her husband. Again this night he had fulfilled his manly needs without her reaping any benefit from the union of their bodies. North Star's thoughts were in the past, when she had shared such intimacies with Red Bear and had been swept away onto cloud after cloud of rapture.

Biting her lower lip, North Star hungered for the feelings that only Red Bear could give her. She longed to be with him, to be *his* wife. How was it that she had chained herself to a loveless marriage? Life was too short. She had to have more.

Slipping from the bed, North Star crept to the open bedroom window and stood in the soft breeze. The sheer curtains rippled and swayed, drifting against her long silk gown. Her fingers went to the soft swells of her breasts beneath her lacy bodice. She could remember Red Bear's lips kissing her nipples to hardness, his hands kneading and fondling her to a dreamy, euphoric state.

"It could be that way every night, now that peace has come to our peoples," she whispered. "We could make love; we could share laughter; we could share everything, now that peace has been made between the Sioux and Chippewa."

She spun around on her heel and stared at Rory, her heart anxious. He really wouldn't miss her. His love was not the sincere love a man should feel for a woman. She was fulfilling his needs. That was all. Any woman could fill such needs. There were many available, for a price.

"Well, my price is too high now, it seems," she whispered. "Or should I say the price I am paying is far too great. I shall not let another night pass without going in search of the man I love!"

Moving stealthily about the room, soundless in her delicate footsteps, North Star gathered together some bare necessities, dressed herself in a heavy riding skirt, blouse, and boots, then quietly left the room without another look at her husband.

Guided by soft waves of light from half-lighted gas wall sconces along the upstairs hallway, she went to

Rory's study and lighted a lamp on his desk. With trembling fingers, fearful, yet eager, she searched and found paper and pencil and wrote Rory a letter.

Rory, I tried. But my heart beckons me back to the forest, to live the life of an Indian. You see, my true roots are there, not here in the house that once housed my mother and Aunt Rettie. No matter that I have been given the white man's way of life; it is the life of the Indian that I have dreamed of and plan now to live. Rory, please understand that I must leave you, to go to the man who has full claim of my heart. I go to Chief Red Bear, the Sioux who I have loved for many moons. You wondered what man had taken my virginity from me. It was he, and it was done so because it was I who allowed it. So you see, Rory, it is he who has had claim on me, way before you and I sought each other out for all the wrong reasons.

Rory, I tried. But you and I were not meant to be together.

She signed her name, placed the letter spread out in a prominent place on Rory's desk, then stole quickly from the room and the house, understanding the dangers of the trail that stretched out between her and Red Bear's newly formed camp. But a strong steed, a rifle, and enough food and supplies, and she would make it, or die trying.

Rory crept from the bed and went to the window

and pulled the sheer curtain aside to watch North Star go to the stables. He had been expecting this and he wouldn't try to stop her. She had just begun to get into his blood—love was inevitable—but now he would have to battle such feelings. She had proven to him in many ways that she could never care for him. In her fitful dreams she had even cried out another man's name. Red Bear. An Indian. Probably a Chippewa, one she had probably known since childhood.

It tore his ego to shreds, realizing that he hadn't had the required skills to rid her of thoughts of an Indian lover. But be as that may, he was going to give her her freedom without a verbal battle. On the morrow, he would even draw up his own divorce papers. He would end this farce once and for all. And should she, for any reason, return, well . . .

Sulking, and in need of a drink, Rory lumbered to his study. His eyebrows raised when he saw a lamp alight on his desk. He then shrugged and went to his liquor cabinet and poured himself a shot of whiskey and gulped it and two more down in quick swallows.

And after a welcome numbness settled his insides, he went and flopped down onto the chair. As he leaned over his desk, a piece of paper caught his eyes.

"What the . . . ?" he said, reaching shaking fingers toward it. When he placed it closer to the light from the lamp he recognized North Star's handwriting.

"Don't tell me she thought at least enough of me to give me a reason why she's leaving," he grumbled, kneading his brow as he slowly began to read.

His hands circled into fists on the top of his desk the more he read, his eyes becoming hot with rage.

Then he crumpled the letter up into a tight ball and threw it angrily across the room.

"A Sioux," he snarled. "She's going to a damn Sioux. She chose a Sioux over me!"

A keen hatred burning his insides, he vowed never to look at another woman, no matter the cause for or benefit from doing so. He was reminded of the worthlessness of his mother.

Yet, there was Judith. She had proven that not all women were cheats. . . .

Chapter Thirty

The Turning of Leaves Moon month of September had arrived in the village of the Chippewa, bringing with it the snappy nights of the north country, which had painted the foliage of the hardwood trees a riot of color. Along the trail were arrayed the deep reds of the oaks, the gold of the birches, and the shady purples of the ash.

All wigwams had been readied for winter. Moss and cornstalks had been placed around the circular base of each, weighted down with large stones. A generous wood supply had been piled high against the great pines, and golden corn lay heaped in sunny spots in front of the wigwams. Before the snow began, the corn would be ground in long, hollowed logs with primitive grinding stones.

There was one exception in this village. At the very outskirts of the village, nestled cozily in the dense growth of pines and hemlocks, a great two-story house stood, with a fresh coat of white paint and neat black shutters at the windows. A stone fireplace stood at one end, puffing spirals of smoke.

Strong Hawk had kept his word and had built Judith a house to her liking. It was now even furnished with the comforts of her choosing, and she was content—snugly content.

The air pulsed with life, an almost insect hum, as the Chippewa worked together as one body, one heart, harvesting the wild rice that grew in abundance in the shallow inlets of Rice Lake.

Even Judith was in the midst of the activity. She was in a canoe with Strong Hawk. While he poled the canoe through the long green rice plants, Judith bent the kernels of rice over the canoe and knocked them off with a flail, a short wooden stick. Over and over again she sent the ripened kernels spilling into the canoe, until the floor of the canoe was covered with what appeared to be grain oats. And then Strong Hawk directed the canoe to shore, for the processing of the rice.

"The good berry will fill our people's stomachs on the cold days of winter as never before," Strong Hawk said proudly, watching the many canoes traveling to and from the tall, swaying rice stalks. "Wenebojo has blessed our people, Judith. We will celebrate our thanks this night with our *manomin* feast."

Dressed in her jeans and shirt, unable to shake her preference for such comfortable attire, Judith stepped from the canoe and helped Strong Hawk drag the canoe onto the banks of the river.

"Do you think Danette and Giles will come to part of the celebration?" she asked, panting as she continued to tug on the canoe. Her hair spilled in gold streamers across her shoulders, her face rosy

431

from the sun as well as the nippiness of the autumn breeze.

"*Ay-uh*," Strong Hawk said, nodding. "They will be here, shortly. By evening we will be sitting around a communal fire, our family together again, if only for a short time."

"I wish Rory—North Star—" Judith murmured, stepping back from the canoe, wiping her brow with the back of her hand.

Strong Hawk made one last yank, finally succeeding in beaching the canoe, heavy with rice, then wiped his sore hands on the sleekness of his buckskin leggings. "That is never to be," he grumbled. "North Star made her choice. She now resides with the Sioux. It was her right, to decide for herself what she wishes out of life. I am just sorry that your brother had to be involved in this, one way or the other."

"It would've been nice to have Rory and North Star married," Judith sighed. "Wouldn't that have made our family so complete, Strong Hawk?"

Strong Hawk went to Judith and drew her into his arms, looking warmly down into her eyes. "How can you say that?" he said hoarsely.

"Say what?"

"That having Rory and North Star married could make our family complete."

"You wouldn't have wanted it that way?"

"*Ay-uh*. I would want them together."

"Then what are you talking about?"

"Our family won't be complete until a child is a part of our family. Mine and yours, Judith."

Judith's eyes widened, her heart raced. Never had he spoken of children before. Nor had she. Strong

432

Hawk was so much a part of her life that she had all that she needed. No, she hadn't thought about a child, not until recently. She hadn't yet told Strong Hawk that she had suspicions of being with child. She had missed her monthly, but only once.

She pressed her cheek against his chest, hearing his heart beat serenely. "Child?" she murmured. "Strong Hawk, do you truly wish for a child?"

Strong Hawk's fingers wove through the silkiness of her hair. "It is the best of times to bring a child into the world of the Chippewa," he said softly. "There is peace, there is food, there is shelter. I see only happy times ahead. A son. I wish for a son to carry on this heritage of peace and love."

"And if I were to tell you that perhaps a child may be in the making?" Judith tested, expecting to be released, for him to look down at her in wonder. Instead, he tensed and held her more tightly against him. But it was the beat of his heart that spoke of his excitement to her as it now thudded wildly through his chest, transferring to her cheek.

"A child?" he said in a shallow voice. "A child is growing inside you?"

"Perhaps."

"You are not sure?"

"I will know soon."

Strong Hawk gently pushed her away from him, his dark eyes heavy with deep emotion. "You make me proud, my wife," he said. "A child will enhance our togetherness."

"*Ay-uh . . .*" Judith said, reaching her hand to the softness of his copper cheek.

Strong Hawk glanced away from Judith and to the

working women, then back to Judith. "You will do no more labor," he said flatly. "We must assure the safety of the child you may be carrying. I have seen too many squaws whose babies were born dead because of their activities while with child. This will not be allowed to happen with you."

"I am not a squaw," Judith reassured. "I am strong. Your worries are in vain."

Strong Hawk's face shadowed into a frown. "My mother was not a squaw, and she lost more than one child in childbirth," he said solemnly. "Surely she thought as you do. So you see, you must take all precautions. We must have a healthy child. If the child is a son, he will be the future leader of our people."

"I understand," Judith said, smiling warmly up at him. "And I promise to not do anything to jeopardize the pregnancy. I will know what's wrong and right. Please trust me, Strong Hawk, to use my own judgment. I'm not the type of person to just sit idly by and watch. I have pent-up energies, which must be used. It would be harder on me to become frustrated from watching and not doing."

She leaned into his embrace and gently hugged him. "Tell me that you understand," she softly begged. "Please, Strong Hawk?"

"I understand your fiery, restless nature," Strong Hawk sighed. "So I must understand how hard it would be for you to behave yourself."

Judith slipped from his arms and looked incredulously up at him. "Behave?" she said, laughing throatily. "Strong Hawk!"

"All right. So I chose the wrong word," he

chuckled. "But what I am trying to say is that, *ay-uh*, you may join in with the women's activities, but do so in moderation."

"Well, that's better," Judith giggled. She looked down at the canoe and at the grains of rice waiting to be spread out on dried birchbark sheets that lay only a few footsteps away.

Then she gave Strong Hawk a half glance. "Shall we?" she said, nodding toward the canoe.

"*Ay-uh* . . ." Strong Hawk chuckled.

Together they began scooping the kernels of rice from the canoe, until the canoe was empty and the green kernels were left thinly spread on the ground to dry for a short time, before being processed, Indianstyle.

Judith inhaled deeply. Strong Hawk had once said that nothing equalled the aroma of ricing camp, with the wood fires burning, the rice drying, and the dewy-fresh air drifting in from the lake; and he had been right. A contented feeling of well-being filled the camp. The first grain of the season had been offered for a blessing from the Great Spirit. The time to partake of the gift would come later that evening. Strong Hawk had told Judith that boiled with venison or with duck or rice hens, the rice was not only delicious, but nourishing.

"I want to help process the rice that is already dried," Judith said, eyeing the many large tubs resting over low fires built in pockets of rocks.

"The paddling is tiresome," Strong Hawk warned.

"I promised to be careful," Judith reassured him. "Now you go tend to your chiefly duties while I tend to womanly duties along with the rest of the women."

"It is time for me to see that the meat is being prepared for tonight's feast," Strong Hawk said, looking toward the large fire in the village.

A shudder coursed through Judith, remembering the animals being cooked whole over the fires the one other time that she was to partake in a Chippewa feast. "Strong Hawk, will the claws, teeth, and skins be removed from these?" she darked to ask.

"Would that please my wife?"

"*Ay-uh . . .*"

"Then it will be done."

"Thank you, Strong Hawk," Judith said, breathing a heavy sigh of relief.

He brushed a kiss against her lips, then hastened away from her. Judith rolled the legs of her jeans up above her ankles, revealing her flesh-toned moccasins with their fancy beadwork. Smiling a silent hello to the women already busy at work at the monstrous tubs, Judith picked up a wooden paddle and sank it down into the bed of green rice. With steady, constant movements she kept moving the paddle round and round, through the rice, keeping the rice from scorching.

As the green husks became heated and browned, Judith's arms began to ache and her eyes to burn from the acrid fumes that rose from the tub. But she had been told that with good, dry tamarack and birch wood to keep the fire burning steadily, the process didn't take long, for not much rice was parched at any one time.

When the husks began to smoke lightly and a popping sound here and there came from the

ndermost layer, the rice was ready for the next step.
he rice was then carried to a jigging tub, a wooden
arrel sawed in half to make it low and squat, sunk
nto the ground to keep it steady. After the rice was
llowed to cool a few minutes, a few scoops were
umped into the jigging tub.

Judith knew that she had come to the point in the
rocess when she could only watch. The women had
een taught the skills of jigging the rice since
hildhood. The ones chosen to do this special chore
f further preparing the rice were already dressed in
heir jigging moccasins made of the softest doeskin.
A new pair was made every year, carefully sewed dur-
ng the long winter nights. Wearing her jigging moc-
asins was one of the squaw's most important events
f the whole year.

Judith stood back in the soft splash of the autum
un and watched as a few women climbed into the
arrel and began to jig, a lively dance in triple
hythm, their feet landing in a sliding, rolling
notion against the rice.

After the jigging process was complete, Judith
oined in again, scooping the rice out of the tub into
andmade baskets of birchbark. The baskets were
ew, the bark smooth and white. Their top edges
vere laced with a light brown reed.

Judith hoisted a basket to her shoulder and
roceeded to a high spot in a clearing overlooking
he lake, where the gentle breeze stirred. She then
ook the basket from her shoulder and with a flip of
er wrists tossed the rice into the air, catching it
gain as it came down. Each time the rice was air-
orne, the breeze blew away some of the loose husks,

so that every time the rice landed in the basket there were more clean kernels and less and less chaff.

As Judith watched the other women do this sh repeated this procedure over and over again. An when she was done, a pound of wild rice lay in th bottom of the shallow birchbark basket, plump clean, uniform in size and color.

Strong Hawk had said that at this stage the rice wa prime. Excluding herself, Judith understood that th rice had been prepared by the masters of th wilderness! Proud of her own minute role in the day' proceedings, she began to carry her basket to place i among the many others. But a movement in th distance, two silhouettes against the horizon, caugh her attention.

Shielding her eyes from the sun with one hand, sh peered with more determination at these two figure on horseback who were poised, quite still on the pea of a hill, seemingly returning Judith's steady stare

Closer attention on Judith's part proved to her tha one rider was female and the other was male, both Indian. But then her eyes focused on the gold of th hair whipping in the breeze. There was only on Indian known to her with such hair, and that wa North Star. And should this be North Star, then he companion must be Chief Red Bear.

Judith became torn with feelings. She wasn't sur what her next move should be. Should she ignor North Star's presence, or should she go to her and invite her into the village? Not knowing North Star' reasons for being there made Judith hesitate in he decision. North Star could be observing the wild ric harvest with her Sioux husband for either of two

asons, or possibly even for both. They were either
ointly spying on the Chippewa, or North Star had
ome to watch, aching to be a part of the upcoming
anomin feast.

"Which is it?" Judith whispered. She knew that it
ould please Strong Hawk if North Star could be
resent at the feast, yet she knew that he would not
elcome Red Bear there, where only the Chippewa
aid homage to the Great Spirit who had blessed his
eople with the great abundance of wild rice.

"But I must go to North Star and welcome her. I
ust," Judith quickly decided. "It isn't right to cast
er from the family because she married a Sioux. I've
ven got to forget how she left my brother's bed to go
o Red Bear. Why can't I remember that Rory is
artially responsible for her doing that? He didn't
ove her at first. . . ."

Turning on her heel, Judith thrust her basket of
ice into the arms of a squaw, then broke into a run
oward the fenced-in horses at the edge of the village.
he chose Strong Hawk's black stallion for speed and
entleness, and hopped on it, to ride it bareback.
Directing it away from the fence, she snapped the
eins and galloped away from the village toward the
ise where she had seen the two lone figures.

Disappointment surged through her when she saw
o one. But she knew that they could not yet have
raveled far. And Judith had made up her mind as to
hat should be, and she was not going to back away
nly because she would have to put more effort into
his decision!

Riding into the wind, enjoying its briskness on her
ace, feeling her hair whipping up from her

shoulders, Judith couldn't deny that her decision to ride after North Star and Red Bear was, perhaps, a selfish one. She had often felt a need to come face-to-face with Red Bear again. She still felt the bond that had developed between them those hours that they had been together, and his friendship was suddenly important to her. It was an attraction unlike any Judith had felt before for a man and she silently thanked God that it was not a sensual, sexual one. It seemed to have been born of the ease she had felt talking with him, and trust, since he had had every opportunity to have her in every way a man desired of woman and had only touched her with his eyes. Somehow, she felt the need to reaffirm this strange camaraderie between them. And couldn't such a relationship even eventually help dissuade tensions from rising between Strong Hawk and Red Bear? The power of a woman, and her viewpoint could weigh heavily in matters, if a husband would so allow!

She reached the rise. She spun the stallion around, looking in all directions. Goldenrod gave the meadows the appearance of yellow velvet. The far mountains, now capped in white, were ghostly apparitions! The forest was a patchwork of color intermingled with the brilliant greens of the pine and cedar trees.

And then she saw the two on horseback as they moved into a clearing and across another flat stretch of meadow.

"Hahh!" Judith yelled to the stallion, thrusting her knees into the horse's ribs. "Show me your stuff, Thunder!"

Judith had only recently been given the privilege of naming Strong Hawk's horse, and he was now as much hers as her husband's.

Thunder rode like the wind now, his head held high, his strong legs lifting and falling against the grassy meadow flow. And then Judith felt close enough to those she gave chase to to yell at them.

She cupped a hand over her mouth. "Wait up!" she shouted. "North Star! Red Bear! Wait! It's me! Judith!"

Judith whispered a small prayer of thanks when she saw that her shouts had not fallen on deaf ears. She found herself now being watched by two sets of eyes and hoped and waited for smiles to follow, sighing heavily when she was afforded even this as she drew rein next to North Star.

Her chest heaving and perspiration lacing her brow, Judith looked from North Star to Red Bear, smiling warmly at each, now feeling foolish for ever having imagined that either of them could be suspected of spying. What purpose would that even serve? The Chippewa had staked their claim to the wild rice at Rice Lake, and the Sioux had now done the same for their own autumn harvest at Stone's Throw Lake, where the Sioux village now grew in leaps and bounds.

"North Star. Red Bear," Judith finally said, after catching her breath. "It's so good to see you."

Judith felt Red Bear's scrutiny of her and returned the gaze in a silent understanding, knowing that he knew that they could never speak openly as friends were wont to do. They would have to pretend to stay aloof, though both knew and felt the friendship that had become so unique between them.

She tore her eyes away and once more focused her full attention on North Star. "Have you come for the *manomin* ritual that is to be held tonight, North Star?" she murmured. "That would make Strong Hawk happy. You know how he feels about family."

"*Ay-uh*, I know that it would please Strong Hawk if I would be there," North Star said, lowering her eyes, still uncomfortable in Judith's presence because of the short marriage between herself and Judith's brother.

"Well, then? Are you?" Judith persisted, noticing something new about North Star's appearance now that she was taking a closer look. North Star's delicate features had blossomed somewhat, and her cheeks had filled out, and beneath the copper sheen of her gorgeous face could be seen a pleasant glow, which was also in her luminous, blue eyes.

Judith's gaze wandered lower. North Star's buckskin dress seemed drawn tightly at her bust. Then Judith's gaze traveled upward. Could North Star be pregnant? Would a child be born into the Sioux camp at almost the same time as in the Chippewa village should Judith be with child?

The thought pleased Judith, thinking these children would be special and perhaps even friends who could forever bind these two tribes of Indians in friendship. Should they be sons, they would both eventually even be the leaders of their people!

North Star raked her fingers nervously through her golden hair. "Strong Hawk would welcome me," she murmured. "But he would not let my husband participate, so I shall not either. Where I go, Red Bear also goes."

Judith knew not to speak for Strong Hawk in this matter, but she could feel free to make a suggestion, for herself. She reached for North Star's hand and gently held it. "North Star, why not come ahead with Red Bear," she encouraged. "I am sure Strong Hawk won't refuse you this night. It won't hurt to try."

"I just don't know," North Star murmured.

"Giles and Danette should be arriving sometime today," Judith further encouraged, then bit her lower lip, seeing Red Bear's scowl, as though he did not approve of her continued interference. Yet he did not speak his thoughts.

"When the full moon tips the trees white, I will make my decision," North Star said, slipping her hand from Judith's. "I do not want to cause a strain in Strong Hawk's village during a time set aside for laughter."

Judith looked over her shoulder and at the billows of smoke rising into the sky. "I must return to the ricing," she said. "Working alongside Strong Hawk's people makes me feel more a part of the Chippewa."

"Being a part of the Chippewa comes easy," North Star sighed. "They are a fine, generous people, filled with love." She gave Red Bear a sweet smile. "As are the Sioux, who have welcomed me as a part of their lives. It seems I am now truly of mixed heritages. I am part white, part Chippewa, and part Sioux."

"Yes. My woman makes me proud, she is so beautiful in her complexities," Red Bear chuckled. "She even blooms in her new environment of the Sioux."

"*Ay-uh,*" Judith said. "North Star does look

radiantly beautiful these days. But why shouldn't she? She has a husband who draws the loveliness from inside a woman because he is so kind and understanding.''

It seemed to Judith that Red Bear had caught the double meaning to her words, and they exchanged silent smiles of understanding. . . .

Chapter Thirty-One

Wood had been carried to the edge of Rice Lake and stacked in a high, teepee-shaped pile. An Indian brave sat beside a lone drum made of deerskin, scraped thin and tightly stretched around a wooden frame. The *manomin* ritual was about to begin.

Everyone in Strong Hawk's village was crowded along the lake, anxiously watching the sky that was already asparkle with teardrops of stars splashed along its black velvet backdrop. There was nary a sound. Even the loon, which usually bounced its song across the lake, seemed to be waiting for the first signs of the arrival of the *manomin-gissis* moon, in its perfect circle along the horizon.

The air hung heavy with pleasant smells rising from the many fires over which meats of all kinds dripped their succulent juices into the flames. Along long tables an assortment of food had been laid out, tempting sneaking dogs and playful children. Squaws still labored at turning spits and preparing even more food and tantalizing, exotic drinks, which

445

would be served once the celebration had truly begun and the moon was high overhead in its utter brilliance.

Judith sat on a blanket watching Strong Hawk who paced beside the piled wood, keeping his eye skyward. He was handsome in his white doeskin tunic and leggings, which were beautifully embroidered in beads and porcupine quills laid on in symbolic designs.

Judith was as dressed in an identically decorated doeskin dress and moccasins, and beads were woven into the sleek braids of her hair.

Beside Judith sat Danette, who was also dressed in her buckskin Indian attire. Her single black, gray-streaked braid was coiled atop her head.

Silver Fox—Giles—sat on the other side of Danette, nothing like Strong Hawk's double this evening. His short-cropped hair was the most distinctive difference between them. Also, he had chosen to wear simple, less ornamented, buckskin attire.

Something kept pulling Judith's eyes to the soft rise of land in the distance where she had met with North Star and Red Bear earlier in the day. Was North Star's devotion to her husband now so steadfast that she wouldn't come—or would her heart once more let her loyalty to the Chippewa guide her to them, to participate in the festival with them, on this very special night?

Judith hoped for the latter.

Her eyes were drawn quickly elsewhere. They were drawn to the sky. She felt Danette's hand slip over hers as the moon began to rise, casting pale golden light from the east over the tops of the pines. Th hush among the Indians was so keen, it seemed that death had come to this village and swept it clean of people. All eyes were on the sky. All hearts were filled with thanks for their wise Chief Strong Hawk and for the blessings of Wenebojo who had led him to this land of paradise.

Then Judith looked toward her husband, pride for him sparkling in her eyes. This would be the first time she would see him perform fully as chief before his people. It sent shivers of anticipation through her, anxious, though she had a lifetime ahead of her of witnessing his leadership. Her breath slowed and color suffused her cheeks when Strong Hawk began the *manomin* ritual.

Strong Hawk's heart began to thump wildly against his ribs, watching the golden light of the moon grow wider in the sky, now casting its reflection almost mystically into the still waters of Rice Lake. He was recalling the many other *manomin-gissis* moons of the past and how he had watched not only his father, Chief Gray Wolf, perform the rituals required of a chief, but also his grandfather, Chief Yellow Feather. Pride swelled inside him that he was now the one to carry on this tradition of his people. And he knew that he could perform as well as all the chiefs before him. He felt the blessing of Wenebojo in the peace that he felt, which seemed to reach clean into his soul.

With his arms outstretched to the rising ricing-moon, Strong Hawk began to chant. The drumbeat began behind him, softly at first, then rose in volume. Strong Hawk's chant continued. All the Indians joined in, their words unintelligible, the cadence

447

always the same ... *tum-tum-tum-tum, tum-tum-tum-tum.*

And when the moon showed its full face, Strong Hawk raised a hand and commanded complete silence from his people. There was an air of anxiety of the air as he was brought a lighted torch. The fire from the torch danced and played on his face as he stepped to the piled wood. Without any words, he tossed the torch into the wood and watched as the flames took hold.

When the reflection of the flames rose into the sky and blended with the shine of the moon, Strong Hawk let out a loud whoop and raised a doubled fist to the sky in victory.

"Mi-nah-wah-ni-gway-dahm! Ish-kway-mah-no-mi-ni-kang!" he shouted. *"Nin-mamoi-awe, Wene-bojo!"*

This was a signal for the rest of the Indians to once more join in. The drum began to boom boom, the furious accent on the first stroke. The men began dancing, bobbing up and down to the rhythm of the drum, their feet beating out the rhythm. Their bodies swayed to and fro, their arms tossed first right, then left as they shuffled about the fire.

Their chant filled the air with *"Hi-ya-ya-ya."* The clap-clap of the hands of the women kept time with the dancing men, who traveled round and round in a rising frenzy of excitement.

A sudden signal from Chief Strong Hawk, and the drum ceased to beat and the men to dance. Strong Hawk once more raised a hand to again command complete silence, then he spoke to his people.

"We are gathered here as one body, one heart, one

448

soul, to give thanks for our blessings," he shouted. "Never before has our people been so blessed! Never before has our people had so much to be thankful for. We have a new land, sufficient for the needs of each of you, my people. We shall not want for food or shelter. Our long winter nights will no longer be filled with the fear of the morrow. When our heads rest upon our blankets beside our firespaces for the night, we can dream pleasant dreams, not troubled ones."

He lowered his eyes and looked softly down at Judith. "We have been blessed with the presence of my wife, Judith," he added, smiling. "Not only her name evokes sweetness and gentleness; she is truly those things, and much, much more."

He reached a hand toward Judith, inviting her to him. "Come. Stand by my side. Let my people feast not only on food this night, but also on your beauty," he said, smiling.

A knot had formed in Judith's throat. She swallowed hard, even having to fight against tears that had swelled in her eyes. Her happiness was complete. With her eyes following the command of Strong Hawk's, she rose slowly to her feet and placed her trembling hand in his, swallowed whole by her intense joy and love of him.

Smiling an almost embarrassed smile, she stepped up next to him and welcomed his arm about her waist. She tremored inwardly when he drew next to her at his side so that their bodies met. A radiant glow seemed to reach out from her and touch the onlooking Indians, for her arrival at her husband's side was received with a burst of savage enthusiasm.

Judith's eyes widened in surprise. She gave Strong

449

Hawk a look of wonder, and received then a gentle kiss in answer to the silent question in her eyes.

"My woman, my wife, you are welcomed with much fervor by my people," Strong Hawk then whispered. "Do you remember the words in Chippewa that I taught you earlier today?"

His cheek was warm against hers as he chose to speak into her ear. "This is when I should say 'I thank you, my fellow tribesmen?'" she whispered back.

"*Ay-uh*. Now is the time. You see, we celebrate more than the ricing-moon this night. We welcome you, formally, into our village of Chippewa, as only the Chippewa know how."

"Strong Hawk, I didn't quite expect this. . . ." Judith gulped, feeling awkward.

"Do you remember the words, Judith?"

"*Ay-uh* . . ."

"Now is the time to prove to my people your willingness to become truly as one of them."

"Now . . . ?"

"*Ah-szhee-gway*. Now."

He urged her around, to face his people, who now had grown stone quiet, watching, waiting.

Judith cleared her throat and squared her shoulders, wishing her heart would be still! Her tongue felt so thick from fear, she wasn't even sure if she had the ability to speak. But speak she must. Strong Hawk and his people were waiting. Much seemed to weigh on her proving herself to them all, even possibly to her own husband.

Judith looked down at Danette, seeing tears in Danette's eyes and a soft smile directed her way.

When Danette nodded, Judith understood that Danette, too, had been tested in such a way, and knowing this seemed to make the chore easier.

Strong Hawk tightened his hold about Judith's waist, transferring his confidence to her. She licked her dry lips, then braved remembering what Strong Hawk had taught her.

"Nin-mamoi-awe, nind-awema!" she said, with emphasis on the words "fellow tribesmen."

Her declaration was met with a quick burst of applause and chants and the resumed pulsating of the drum. And to Judith's surprise, the head of each household approached her, one by one, moving slowly and with great and solemn dignity, each placing hands on her shoulders.

"You are now my tribeswoman," each one said. "I pledge you my everlasting devotion and friendship."

This was followed by lips being pressed to one of Judith's cheeks and then the other, until all had given their approval in this way, astounding Judith, leaving her breathless.

"We shall now share in a feast of feasts!" Strong Hawk shouted. Then his eyes narrowed as a sudden hush fell over his people as they stepped aside to reveal some newcomers to the celebration. Strong Hawk circled his hand into a fist at his side and glared at Red Bear as Red Bear escorted North Star through the silent Indians.

Judith's heart skipped a beat as she felt Strong Hawk's arm tense around her and then slip away from her, to fold his arms across his chest. She let her gaze travel from North Star to Red Bear. They had left their horses behind and were now on foot, dressed neatly in buckskin for what had been a festive occasion before their arrival. Now Judith didn't know what to expect.

Red Bear guided North Star onward until they were standing before Strong Hawk. Red Bear's dark eyes were void of emotion, his face a mask devoid of expression.

"*Weh-go-men-dush-wi-szhis-chee-gay-yen?*" Strong Hawk growled, directing his full attention to Red Bear. "You enter the village of the Chippewa? Do you not see that you have interrupted the *manomin* festivities?"

Strong Hawk dared not look at North Star for fear of seeing the hurt in her eyes. But it was enough to have to get used to being acquainted by way of marriage to the Nadoues-Sioux, let alone have to share him in other ways with North Star.

And Strong Hawk didn't want his people to be forced to be polite to the Sioux, when in truth they most still surely looked to him as their enemy! Didn't their strained silence and the drawn, cold looks on their faces prove this?

"It was in my woman's heart to join her people this night," Red Bear said dryly. "But she would not come alone. To please her, I accompanied her here. I have come in peace, Strong Hawk. Or do you forget that we have already shaken hands in friendship for the sake of our peoples?"

"*Gah-ween,*" Strong Hawk grumbled. "No. I do not forget such words, which could mean whether or not survival is assured for our people."

"But still you lock your arms in stubbornness across your chest?" Red Bear said scornfully. "Your

452

eyes are still shadowed with hate when you stand face-to-face with me?"

"Your entrance into my village at any time would in the past stir my braves to arming themselves," Strong Hawk growled. "You are lucky they did not this time. Their trust in you wears thin. Even I still am filled with doubts. So how must I react when you so boldly arrive, unannounced?"

"You must have faith, Strong Hawk," Red Bear said, raising a hand, offering another handshake of friendship. "If not for me, for North Star?"

Strong Hawk let his gaze move slowly to North Star, seeing the radiant beauty in the glow of her copper face and the golden shine of her hair as it lay across her shoulders. The fire's shine showed the clear blue of her eyes and the pleading in them. He had always found it hard to deny her anything, and now was no different.

Unfolding his arms, Strong Hawk slowly lowered a hand to where Red Bear's stiffly waited. "For our people," he said, not wanting to appear weak in Red Bear's eyes by letting the Sioux see that his decision had been swayed by the persuasion of a woman, though this woman was his *gee-dah-way-mah*—his cousin. "You are welcome to join my people in the further festivities. A feast of all feasts has been prepared. It would please me if you would sit with me, along with the rest of my and North Star's family."

Strong Hawk clasped his hand into Red Bear's and gave it an eager shake. Then he motioned Red Bear and North Star to his left side and raised his hand, an indication that he once more had a need to speak

453

to his people before partaking with them in the prepared food.

"My people," he said in his authoritative voice, "Please welcome North Star and her husband, Chief Red Bear. My people, let us celebrate for even one more reason this night. Let us celebrate the warm touch of peace. The Sioux and the Chippewa will from here on out coexist without bloodshed, hate, mistrust. Show your joy in the knowledge of this. Share with the Sioux this night! The rewards of a bright future will be awarded you for your kindness and understanding!"

Silence rippled through the Indians as they pondered this latest request of their new chief. Then one by one, low grunts of *ay-uh* were heard from all the men, and it was confirmed that they were willing to at least give this new chief of the Sioux a chance to prove that his words and actions were spoken from the heart.

Strong Hawk would have wished for a more hardy response from his people, but understood their hesitation and so accepted what they had given him back in trust. He forced a laugh, to lighten the mood of his people, hoping to see merriment once more etched across their now somber faces.

"Let me hear the drum!" he shouted, flailing his arm into the air. "Let me hear songs! My people, let's fill the air with that never witnessed before by the *manomin-gissis* moon or the sequined stars! *Bah-pin! Nah-gah-mun! Wee-si-nin!*"

The night was once more filled with a frenzy of drumbeats and dancing, bringing a pleased smile to Strong Hawk's face. He curved his arm about

454

Judith's waist and gestured with his free hand toward Red Bear. "Let us join my mother and brother by the fire," he said. "We shall fill our stomachs now that our hearts are warmed."

Danette rose to her feet to meet Judith's approach and gave her a tender hug, then did the same to North Star and welcomed Red Bear. They all settled down on blankets about the fire. Soon birchbark platters and wooden bowls of food were passed around. Each was heaped with rice, all sorts of meat, fish, parched corn, and bowls of crunched maple sugar. There were strips of pumpkin and pumpkin seeds, which had been spread out to dry in the sun and were now nutty-flavored dainties that were considered special treats to the Indian children. And then the drinks were served, in tin cups; they had been made by adding wild cherry twigs to water. And now the feast was well underway.

Later, Strong Hawk patted his full stomach. He leaned over to speak to Red Bear, around Judith. "Ah. And will your *manomin* feast be as great?" he bragged.

"And why shouldn't it be?" Red Bear challenged. "Our rice plants bend with much weight. Yes. We can expect to have as great a feast."

Red Bear paused, placing his empty wooden bowl on the ground before him. "And will you and your wife be guests in the Sioux village for the celebration?" he asked, forcing a smile.

Strong Hawk was taken aback, not expecting this so soon from the Sioux. He accepted his colorful, long-stemmed pipe as a young boy brought it to him already prepared with tobacco. He contemplated his answer as he lit the pipe with a burning twig, all the while studying Red Bear out of the corner of his eye.

"Well? What is your answer to be?" Red Bear persisted. "My village? You will come? You will show my people that peace is a reality?"

Drawing deeply on the stem of his pipe, letting smoke curl from the corners of his mouth, Strong Hawk nodded, then offered the pipe to Red Bear.

"*Ay-uh*," Strong Hawk said hoarsely. "My wife and I will come. Now let's talk no more and enjoy the pipe of peace."

Red Bear accepted the pipe and placed it between his lips.

Stuffed to the brim, Judith clung to Strong Hawk as they walked beside the lake, bathed in the lingering moonlight.

"It couldn't have turned out any better had it been planned," Strong Hawk chuckled.

"What couldn't?" Judith asked, her eyes following his perfect Indian profile in the moonlight.

"This thing that has happened with Red Bear."

"Oh. You mean having become friends."

Strong Hawk once more chuckled. "Friends? Never friends nor allies. But peace. That is something between us much more important than the word friend. Peace is for my people as a whole. Friendship could not be felt as deeply as a group as peace is felt. It touches everybody's lives. It is to be nurtured. I must see to it that nothing interferes with this newly found peace with the Sioux."

"And nothing will," Judith sighed, leaning more

into his embrace. "And isn't everything just perfect? I've never been happier, Strong Hawk. And you? How are you feeling?"

"Content," he said hoarsely. "I'm warm with contentment."

"There is only one thing missing," Judith openly pouted.

Strong Hawk swung her around to face him, his smile erased by her words. "Nothing is missing in our lives," he growled. "Even a child is possibly growing in your womb. What did you mean by saying that?"

Judith eased past his arms and fit her body into the muscled strength of his. She stood on tiptoe and brushed a gentle kiss against his lips. "Do not worry so," she teased. "What I am missing is a kiss. It has been hours, Strong Hawk, since you kissed me. I think I shall die if you deny me that for even one more second."

Strong Hawk's eyes took on a haunting gleam as he framed her face between his hands. "My beautiful wife," he said huskily. "How could I ever deny you anything?"

"Then do it, silly," she sighed, moving her lips to his. "Kiss me. The seconds are turnng into minutes." She let out a throaty gurgle of pleasure when he placed his hands at the back of her head and forced her lips hard into his.

Strong Hawk felt the heat rise in his loins, already stimulated by the pleasures of the full night's gaiety, companionship, food, and drink. He lowered his hands to her buttocks and drew her into his risen sex and began a sensual movement against her.

Judith's fingers locked around his neck. She lifted a leg about him, savoring his male hardness against her abdomen. She accepted the softness of his tongue as it probed between her lips and trembled as it explored inside her mouth.

Her hands went wild with need of him. She let them travel across the tightness of his back through his shirt and then crept them up inside his shirt and enjoyed the smoothness of his flesh. Then her fingers began a trail following the path of the waist of his breeches and lowered them to envelop the throbbing hardness of him through the sleekness of the material. She rubbed. He moaned. She welcomed his hands, which now were on her breasts, caressing them through the softness of her dress.

He drew his lips away from hers. "Let us make love beneath the stars," he said huskily. "Now. Beside the lake that has been so good to my people."

Judith glanced back over her shoulder at the fires that were still burning in the many outdoor fire-spaces. "We will be seen," she whispered. "Your people are not that far away. And the moon. It is like many lanterns lighted over us."

She turned her gaze back to Strong Hawk and placed a hand to his cheek. "Have you no shame, Strong Hawk?" she teased.

"Danger enhances pleasure," Strong Hawk chuckled, already reaching to release the beads braided into her hair.

A cool breeze whipped across the lake, settling on Judith's bare arms and face. "We'll freeze," she softly argued.

"I will fully warm you," Strong Hawk argued back, his fingers loosening the braids, now tossing the beads aside, into the lake.

"But, Strong Hawk . . ." Judith sighed.

"Hush, my woman," Strong Hawk growled, already slipping her dress over her head. "I know what is best for you."

Judith laughed softly, tremoring as she now stood perfectly nude beneath the eyes of the winking stars and the bold white face of the moon. "All right, my love," she whispered. "Your turn. Let's see if you are brave enough to also bare yourself for the world to see."

"That will not be an impossible feat," he chuckled. "You are my world, Judith."

He quickly removed his fancy attire and his moccasins and soon stood before her naked, his magnificent body shining in the moon's glow.

"You are so beautiful," Judith sighed, splaying her hands against his chest. "So absolutely beautiful."

Strong Hawk covered her hands with his. "A man is not beautiful. Only a woman is," he said huskily, urging her down to the ground to lie on their layers of discarded clothing. "And no other woman is as beautiful as you."

Accepting the softness of doeskin against her back, Judith stretched out and indeed welcomed the warmth of him as he spread himself over her. Once more her fingers traveled over his lean, sinewy body. She could feel his animal heat as he coiled his arms about her and drew her fully into his embrace. Shimmers of desire soared across her flesh. He stole her breath as his lips possessed her in a blaze of urgency, while his hand stroked the silken curves of her thighs and moved to the most sensitive pleasure point she possessed.

Judith flowered herself open to him and became lost in a gentle passion as his fingers became the artist, she the canvas.

His kiss lengthened; her ecstasy mounted. Her arms twined about his neck and she caressed his skin lightly with her fingertips.

A tremerous sigh broke free from inside her as Strong Hawk lowered his lips to fully capture her breast. Judith's heart seemed to be melting, her brain a fuzzy mass of euphoria.

And then he entered her, filling her magnificently with his hardness, and began his movements inside her. She clung. She sighed. Her hips lifted to draw him even more fully into her. The friction of his movements was making the curl of heat spread inside her. She dug her fingers into his shoulders. He burrowed his nose into the soft curve of her neck, and thick, husky moans emitted from him as the fire inside him exploded into a blinding sensation of rapture.

Judith felt his quiverings, and this sparked her own release. She responded, in her own momentary state of bliss, letting a soft cry of joy escape her lips as he once more kissed her with fervor.

Then Strong Hawk nuzzled her neck as they still lay in their intimate embrace, at this moment one person, fused in every meaningful way.

"Gee-mee-nwayn-dum?" he whispered, his hot breath against her neck sending a sensual thrill through Judith.

"Ay-uh. I am happy," she whispered back.

Strong Hawk eased away from her, chuckling. "My woman learns more words in Chippewa," he said.

"How could I not know the word happy, Strong Hawk, when I'm filled with such marvelous feelings?" Judith sighed headily.

"The long winter months ahead will afford us many such opportunities to share in this happiness," Strong Hawk said. "The Chippewa family's outdoor activities are curtailed. But inside? Many babies are made when bodies warm and entertain each other."

"But our child will be the first," Judith giggled. "We didn't wait for the long nights of winter to share our love."

"Then you do believe you are with child?"

"Almost certainly."

"Ah, *see-gwun*," Strong Hawk sighed. "Spring. It is the season of the Chippewa. The promises of spring are fulfilled each summer when the ripened products of field and stream are harvested. This is also courting time for the marriageable, who will be brought together by formation of rounds of social activities. But most prominent of all are the many births into the village of the Chippewa, the harvest of the long, sensual nights of winter."

"I'm anxious to experience all the seasons with you and your people," Judith said, placing her hand gently to his cheek.

"And you will," Strong Hawk said. "The time for tormented separations is a thing of the past, my sweet wife."

He rose away from her and offered her a hand. "*Mah-bee-szhon.* Come. Let us dress and go to our home," he said. "In it we have already begun to build memories for our future."

"*Ay-uh*," Judith murmured, taking his hand, her happiness a radiant thing to behold. . . .

461

TO MY READERS:

Thank you for buying my book. I would enjoy hearing from you. I respond, personally, to all letters. If you wish to write, please address your letters to:

> CASSIE EDWARDS
> P.O. Box 450
> High Ridge, Missouri 63049

YOU CAN NOW
CHOOSE FROM AMONG JANELLE TAYLOR'S
BESTSELLING TITLES!

BRAZEN ECSTASY	(1133, $3.50)
DEFIANT ECSTASY	(0931, $3.50)
FIRST LOVE, WILD LOVE	(1431, $3.75)
FORBIDDEN ECSTASY	(1014, $3.50)
GOLDEN TORMENT	(1323, $3.75)
LOVE ME WITH FURY	(1248, $3.75)
SAVAGE CONQUEST	(1533, $3.75)
SAVAGE ECSTASY	(0824, $3.50)
STOLEN ECSTASY	(1621, $3.95)
TENDER ECSTASY	(1212, $3.75)

Available wherever paperbacks are sold, or order direct from the Publisher. Send cover price plus 50¢ per copy for mailing and handling to Zebra Books, Dept. 1739, 475 Park Avenue South, New York, N.Y. 10016. DO NOT SEND CASH.

CAPTIVATING ROMANCE FROM ZEBRA

MIDNIGHT DESIRE   (1573, $3.50)
by Linda Benjamin
Looking into the handsome gunslinger's blazing blue eyes, innocent Kate felt dizzy. His husky voice, so warm and inviting, sent a river of fire cascading through her flesh. But she knew she'd never willingly give her heart to the arrogant rogue!

PASSION'S GAMBLE   (1477, $3.50)
by Linda Benjamin
Jade-eyed Jessica was too shocked to protest when the riverboat cardsharp offered *her* as the stakes in a poker game. Then she met the smouldering glance of his opponent as he stared at her satiny cheeks and the tantalizing fullness of her bodice—and she found herself hoping he would hold the winning hand!

FORBIDDEN FIRES   (1295, $3.50)
by Bobbi Smith
When Ellyn Douglas rescued the handsome Union officer from the raging river, she had no choice but to surrender to the sensuous stranger as he pulled her against his hard muscular body. Forgetting they were enemies in a senseless war, they were destined to share a life of unbridled ecstasy and glorious love!

WANTON SPLENDOR   (1461, $3.50)
by Bobbi Smith
Kathleen had every intention of keeping her distance from Christopher Fletcher. But in the midst of a devastating hurricane, she crept into his arms. As she felt the heat of his lean body pressed against hers, she wondered breathlessly what it would be like to kiss those cynical lips—to turn that cool arrogance to fiery passion!

Available wherever paperbacks are sold, or order direct from the Publisher. Send cover price plus 50¢ per copy for mailing and handling to Zebra Books, Dept. 1739, 475 Park Avenue South, New York, N.Y. 10016. DO NOT SEND CASH.